By J.S. COOK

Because You Despise Me

KILDEVIL COVE MURDER MYSTERIES
Dark Water
Dark Mire

Published by DSP PUBLICATIONS
www.dsppublications.com

DARK
WATER

J.S. COOK

DSP PUBLICATIONS

Published by

DSP PUBLICATIONS

5032 Capital Circle SW, Suite 2, PMB# 279, Tallahassee, FL 32305-7886 USA
www.dsppublications.com

Dark Water
© 2021 J.S. Cook

Cover Art
© 2021 L.C. Chase
http://www.lcchase.com
Cover content is for illustrative purposes only and any person depicted on the cover is a model.

Trade Paperback ISBN: 978-1-64405-916-6
Digital ISBN: 978-1-64405-915-9
Library of Congress Control Number: 2020947385
Trade Paperback published March 2021
v. 1.0
First Edition
Previously published as Wind and Dark Water by Dreamspinner Press, March 2020.

Printed in the United States of America
∞

This paper meets the requirements of
ANSI/NISO Z39.48-1992 (Permanence of Paper).

To my sister Jen, who reads everything I write.

Acknowledgements

Thanks as always to Elizabeth North for saying yes to this book, and to my editors, Andi Byassee and Nicole Dowd, who made sense of my confusion. Heartfelt appreciation to L.C. Chase for an absolutely gorgeous cover, and to everyone at Dreamspinner who made sure this novel saw print. I am forever in your debt.

DARK
WATER

J.S. COOK

CHAPTER ONE

TWICE NOW Deiniol Quirke had pulled off the highway, intending to turn around and head back to the city. Twice he had talked himself out of it. At Whitbourne he'd stopped to get gas before the turnoff, arguing with himself while he filled the tank. The wind was straight out of the northwest, and it poured cold down on him like water. Why was he always having to deal with things like this? And it wasn't like his sister, Sandra, was going to get up off her arse. She'd always had a knack for avoiding anything unpleasant to do with family, and he was usually the one left holding whatever bag the unpleasantness happened to be in. "Are you sure you're not coming?" he'd asked her for what felt like the thousandth time. "He was our grandfather, Sandra."

"I know what he was," she told him. "Believe me, Danny. I know what he was. Better than anybody."

He'd been lulled almost into insensibility by the endless road when he saw the turnoff for the small Newfoundland town of Kildevil Cove late that October afternoon. The place hadn't changed a great deal, but it never did, and he suspected it never would. He could come back here in a thousand years' time, and it would be exactly the same: the same long sweep of hills coming into and going out of the village, the thin ribbon of road leading down to the sea, the post office, the little shop. It was a place caught deep in the onward course of time. He'd driven from town in a record hour and a half, ignoring the posted speed limits, overtaking every other vehicle on the road. Why the hurry? It wasn't pleasant anticipation that drove him, but a clear and present sense of dread, knowing this was something he had to take care of, but not liking the idea one little bit. "Needs must," as Nan would say, "when the devil drives."

He slowed his car by the white house that marked the beginning of his grandfather's lane, but turned in the other direction, away from it, and followed the patchy strip of asphalt towards the sea. It was early still; he'd awakened at four thirty that morning, dragged out of sleep by another of those godforsaken dreams. Maybe it would stop, in time. At least that's what they'd told him. He didn't believe a word out of their mouths, any of them. What the hell did any of them know about it? It hadn't happened to them. It had happened to him, and he would never be able to successfully scrub it from his memory. It would follow him to his grave.

At the end of the road, he saw the familiar shape of a white saltbox house, its bland face turned towards the ocean. The winds today were brutal, dashing enormous waves against the rocks, and the tide was high. There would be a full moon that night. He pulled his rented car onto the gravel drive, as close as possible to the house. The cliffs in the area had been unstable as long as he could remember, and he didn't trust the peaty, saturated ground to hold. The house was just about hanging off the cliff. Some stormy night during a November gale it would tip over the edge, give itself up to the icy North Atlantic. Good riddance to it. There were no good memories for him here.

He'd only packed the one bag, a leather holdall that he'd had forever and a day. It had been all around the world with him, to conferences and seminars where all the great crime-solving minds met to pick each other's brains, drink and flirt, and screw each other in any number of faceless hotel rooms. Year before last it had been Taiwan. Before that, Australia. This year it would be nowhere at all. He fetched the bag out of the back seat, handling it as carefully as a holy relic. It contained a bottle of his favourite Scotch, twelve years old, single malt, capable of obliterating insomnia and nightmares no matter the strength. Wonderful, peace-giving booze.

The gravel drive was merely an illusion, as was the narrow strip of grass at the front. He'd forgotten all that. There was more land at the back, tussock and ground juniper, overlaid in places with yellow autumn grass. The wind howled, shuddering the ground, rocking the rental car where it stood, scouring the skin of his face and making his hair stand on end. Good to be home, he thought sourly. But the air was fresh here and smelled of salt and peat—earthy smells, not like the crowded cities of the world. He filled his lungs with it, sucked it down like water. He could almost believe he was out of the world altogether. He'd been gone for a while, seconded overseas to the main Irish police station in Dublin, loaned out to the Garda Síochána because a serial killer had decided to cut a swath through that spring's latest crop of debutantes. Bloody upper classes. Leave it to the fucking quality to find trouble in the last place anybody would expect. And here he was, home again, but not because he wanted to be; he had no choice, not really. Lucky enough he didn't have to stay. With his severance pay and the savings he'd put by over the years, he had secured a rental apartment in St. John's with a good view of the Narrows and the Southside Hills—the standard postcard optics.

He climbed the front steps—wooden, weathered, far too steep, or maybe that was his advancing age— and dropped his bag on the landing. The agent had messengered the keys to him the week before, and he fumbled in his pockets for them. He got them out and promptly dropped them. His hands were none too steady anymore. There was a time he had the steadiest hands in the world, but not now. Not now and never again. He bent with a muffled curse and picked the keys up, fitted the right one in the door, and pushed it open. *Welcome home, Danny my boy. Here's right where you've landed, arse over teakettle.*

He pushed the heavy wooden door closed, shutting out the keening wind, and sighed with something like relief as he turned the key in the lock. Bit of bloody foolishness that was. Nobody had cause to lock their doors around here, and no one ever did. These people didn't worry about some great big fucker with a sawed-off shotgun forcing his way in at some ungodly hour of the morning, or a disheveled smackhead taking up semi-permanent residence in one of the outbuildings. Nothing here to be afraid of, Danny. Don't be so frigging foolish.

He could have stayed in Grandar's house, except it seemed too ghoulish, even for him. The old place had been empty for weeks now, but he felt it would be wrong. Grandar had died in that house. To walk in there now would feel far too much like trespass—and this was close enough, the now-vacant home of a local family who'd pulled up stakes and moved to Alberta. The town, though, was just the same, the place where Danny had spent his formative years getting into fifty kinds of trouble, chasing the local sheep around, and pestering the old people, getting underfoot and in the way. He'd played here, going past the house out to the point of land where it narrowed dangerously to a thin slice of cliff that dropped four hundred feet to the sea below. He was never afraid in those days. There was nothing to be afraid of.

He could have bought this house if he had the money, and supposing that was what he wanted. The real-estate agent was an old friend, and she quoted him a good price. He could have paid for it in cash, no questions asked—except he knew if he came back to Kildevil Cove permanently, he'd take to drink. He'd crawl inside a bottle and never come out.

He was deathly tired… of everything, but especially of questions. He didn't want to answer any more questions. He wanted somewhere quiet to lay his head and be left the fuck alone. The investigation had sucked the life out of him, hours and days in that goddamn interview room with those two bastards from the internal investigations unit of the Gardaí, asking him the same questions over and over again.

"Do you recall what you said?"

"I told him to let the girl go and come down off the wall."

"So he shot himself because…?" A cynical question voiced by a cynical senior officer, tall and skinny Joey Doyle, the bastard who knew everything.

"I don't know why."

"Could you recount the events for us? In your own words, of course."

There weren't any more words he could say. He'd said them all. A particle of memory replayed itself at intervals inside his head: standing in the pouring rain, his clothes plastered to his body, shivering with the awful anticipation that the man with the gun was going to use it… and he did.

"So he had the gun up to his head, and you said what, exactly?" The interview room was a big glass box, dominated by a shiny conference table with padded chairs set about it at intervals. Besides Danny there were six others—four men and two women, each holding a high rank in the Gardaí, each there to judge and condemn him.

"I told him to come down off the wall. 'Come down,' I said. 'Come down.'"

But Eamonn Nolan had no intention of coming down. He had other plans instead.

Danny shook off the memory and went into the kitchen, where he laid his bag on the floor. The room was the same as always, Enterprise wood-and-oil stove, old wooden table and mismatched chairs, hand-sewn curtains at the window—raggedy lace turned yellow from thirty years of sun, falling into holes now, useless and threadbare. He reached across the sink to open the window even though it was hardly warm outside. He needed to feel the air against his face. He turned on the taps, cupped a hand, and tasted some of the water. It was icy cold, delicious, with a faint tang of salt. "Right out of the rock," his grandfather used to say. "That's the best water there is, my son."

The place was spotless and smelled of Sunlight soap. He knew that his late grandmother's best friend Hetty Jamieson had most likely been in the last day or so, scrubbing the place clean. He'd been sure to hire her long before he ever stepped foot inside the house. He didn't want to smell anything except lemon soap and the blacking Hetty would have used on the old stove. He had no interest in smelling more recent memories, the scent an after-image of happier times.

He conducted a review of the upstairs, the bedrooms with their too-soft mattresses and iron bedsteads, each one only enough to fit two people—two slender people, probably stacked on top of each other, he amended—a washstand and basin in each room, and old-fashioned chenille bedspreads on the beds. To the right of the upstairs landing was a clothes closet, a small room with racks and shelves for storage. He'd make sure to stack his chinos in there, and his woollen jumpers, the cold-weather uniform he wore almost every day of his life. Danny himself would be the first to admit it: he was a creature of habit who liked his world to be orderly and sane and who was vastly uncomfortable with surprises and the unexpected. Strange to think he'd gone into police work, where everything was surprising, uncomfortable, and violent.

He chose the bedroom he wanted, the larger of the two at the back of the house, not near the sea. Sleeping with the window open, the roar and chuff of it would keep him awake, and he'd come here to rest. He tossed his holdall onto the bed and started pulling things out of it, using the opportunity to change into baggy jeans, a faded grey sweatshirt with a university logo on the front, and a pair of fluffy wool socks, a leaving present from Arlene Devlin, the Scottish departmental secretary in Dublin. She'd knit them herself out of the softest merino wool, and she'd worked an intricate Fair Isle pattern around the tops. He remembered his grandmother knitting his mother a Fair Isle sweater once, a long time ago. Pale pink it was, with a moss-green pattern worked into the yoke, accented with dark blue and ivory. It was a beautiful sweater. His mother had neglected to store it properly and the moths got at it. The last time he saw it, the poor old thing was a holey ruin, not even fit for a cloth to wash the floor with.

He padded downstairs and put the kettle on, then opened drawers and cupboards, looking for cups and spoons. Hetty had laid in groceries, too, a quart of milk and a loaf of homemade three-bun bread, tea and sugar and butter, a tin of biscuits the same kind his grandmother used to buy, a tub of molasses. She'd seen that the house was stocked with anything he might need, right down to clean linens in the bedroom and fresh towels in the bathroom. The unexpected kindness touched him. So many things did nowadays, and his emotions were always too close to the surface. He angered easily, shouted like a lunatic, maybe slammed his fist down on the nearest desk, but that was it. The storm was gone as quickly as it had come, and he usually went about apologising for it. He cried as easily, often at insignificant things, embarrassing himself. He would probably end up as one of those foolish, weepy old men, snotting and bawling over the obituaries in the newspaper.

He made a sandwich while the kettle boiled, and ate it at the ancient kitchen table, paging through a copy of the *Register*, the only remaining local newspaper. Everything had gone digital, or so people said, and those who wanted their news printed on paper were fewer every year. There was nothing here for young people, who left as soon as they got the chance and didn't come back, headed for the city and good-paying jobs on the oil rigs. Every year the population counted a few less souls as the old people died off and hordes of "come-from-aways" bought up their empty houses to use as vacation homes. There were strangers in the shops now, people nobody knew, with disparate accents from other places. There were foreigners with cameras every summer, clambering over the hills and barrens, taking pictures of all sorts, chattering excitedly amongst themselves about things that islanders took for granted. They boarded whale-watching tours in their pitifully inadequate clothing, returning off the water bright red and chilled to the bone, wondering why no one had told them. Surely the fact that the locals all wore rubber boots, knitted caps, and mitts and heavy wool jumpers should have alerted them to the fact that maybe this place wasn't Florida. Still, it was better than the houses sitting empty, rotting away and falling into disrepair. At least the come-from-aways spent money in the local shops and paid retired fishermen to take them out iceberg hunting in the spring. It helped to keep the place going.

The *Register* featured the usual wedding announcements, with lavish descriptions of the marriage attire, often with unfortunate spelling errors ("the groom wore a bright purple cumberbun"), and obituaries full of weepy poems culled from some ladies' book of days… "I am not dead, I do not sleep…." *Yes, you are*, he thought with a shudder that ran the length of his entire body. *Yes, you are, and you'll never be anything but that.* His hand crept to his face, wiping quickly, scrubbing it away, that trickle of wetness. It was always so surprising, death, and so final.

His grandfather's obituary was there, halfway down the first column on the last page.

Eleazar Quirke lately of this town, passed peacefully in his sleep, leaves behind one grandson Danny, one granddaughter Sandra. Predeceased by son Gareth and daughter-in-law Lena. In lieu of flowers, donations to the Knights of Columbus.

That was it. Simple and direct. Danny had written it himself. The old fellow had passed peacefully in his sleep while Danny was on his way across the Atlantic, a late flight out of Dublin with a strong headwind that kept him in the air for nearly six and a half hours. There was no formal reading of the will; the little that Grandar owned was disbursed by a lawyer in Clarke's Beach, an old friend of the family. He'd filed the necessary paperwork and took care of the rest of it, sending cheques as small tokens of gratitude to those who'd been kind to Grandar during his final weeks and months. *God love them. The kindness of the ignorant.*

He finished the sandwich and dumped the crusts in the bin, boiled the kettle for a second cup of tea. The daylight this time of year was short, the opposite of midsummer nights where a pale blue illumination glowed along the horizon until after ten o'clock. He went about the house, turning on all the lights, then went about again and turned them all off except the single pole lamp above a wingback chair he'd already designated as his reading place. It was opposite a small fireplace of dark mahogany with polished brass accents, a real work of art salvaged from old Simmy Bailey's house on Southwest Path. Some thoughtful soul—probably Hetty—had left kindling and old newspapers in an antique coal hod on the hearth, and he used these to start a small fire, amazed that he still remembered how to do it. He was a long way and many years beyond such simple, ordinary things, but it gave him comfort, grounded him in a way few things could.

He sank into the chair and opened a novel he'd brought with him, a lengthy work of nearly four hundred pages about the survivors of the Bosnian war. The night folded itself around him, and the wind rose, roaring around the corners of the house and rattling the windowpanes. There was no other sound except the quiet ticking of the clock.

CHAPTER TWO

TADHG HEANEY—WHEN he was a boy, everyone had trouble with the pronunciation of his archaic Celtic name, voiced like the first syllable of the word 'tiger'—tried to suppress the sick feeling in his stomach, watching from the side as Tom Single's digger lowered the stone down onto fresh cement. Five years since his father had died and they were only now getting around to this, him and his brother Declan. It was Dec's fault, but it always was. He was gallivanting around Australia or somewhere with his latest conquest, a tender young thing named Ariadne or Helena or something like that. Tadhg didn't remember and he didn't really care. All he knew was the girl was Greek and her father was a shipping magnate, a real Onassis type who had more money than God.

I think it's best if we agree on the design as soon as possible. That way, we can get the stone placed before the frost sets into the ground. He'd emailed Declan in care of his company, a London banking firm that sent him all around the world doing God knows what while they paid him a hefty salary and gave him an expense account to rival the riches of Croesus.

Dec replied he didn't care what Tadhg put on it. *Just be glad the old fucker is in the ground.*

"What's that look like to ye, Tadhg?" Tommy Single leaned out of the cab and shouted over the engine noise. "Is it straight?"

Tadhg stepped forward and regarded the flat slab of granite in the last of the late afternoon's fading light. "Looks good," he said. "Finest kind, my son." He wanted this over and done with. He hated this time of year and this time of day when the light went away early and didn't come back for far too long. As a young boy he'd dreaded winter with its early dusk and interminable nights, sitting with the family in the living room and feigning interest in the six o'clock news and the game shows that came afterwards. His mother sat sewing in the rocking chair, pushed so far back into the corner that she didn't even seem to be in the room. And his old man, front and centre in the easy chair, legs spread wide on the footrest, argued with the television as if the people on there could hear a word he said, the volume up on bust. He always had to get the last word.

"So you're all right with that?" Tommy turned off the machine and hopped down out of the cab. "If you're not, I don't mind—"

"That's fine," Tadhg cut in. He realised how abrupt it sounded and softened it with a grin. "Honest, Tommy, it looks grand." He reached into his hip pocket and brought out his wallet, counted out some bills, and handed them across. Tommy flicked through them, then looked up at Tadhg with a confused expression.

"You gave me too much, bhoy." He peeled off the excess and made to give it back. "We said forty dollars, and that's all I'm charging ye."

"Keep it," Tadhg said. "Please." He felt absurdly grateful to Tommy, who had made this distasteful task so much easier. "God love ye, give it to Margaret for her Christmas baking." Tommy's wife Margaret made almost all the holiday cakes for the little town of Kildevil Cove and even exported some to area shops and restaurants. She inevitably took top prize at the community fair every fall for her dark boiled fruitcake.

"You're sure?" Tommy hesitated, the money still in his outstretched hand.

Tadhg reached out and closed his fingers around it. "Take it." He bent in the growing darkness to look at the simple flat plaque resting on its bed of fresh cement. It had his father's name and his birth and death dates. That was it. Tadhg didn't have the stomach to include a flowery sentimental phrase. Sentiment wasn't something he felt when he considered his father. Besides, what was the old bastard going to do, rise up out of the ground and smack Tadhg a good one in the back of the head? *You did enough of that when you were alive, you old cunt.*

The placement of his father's headstone coincided with this trip to Kildevil Cove. Old Eleazar Quirke was dead, and Tadhg hoped to snatch up the now-empty family homestead and turn it into a holiday let. Mainlanders and other come-from-aways loved the island, now that it was prosperous; there were expensive foreign cars on the roads and private sailing clubs for the oil company executives and their skinny trophy wives. True, most of them lived in the city, but they were always looking for the perfect weekend getaway, and rural Newfoundland, with its close resemblance and relative proximity to Ireland, seemed tailor-made for them. Tadhg didn't anticipate any difficulties in procuring the property. Old Eleazar's only living relatives were his grandchildren, Danny Quirke and his sister, Sandra—and Danny was in Ireland, seconded to the Garda Síochána from the Royal Newfoundland Constabulary. He couldn't see Sandra coming back to Kildevil Cove any time soon. Like him, she'd been keen to get away after high school. Also like him, she was out the door the day she passed her final exams. The last he'd heard, she had become a successful jewelry designer and was living in Portugal with a man friend, or maybe he was her common-law husband. Tadhg hadn't seen her in nearly thirty years. It had been almost that long since he'd last seen Danny.

He was reasonably sure Danny wasn't interested in seeing him.

Tadhg had done well since high school. He went on to university where he studied business and commerce, like his old man wanted him to. He'd had no choice. He knew he wouldn't get one red cent unless he did what his father wanted, and what his father wanted was for Tadhg to eventually take over the family business. Tadhg was the natural choice—Declan wanted nothing to do with the Heaney's fleet of seagoing vessels and even less to do with the Heaney Ocean Group, the fish processing plant they owned—but at the last minute Tadhg had confounded his father's expectations and set himself up as a property developer.

His old man had been livid. Tadhg had driven from town on a Sunday morning to have dinner with his parents and tell his father the news. He was twenty-five and had closed a deal worth two million dollars to develop a new subdivision outside Carbonear, a bedroom community to accommodate the hundreds of new oil-patch workers and their families. He'd acquired the land for a song from the grieving grandchildren of a recently deceased fisherman who had inherited it from his grandfather. Tadhg told them he intended to use the land as a history and heritage site, a green space for the community. Plans were being drawn up, and consultations with local government officials were underway. By the time they realised his true intentions, the deed had been signed over to him, and the first phase of site-clearing work had begun.

"You made a promise." The daughter had shown up at the site one Monday morning. She found Tadhg sitting in his pickup truck, looking over the plans. "You said—"

"I changed my mind."

"That land belonged to my grandfather! My ancestors came over from Bristol with John Guy."

Tadhg shrugged. "And mine came from County Wexford. Big deal."

She stared at him, her face expressionless. "I can't believe you. You don't care about nothing, do ye?"

It was mostly true. He cared about money; he cared about Lily. That was it. What else was there? His father had been pissed off. He turned the family dinner into a battlefield, roaring and ranting, pounding on the table so hard he made the glassware rattle. He kept Tadhg behind for hours after the meal had finished, haranguing him, attempting to manipulate with recriminations and yes, even tears. If an argument wasn't going his way, he'd switch into what Tadhg thought of as Good Father Mode. "I loves all my children the same," he'd say. "You and Declan, you're everything to me. It's just too bad you don't see it, Tadhg." He'd walk around the room, praying aloud, "Oh lord Jesus, please forgive your wayward son, a sinner." It was a sickening spectacle, and Tadhg had long since grown weary of his father's perverse attempts at emotional manipulation.

"I won't run the fish plant," he said. "I've got plans of my own."

"You'll do what's right, my son, or else. It says in the Bible to honour your father and mother."

Tadhg had calmly told him to fuck off. His father's face had turned a shade of red he'd never seen. "Oh, you can curse and swear as much as you like. Won't change the truth."

Tadhg watched now as Tommy climbed aboard the digger and backed slowly out of the cemetery, turned, and drove away. Tadhg felt sorry for anybody stuck behind him on the road, but then again, this was Kildevil Cove. The rate of traffic was maybe one vehicle per hour on a busy summer weekend, three or four if there happened to be a funeral passing by.

When he arrived at the family home twenty minutes later, the door was locked, and all the windows were dark. He hadn't expected any different. No one had lived there for the past five years, ever since his father died. Neither he nor Declan had expressed any interest in opening the place up. Tadhg supposed he could have had a key cut, but he had no desire or reason to go inside. He'd made a home for himself and Lily on Eigus, the largest of the smaller islands in Conception Bay, and that was more than good enough. He'd bought the island outright for less than half its value and erected a huge house. Truth be told, the house was much too big for only him and Lily, but wasn't that the point? People judged you by what you owned and how much you had, and Tadhg had lots.

He parked his Range Rover and got out. He had never been able to drive past the old place without at least a look. It was cold. He could see his breath steaming out in front of him, dispersing into eddies in the indigo twilight like the swirling shapes around Van Gogh's illuminated stars. His fingers cramped with pain, his Raynaud's Syndrome making them stiff and clumsy. He tried to push his car keys into his pocket but dropped them on the ground. It was still there, etched into the cement of the foundation: TADHG 1986. He'd written it one hot July day when the new house—this house—was being built. It seemed an appropriate thing to do. He was nineteen, home for the weekend from the university's summer session, and at loose ends. Danny Quirke was home too, and from the same university—indeed, he and Tadhg were in some of the same classes—but ever since Tadhg's disastrous involvement with Danny's sister, Sandra, Danny wanted nothing to do with him. As for Sandra…. "The best thing for you to do," Danny had said, "is to fly the fuck out of here. You done enough damage already."

Tadhg had kept himself informed of Danny's career via social media and the local papers. After two years in university, Danny had gone for police training and had spent the intervening thirty years working his way up the career ladder. From traffic patrol he moved to the detective division, becoming a detective constable a mere two years after he'd joined up. A promotion to detective sergeant quickly followed, then inspector. He and Tadhg were the same age; Tadhg couldn't figure out why the silly fucker hadn't taken early retirement. The *Evening Telegram* and the *Sunday Herald* printed some police-related story nearly every day, and Danny was featured in a fair few of these. He seemed to deal mostly with kidnapping and domestic violence, child abuse, and the one or two murders that occurred in the city every year. In 2017 he'd been seconded to the Garda Síochána in Dublin as part of an officer exchange program. It hadn't gone well for him. There had been some kind of altercation with a suspect, and Danny had narrowly escaped criminal charges. Since then, he'd vanished off the radar.

It had been a very long time since Tadhg had seen Danny, but his feelings for his old friend remained unchanged. As children, they'd been close, sharing a David-and-Jonathon relationship "passing the love of women." Danny told Tadhg things he had never told another living soul, and Tadhg confided the often-painful details of his family life to Danny, knowing it would go no further.

Tadhg stood up, cursing the pain in his knees and the tightness of his calf muscles. This getting older bullshit was depressing as hell, he thought. Bad enough he had to use reading glasses now without the rest of it. He went round to the south side of the house, climbing onto a short stack of cinder blocks to look in the window. Why, he didn't know. He'd seen it all before. There was the kitchen with its gorgeous labradorite countertops, the butcher's-block table his mother used as a work surface, and the enormous Wolf stove, special ordered from the States. You couldn't get a stove like that in town, even in the city, in 1986. "Nothing but the best," his father had said. "I don't want no old garbage." The old man insisted on spreading his money around. It was the only thing he had to give, and the only thing he cared about.

On the opposite side of the house was the dining room with its three-paned french window opening onto a teak patio. Tadhg remembered they had a barbecue once: hamburgers and hotdogs for himself and Declan, steak for his parents. The charcoal never really caught fire well enough to roast the meat, and his father, out of patience, hurled the entire thing into the yard. After that, the patio became a storage place for the lawn mower, rakes and shovels, and occasional bags of potting soil his mother bought for her houseplants. He hoped there were at least one or two indoor plants where she was now.

Tadhg's mother had developed Lewy body dementia shortly after her fiftieth birthday. At first her condition seemed innocuous, merely some difficulty picking things up and holding on to them, or problems navigating the stairs in their home. She became abnormally forgetful, pouring a cup of tea and wandering off without drinking it, then returning to the kitchen several more times to make more tea that she also forgot about. It wasn't uncommon for Tadhg to turn up and find ten or more mugs of tea lined up across the kitchen counter. His father had to buy a kettle with an automatic shutoff, because she would turn it on and forget about it, leaving it to boil dry. She left the stove on, opened windows in the middle of foul weather and forgot to close them, hung dirty laundry to dry outside in the yard. His father, predictably, saw all this as an attempt to irritate him.

"There's nothing wrong with her. She just does it now to spite me." The conversation with Tadhg's father took place over the telephone. He'd been home once since the onset of his mother's illness—arriving on a Sunday for dinner and planning to stay the night—but left early when his father's behaviour became too much to bear. He'd sat at the dining table complaining as his wife struggled to put the meal together, and nothing she'd cooked suited him. The potatoes were undercooked; the carrots were mushy; the portion of salt beef she'd given him was too fatty. His mother tried to put the best face on it, chatting with Tadhg and asking where his sister was, and why hadn't she turned up for Sunday dinner?

"I haven't got a sister, Mam." Tadhg ignored his father's derisive laugh. "It's just Declan and me."

"Who am I thinking about, then?" She struggled to remember.

"Probably Aunt Joyce. That's your sister."

His mother looked for a long time at Tadhg's father. "I didn't think you worked here," she said. "Who's Declan?"

It went downhill from there. By the time the meal was finished, Tadhg's throat was so tight he could barely swallow. He helped clear the table and washed the dishes, then collected his coat and car keys and left. His father met him in the front hall. "Where the Jesus do you think you're going, then?"

Tadhg didn't even bother saying anything. He just left. From time to time, he would call his mother, but her conversation made little sense, and she was frequently too afraid to speak on the telephone, fearing that someone was listening to and recording her conversation. Tadhg's father rang him late one night at his home on Eigus. "I think she's after losing her mind. Somebody got to do something with her. She's off her head."

As usual, Declan was unreachable. Tadhg called his office and left a message with the receptionist. Then he arranged an appointment with a neurologist in the city, who ran a series of tests. Dementia with Lewy Bodies, he said, "…but not to worry. Many people live for five to eight years after diagnosis." In the end it wasn't an issue. Tadhg's mother developed pneumonia and died in hospital eighteen months later. He managed to track Declan down in Austria. His brother showed up drunk to the funeral with a woman in tow, a nice enough girl who spoke barely any English. As soon as his mother's coffin was interred, Declan was gone again. Tadhg stood over the grave after the rest of the mourners had left and remembered something he'd said to Danny Quirke when they were teenagers: "My whole fucking family is good for nothing."

And now Eleazar Quirke had finally kicked off, and Danny would come back to Kildevil Cove. It wasn't an idea Tadhg relished, but he knew he would have to face Danny sometime. Better sooner than later, he supposed, and now that Eleazar was gone, there were some things he needed to tell Danny, things Danny very much needed to know.

DANNY WOKE the next morning to the insistent buzzing of his phone. He'd put aside his book somewhere after midnight and had the first good night's sleep he'd had in a while. He picked up the phone and glared at it. "Danny Quirke."

"Danny! Good God, did I wake you? I'm so sorry." Rosemary Dean's bright voice exploded in his ear. The goddamn woman was too cheerful for this time of the morning. "I wanted to go over a few things before the viewing."

He hauled himself out of bed and rubbed a hand over his face. "Right."

Rosemary was a one-woman powerhouse of real estate. She could sell anything to anyone. He'd known her since university, and in all that time he'd never seen her disappointed by setbacks or anything less than all in when it came to business dealings. "Noon," she reiterated, "at your grandfather's house. Are we clear, Danny? I don't want to hunt you down, but I will if I have to. You are not messing this up for me, are you listening? This buyer is very eager, and he's got the cash, you can rest assured of that."

He nodded, even though he knew she couldn't see him. "Be there soon," he said and hung up. Rosemary regarded herself as a kind of unofficial agony aunt, the person everyone called when they were having problems. She was always up for a glass of wine and a chat about whatever was bothering him. Some people disliked her forceful, direct personality, but that was just her way. Danny found her honesty refreshing, even if she was handing out truths he didn't necessarily want to hear. Unlike a lot of people in this day and age, she genuinely cared about her friends, and this earned her their loyalty.

Danny got up, still feeling unreal and strange in the house he hadn't seen for thirty years. He took a shower and shaved, carefully avoiding the mirror, which was also good at handing out truths he didn't want, as much as possible. That horrible business at the Clontarf sea wall had aged him, and he knew he looked haunted and old, haggard beyond his years. After his shower he made a simple breakfast of tea and toast, unable to stomach anything more complicated, and brought it out to the patio some previous owner had built onto the side of the house. It hadn't been there when he was a boy, which felt like centuries ago, to be sure, and good riddance. Some corpses deserved to stay buried. The past was the past.

He stepped back inside to fetch a blanket, then wrapped it around his shoulders before going back out again. The morning was cool, and there was a latent mist hanging over the ocean. It was calmer today, and the wind that had rocked him to sleep the previous night had by now died away. He ate his toast and drank the tea, scalding his tongue in his haste. He didn't want to be late. Rosemary was expecting him. Time to do what had to be done.

DANNY'S GRANDFATHER'S house was located at the end of a gravel road, a white biscuit box with white rail fences and a big garage set some distance away. He knew without looking that the property had a root cellar, a stable, and a well with sweet water he hadn't tasted in years. As he pulled into the drive, he saw two cars parked there—Rosemary's sleek silver BMW and a big Land Rover. He didn't recognise the latter, so it must belong to the buyer. He was halfway to the front door when Rosemary came running to meet him, her stiletto heels sinking into the soft earth. She was a tiny woman, not much over five feet tall, and dressed as always to the nines. There was a fit, slender man about Danny's own age walking beside her, the kind of slick sleveen who would probably sell his own grandmother. His heart stuttered when he realised who it was. *Oh Christ, no.*

"Danny, this is—"

"Tadhg Heaney." Danny barely resisted the urge to turn aside and spit. Tadhg was as confident and self-assured as ever, easy in his own skin, rich as Croesus and, Danny was certain, especially beloved of God. He'd made a lot of money as a real-estate developer, a man with the knack to recognise significant opportunities that others overlooked.

"He's buying your grandfather's house," Rosemary said quickly. "I believe he intends to put up... what is it? Seniors' condos? Holiday cottages? Holiday cottages, he says. It's his latest project."

"No," Danny said. "He's not buying it. He's not coming near anything of mine." His hands clenched into tight, painful fists. "He's not buying this house." He forced himself to meet the other man's gaze. Yes, the bastard was as comely as ever, and him smiling then, those straight white teeth all but flashing in the hazy sunlight. How the hell did you make your teeth flash, Danny wondered bitterly. If it could be done, Tadhg would see to it. He had the magic touch, he did so.

"It's been a while, Danny." Tadhg held out a hand. Danny ignored it. "You look good. You've been keeping well?"

"As well as can be expected," Danny said tightly.

"You've already agreed in principle to the sale," Tadhg said lightly. The smile didn't waver, even for a second. "So I can't think why you're holding it up." The grin seemed to say, "Don't be like that, Danny old son, we're friends aren't we? We're real good pals, me and you." His dark hair had given way to a premature grey, glossy and silver as a seal's back. His tightly groomed beard was slightly darker than his hair, and so were his eyebrows. He was as beautiful as ever he'd been, and wore his maturity well. He had the same skeptical expression as always, underpinned with a selfish delight, as if he couldn't believe the world in all its wonders was laid out there for him. Danny itched to smack the smile off his face.

"What the hell are you doing here?"

Tadhg laughed in apparent disbelief. "Didn't you hear the lady? I'm buying this house."

"No," Danny repeated, "that you're not."

He turned and headed back towards his car. His heart was drumming hard enough to burst his chest, and the swish of blood in his ears was deafening him. His mouth filled with hot saliva, but it was impossible to swallow, his throat closing. He reached his car and spent several seconds fiddling about with the keys until he found the right one. His shaking hand could hardly put it in the lock.

"Danny! For the love of God, don't be a fool." Tadhg caught up with him. "I'm willing to pay whatever you want." He reached into his jacket and came out with his chequebook, flipped it open to a clean form. "Look, whatever amount you name, it's yours."

Danny reached for Tadhg, slapped the chequebook out of his hand. "You can keep your fucking money," he said viciously. "I would rather burn the whole goddamn thing right to the ground than sell it to you." He ripped open the driver's side door and got in.

Tadhg came round and stood before him, one hand lying flat on the car roof. "Surely to God we can talk about it." His expression and his voice were both conciliatory. Tadhg did conciliatory better than anyone. It was like meat and drink to him.

Danny put the key in the ignition and started the car. "Get out of my way."

Tadhg stood his ground. "I will not."

Danny gunned the engine hard. He was, he knew, behaving like a fourteen-year-old, but he couldn't help it. "Move."

"No."

Danny put the car into gear and started forward, startling Tadhg, who only just managed to jump out of the way. He pulled away, gravel flying, Tadhg cursing and shouting behind him.

"You're a fucking maniac, you!"

In other circumstances, Danny might have been laughing, but it wasn't funny. With everything he'd been through this past year, seeing Tadhg again was too much. And him wanting to buy Grandar's house? *I would rather burn the whole goddamn thing right to the ground than sell it to you.*

He'd barely reached the end of the lane when his cell phone buzzed. He picked it up and glanced at the screen. Rosemary. "What?"

"Tearing off in a mad rush isn't helping anything." Her voice was high and tight. She sounded fit to be tied. Losing this sale would mean the loss of her commission.

"Rosemary, you can say what you like. I will not sell my grandfather's house to that son of a bitch."

"Danny, you didn't even listen to what he had to say."

"I didn't care to hear it."

"I expect there's lots you don't care to hear," she said. There was silence. Probably she expected him to say something else. "Listen, Danny, the market for real estate around here is as soft as shit. Nobody else is going to buy that house, I can tell you that for certain sure. So get your head out of your arse and sell. Do you hear me?"

He was at the turnoff for his road. "I've got to go."

"Will I come over later on?" she asked. "Bring a drop of stuff? Maybe we can watch a movie." No doubt she thought to work on him, bring him round to her way of thinking. Danny was far from stupid; he knew what Grandar's house was worth in the current real-estate market. Rosemary stood to make a nice bundle if the sale went through—maybe enough for an expensive holiday in Mexico or Cuba, get together with the girls and drink till they were well cut, take the cabana boy upstairs and fuck his brains out. She'd like that.

He sighed. *Stop making up movies in your head.*

"Haven't got a television," Danny said. "Look, Rosie, the reception's not the best. You're starting to break up, so I'll say goodbye now." The reception was as good as anywhere else on the island, and both he and Rosemary knew it, but he had no more patience for argument. Seeing that bastard Tadhg Heaney after so many years had been an unpleasant jolt, almost an ache in his bones, an unwelcome surprise that left him feeling sick to his stomach. There was no way to forget or overlook what Tadhg had done to Danny and his family.

He pulled the rental car close to his house. The winds had come up again, and the sea was licking hungrily at the cliffs, tearing at the land. A strong nor'easter was forecast to travel up the coast later that night, with heavy precipitation and gale-force winds. Already the clouds were spitting rain, and Danny wasted no time getting inside. He slammed the door on the wind and wrenched off his coat and shoes, not caring where they landed, then got the bottle of twelve-year-old Glenfiddich out and tossed three fingers into the first glass tumbler he found. It went down burning, and he poured another, then another. By the time he made it to his favourite chair, he was half in the bag, eyelids sagging, the hard knot of tension inside of him dissolving, fading away to nothing.

He woke up hours later, groggy and cotton-mouthed, unsure for a moment where he was or how he'd gotten there. The wind roared around the corner of the house, and the rain beat hard on the roof. Yes. Grandar's place. Rosemary and... *him.* Tadhg Heaney, the fucking arsehole.

He got up and turned on some lights, moving from room to room, eager to banish the dark. Right now it frightened him as it seldom did, not anymore, but waking up alone always unsettled him, made him feel like the last man alive on earth. He knew the sorts of awful things that could happen while you were asleep, how people you loved and counted on could go away forever. He went into the bathroom and ran the tap, sluicing cold water over his face, rubbing it into his cheeks and forehead. Then he brushed his teeth, rinsed his mouth, and dragged the brush through his thick light brown hair. He still had his hair, something for which he was eminently grateful, and he'd managed to delay the creep of middle-age spread. His belly was as flat now as it had been in his twenties, owing to his daily running regimen and a careful diet, but there were fine lines at the corners of his eyes, lines bracketing his mouth. He dabbed at his face with the towel, wiping at the wetness on his cheeks. "It will fade in time," his doctor had said. "It isn't real. It's the body's way of processing the trauma so you can move on with your life." Move where, Danny wondered. Was there somewhere he was supposed to be? Memories were sticky like that—sticky like old blood and as hard to scrub away.

He went downstairs carefully, still half-drunk and weak from not having eaten all day long. There were bread and luncheon meat in the fridge, tomatoes, cheese—he'd make a sandwich. He laughed. Another sandwich. It was all he ate these days. Sandwiches with a side order of whisky. He finished eating and put the plate in the sink. He'd wash it later. He poured another two fingers of Glenfiddich into his glass and headed into the living room.

Above the noise of the rain beating on the windows was another noise; someone was pounding on the door. Fucking Rosemary, probably, even though he'd already told her no. He went without thinking and yanked the door open. The rain was coming down in sheets, like water tipped out of an enormous bucket. Tadhg was standing on his porch, soaking wet, his trousers sticking to him, his thin cotton shirt translucent in the rain. "Danny."

"What the hell are you doing here?" Danny asked. He was tired. Seeing Tadhg made him feel a thousand years old.

"I need to talk to you." Tadhg swiped water from his face. "It's important." They stared at each other for a moment; then Danny moved to shut the door. "Wait." Tadhg put his hand on it like he'd done earlier that day with the car. "Can we not talk civilly for a minute, like we used to?"

TADHG ACCEPTED the towel Danny handed him, and the whisky. "I thought you were in Ireland," he said. "You were with the cops over there, weren't you?"

"I was."

"But you're not now."

"No."

"So I guess you're working with the constabulary, are you? In town, I mean. Not here."

"No."

Jesus, this was getting on for desperate. "What is it you're doing?" There could be a million things Danny wasn't telling him, and Tadhg wanted to know. "Surely to God you can tell me. I'm your oldest friend." He swabbed the water from his face and neck with the towel. It smelled like lavender and lemon and cedar wood shavings.

"I... I was in charge of a case, and something went wrong. There was an internal investigation." He raised his shoulders and let them drop. "That's it."

What a load of shite. Of the two of them, Danny was always the strong one, emotionally. He was the most compassionate man Tadhg had ever known, but also resilient. He had to be in his line of work. "You're not a cop anymore."

"I'm not."

"Sure what'd you do with your badge?"

"I kept it for a fucking souvenir, all right?" Danny exploded. "Jesus Christ, do you need to go on about it?"

Good, now we're getting somewhere. "What happened, Danny? Are ye going to tell me, or do I have to drag it out of ye?" Danny had always been like this, stubborn, reluctant to open himself to anyone who actually cared about him. The surest way to shut him down was to tell him that you loved him. He would accept the sentiment readily enough, but then something inside of him pushed it away. Tadhg had seen it firsthand more times than he liked to count. It was a personal defeat for Danny. He'd lost and you'd won because you found a way inside of him, and he hated that.

"There was an incident... during a case I was working." Danny stared into the fire, head slightly bowed. "A suspect...." He was quiet for a long time, gazing ahead with unfocused eyes, lost somewhere inside his memories. "Well." He jerked his head up and offered Tadhg a thin little smile. "It didn't end well. I was invited"—the smile vanished—"to tender my resignation." One shoulder twitched involuntarily, a quick little movement like a shrug.

"I'm sorry," Tadhg said. "From everything I've heard, you were a good cop."

He huddled near the fire while Danny fed the flames with several stout birch logs. He sat back on his heels and gazed at Tadhg. "Yeah? What did you hear?"

"That you joined the constabulary after university, worked your way up to sergeant and then detective." Tadhg pulled his wet shirt away from his abdomen, where it was sticking to him and itching. "Out there making a difference in the world." Too late he realised it sounded cynical and snarky.

"Oh, right on. So that's what you heard." Danny's hollow laugh had no humour in it. "You don't know much about the way the justice system works is all. Sure you can do what you like nowadays. Run someone down with your car. Steal from old ladies." He grabbed the poker and shifted some of the burning logs around. "You could beat somebody's head in with a hammer and get away with it because you're young and pretty and female, and you can pretend to have mental problems so you don't know what you're doing."

Tadhg remembered it clearly. "I heard about that case."

"Not criminally responsible," Danny said. "Didn't know what she was at. She knew enough to get rid of the murder weapon afterwards, though." He stood up, grunting a little when his knees cracked. "Are you hungry? Did you eat anything today? Or are you running on strong coffee like you used to do in high school?"

It was true. Tadhg hadn't changed his habits in university or since. Tim Horton's house blend was his go-to drink during exams, that and Diet Coke. He used caffeine like some other people used speed—to stay awake, to sharpen his mind. It was better than drugs and didn't seem to cause him any lasting harm. Nowadays he made some of his shrewdest investments while buzzed on Red Bull and espresso.

"Not hungry, thanks anyway," Tadhg said sharply. He stood up and leaned against the mantelpiece. "You came back for the funeral." The whisky wasn't his customary brand. He seriously doubted Danny could afford the one he usually drank, not on his salary. His former salary.

"Of course I came back for the funeral," Danny said. "He and my nan raised us, me and Sandra. You know well and good—" He huffed out a breath. "Why are you here? What is it you want? You got something to tell me? Go on, then."

Best to get it out in the open right away. "Danny, I have a daughter."

A ponderous silence fell between them, the only sound the wind lashing the rain against the windows. "A daughter," Danny said. He bent to push another birch log into the fire. The firebox was by now crammed so full of wood there was barely room for the flames to breathe. "You."

Tadhg's guts twisted. "Is it that fucking hard to believe? That someone could want to have a baby with me?"

Danny moved to retrieve the whisky. "I'm thinking I'll need something to prop me up for this." He refilled his own glass and proffered the bottle to Tadhg. "'Nother drink?"

It was bloody tempting for sure, but he needed a clear head. "No. You go on." Where the hell should he begin, to tell something like this? He searched his memory for some suitable starting point but there wasn't one, so he started at the beginning. "Back a few years ago, I was in Scotland for a bit, way up past Inverness...." Inverness. Fuck if that wasn't one of the most beautiful places he'd ever been, a perfect little city nestled near a lovely river, solid stone houses and shops, more pubs than you could shake a stick at. There were plenty of gorgeous people in the pubs, and even more in the discos and dance clubs, and Tadhg saw no reason to deny himself the pleasures of the flesh. He got busy working his way through Inverness, one hookup at a time. "Looking after a house for a friend of mine, fellow I met working in construction over in Dubai." He tried to take a deep breath, but his chest was tight as iron bands. It always sounded like he was bragging, but he wasn't. People often got their backs up when Tadhg said such things, even though it was his life's experience and not some half-arsed attempt to make someone else feel jealous. "Anyway, he was going to be gone for three months, and he didn't want to leave the house empty. I said I'd stay in it and look after Jock, his dog." It was a nice house, a renovated chapel that had lain empty for a while, with a small salmon stream nearby and quiet country lanes where he'd often take Jock walking.

"Sounds uncomplicated so far," Danny said, but there was contempt in his sour expression and his raised eyebrow.

"It was." Tadhg rubbed a hand across his forehead. He couldn't tell if the wetness there was rain or sweat. "Couple of weeks in, I was out walking, and I saw this woman. Kind of fey-looking, all this long red hair and pale skin. Bright green eyes of the sort you'd never think to see on an ordinary human person. Jesus, she was like a fucking changeling, so beautiful."

"Mm," Danny said. "I bet she was."

Tadhg ignored the scorn apparent in Danny's voice. "So between the jigs and the reels we ended up getting together one night. Midsummer it was, gorgeous weather. We sat outside for a few drinks, listening to music, when all of a sudden she stands up and says we ought to dance. Jazz music it was, that slow kind. We weren't together five minutes before she—"

"That'll do," Danny said, holding up a hand. "You don't need to go into the minor details." He threw back the rest of his scotch and reached to refill the glass. "So I'm guessing the two of you fucked. That's how it usually goes with you, isn't it?" He uttered a short, sharp noise that Tadhg supposed was meant to be laughter. "Fuck and run?"

He fumbled for his phone and clicked through to the camera roll. "Danny, just because—"

"Spare me." There was still a great bitterness there.

Tadhg scrolled until he found the picture he wanted: Lily, age seven, sitting on a carousel horse in New Orleans, wearing her favourite sundress and a floppy hat she'd begged him for at a street market. He remembered it like yesterday, the same way he remembered everything else about his daughter. "That's her. Gwen was six months pregnant before I even realised." He reached over and handed the phone to Danny. "She was born early, a bit premature, but she caught up all right." He pointed to another favourite picture of her, standing beside the water fountain at her school, wearing her first long dress and smiling all over her face. A shard of pain went through him, but he managed to suppress it before he embarrassed himself. "Her name is Lily. It's Gwen's mother's name."

Danny handed back the phone. "So where is… Gwen, is it?"

Tadhg shook his head more vigorously than was necessary. "She's no longer in the picture. Having Lily interfered with her career. She's a dancer. After Lily was born, Gwen wanted to put her up for adoption, but I took her to raise instead. The bitch made me prove paternity, of course, so DNA tests and blood and all the rest of it." A cold fist squeezed his heart. "She's fourteen now. She lives with me on Eigus." The small island sat close to the main land mass in Conception Bay, far enough from shore for true privacy, but a quick enough trip in a motorboat whenever the need arose. Tadhg had bought the entire island for a song from an old man who was retiring to Toronto—although why in the name of Jesus anybody would want to live in Toronto was something he couldn't figure. "It's about an hour outside town, but going the other way, down the shore. I got a house out there, and there's a girl to come in and clean."

"You didn't bring her with you?" Danny asked. "Lily, not the girl. Although knowing you—"

"She's not well. I hired a live-in nurse some months back, when…." There it was, that solid punch to the gut. He ought to be used to it by now. "Cancer. Neuroblastoma, they call it. That's the fancy name for it. Really, it's a fucking bastard piece of shit disease that likes to hurt little children." He turned away, forcing back the traitorous tears that filled and blurred his vision. "Uh…." He cleared his throat and turned back. "It was pretty far advanced when it was discovered, so I've had to take her elsewhere for treatment. Sloan-Kettering in New York, do you know it?"

"Yes." Danny got up, and for one horrified moment Tadhg was afraid the other man was going to hug him, but Danny only filled a glass and passed it to him. "I'm sorry." He gazed at Tadhg, his own blue eyes swimming in tears, but that was Danny. He felt the sorrows of other people more strongly than his own. He should have been a priest, that one.

"How is she?" Danny asked quietly. He sat down, warming his whisky glass between his hands.

"She's in remission," Tadhg lied. Maybe he shouldn't have said it. Perhaps saying it aloud meant he'd jinxed himself, and her. "We're 'cautiously optimistic,' as they say."

"Well, that's good."

"It's expensive, getting her treated in the States." Tadhg continued, "and I don't want to leave her to go away working, so I've been developing some properties around here. Lily, she loves this area. I thought it would be nice to have a foothold." He drank some of the whisky, relishing the deep burn it made as it went down. "I've got some put away, but you always worry that it won't be enough." He risked a long look at Danny. "I didn't come back here to fuck with your memories, Danny. The property came up for sale, and I figured you'd not want some arsehole mainlander buying it." He wiped his eyes with the tips of his fingers, no longer caring if Danny saw it or not.

"So what now?" Danny asked. "With Grandar's house?"

"Eh…." He cleared his throat and made and effort to govern his emotions. "I'm thinking of leaving it the way it is. Renovate it to period, the 1940s." Danny's grandfather had built the house after he'd returned from the war. "Get rid of the 1970s wall paneling, put in some vintage or repurposed appliances, and rent it for holidays."

"So you're not going to tear it all down?" Danny asked. "Bulldoze the lot of it?"

Tadhg was surprised that Danny would even think this. "No, absolutely not. There's land up the back where I want to put three or four small cottages. I'm not sure how many yet since I've not decided on the size." He sniffed, wishing he had a Kleenex. As if reading his mind, Danny handed him a box from one of the end tables.

"Move here, will you?"

"No. I'll stay on the island, at least for now." He put his glass on the mantelpiece. At least for now while his daughter was still alive. At least for now while the disease that was eating her body and bones had been successfully anaesthetised. He'd made himself content enough, if not actually happy. "There's something else."

Danny's entire body stiffened like an electric current had passed through it. "Yeah? Something else like what?"

"What happened with Sandra—" The expression on Danny's face stopped him dead.

"Don't you be speaking her name," Danny whispered.

"Yes, but you don't understand what—"

"I don't want to hear it."

Tadhg, stupidly, persisted. "It's not what you think it was. Me and Sandra."

Danny stood up, looming over Tadhg, and he was every inch the cop. "Shut it." Tadhg wasn't about to continue the confrontation. He knew Danny could slap him down so fast his head would spin.

"I should get going," he said quietly. "I just wanted… we haven't talked in donkey's years." He'd tried to tell Danny the truth, but Danny wasn't having it. Now Tadhg wanted to scurry away and crawl in a hole somewhere. He didn't like being vulnerable. It felt like a psychic wound to him. He stood up.

"Don't run away." Danny caught up with him as his hand was on the door. "You're still coming to the funeral, right?"

"Do you want me there?"

"Yeah." Danny laughed mirthlessly. It was a raw, vicious sound, and it made Tadhg shudder. "Say a prayer for the repose of his soul, sure. The old bastard could do with that." He shut the door, and Tadhg was outside again, and the rain had stopped.

CHAPTER THREE

THE MORNING of the funeral had dawned bright and clear, but by eleven the skies were cast across with scudding grey clouds, driven by a relentless northeast wind. Danny woke late but had no stomach for breakfast, so he made a pot of tea and sat down to look at his email. He had a couple of hours or so to waste, and he wasn't keen on wandering around the house, peering out of windows like a sad old bastard with nowhere else to go. He'd discovered more grey hairs that morning, silvering the top of his head and his temples, and he kidded himself it didn't look that bad. *You look like a fucking badger.* The sight of his own face irritated him. There was an email from Sandra, currently living in the Algarve with her latest fling, an Australian with an impenetrable accent and a tan so deep it looked like he'd been shellacked. The email was dated five days earlier.

I can't get back for Grandar's service. There's a storm coming across and they've grounded all flights. Give everyone my love.

Give everyone my love. Apart from the token apology, she didn't seem all that sorry. To be fair, Portugal was a hell of a long way from the island, much too long to come for a funeral and an informal wake of a couple hours' length with more whisky than food. And Sandra had her reasons for wanting to stay away. He didn't blame her at all for the way she felt. Grandar had been hard on Danny when he was young, but he rode Sandra mercilessly. He'd had the idea that she was some kind of village bike, the town slut that everybody'd had a go at. Nothing could have been further from the truth. From the time she'd first laid eyes on him when they were at primary school together, she'd noticed nobody but Tadhg Heaney. He'd been the great love of her life. In a lot of ways, he'd been Danny's too. But of course he never said such to anyone. Growing up on the island, you learned early on to stay inside the lines. Maybe it was different for the younger people nowadays, but when Danny was a teenager, you went to church on Sundays and kept your hands to yourself.

Sandra's jewelry designs had begun to sell at various craft fairs around the world, and she was gaining a reputation as a skillful artisan, but she hardly had money to burn, and as for the Australian, Danny had no idea what he did. Not much by the looks of things. Every picture Sandra had ever sent showed her new man lying in the sun beside a swimming pool or spread on a towel on some sun-soaked beach, baking himself to the colour of a meerschaum pipe. The last time Danny had ventured onto a beach, he'd scorched nearly every inch of skin to a dark and painful red—so painful that he'd had to drive himself to hospital in the middle of the night for an analgesic injection. Days later, his charred epidermis erupted into enormous blisters that later burst and sloughed off in long wet sheets of corrupted skin. It wasn't an experience he was eager to repeat.

Danny typed a short reply:

Sorry to miss you. Give my best to Mr. Melanoma.

The inbox flashed blue; she'd replied already.

Have you seen Tadhg Heaney? I had an email from him a couple weeks ago. He was looking for you.

His face prickled. Why would Tadhg Heaney have been looking for him then? Unless it had something to do with the house, there was no need or reason for them even to speak to each other. Danny's fingers hovered over the keyboard. Sandra's bullshit detector was knife sharp and deadly accurate. If he lied, she'd catch him out immediately, and there would be hell to pay.

Yes.

He waited. The inbox flashed blue again.

And? Look, go to instant message. I'm going cracked waiting on this back-and-forth.

He clicked on the little message icon in the lower corner of the screen. Sandra's avatar popped up immediately: a cartoon sunflower with a broad grin.

Has he been to see you? Andy Graham said Tadhg was going to buy Grandar's place.

How much was Danny willing to tell her? Sandra was his twin, considered it her right to poke as deeply as she wanted into his personal affairs. She probably knew Tadhg better than anyone.

I saw him yesterday.

He clicked the Send button and waited. Outside the wind was rising, rattling the windowpanes and funneling down the fireplace flue. It wouldn't surprise him if there was snow before day's end. The island's capricious climate frequently cycled through all four seasons in a matter of hours. He made a mental note to wear his heavy woollen overcoat. Standing at the side of a grave was the coldest place on earth.

He wants to make the old house into a holiday cottage. That's nice, isn't it? Sandra was one of these glass-half-full people, always looking on the bright side, forever optimistic. It was surprising, considering what she'd been through in her life, or maybe she was the stronger sibling. *He always thought the world of you. Why don't you get together with him?*

A flash of temper sent hot blood surging into his face. Tadhg Heaney thought the world of exactly one person: himself. *I don't think that's a good idea.*

A red and yellow smiley cat burst onto the screen. *You used to be best pals.*

Danny was surprised to learn that Sandra and Tadhg had kept in touch. *That was a long time ago.*

There was a long pause while he watched the blinking cursor. Then, *Ye got to let stuff go, Danny. I have. I don't blame Tadhg anymore.*

His skin prickled with annoyance. Sandra had never been the forgive-and-forget type until she met the Australian. Doubtless this was more of his New Age kumbaya shite. *After what he did? Yes, mind out now.*

The smiley cat popped up, blinked, and morphed into a sunflower. *You don't know everything.*

Danny's hands clenched into fists. *Says you.*

Without waiting for her reply, he closed the chat window and shut the cover of his laptop like he was closing the lid of a coffin. He gazed at his own reflection in the darkened window opposite. He looked angry. Lately, he always looked angry.

TADHG STEPPED out of the shower and reached for the towel hanging from the rack near the sink. He turned his back to the full-length mirror mounted on the door, checking the scars. They were new, a series of puncture wounds low on his hips, surrounded by deep bruising and dotted with tape burns. It had been nearly a week since the surgery, but the wounds were still sore, and even the light pressure of the towel caused him pain. He was more tired than usual and needed a couple of brief naps to get through the day. The transplant specialist had warned him to avoid strenuous physical activity for at least three weeks after the harvest, but the enforced inertia irritated the bejesus out of him. The procedure itself had been done under general anesthetic, so he'd been insensible to the thirty separate passes surgeons had made into his pelvic bone with hollow needles. It only hurt like hell after he woke up, but that didn't matter. His bone marrow was a perfect match for Lily. He would endure any amount of pain for her.

The Skype application was chiming on his laptop when he came downstairs, dried and dressed. Like Danny, he was staying in Kildevil Cove for the next couple of days. Unlike Danny, Tadhg owned this house and two or three others in the small town. As the older people died off, their houses came on the market, selling for far below their market value. The remaining relatives, children, and grandchildren, had no intention of staying in Kildevil Cove. In most cases they couldn't get clear of it fast enough, which meant Tadhg was able to pick up some decent real estate for not a lot of money.

He sat down and pulled the computer towards him, accepted the call. At once the screen filled with Lily's face, unnaturally pale and with violently coloured eyelids. "Forget it," he said.

"But Dad!"

"Did you get that from Gemma?" She looked, he thought, like a drag queen.

"It's a new kind of makeup," she said. "Her sister is selling it, and I told her I'd try it for her, to see how it looks." Her hair had begun to grow back in after the latest round of chemo, so she was still nearly bald, but she refused to wear a wig. "Everybody's shaving their heads now," she told him. "It's really cool." She looked a bit like Sinead O'Connor and thinner than she had been before the cancer returned, but he knew she'd pick up once she started eating again. He'd left strict instructions with Yvonne, Lily's nurse, that she was to eat three good meals a day according to the dietary plan set out by the nutritionist they had consulted. For a girl of Lily's age, that meant lots of fresh fruit and veg, milk and nuts and grains. She liked none of it, so Tadhg bought an expensive blender and they made smoothies that Lily grudgingly drank. He supposed it was better than nothing. Even before her diagnosis, she'd been a remarkably picky eater, and he'd weathered many dinner table arguments that usually ended in a tantrum or tears. "Does it make me look older, Dad?" This was a touchy subject. Whereas other girls her age were growing breasts and starting to notice boys (or girls), the chemo had delayed Lily's puberty indefinitely. She was flat-chested, shorter than other girls her age and, at least to his eyes, still very childlike.

He sighed. "It's too much, Lily. You don't need all that… stuff on your face."

The corners of her mouth pulled down, but she fought it, trying valiantly not to cry. She was so sensitive, everything she heard and saw affected her so much more deeply than it did others. "It makes me look pretty," she said quietly, and Tadhg's heart shattered into a thousand pieces.

"You are pretty," he said, his eyes suddenly full. "You are beautiful."

"You only say that because you're my dad."

"I say it because it's true." In a minute he was going to start crying and make a complete idiot of himself. He drew a shaky breath. "How are you feeling?"

"All right. Gemma and I might bicycle down to Languille Cove later on and take a picnic." Gemma had been Lily's best friend since kindergarten, a freckled, gum-cracking tomboy. Many of Lily's schoolmates had deserted her once it was made known she had cancer, but Gemma had stayed. For that, Tadhg was eternally grateful to her.

"Are you sure you're up for that?" The engraftment of the donor cells—his cells—had been accomplished quickly, but she was still feeling tired and had to be careful not to overdo it. In addition to the special nutritional requirements, she was on a heavy regimen of antibiotics and antirejection drugs, as well as filgrastim to encourage her body to make new blood. They wouldn't know right away if the graft had been entirely successful, but early indications were encouraging. "Maybe you and Gemma can watch a film, instead."

"But Dad, it's only a quarter of a mile."

"Lily. It's cold outside."

"I feel terrific, Dad, honest! And I've got my phone, and Gemma will have her phone, and I promise not to go any farther than the beach."

Christ, she made it hard sometimes. "Did you take your pills?"

"Yes, and I took my vitamins, and I drank my breakfast smoothie." A beat while she waited for her plea to sink in. "Just a picnic."

"Do kids still do that?" he asked. "Didn't think your generation wanted anything to do with such arcane amusements."

"Dad." She rolled her eyes. "So is it all right for me to go out with Gemma?"

"Of course. As long as you wash that rubbish off your face." He laughed at her aggrieved expression. "I love you."

"Mmm…." She huffed out an irritated sigh. "I suppose I love you too. Bye, Dad."

"Talk soon, darling."

He closed out the call just in time, was immediately racked by violent sobs. He bent forward from the waist, hands pressed against his mouth even though there was no one to hear. He cried that way for what felt like forever, on his knees on the living room rug, rocking back and forth, nearly demented by the grief that rose to swallow him alive. After a while the tears stopped, and he sat back on his heels, breathing in the silence. He was exhausted, his face hot from crying, tight with salt. He rubbed his eyes with the palms of his hands. *Jesus, Tadhg, you can't just go to pieces like that.* Lily's neuroblastoma had proven difficult to treat because the cancer had spread beyond the origin site before they'd caught it, metastasising in her bones and other organs. She had been diagnosed at ten, and this was her fourth go-round with the disease. Each successive bout of chemo weakened her further, and did little to stop the cancer's aggressive growth. Tadhg gave himself permission to hope, but he was a practical man. Four bouts of chemo, bone marrow transplants, stem cell therapy, the very best patient care that money could buy, but in the end her disease would have the final say.

He made himself get up, go into the kitchen, and drink a glass of cold water. He ran the tap again, filled his hands, and pressed his palms against his heated face. The water ran down his neck, collecting in the hollow of his throat like a kiss. Enough of this ridiculous snotting and bawling; he needed to man up. He couldn't be the strong father that Lily needed if he fell apart. She was counting on him, and he was counting on himself. They were going to survive this, and she would go on to a wonderful life. She'd meet someone, fall in love, and he'd walk her down the aisle, dance with his daughter at the wedding. Every victory between then and now, no matter how small, would be celebrated. He and Lily would get through this, the two of them.

Maybe he'd have met someone by then, and they would be somewhere close by, a solid and supportive presence, loving and helping him. He wouldn't have to do it all alone. Even a good friend would be comforting. He didn't need to sleep with someone…. *Go on with ye.* The inner voice was caustic, nasty, and sounded a lot like his old man. *Sure you'll have anything with a pulse.*

THE SMALL white wood-frame church was far from packed with people, and only a scattering of them remembered Danny or knew who he was.

He recognised Flora MacInnes, who had taught him in elementary school, and Dora Belbin, an old friend of his mother's. She caught his arm as he went by and pulled him into a hug. "I'm so sorry about your grandfather," she whispered. "He was a good man." It was the sort of lie people always told at wakes and funerals, preferring to confer angelic status on the newly deceased, as if they might be listening. Dora had been at his parents' funerals as well, when he was so much younger. He remembered she gave him peppermints from her purse and hugged him, told him he was a good boy. Gord Trimm patted his back as he stepped into the pew. Gord was deaf and unable to speak, the result of a childhood bout with meningitis. He was a few years older than Danny and had been ahead of him in school. He and Danny's sister Sandra had dated for a little while in the twelfth grade, but nothing came of it. Sandra was flighty, and Gord was much too staid for her tastes. He intended to stay in Kildevil Cove and farm the land his father had, invest in a herd of beef cattle, expand the old dairy on the property. Sandra wanted to move to the city, where she intended to get drunk a lot and party. The two of them would have never worked out. Nina Single was there, dressed primly in a navy-blue suit and a wide-brimmed hat with a flower, more suitable for a ladies' luncheon than a funeral, but that was Nina. She never missed an opportunity to make an impression.

Danny ducked his head and pretended to be looking at the order of service, a printed pamphlet informing attendees which hymns would be sung, who would read, and what they might say. He'd been approached by Glenda, the minister, to do a reading but had turned her down. He wasn't afraid of speaking in front of people, but he knew a few words about his grandfather and the brief recitation of some poem he'd learned at school was hardly sufficient. They hadn't always had an easy relationship. The old man was often mystified by him, couldn't comprehend his motivations. This was a gulf that grew wider once Danny went away to university. Grandar had no real education to speak of. Indeed, he'd been pulled out of school at the age of nine to go fishing with his father before he'd completed grade three. He could read and figure sums, but that was it, and Danny, returning from school with a head full of criminal psychology and behavioural theory, might as well have been a kraken. Once Danny left for good, his visits home naturally tapered off, and the closeness he and Grandar shared began to be eroded by Danny's changing role in the old man's life. In recent years, as his grandfather's health failed and the years of hard work began to take their toll, their relationship devolved into a superficial exchange of news and gossip, desultory talk about the weather.

The entire church service passed him by as if in a dream. He was aware of the play of light and shadow on the floors and walls and the slow drift of fallen leaves outside the window. His grandar wasn't in that fancy wooden box up at the front, nor would he be in the ground later on that day. No, his grandfather was away to the summer fishing grounds in June, rowing his bright yellow dory, or he was over in the barrens, gathering ripe red lingonberries or fishing for trout in the pond. At suppertime, when the sun was drifting towards the west, he'd come whistling out the path, his creel full of speckled rainbow trout and plump German brown, his old dog Toby by his side. They were all gone now, Nan and Grandar—dear Toby was twelve years in the ground. It was all so fucking senseless, he thought bitterly, that you were born into this world and given other souls to love with the knowledge they would be taken from you, and there was nothing you could do about it.

"Everybody dies, love." He could almost hear Alison's voice in his head. They had a long history together; she had been there at his first homicide. He was finishing up his last year of training, working extra nights and weekends to gain experience, when a call had come in about a young woman who'd been heard screaming from a house on Lime Street. The neighbour who called it in said the young couple who lived there were always at odds, and there were loud fights at all hours. Danny answered the call and was told a second constable was en route and would meet him at the scene. He got to the house and found the front door wide open and a long, sticky trail of blood from the kitchen to the back porch. He found the girl lying on her side next to a washing machine that was still running, loud and irritating in the small space.

"That's not very nice," a woman said, nodding at the girl on the floor. "I hope that dirty bugger burns in hell for it."

She was about his own age and nicely put together—although Danny later blushed to admit he'd noticed this—with long dark hair pulled back in a tidy ponytail, big blue eyes, and a soft pink mouth that reminded him of the petals of a flower. She must have been seconded from CID, the major crimes unit, because she wasn't in uniform.

"Don't take it to heart," she'd said. "You do that, and after a while it eats at you. Keep telling yourself it's just a job."

"About bloody time you got here," Danny said. He couldn't think what had kept her, not that hour of the night.

"I'm Alison Dawe," she said. "Could you help me turn her over?"

He took hold of the dead woman's shoulder while Alison did the same with her ankles. They rotated the body onto its back.

"She was a pretty girl," Danny said. "Too bad."

"Oh?" Alison raised an eyebrow at him. "So it's okay with you if the ugly ones get killed?"

"Don't be so bloody foolish."

The girl had long dark hair and big blue eyes, wide now and staring at nothing, her pink mouth slack and open. Her creamy complexion had begun to fade towards the greyness of death, the colour shading darker as the cooling blood settled into livor mortis. The hair on the back of Danny's neck stood up stiff as iron nails. He'd learned this was a habitual reaction for him, that he perceived many of the dead still in their bodies, watching him from behind their lifeless eyes.

"Sin. She was lovely." He shoved his shaking hands into his pockets.

"I know." Alison patted his forearm briefly. "But at least he didn't touch her face."

It was true. Her killer had left her beauty entirely intact—except for the screwdriver protruding from the nape of her neck. Danny sighed and sat back on his heels. "Son of a bitch didn't have to."

Danny rose with the other pallbearers and went to shoulder his grandfather's coffin, numbly followed the rest of the mourners to the gravesite across the road from the church and up a small rise to the old cemetery. The sun came out from behind the clouds for a moment, a bright flash amongst the ancient headstones, but the wind was raw from the northeast, and Danny was chilled to the bone. He shivered as the coffin went into the stony ground, too quick for actual time, and then he was bending with the others to scrape up a handful of the peaty soil and cast it down. Too well he knew how life could break your heart.

"Danny."

He turned at the sound of Tadhg Heaney's voice. The other man was standing a little distance away among the gravestones.

"Didn't know you'd be here," Danny said. "You weren't in church." Tadhg looked as weary as Danny felt, and there were dark circles beneath his eyes. He felt a pang of sympathy for the man, a single father struggling to care for his dying child. Tadhg was a bastard, but even a bastard like him didn't deserve that.

"I was," Tadhg said. "I had to come. I knew him." He moved to where Danny stood, nodded towards Nina Single and her lawyer husband, who were standing some small distance away. "Did she say anything to ye?"

"Oh yes," Danny replied. "So very sorry for your loss. He was a real pillar of the community. We should all try our best to remember."

"The usual mealy-mouthed shite she's known for," Tadhg said. "She's a cold fucking fish, that one." He huddled farther into his overcoat. "It's an awful business, funerals."

"It is that." Danny grudgingly offered his peat-damp hand, and Tadhg took it, held it for a moment, pressing Danny's cold fingers in his own warm ones. "Will you come for a drink at the house?"

He wanted Tadhg to come, even if he didn't really know why. There was no buttress for him against the collective grief of other people, his grandfather's friends, their murmured words of sympathy and proffered comfort. No one he had known in childhood still lived here; his schoolmates had all gone elsewhere to look for work, start families, build their lives. The village was a hollow shell of its former self. Tadhg at least was familiar.

"Do you want me there?" Tadhg asked.

"Yes," Danny told him. "I do."

Several of the mourners from the church were already at the house when he and Tadhg arrived, and most of the women had stayed back from the funeral in order to prepare the food and drink and get the house ready for visitors. Hetty Jamieson met Danny and Tadhg at the door with a glass of whisky in each hand. She reached to embrace Danny and kiss his cheek. "God love ye," she murmured. They followed her into the kitchen, where most of Kildevil Cove had gathered, those who knew his grandfather personally and those who knew him only by reputation. Some of the visitors had brought family with them from other nearby villages—aunts and uncles, cousins and children and babies. It ought to have made for lovely company but was merely a godawful din.

"Christ," Tadhg murmured, moving into the kitchen. "The world and its wife is here." He glanced at the assembled crowd. "All these people knew your grandar?"

Danny shrugged. "Or think they did."

Tadhg gave him a searching look. "He and my grandfather were at school together. The old school"—he gestured vaguely—"over on Belvidge Road there."

Danny found this hard to swallow. Tadhg Heaney's grandfather was descended from one of the original fish merchants, men whose power in a small place like Kildevil Cove was absolute. Using the notorious "truck system," a merchant would bind a fisherman and his family in perpetual servitude by offering necessities like food, clothing, and fishing gear on credit. When the fisherman returned at the end of the season with his catch, ready to settle up, the merchant would suddenly raise the prices or impose grossly inflated interest on the loan, leaving the fisherman with almost nothing. Many fishing families in Kildevil Cove, most of whom worked for the Heaneys, were in thrall to them from the cradle to the grave. "Your grandfather and mine went to school together?" Danny said. "First I've heard of it."

Tadhg's eyes darkened with anger. "Yes, and you fucking know everything, don't ye?"

"Not too much changes round here," Danny said. "You can't help being a proper cunt." Stung, he turned and left Tadhg where he was.

He spent some time going round the room, thanking everyone for the courtesy of their presence, exchanging anecdotes about his grandfather, accepting drinks and hugs. It felt surreal and strange, like he was standing outside his body and watching everything from a distance.

Someone filled a plate from what was laid out on the table and handed it to Danny, who refused. The last thing he wanted was food. "I'm not hungry." He drained his glass of whisky in one go. He felt wobbly on his legs, unsteady. The room had begun to slowly revolve around him, and his eyes wouldn't focus. A hand fastened on his elbow. "For fuck sake," Tadhg said, "look at the friggin' state you're in."

"Leave me be," Danny said. What did it matter if he was sober or completely legless? Drinking and eating changed very little in the world; whether you slept or ate or walked or didn't, you personally affected nothing.

"That's utter shite," Tadhg said.

Danny turned, surprised to see Tadhg was still there. "What?"

"You," Tadhg replied sourly, "the policeman philosopher. What, are ye turning into a poet now? Pissed to the eyes and spouting wisdom."

Tadhg's face wavered in front of him. *Yes, I am very drunk right now*. This wasn't like him. He drank, of course—everybody did—but never like this. Good thing Alison wasn't here to see this. "You'll be throwing up your guts tomorrow morning. What are ye doing to yourself?"

"Keep the A.A. rubbish to yourself," he said. "I've no head for hearing it."

Tadhg lifted a full bottle of whisky from the kitchen table. "Come on," he said, tilting his head towards the back of the house. "It's like a bloody hen night in here." He led Danny out into the yard and opened the door of the garden shed. "This is better." They could still hear the gabber from the house, so he closed them in, pulled the cork with his teeth, and poured them both a healthy portion. Danny tossed the whisky down his throat and held out his glass, his arm swaying back and forth.

"You're best easing off on that," Tadhg said. "You'll be sick as a pig in the morning. Not to mention you're drinking on an empty stomach."

Danny shook his head, grabbed the bottle, and poured, filling his glass to the brim. What was he trying to do? Some small, sane part of him protested that this was a bad idea, that he shouldn't get drunk, not now. He would end up embarrassing himself, say something he'd later regret, make promises he couldn't possibly keep. What had happened to his habitual caution?

"I'm glad you came," Danny said. He didn't look at Tadhg but down into his glass instead. "I didn't expect to see you."

Tadhg paused, gazing at him as if trying to memorise Danny's features. Then he reached out and drew him into a one-armed hug. He smelled really good, the way Tadhg always did, like fresh cold air with a hint of green citrus. His cologne was probably distilled mountain water, brought in from the Himalayas especially for him. Christ knew he could afford it.

"I'm glad we came to an understanding, Danny," he said, his mouth against Danny's ear. "It's important to me. I couldn't proceed without your blessing." He clasped the back of Danny's head, held him close. "Thank you so much."

It was said with a certain self-assurance that rankled. Danny pulled back, causing Tadhg to drop his arm. "What do you mean?"

"Your grandfather's house." Tadhg took a sip of whisky, gazing at him over the rim of his glass. "I'll have Rosemary draw up the deed of sale—"

"Will you now?" The venom in Danny's voice left Tadhg gawping like a landed fish. "I already told you, I will not sell to you." Danny was paying attention now, no longer wobbly and muzzy-headed from the drink.

"Why?"

"Because it means nothing to you," Danny spat. "It's another property, a business investment, a way for you to add more to your burgeoning millions. You're a shark, Tadhg, another money-hungry sleveen who cares about nothing and nobody."

"That is not true," Tadhg said flatly. "I want to buy your grandfather's property to preserve it, I already told you that." His gaze slid over Danny's face. "I don't intend to make a mockery of it. Danny, I want us to—"

"You will," Danny said sharply, cutting him off. He was beginning to slur his words, but he no longer cared. "You don't give a fuck as long as you get what you want. You'll tell anybody anything." He laid his now-empty glass down and grabbed Tadhg's lapels. "You're a fucking liar, that's what—"

"Shut up, for fuck sake." Tadhg pushed him away, probably harder than he intended. Danny hit the opposite wall, caromed off a low shelf, and fell to the floor.

"Son of a bitch," he said, not really meaning it. "I didn't come here to be hove around by you." He'd returned to Kildevil Cove for Grandar, and only for Grandar, to see to the funeral and the sale of the old man's house. "Put your hands on me again and I'll fucking blind ye." He tried to stand, failed, and sat down hard on the wooden floor. Fucking legless, he was. The only thing for it now was sleep. Yes, that's what he'd do. He'd go to sleep and be well out of it. Danny leaned against a pile of dusty, half-rotted old fishing nets and fell gladly into the arms of Morpheus.

IT WAS full dark when he woke, and for a little while he had no idea where he was. The light inside the shed had been turned on, and the door was open a crack, letting in the cold night air. He blinked and squinted until the shape across the room resolved itself into Tadhg, sitting with his knees drawn up, a half-empty bottle of Glenfiddich clasped between his hands.

"About time you rejoined the living," he said. He raised the bottle to his lips and took a long drink. "Everybody's gone home. I went inside before they could come looking for ye, told them you were overcome with grief and wanted to be on your own." Another slug of whisky. "Ye can thank me later."

"You're still not getting the house," Danny said. A wave of sickness rose in him, and he headed for the door, crawling and stumbling and finally falling face first on the brown October grass. He managed to brace himself on his knees and elbows, vomiting until there was nothing coming up but bile. Someone—Tadhg—caught him under the arms and hoisted him to his feet, frogmarched him towards the house. He lurched up the front steps and then fell against the door, Tadhg reaching around him to open it. "Get in, you friggin' fool. You're fucking shitfaced, you are." The sofa came up to meet him, and he dropped onto it, his head slumped against the back. He was swimming in and out of the world, and that was all right because Tadhg was here to help him. Tadhg would help him. Tadhg was good for that, at least. He closed his eyes.

In the darkness behind his lids, he saw himself standing on the Clontarf sea wall in the pouring rain while storm-driven waves lashed at his feet. It was late afternoon and already getting dark, the streetlights coming on in quick succession. The area had been cordoned off with fluttering police tape, and red and blue lights at either end of the street washed the surreal urban landscape with strobing strips of colour. A young man in dark jeans and a rain-soaked jumper sat astride the sea wall, legs dangling, his face twisted in anguish and despair. He held a gun against his temple, teeth bared like an animal in mortal pain. He was screaming something unintelligible, a series of guttural syllables that sounded nothing like actual words. Danny's perspective changed constantly: one moment he was close to the boy, close enough to touch, and in the next moment he was miles away, staring at the scene in horror.

Give me the gun.

Please give me the gun.

You don't want to do this. Just give me the gun.

His perspective wavered, snapped shut like a trap, and he was right there in the young man's face. *Please, Eamonn, give me the gun.*

Every time, he told himself he was ready for it. Every time he told himself it would be different… and every time the gun went off with a deafening report, and there was blood in his face, blood running into his eyes, not his own blood—

Danny woke with a gasp. The room was dark, and it was night outside, with a thin fingernail slice of moon riding just above the horizon. He was stripped to his underwear and lying in his own bed. The digital clock on the dresser read 4:29 a.m.

As usual, Tadhg was gone.

CHAPTER FOUR

THE CHARTER Club was packed to the walls, and it was very late, but Tadhg didn't know what time it was. He didn't care. He assumed he was still in Amsterdam, crushed into a banquette seat with five other people, two men and three women. Someone had their hand on his thigh, kneading the muscle slowly and deliberately, but the booze and the darkness, the pounding music, and the drugs he'd ingested dulled his senses. The room and all its contents, human and otherwise, were saturated with darkness, soaking in it, and he was dark as well, as dark as unholy fuck. He closed his eyes as the hand on his thigh slid up, cupping the growing bulge at his crotch. He raised his head to watch as a woman straddled his lap, her naked thighs clenched around his hips.

The club had disappeared. The silence was deafening. He shifted himself on his chair as the woman undulated on top of him, grinding her pelvis against his, her head thrown back and her mouth open in simulated ecstasy. *Lap dance,* he thought. Had he paid for this? Where was his wallet? Rutger had been paying for the drinks. He'd taken one of his credit cards out before he left the hotel and stuck it in his back pocket, but every time he tried for pay for anything, Rutger or one of his friends waved him off. It didn't bother him, not really. Nothing bothered him now. Where the hell was his wallet?

His head was going round, and it was hard to figure anything, his thoughts moving slow as oil. What the hell had he taken? This wasn't coke or crystal or E but something else. He had been sitting at a banquette surrounded by other people while the woman next to him caught his chin in her hand, opened her mouth, and kissed him. He'd hardly felt the trespass of the tiny piece of blotting paper, and by then it was too late— it had already begun crackling along his synaptic pathways, shattering reality. People in strange costumes were walking back and forth in front of him; he was in a hallway or corridor, maybe backstage at some kind of play, while the performers moved past him, going somewhere else.

You shouldn't even be here. You should be home with Lily. What kind of bullshit is this? Business. It was business. This was an important deal he was making, and it was important to romance the client. Wasn't that the point?

A buzzing noise cut across his senses, as insistent as a bullhorn, and he reached out towards the source of the sound, grabbing his iPhone from the bedside table. "Mmm."

It was still night outside the windows of his hotel room. He'd gone to sleep fully dressed and with the drapes open. It was his habit not to close them whenever he slept away, because he liked to wake to natural light in the room. "Tadhg?"

"Yes." The manic high of the previous night was gone, and he felt faintly afraid. How had he gotten back to his hotel room? Who had unlocked the door and put him to bed?

"Where are you?" The voice was a woman's, but he didn't recognise it, not right away. The woman was somebody important. He knew that much.

"I'm in Amsterdam. I had dinner last night with Rutger van der Heide from Naxco." Rutger had picked him up at his hotel in a taxi, and they'd driven through the darkened city to a small restaurant tucked away on a dead-end street. He'd intended to pin Rutger down on the possibilities for the project they'd initially discussed, but there was a lot of drinking, and eventually they'd gone on to the club, where Rutger had introduced him to some friends. "I'm flying back day after tomorrow." Yvonne, he thought. The woman's name was Yvonne. She was his daughter's nurse. His daughter—wait. "Is something wrong with Lily?"

"She had a bad nosebleed early yesterday morning, but it stopped. Dr. Stack said she's holding her own for now. We thought that was the extent of it, but then she spiked a slight fever last evening, so he thought it best to admit her."

He threw back the covers and put his feet on the floor. "Which hospital?"

"The Janeway. They want to keep her in overnight."

"I'm coming home." Fuck Rutger. They hadn't been able to reach any kind of agreement the night before, and their business dinner had turned into an evening of debauchery. "Call Dr. Genge at Sloan-Kettering in New York. His number's already programmed into the landline. I'll get the next flight out." He paused to draw a deep breath, attempting to calm his racing heart. "Get hold of Robbie Tuck at Cougar, have him put one of the Sikorskys on standby, just in case we need it." He would charter a helicopter for her, of course he would. She was his daughter. He'd get a bloody flying carpet if that was what it took. "It's probably not necessary. Dr. Stack said she's stable." She was right, of course. Was he jumping at shadows? No, he knew the truth about Lily's condition even if she didn't. The latest transplant had been a gamble and a leap in the dark, a last-ditch effort to stop the relentless progress of a cunning and deadly disease.

If her marrow failed to regenerate, then his daughter was dying. She had been dying for a long time. A very long time, and she must be exhausted by now. A wave of sadness washed over him, and he forced it back. This was no time to get mawkish.

"It's fine," he said. "I'll call you once I've booked the flight." He rang off and reached into his inside pocket for his wallet. It was missing. Had he left it at the club? Had someone stolen it? He went to where his suitcase sat against the far wall and rifled through it, tossing clothing out onto the floor, searching all the individual pockets on the sides. Nothing. Oh sweet holy Christ, his entire life was in that wallet. *Don't panic, Tadhg. You've had worse than this, you have so.*

A thorough search of all the drawers and cupboards brought nothing. Where was it? It didn't make sense. He'd had it when he went to the club, and surely he hadn't left it in the bathroom. He'd gone in for a quick piss, washed his hands, grinned at himself in the mirror, and went back out. Everything was exactly right. Nothing had moved. The people round the table were the same as when he'd gone in. His half-empty whisky tumbler was where he'd left it, its heavy glass bottom inscribing a circle of dampness on the tablecloth. That had struck him funny at the time—a nightclub with tablecloths. Then again, it was a rather chi-chi kind of place, fancy light fixtures in the ceiling, luxurious chairs and banquette seats set at tiny tables, everyone squeezed together. A girl in a silver cocktail dress had been sitting next to him, her thigh against his. She'd been touching him, running her fingers lightly up and down his leg….

Yes, the lap dance girl, twisting and grinding, riding him until he'd climaxed messily in his pants, disgusting himself. *You're such a fucking boy, that's what you are. A friggin' little boy in a man's body.*

The armoire on the other side of the room held a flat-screen TV set and had two lower drawers for extra bedding. He checked the top drawer and then the bottom. Nothing. His cell phone rang; the Uber taking him to the airport was here. "Can't you wait a minute?"

"I'm parked in the fire lane," the man said, "and I have to go now. You'd best get down here."

He called down to the front desk and spoke to the night manager. Had anyone turned in a man's wallet? The cash was incidental. All but one of his credit cards were in there, and pictures of Lily as a baby and…

…a picture of him and Danny when they were lads, arms wrapped around each other and grinning like fools. He remembered when it was taken, on a hot July afternoon they'd spent swimming and larking in Church Pond. It was snapped long before digital cameras, and the dog-eared snapshot was the only copy he had. He didn't need it to remember since he'd looked at it a hundred times, but that wasn't the point. It was one thing from his past he wanted—no, needed—to hold on to, seeing himself and Danny grinning like fools back in their glory days.

At least he had a credit card. That would get him home. He left word with hotel reception that his wallet had gone missing. They promised to contact him if and when it surfaced.

He was lucky enough to find the single remaining seat on a flight to London that connected with an overseas one that would land him on the island late the next afternoon. He called Rutger's office from the airport and got his secretary. He left a message that he'd been called away, and Rutger could ring him if he wanted to. He was more than a little annoyed that Rutger had blown off what was supposed to be an important meeting. Did that fucker think he had time to burn? This was business, goddammit. Then his flight was called, and he took his seat, popped an Ambien, and pulled down the window shade. The last thing he remembered was the earthwards thrust of the engines as the plane lifted into the air. Then he was gone. The landing at Heathrow was quick and painless. Less than an hour later, he was in the air again, heading for home.

He woke while the plane was somewhere over the Atlantic, still too far out from the island to see anything besides choppy grey water. He checked his phone, expecting to see a message from Yvonne or even from Lily, but there were three missed calls from Danny. He listened to his voicemail with weary detachment. The first two were hang-ups, which meant Danny had started to call him, then thought better of it. The third was a short voice message.

Tadhg, it's Danny. I've changed my mind. Call me.

It was late afternoon when he landed, and the city was cold and sere, with a damp wind blowing straight out of the northeast. He tried to return Danny's call while driving from the airport to the children's hospital, but there was no answer. He contacted Yvonne, Lily's nurse, who replied on the first ring. "Where are you?" he demanded.

"They've admitted her, like I said." She knew better than to give him false hope. "We're on the ward now."

"There as soon as I can," Tadhg said and rang off. He found a parking spot in the underground lot next to the hospital and took the tunnel from the parking garage. He caught the first elevator available from the main lobby and rode it to the fourth floor. He knew where Lily would be. They'd gone through this many times before.

"Mr. Heaney!" The charge nurse slipped out from behind the desk and stopped him in the hallway. "Wait." She was short and neat, around Tadhg's own age, with a no-nonsense attitude and flaming red hair. Her nametag read Marion Rendell.

"I need to see my daughter," he panted. Christ, he was out of shape. Time to get back on the bike again, or maybe take up running. Yes, he'd take up running. Didn't Danny run? He'd go running with Danny, and why the hell was he thinking this now? "Where's Lily?"

"She's in isolation. Early this morning Yvonne alerted us that Lily had had a fairly severe nosebleed. We've isolated her for her own protection." She went into a closet to one side of the desk and brought out a set of hospital scrubs—a yellow paper gown, and a blue cap with matching shoe covers. "Put these on. I'm sure you know the drill." He did as he was told; then Marion led him to an isolation unit at the end of the hall. Lily was sitting up in bed, playing a game on her iPhone. The breath went out of him in one huge gust of relief. Yvonne sat in a recliner in the corner of the room, reading a magazine. She stood up when he came in. "I'll leave you two alone," she said. Tadhg thanked her and went to sit on the edge of the bed.

"So what's the big idea?" he asked. "Is this some sort of ploy to make me come home?"

"Dad." She rolled her eyes.

"Don't roll your eyes at your old dad." He leaned in and kissed her. "You scared the bejesus out of me, and I'm sure you scared Yvonne. What did you do to bring this on?" She was avoiding his eyes. "Lily?"

"It was nothing. Like I told you, I went out with Gemma. You said I could go."

"Right, and where did you and Gemma go?"

"Mr. Fahey's rabbits had babies." Fahey was an old landowner whose family had originally owned the island; Tadhg allowed him a smallholding at the other end of Eigus in return for some gardening or other trivial tasks.

Oh Christ. He squeezed his eyes shut. "Lily, you know you aren't supposed to go near animals! What possessed you to go to Fahey's farm?"

"I'm so sick of it," she said. She tossed her phone aside. "Sitting in the house with Yvonne and watching television or playing on the computer. I'm never allowed to *do* anything."

"I'm sorry it has to be this way." Panic began to flutter in his chest. He and Lily had always been able to talk honestly, but this had become more difficult as she got older. Now it seemed there were myriad unwritten rules of communication that he couldn't begin to understand, all of which served to distance him from his daughter. She was more defiant now than she had ever been, questioning and contradicting him, refusing his requests outright—and she knew the truth of her own condition, or at least, some of the truth. She knew she was very ill. She didn't know this had been the last failed transplant, and there would be no more after this.

"You cannot be around farm animals or anywhere there might be the possibility of infection," he said.

"I'm not allowed to do sweet fuck all," she said sourly.

"Do not use that word." He tried to be stern and failed, offered her a watery smile instead. *Keep it together, Tadhg. Don't frighten her. Be calm.*

"Why the fuck not?" She scoffed. "It's not like it matters. I'll be in a body bag soon enough."

Tadhg sighed and pressed the heels of his hands into his eyes. "I am not having this argument now." He stood up. "I'll stay in town for tonight." No sense in driving all the way to Portugal Cove, where he kept his motor launch moored. He'd only be on Eigus for the night before he'd have to come back and fetch Lily and Yvonne in the morning. "Tomorrow we'll all go home together. Okay?" When she didn't answer, he said, "You know I love you."

"I love you too, Dad." Her expression said otherwise. He leaned in and kissed her again, lingering for a moment, breathing in the clean smell of her. She still smelled the way she did when she was a baby. "I'll see you tomorrow. Get some rest." Marion was at the nurses' station when he went out. "I don't suppose Dr. Stack is around?" he asked.

"Sorry. He's in surgery right now. Is there anything I can help you with?"

"I'd hoped to get a rundown of Lily's condition. She's admitted to being around animals, as I'm sure you know. Is there any evidence of infection?"

Marion went to the desk and tapped on a computer keyboard. "When Dr. Stack initially saw her, she was feverish and eosinophilic. Some rash on the palms and soles, possible GVHD." Graft-versus-host disease. The worst possible outcome of the transplant. Tadhg's heart stuttered for an instant in his chest. "We've taken a biopsy from the sole of her foot, and we're waiting on the results. Dr. Stack may want to do a chest X-ray, depending on what the biopsy shows. We're always worried it's gotten into the lungs, so it's best to get hold of it and treat it right away."

"Can I stay with her? What time is Dr. Stack going to be out of surgery?"

"If you limit your visit to a few minutes, all right. Lily needs to rest." She checked her watch. "He's due to come back later this evening. Is there a number where I can call you?" She was brisk and professional, her face betraying nothing, but Tadhg knew. There was nothing more that Stack or any other doctor here could do for Lily. It felt like someone had sucked the air out of his lungs. It was too soon, much too soon. *I'm not ready to lose her yet.*

He assembled his features into something approaching normalcy. "You have my cell phone number, I think." He gave it to her again, just in case. "I'm staying in town for the night. You will alert me if there's anything… anything at all?"

"Of course."

"I will probably take her to New York after she's been discharged," he told her. "Their facilities are top of the line—" He stopped, suddenly ashamed. He hadn't meant to criticise. This hospital had done all they could for her, had taken extraordinary measures. "I'm sorry, I didn't mean…." He squeezed his eyes shut. *Maybe I'll count to ten, and when I open my eyes, everything will be normal. She won't have cancer. We can go home, and she'll be my little girl again.*

"You don't need to apologise." She laid a hand briefly on his arm. "Mr. Heaney, you know we have done everything humanly possible to do in your daughter's case. Think carefully about where you want to go from here. For her sake."

He went into Lily's room. She had abandoned her game and lay asleep, her naked head looking small and vulnerable against the pillow. With the two of them together here like this, he still felt more alone than he had in his life. He bent low and kissed her forehead, murmured that he loved her. *Let nothing happen to her in the night,* he prayed. He lifted her small hand with its bitten nails and chipped nail polish, the friendship bracelet from Gemma around her wrist, and kissed the backs of her knuckles.

"I'll ask the charge nurse if I can get Gemma in to see you," he said. "Would ye like that?" Gemma would bring her native cheerfulness with her, and shine a light for Lily, and they could whisper and giggle and be girls together. "Dad will see you in the morning." He kissed her knuckles again and laid her hand down by her side. "I'll be back to see you."

He stepped out into the corridor, pain stabbing at his chest, and leaned for a moment against the wall. It was hard to breathe. He forced himself calm, drawing in slow breaths and pushing them back out again, over and over, until he felt strong enough to go on. He went to find Yvonne, nearly ran her down as she came off the elevator. "God, I'm sorry," he said. "I wasn't watching where I was going."

"You look like shite," she said frankly. "What'd you get up to in Amsterdam?"

"The usual," he sighed. He'd known Yvonne too long to even consider lying to her. "And someone stole my wallet."

"You'd better cancel all your credit cards," she said. "I've heard horror stories. Some people have even had their identity stolen."

"I'm going to call as soon as I get to the hotel," he said. "I'm staying in town tonight. I'd rather we all go home together tomorrow. Much less hassle." He didn't mention his thought about taking Lily back to New York. There would be time enough to tell Yvonne about it once the travel arrangements had been made.

"That makes sense," she said. "Marion is going to put me up for the night, so I'll see you tomorrow."

"Are you sure? I'm happy to pay for a hotel room."

"No, it's fine. We were at nursing school together," Yvonne said. "It'll be fun."

"All right. If there's any change—"

"I will let you know."

He left reluctantly, feeling like he'd abandoned Lily, and drove downtown where he found a room at the Sheraton on Cavendish Square. He went up in the elevator, unlocked the door, and threw his leather weekend bag at the bed. It landed, bounced off, and fell onto the floor, and he heard something inside crack. "Fuck." He got the bag open and saw that the snow globe he'd bought in Amsterdam for Lily had broken and was leaking water. "No." Lily loved snow globes. She'd collected them ever since she was a small girl. Wherever Tadhg went in the world, he bought one for her, and she had amassed a sizeable collection over the years. "Fuck," he said again. She would be so disappointed when he told her it was broken. He'd have to buy her something else here in the city, but it wouldn't be the same.

He threw the broken snow globe away, then stripped and ran the shower warm, hoping to lull himself into an early bedtime. A kettle was provided in the room, so he made some hot tea to take to bed with him. He felt about a thousand years old. Had it been only yesterday that Yvonne had called him in Amsterdam? It seemed more like months had passed between then and now. He rummaged through his bag and found a pair of lounge pants and a T-shirt, still miraculously dry, and pulled them on, then got into bed. What time was it? Nine o'clock, which meant it was seven thirty in New York, too late for anyone to be in the office at the pediatric cancer care centre at Sloan-Kettering. He could call the direct access number, but all that would probably get him was a recording asking him to leave a message. He stuffed three pillows behind his back and sipped at his tea. The earliest he could call was nine thirty local time, so there was nothing to be done until tomorrow morning. He picked up his phone and stared at the icons on the screen. Danny had called and wanted Tadhg to call him back. He swiped through to Danny's number and tapped the screen. The call connected, ringing on the other end.

The wind had risen outside, battering at the hotel windows. Leaves and other debris were caught by the external security lights and rendered in surreal detail as they went whirling past. A door slammed somewhere down the hall.

"Hello?"

"Danny." *Please don't hang up.* He needed desperately to talk, and there was no one, only Danny. "It's me, Tadhg."

"Tadhg," Danny said, "I wasn't sure you got my message." He sounded tired. "I've been in to Grandar's house most of the day, cleaning the place."

"Why?" Tadhg was puzzled. "There's been no one living there since—"

"I know," Danny cut him off. "The door must have blown open in the night. There was rubbish all over the place."

"Rubbish?" The back of Tadhg's neck prickled. "What kind of rubbish?"

"Empty beer bottles, chip bags, chocolate bar wrappers, energy-drink tins, torn clothing—might have been forcibly removed, or maybe the spirit simply moved them"—Tadhg couldn't help himself; he smirked at that—"and a fuck of a lot of used condoms." Danny sighed heavily. "I was at it all day."

"You said… you left a message that said you'd changed your mind." Tadhg swallowed some tea, wishing it were whisky. "I wondered what you meant."

"Oh, that." Danny cleared his throat. "If you want the house, it's yours."

"Oh." Why the sudden change, he wondered. He hadn't said anything particularly persuasive to make Danny do a complete one-eighty. "You said you'd rather burn it to the ground. You were quite firm on that point, if I remember." He couldn't stop himself needling Danny. The urge was like an itchy insect bite he had to scratch.

"I don't want to fight with you," Danny said. "I'm too bloody tired to fight with anybody."

"Well, thank you. I appreciate it." He paused. "Lily is in hospital."

"What?"

"She had a nosebleed this morning… no, that's a lie, it was yesterday morning." The sense of strange time was still with him. "They've admitted her to the hospital for overnight."

"Christ, Tadhg. I'm sorry." Danny's voice was warm and close, almost as if he were sitting beside him… almost as if he and Danny were still friends. "Do you need me?"

Tadhg's eyes blurred with tears. "Would you come if I asked?"

"Are you asking?"

"No, it's not necessary." He shook his head, even though Danny couldn't see him. "She'll be released in the morning." A sob rattled in his throat; too late he tried to force it back. "I'm taking her home to Eigus with me."

"Jesus, Tadhg." Danny's voice was sad. "I can meet you at the pier tomorrow morning if that's what you want." Danny—sensitive, intuitive Danny—had correctly perceived what he meant when he said "home to Eigus."

Home to die.

"Is that what you want, Tadhg?" Danny asked.

"Not much choice, really." He forced a note of practicality into his voice. "So I'll see you at the pier?"

"I'll be there."

THE ISLAND of Eigus had at one time been nothing more than a place for local farmers to put the sheep in summer for grazing, until Tadhg bought it, built a big house on it, and turned acres of rocky soil into an all-season playground for his well-heeled friends. It was a handy place to invite prospective investors whose time, attention, and money he hoped to attract to his real estate development business. Danny had never been to Eigus, and despite living a mere ninety minutes' drive away, Tadhg had never bothered to ask him. Of course, ever since the final rupture in their relationship, it was unlikely he'd go hunting for Danny so he could invite him to his private island. "I can't forgive this," Danny had said. "So don't even ask. I will never forgive you."

He waited now in his car, parked next to Tadhg's private pier. A huge white behemoth of a yacht—it was far too big to be thought of as a mere boat—rode the waves, tethered to a bollard by heavy mooring lines. He'd been there for an hour, looking out at the water and wondering what he was going to say to Tadhg. "Sorry your daughter is dying"? "I didn't know"? Or should he just pretend everything was normal, greet Lily like she was any other teenaged girl, ask teasing questions about boys?

I didn't know. I'm so sorry, Tadhg. I didn't know. Would that be the right thing to say? He was supposed to be good at this sort of thing. How many times had he been required to deliver bad news to the loved ones of a murder victim? He was often among the first responders at bad accident scenes, the first to witness untold horrors that normal people, regular citizens, couldn't possibly imagine. Danny was the one who informed parents that their child hadn't made it home from school, that their body had been found floating face down in the harbour, that they'd been kidnapped, violated, and killed by a pervert with no conscience. *I'm sorry to have to tell you… your son… your daughter… your spouse….* He'd had years of practice at this sort of thing, but he was never able to detach himself, as some of his colleagues did, from the situation. Danny's emotions were powerful, often ungovernable, and he felt things far deeper than most people. He cried easily, far too easily for a career police officer, some would say, and his joy was large and overwhelming. His empathy for the victims of crime and those who had lost someone often brought him to the brink of tears and strengthened his resolve to bring the perpetrator in. He'd often wished he were less emotionally labile—or emotionally incontinent, as Tadhg had once called it—but at this stage of his life, he understood this was an integral part of his personality, as natural to him as his dark blond hair or the freckles on his nose and forehead.

He glanced up, drawn out of his musings by the sight of Tadhg's black pickup truck. Like everything else Tadhg owned, it was huge, ostentatious, and had more options than a special-order sex toy. The cab was so high it almost needed a stepladder to reach, and there were no less than four shiny chrome exhaust pipes coming out the back. He waited until Tadhg had parked before getting out.

"Danny." Tadhg looked haggard, tired, and old, even worse than the last time Danny had seen him. "I'm glad you're here." He turned to help a middle-aged woman down from the truck, introduced her as Yvonne, Lily's nurse. "And this of course is Lily."

She was beautiful, but terribly pale and oh-so-thin, her eyes sunk deep into her skull, her lips as white as paper. She wore a brightly patterned silk scarf on her head, and Danny assumed she'd lost her hair to chemo. What a damn shame, he thought bitterly. She was, what? Fourteen years old? She didn't seem to expect a handshake, and Danny didn't offer it. "Danny—Inspector Quirke—is my old pal," Tadhg lied. "We were boys at school together."

"Hi," she said listlessly. She was clearly very tired, the kind of tiredness Danny had seen in people at the end of their lives. Alison had looked that way right before she died. "Okay if I go aboard?" Lily asked, turning to her father.

"Of course, my darling. Yvonne, can you help Lily?"

The nurse came forward and took Lily's elbow. "Nice to meet you," Lily said politely. She went with Yvonne, who supported her up the gangplank and onto the boat. Tadhg's gaze followed her every move.

"She's not well, is she?" Danny asked. There was no point in avoiding the obvious. "It's palliative care, isn't it?"

"Yes." Tadhg turned to him, his eyes red-rimmed. "Look, Danny, I don't expect you to just forget what happened between us. I don't think anybody could be expected to do that. And I don't expect forgiveness either. I just want—"

"I'm here," Danny said firmly. He needed to put a stop to Tadhg's overemotional rambling. "I'll help in whatever way I can."

It took twenty minutes to travel from Portugal Cove to Eigus, and Danny spent all of it on deck. He loved the sea, had often gone fishing with his grandfather as a boy, and even though the early November air was cold, it refreshed him and cleared his head. He'd been of two minds whether to call Tadhg the other day, but something prodded him, flicked impatient fingers at the back of his mind until he was forced to give in. He wondered whether his grandfather hadn't taken to haunting him. As far as he was concerned, he and Tadhg had parted ways the night after the funeral. He had nothing more to say to Tadhg, and presumably Tadhg had nothing more to say to him. But Tadhg was never far from his thoughts, and even when he forced himself to think of something else, some memory or other would resurface to remind him; he and Tadhg had loved each other once.

They'd been an unlikely pairing—the spoiled, indulged son of the local ruling fish merchant, an oligarch of cod, and the orphan son of two very ordinary people who'd died innocuously when their car had collided with a moose one dark November night. Danny was smart, quick to learn, and fiercely independent, while Tadhg was lazy and shiftless, indolent in the extreme. Tadhg's family lived in a huge house out on the point, overlooking the sea from which they drew their wealth, while Danny's grandparents, already in late middle age when his parents were killed, occupied their modest wood-frame cottage with a palpable resentment. Tadhg's family ate in the dining room, with candles and wine and a proper cloth on the table. They went on holiday in the summertime, to the mainland or even abroad. Tadhg and his brother, Declan, had passports with their pictures in. Danny and Sandra might get a Sunday afternoon picnic at New Melbourne Beach if their grandparents felt up to it.

But Danny didn't care about Tadhg's money, no more than Tadhg cared about Danny's relative poverty. Danny read a lot of books and always had interesting tidbits of information to share. Tadhg was funny, willing at a moment's notice to engage in whatever foolishness he or Danny had thought up. They rode bikes together and swam in the summer, and Danny defended Tadhg against the bullies who considered him a worthy target of their abuse. They had sleepovers in a tent in Tadhg's backyard, practised smoking purloined cigarettes, and wrestled in Tadhg's huge bedroom, throwing each other onto the bed and bouncing off the walls.

They told each other secrets. Danny first noticed the scars when they were changing for gym class one day in the eighth grade—livid dark red stripes lying in parallel lines across Tadhg's shoulders and lower back. Danny had never seen anything like it.

"Lord Christ, bhoy, what happened to your back?"

Tadhg had merely shrugged. "Dad did it. My own fault, I suppose. I punched Declan in the mouth and broke one of his teeth." Danny couldn't get the image out of his mind. Not of Declan's damaged mouth, but the long red stripes on Tadhg's pale skin.

"Does it hurt?"

"It hurt when he did it, but not now." He'd glanced nonchalantly at his back in the mirror. "Looks some bad, though. You'd think he was after killing me." He caught Danny by the arm as he turned away. "Don't go saying nothing, okay? Keep it to yourself."

THEY SPENT the day together, Tadhg showing Danny around the island and the property, and in the evening Tadhg fired up the huge outdoor barbecue and they grilled steak and salmon. By eight, Lily was tired, so Tadhg saw her up to bed early and tucked her in. "Do you want to be read a story? 'Three Little Pigs' or something?" She rolled her eyes. "Keep doing that," Tadhg said, "and one of these days they'll get stuck that way."

"Dad, that's an old myth." She slid down in the bed and drew the duvet up to her chin. She looked like a child, Tadhg thought, like the little girl he remembered. "Can I have some hot cocoa?" she asked.

He pretended to be annoyed with her. "What do you think this is? The hospital? You'll not get waited on hand and foot here, missy." He left her and went downstairs, made a cup of cocoa in the microwave. He fully expected her to be asleep when he returned, but she was sitting up in bed, looking at something on her iPad. "Your cocoa, m'lady." He handed her the cup. "Careful now, that's hot." He sat on the end of her bed, nodded towards the iPad. "What are you doing? Planning to take over the world?"

She turned the tablet so he could see the screen. "I'm making you a memory book." He leaned in to take a closer look. She had uploaded various photos from different times in her life, some of her by herself, some with friends, and others with him. "That's very nice," he said. "So are you going to set up a blog? Is that what they call it? Where you write in it regularly, tell people what's going on."

"No." She sipped her cocoa and made an appreciative noise. "It's just for you." He gazed at her, wondering what she meant.

"Just for me?" he asked.

"After I'm gone," she said. "It'll be so you can remember me."

"What…?" A chill sliced him through, and he was suddenly sick to his stomach. "What do you mean? Lily, what did they tell you at the hospital? Has someone said something?" He caught her by the upper arms, gently. "What did they say?"

"I know the graft didn't take," she said calmly. "I heard the nurses talking about it. I'm not strong enough for another bone marrow transplant. There's nothing else they can do." She reached out and cupped his cheek in her palm. "Don't cry, Dad, please. Honestly, I don't mind."

"What in Christ's name do you mean, you don't mind?" He bolted off the bed and walked to the window, looking out but seeing nothing. It had been dark since four that afternoon, and the dim light from the room behind him reflected the image of his own face on the glass. "I'd like to know who saw fit to talk about it right in front of you." He wrapped his arms around himself, clasping his elbows. He was so angry he could feel it vibrating in his bones. "I'm going to call that hospital and get to the bottom of this. Just you wait—"

"Dad!" Her voice stopped him cold. She was crying silently, tears slipping down her pale and sunken cheeks. "You have to *stop*." She dropped her head into her hands. "You have to stop now. Please. I'm tired."

He sat on her bed and took her into his arms. "I can't stop," he whispered. "When it's you I can't ever stop, do ye hear me?" He held her a little distance away and looked at her. There was time. There had to be time. She was so young, still. "Please don't make me." *You're all I've got.* "We can try at the hospital in New York. They're world-renowned, cutting-edge. They've got technologies and medicines they've never even heard of around here. We'll see the same doctor as last time, what was his name? He was nice, wasn't he? You liked him." He clasped her hands in his, his thumbs drifting over her bitten nails. "When are you going to stop doing this, eh? You've nearly gnawed them to the elbows." He reached out and wiped her tears with the tail of his shirt. "Enough crying, now. Your old dad will fix it. Don't I always?"

"Of course." She nodded. "You always do, that's right."

"Okay. Drink your cocoa." He kissed her cheek and blew a raspberry on her neck, something that had always made her giggle and scream. "Good night."

"Good night, Dad."

He paused in the doorway. "Do you want this open or shut?"

"You can shut it." She was already immersed in her iPad again and didn't look up. "I'd like it shut."

Tadhg went downstairs to find Danny examining the bookshelves in his library. "So have you actually read any of these?" he asked when Tadhg showed up. "Or are they just for show?" He held up a first edition of Fitzgerald's *The Great Gatsby*. "Right, what's the first line of this one?"

"Let me see...." Tadhg squinted, pretended to be searching his memory. "'In my younger and more vulnerable years my father gave me some advice that I've been turning over in my mind ever since.' Is that right?"

Danny flipped to the first page. "Completely. Aren't you a nine-day wonder."

"Do you want to have a swim?" Tadhg asked. "I didn't show you the pool, did I?" His conversation with Lily had unsettled him. He wanted something to take his mind off the things she'd said and the way he had responded. He still felt perilously close to tears, and he didn't want to cry in front of Danny.

"I didn't bring anything to swim in," Danny said. "Can I borrow something of yours? Or do you not want my boys being where your balls have been?"

Tadhg laughed. "I'm cut to the heart that you would even think that." They went down to where a vast indoor pool was installed in the basement of Tadhg's enormous house. "Have a look in there." He nodded towards a small changing room on the opposite side of the pool. "There should be something to fit." While Danny closed himself away with Tadhg's spare swimming trunks, Tadhg made a quick call to Robbie Tuck at Cougar Helicopters, asking if he could rent an aircraft and hire a pilot. "If I need it for tomorrow morning," he asked, "and it might be quite early, would that be all right?" Normally Cougar flew oil-patch workers back and forth to the offshore rigs, but their helicopters were available to private individuals, and Tadhg had rented from them before. "We'll need landing permission from New York. Yes, that's right, New York."

Danny slipped out of the change room wearing a modest pair of navy-blue swimming trunks. Tadhg was still on the phone. He could see Danny out the corner of his eye, wandering around the room, trying to seem casual. Danny's interpretation of "nonchalant" had always been crap; he couldn't act to save his life. He stopped in front of a picture mounted on the wall: Tadhg, Danny, Trevor King, Al Bailey, and Rosie Tuck. They were all about sixteen in the picture, still kids at school. Tadhg closed out the call and went to where Danny was.

"Have you seen any of them recently?" Danny asked, gesturing at the photograph. "Trevor and Al, that crowd."

Tadhg shook his head. "Last I heard Trevor moved to the mainland— Alberta or somewhere like that. Al disappeared after school, and I guess you heard about Rosie." Danny hadn't. "Pancreatic cancer," Tadhg told him. "Saddest bloody thing you ever saw. Six weeks after diagnosis she was gone. I used to get her husband in for cost estimates sometimes. He's a brilliant finish carpenter." He looked Danny up and down. "Holding up well for an old man," he kidded, aiming a pretend punch at Danny's midsection. "How long till you're fifty?"

"Same time you'll be fifty, you arsehole. Are we swimming, or what?"

Tadhg went to change into swim trunks while Danny leaned against the doorjamb and watched. "D'ye mind not gawping?" Tadhg said, mock-angry.

"Why? You got something to be ashamed of?" Danny drifted a bit closer. "You've beat the hell out of your back, have you? Jesus, Tadhg, those are some impressive bruises. How did you…?"

Tadhg watched as the penny dropped.

"You… you donated bone marrow," Danny said. The bald truth of the statement dropped into the space between them. "For Lily."

"Yeah." He turned away, not wanting Danny to see his tears. "Not that it matters now."

Danny laid a hand on his back, kept it there until Tadhg pretended to have an itch so he could shrug it off. "Why doesn't it matter?" he asked softly.

Tadhg figured he'd best tell the truth. "She's not getting any better. In fact, the doctors say there's nothing else they can do for her." He turned to face Danny. "I want to take her to New York again. The treatment might put her into remission. You know?"

"Right," Danny said. "I overheard the conversation you and Lily had. I didn't mean to, but she was shouting."

"Yeah." Tadhg's eyes filled with tears. Christ, he was turning into a little fucking girl. "I want to take her to the States, and she doesn't want to go. Teenagers. You can't tell them nothing." He sniffed, then tapped Danny on the shoulder. "Come on. It's warmer in the water."

They swam lazily, a few laps up and down the pool. The water was as warm as a bathtub. Danny floated on his back for a while, gazing up at the ceiling. Tadhg appeared beside him. "What're ye doing?"

"Wondering why you don't have a bloody great picture of yourself painted on the ceiling." He grinned. "It's a lovely house. You've done well, Tadhg. You should be proud of yourself." He paused, his hands stirring the water at his sides. "What are you going to do?"

"About Lily? She's fourteen, so legally she's still in my charge. I could force her to go." The idea didn't appeal to him, but what else could he do? If he didn't intervene, Lily would die. "She said…." He was forced to stop for a moment. "She said she didn't mind dying."

Danny looked appalled. "I'm so sorry."

Tadhg nodded tightly. "Yeah," he said. "So am I."

A heavy silence descended between them.

"Sometimes I think I'm being punished for my sins," Tadhg said. "All the shite I've done to others over the years."

Danny shook his head. "No, that's bullshit. I don't believe that." He reached out and laid a hand on Tadhg's arm. "I don't believe that."

CHAPTER FIVE

DANNY PULLED the felled fir tree closer to the fire, its blasty red limbs catching almost immediately. "That's it," he said. "Burn, you bugger." He dusted his hands, sticky with turpentine, on his jeans. "How's that?"

Tadhg grinned and saluted him with his beer bottle. "Looking good from here, boyo." He draped an arm around Lily, who was wrapped in a thick tartan blanket and sitting on one end of a long wooden bench. "What d'ye think?"

"It's wonderful," she said. The blaze reflected off her eyes, and her gaze was full of shadows and strange light. She looked otherworldly. "So why are we burning things?"

Danny looked at Tadhg, who pretended to be shocked. "Did ye hear that question, Tadhg?"

Tadhg shook his head. "I've been neglecting the young maid's education." He moved over to allow Danny to sit next to him. "Did you ever hear anybody say, 'Remember, remember, the fifth of November'?"

"Only in that movie with Natalie Portman," she said. She reached for Tadhg's beer, and he handed it to her with a look at Danny and a shrug. The gesture seemed to say, "What difference does it make?"

"It's Guy Fawkes Night," Danny said. He reached into the picnic cooler to one side of the bench and pulled out a beer of his own. "Nasty man who thought to blow up the parliament building in England a long time ago."

"Right." She took a healthy swig of Tadhg's beer and handed it back. "So people burn things to remember it?"

"Yes."

"That's insane." She shook her head, the tails of her scarf slipping to and fro like brightly coloured wings. "Are you sure, Dad?"

"Well yes," Tadhg said.

"And it gives us an excuse to burn things," Danny added. "We like to burn things." He took a long drink. "Brings us back to the days when we were blue-painted savages with big long spears."

Lily huddled into her blanket as a tremor passed through her.

"Are you tired, love?" Tadhg asked. "You want to go to bed?"

She nodded. "Sorry."

"Don't be sorry," he said briskly. He got up and swept her into his arms, blanket and all. She couldn't have weighed more than sixty or seventy pounds, Danny thought, soaking wet and carrying bricks. Tadhg dipped her towards Danny as he passed by. "Going to give your Uncle Danny a kiss goodnight?"

"Tadhg," Danny warned, "don't tease." He didn't know Lily well enough to assume any kind of liberties. She wasn't his daughter. She was Tadhg's daughter.

"It's the God's honest truth," Tadhg said. "She fancies you, isn't that right, Lily?" She reached out her arms and wrapped them around Danny's neck. "There, you see?"

"Good night, Danny."

"Good night, Lily." He watched them move towards the house and reached into the cooler for another beer. It wasn't a brand he liked. "Why does he buy this shite?" he wondered aloud. The evening was clear, the bands of the Milky Way galaxy spangling the velvet sky like a handful of diamonds. He'd agreed to stay on Eigus for the night after Tadhg insisted they were both too drunk to take the motor launch across to Portugal Cove. Their swim in Tadhg's pool had culminated in a tasting tour of his impressive whisky collection, with predictable results. Danny had fallen asleep on one of the sumptuous couches in Tadhg's den and woke, muzzy-headed and cotton-mouthed, late in the afternoon.

"Too late to take the boat out now," Tadhg said. "The wind's come up, and there's a fierce lop on the water."

"I should get back," Danny protested. Tadhg didn't seem to care.

"D'ye have anything in particular to get back to?" It was cruel, but that was Tadhg. In all their many years of acquaintance, Danny could never figure out if Tadhg was deliberately trying to hurt him, or if he asked such things because he was genuinely that obtuse.

Danny's mouth twisted. "Not anymore."

"Jesus. I did it again, didn't I?" Tadhg winced. "I'm…. Jesus, Danny, I'm sorry."

"It's fine."

He was suddenly restless and got up from his seat, leaving the shite beer behind. Apart from Tadhg's house and the attached outbuildings, the island of Eigus was dark, its low shape a blacker colour against the steel-grey sea. The noise of the fire faded to a muted crackle as he moved away. Eigus was flat, green in spring and summer, and one could stand on any point and see for some significant distance in any direction. There was nothing much to see: the North Atlantic spread under the night sky like a ridged carpet, and the dark bulk of Bell Island to the west, crouching in Conception Bay like a recumbent colossus. Danny was reminded of the Shelley poem "Ozymandias", the "vast and trunkless" stone legs lying abandoned in the desert. Maybe at one time these islands had been giants who found themselves far away from home and lonely. Maybe they simply lay down and stayed.

"Contemplating life?" Tadhg's arm came around his shoulders, holding a blanket. Danny took it gladly and wrapped himself in it. The cold had crept up on him while he was musing, lost in his imagination as he was so often wont to be. When they were boys, Tadhg teased him about forever being "away with the fairies." His tendency to daydream was legendary among his friends and classmates, but he couldn't help it. His mind was forever conjuring up any number of answers to life's what-if moments. "Get yourself warm," Tadhg said. He stopped, facing Danny, and adjusted the blanket around his shoulders. "There ye go. Right snug and pretty."

"You'd make somebody a good wife," Danny said. Tadhg looked into his eyes and smiled.

"Do ye ever hear from any of the old crowd?" he asked. It was the same question Danny had asked him earlier, when they were in the swimming pool.

"Nope." Danny scuffed a half circle in the dust with the toe of his boot.

"I know there's no point in taking her to New York," Tadhg said abruptly. "We've been through this before. They told me if this latest transplant didn't take, there was no point in putting her through it again. She won't survive another transplant—marrow or stem cells, it doesn't matter."

Danny knew this chapter and verse. His nan had died of stomach cancer that had spread to her bones and esophagus. By the time she died, she had lost the ability to speak or swallow. Her body had begun to literally consume itself. "I'll stay as long as you need me." He laughed humorlessly. "Like you said, I've nowhere else to go." He turned back towards the house. "Come on. Getting fucking cold out here."

They went inside, and he waited while Tadhg locked up the house and activated the security system. Why, Danny didn't know. Eigus was in the middle of Conception Bay, itself part of the North Atlantic Ocean, and he and Lily were the only permanent residents, apart from a farmer at the other end of the island. Some of the local men over in Portugal Cove had received Tadhg's permission to transport their sheep to the island in summer to graze, but they were gone now. What was Tadhg afraid of? "Keeping the ghosts out?" he asked playfully, hoping to coax a smile from his friend. "Not sure the security lights are going to do it."

"Force of habit," Tadhg said. "Not like being in St. John's, is it?"

"Well, there's some sly-looking rabbits and squirrels around here," Danny said. "Not sure I'd take any chances."

It was true what Tadhg had said about the city. For hundreds of years, it had been one of the safest places on earth. Then the oil came: four billion potential barrels, 12.6 trillion cubic feet of gas, and an explosion of prosperity via high-paying jobs that the island had long hungered for. Other things came with the new prosperity, including a rise in violent crime, centred mostly around organised gangs of thugs who seized upon the opportunity to set themselves up as crystal meth kings. Prostitution was now more visible than ever, with girls working the downtown streets on any night of the week. Some were local while others were recruited from the tiny fishing villages along the coast, seduced to the city with promises of modeling jobs, the opportunity to make a lot of money. In truth, girls as young as twelve were drafted into the brutal world of street prostitution in exchange for a place to sleep and illicit drugs. Danny had seen it firsthand, young people forced to pose for pornographic photos or in front of streaming webcams, performing disgusting, unnatural acts that some sick fucker on the other side of the world got off on. In his years with the constabulary, he'd confiscated literally thousands of flash drives and filthy DVDs, all traceable back to the same three or four sons of bitches who'd "acquired" the girls in the first place.

There were more tankers in the harbour now, and dozens of heavy-duty supply ships used to bring necessary things offshore—food, supplies, fuel—were berthed along the waterfront. The sound of helicopters was constant, ferrying workers to and from the offshore rigs. It was a different island than the one Danny and Tadhg had grown up on.

"You're awful quiet all of a sudden," Tadhg said. They were in the kitchen, and he had fetched down a couple of tumblers and some ice.

"Have one with me before bed, will ye? At least that way I'll sleep." He splashed a couple fingers of Macallan into each of their glasses.

"Macallan?" Danny asked. "Are you sure I'm worth it?"

"You'll do," Tadhg said. They stood in silence for a moment. Then Tadhg said, "I don't know what to say to you." He shook his head, seemingly unable to meet Danny's gaze. "I tried to tell you, even back then. It wasn't like you think."

"Are you talking about Sandra?" Danny asked.

"Yes." Tadhg took a slug of whisky, wincing as it went down. "Danny, there was someone else in the picture, and I swear on my grandmother's grave—" Lily called out from upstairs, and Tadhg stopped talking.

"Maybe this isn't the right time to talk about this," Danny said diplomatically. He wanted Tadhg to stop raking over the past. Since his grandfather's funeral and Tadhg's reappearance in his life, he had let go of some of the bitterness. He'd never forgive Tadhg completely. He knew he didn't have it in him. Some wounds were too deep to be cleansed by even the most generous application of remorse. But he was willing to try for some kind of détente, if that was what Tadhg wanted. Tadhg was the only person left in his life now. Everyone else was gone—and he wanted a relationship with him, whatever that relationship might be. Danny was, he realised, ferociously lonely, and he'd take whatever was on offer. He'd accept whatever Tadhg wanted to be.

"Maybe you're right." Tadhg drained his glass and laid it down on the countertop. "I need to go see to her. We can talk another time." He sighed. "Want to bunk down on the couch? Or ye can sleep upstairs. There's enough room for a fucking army."

"The couch will do me," Danny said. He wasn't sure what Tadhg was insinuating. "Give us a pillow and a blanket, will ye? That's all I want."

Tadhg got two hefty feather pillows and a down-filled duvet from the hall closet and handed them to Danny. "Are ye sure this'll do?"

"I'm sure."

"All right. Well…." Tadhg hesitated for a moment, seemingly on the verge of saying something. "Good night, then."

Danny lay down and tucked the feather pillows under his head. He heard Tadhg going up the stairs, the measured tread of his footsteps on the landing above. *Maybe I should have asked him what he meant,*

Danny thought, but that was all. The couch was wide and soft, and he fell asleep almost instantly.

DANNY WOKE early the next morning, before the rest of the household, and made coffee in Tadhg's shiny big kitchen. Predictably, there was nothing much in the fridge to eat except a half tub of plain Icelandic yogurt, some bread and marmalade, and a case of high-protein liquid meals, probably for Lily. He rooted around in the cupboards and found a mug, poured himself a cup as soon as it was brewed. At least there was cream and sugar.

Adjacent to the kitchen was a family room—at least, that's what he supposed it was—a large space with an impossibly high ceiling and expensive hardwood floors. One wall was glass, looking out over the Atlantic as it roared and foamed against the cliffs. Typical Tadhg to have something ostentatious where ordinary folk would have been satisfied with a couple of nice windows. But he had to admit the view was spectacular, even on a day like today when the sea was relatively quiescent. He could imagine what it might look like in the midst of a gale, rain pounding on the roof, slashing across the windows. Alison would have loved it here on Eigus. The weather was one of the reasons she loved Newfoundland the most. "It's so dramatic," she often said, "everything always in motion. It's much better than sun and sand." She loved to stand on the headlands during a rainstorm, face turned up to the sky, her arms spread wide to catch the wind. "Do you realise how *lucky* we are, Danny? To live here?"

He had loved Alison with everything in him and then some. She wasn't hard to love. She was beautiful and funny, honest and sensitive and kind… but for some reason it never felt as permanent as it should have. Alison was perfect for him; she was everything he'd ever wanted, so the contradiction was worrisome. The whole while they were together, he'd lived in a quiet agony of waiting, knowing that something would someday take her from him. It was as if he knew their time was limited, that she would eventually leave, or they would be somehow parted. He knew the very notion was morbid and self-defeating, that he was afraid of being alone and had always been afraid, except—

"Nice view, isn't it?" Tadhg's voice cut into his thoughts, and Danny jerked back, away from the window. "I can take you back across now in the motor launch."

Tadhg's presence went through him like a spear, catching him flat-footed, tongue-tied. "Uh… well… I made coffee, if you want some." His gaze was filled with Tadhg, as if the other man were his world now, whole and entire.

"Whenever you're ready," Tadhg said. "There's no rush. You said there's coffee?" He reached out and clasped a hand around the back of Danny's neck, the heat of him burning into Danny's skin. "Come on, then. We'll go together."

They went into the kitchen. Danny sat on one of the high stools at the counter while Tadhg put bread into the toaster and fetched out the butter and marmalade. "How did you sleep on the couch?"

"Not bad," Danny said. "It's comfortable enough."

"You could have slept with me," Tadhg said without looking up. He missed the bright red blush that instantly suffused Danny's face. "Big bed upstairs, lots of room."

Danny laughed in spite of himself, shaking his head. "You never do change, do ye?"

Tadhg spread his arms in a dramatic gesture. "Just common sense is all. It's cold. We'd have to huddle together for warmth."

Danny gazed at him for several long moments while Tadhg pretended not to see him. The toaster obligingly spat out its offering. Tadhg took down a plate, then got out a knife and started buttering.

"How long has it been?" Tadhg asked quietly.

Danny said nothing. How had they gone in the space of a few days from cold almost-strangers to this? The intimacy between them now, in this moment, ought to feel forced, but it didn't. The ease with which they'd fallen into their old roles should have alarmed him.

"Since what?"

Tadhg put two buttered slices on a second plate and pushed it across to Danny. "I know she died."

Danny raised one shoulder and let it drop. "A year and… some." A year and four months. He knew exactly to the day—no, to the minute—when Alison died. He'd lain alongside her in the hospital bed, cradling the back of her skull in one hand, smoothing her face with the other. "It's gone all wrong, Danny. It wasn't supposed to be this way." She was troubled at her impending death, as if continuing to live was something she'd forgotten to do. "I'm so sorry."

She had nothing to be sorry about, but he didn't say that. By then the disease had so destroyed her reason that even their most obvious reality had, for her, the quality of a dream. "Tell me where we're going, Danny. We're to get the ferry, I remember you said. I remember now." He shivered, pushed the memory back into the far corners of his mind.

"I'm so sorry." Tadhg reached out and brushed his thumb over Danny's knuckles. "And you've been alone ever since, I suppose." His green eyes sought Danny's gaze. "I know you. You'll have kept yourself as solitary as possible."

"No." Danny shook his head briefly. "I've put myself out there." A woman he'd met on a policing conference in Cardiff, a real Welsh beauty with glossy dark hair and skin like cream. They'd stayed at a bed and breakfast in a tiny village outside the city, far enough from their colleagues to forestall the possibility of unwholesome gossip. And then a night out in Maastricht, clubbing with a group of people he'd met that afternoon on a walking tour of the city. He'd gone to the bar to get a refill on his pint of Amstel when a younger man, perhaps in his midthirties, had offered to pay.

"You're an Englishman, aren't you? I can tell."

That had made Danny laugh. "I'm from Scotland, actually," he lied.

"Even better." The young Dutchman's somewhat craggy features, his lean and hungry look, made him more appealing than if he'd been cookie-cutter handsome. He was a redhead with the most incredible blue-green eyes and a shy intelligence that hinted at considerable creative depth. His copper beard was tightly groomed and trimmed close to his face, framing a sensual mouth.

"What do you do?" Danny asked. "Are you a student?"

"I am. I study art at the Jan Van Eyck Academie."

He fascinated Danny. "A painter?"

"A street artist. Which way did you come into the city?" And when Danny told him, he said, "You will have seen the large mural out by the university." He remembered it, a dazzling, kaleidoscopic interpretation of wild irises, their stalks thirty feet high.

The Dutchman was more subtle than most. His prurient interests hadn't emerged until much later in the evening, after several beers and some tequila shots. He and Danny had gone outside to smoke marijuana

("Quite all right," the Dutchman said when Danny had temporarily protested, "it's legal here.") and he'd pressed Danny against a wall and kissed him. The pot they smoked was strong, its hallucinatory effects swirling in Danny's head, and he'd kissed the young Dutchman back eagerly, his hands seeking ingress beneath his shirt and sweater. They had gone to his apartment, a tidy flat over a shop, and made love, then talked late into the night.

"You'd be surprised," Danny said to Tadhg, "at some of the things I've done." He wanted Tadhg to understand he was no prude. Like Tadhg, he took his pleasures where he found them, as long as there was clear understanding on both sides that no emotional connection existed.

"Is that right?" Tadhg spread marmalade on his toast, his lean hands moving in easy, fluid strokes. "And I'm expected to be impressed."

The bite of toast he'd taken stuck in his throat. He swallowed some coffee in an effort to force it down, but the hot liquid burned him. He should have known better than to confess himself to Tadhg. "Look, maybe I'd better just go." He turned away, leaving the rest of his breakfast untouched.

"Danny, wait…." Tadhg caught up with him in the front hall.

"It's fine." Danny shrugged Tadhg's hand off, bent to put his boots on. "I'll walk down to the pier by myself." He drew his coat on, buttoning it against the early morning chill. "I'm sure I can find the way." And he was gone.

WELL, YE fucked that up, didn't ye? Tadhg should have known better, ought to have remembered how sensitive Danny could be and how much he hated being teased. His experience in Ireland must have been fresh in his memory, dragging on him like a dead weight. The visit to Eigus was supposed to be a pleasant experience, yet Tadhg had ruined it.

He dumped Danny's uneaten breakfast in the bin and went upstairs to wake Lily.

CHAPTER SIX

DURING HIS years on active duty with the police force, Danny had disciplined himself to run every day, as a means of enhancing his general health but also because it gave him an edge when chasing down a suspect. He had once spent three days a week lifting weights at a gym on Blackmarsh Road in the city, not too far from his home, because sometimes chasing down a suspect also meant restraining them, and he needed to be good at that part of his job. Once he moved into detective work, he let the weightlifting slide, except for occasional forays into his home gym, where he watched British crime dramas on the internet while performing the requisite number of squats, lunges, and preacher curls. He still ran, though, because he'd long since realised that running was his sanity, the place he went when he needed to get his head straight. Ever since he'd returned to Kildevil Cove, he'd gone running every morning, rising about seven and pausing only to splash some water on his face and brush his teeth before he was out the door.

It was mid-November, ten days or more since he'd left Eigus, and he hadn't seen or heard from Tadhg, not once. It was… beyond strange. Yes, he and Tadhg had quarrelled, after a fashion, about Danny's sister Sandra, but surely to God something so trivial hardly deserved this level of silence. He wondered what he'd done wrong and debated whether to call or text. Once, he was sure he'd seen Tadhg's Land Rover in Kildevil Cove, parked in the drive of his grandfather's old house. The For Sale sign was still nailed to the front gate, but Danny hadn't heard a peep out of Rosemary, Tadhg's real estate agent, so he assumed the potential deal was dead. Whether the car he'd seen belonged to Tadhg or not, he didn't know. It could have been any number of people interested in buying the house. There was no law against looking.

He took the turning at the main road that led towards the shingle beach where his grandfather and the other men used to pull their boats ashore. The fishing huts that once populated the area were gone, but not an old root cellar, famous in Kildevil Cove because it was where his grandfather had spent three weeks as a young man, recovering from snow blindness in late April, tended to by family members who brought him food and drink. To the right of this was the shop owned by a distant second cousin and his wife, converts of the local Pentecostal church who refused to sell alcohol or pornographic magazines and who went every August to the local swimming pond to renew their faith through full immersion baptism.

He stopped before he got to the beach and began to methodically stretch his calves, pulling his legs up behind him, then releasing each one and bending low over it, feeling the pull of his already aching muscles. At twenty he could run loops around the town without even breathing hard and finish off with a sprint up Robber's Hill. If he tried that now, he'd probably drop down dead.

When he was done stretching, he went down to the water's edge and bent to put a hand in the sea, trailing his fingers through wispy fronds of sugar kelp and rubbery mats of bladderwrack. The tide was out, the ocean fairly calm, a dark grey sheet being endlessly pulled ashore and sucked back out again. The sugar kelp waved languorously, pale bronze and dark brown…

…not kelp. Hair.

It looked like hair.

It was hair.

The swell of the waves gently lifted and dropped the bones, the only artifacts remaining of what was almost certainly a disarticulated human skeleton. The skull was still intact, hence the strands of hair, and Danny recognised a femur, the fragment of a collarbone. *Jesus.*

He fumbled for his mobile to call the RCMP detachment in Harbour Grace, twenty-five miles away. It was the nearest and only police station in this entire area. People in Kildevil Cove didn't go in for the really big crimes, and the murder rate was quite literally nonexistent. The only death Danny could remember being investigated occurred when he was a small boy. An old man from Kildevil Cove had gone into the forest with his horse and sled to cut wood, and never returned. The horse found her own way home with the sled still attached, and a search party of local men found his body lying under a tree. The official ruling was he'd had a heart attack.

The bones in the water, the bones that would very shortly be taken from the sea, had probably belonged to someone who died by drowning, maybe a local fisherman who'd fallen from a boat. They didn't bother learning how to swim, the old men, because they knew they'd not survive more than a handful of minutes in the icy North Atlantic. Why prolong the misery attempting to swim for shore when the cold was going to kill you long before you reached it?

Danny's call was answered after one ring. Slow day, probably. He gave the officer on the other end a thumbnail sketch of the situation, then sat down on an upturned boat to wait. The Mounties had best hurry; the tide was coming up, and if they waited too long the victim could be dragged back out to sea.

So much for rural peace and quiet.

IT TOOK a little under forty minutes for two CID constables to arrive, and by then the keel of the upturned boat was cutting into Danny's backside. They were both men, probably early to late thirties, rather keen-looking and eager to get on with things. A little too keen and eager. He allowed himself an inward sigh. You had to take what you could get in the more rural areas. The younger of the two introduced himself as Barry Thomas and asked Danny all the usual questions while his partner took notes. "Any idea how long it's been in the water?"

"I have no idea," Danny said. "It's hard to tell since it's just bones." He'd had time to examine the bones in their watery resting place, and he'd concluded they weren't those of an adult. A child, then, or a teenager, had fallen or been pushed into the water and died there… but nobody had drowned in Kildevil Cove for a very long time, at least thirty years. Could human bones survive for thirty years in icy-cold sea water? The only case of drowning he could recall….

Best not entertain that thought. There was no way it could be…. Danny took a deep breath and straightened up. There was no way. That body—*his* body—was long gone.

The two constables exchanged glances. "Are you a police officer?" Thomas asked.

Danny shook his head. "Leave of absence." He didn't feel inclined to say more than that.

"Detective?" the other constable asked. His nametag read Barnstable. Not a local boy, then.

"Yes, detective." Danny rubbed his cold hands together. "Well, I'll let the two of you get at it. If you have any questions for me—"

"Just a second." Thomas nodded at the other constable, indicating he should continue to take notes. "What was your name, again?"

"Deiniol Quirke." If he didn't get away from them soon, he could end up here for hours, answering the same questions over and over. He knew how this process worked.

Thomas looked at him quizzically. "Spell it?" Danny did. "Are you Welsh?"

"No," Danny said. "My mother just liked the name." He made a show of checking his wristwatch, which wasn't really a wristwatch but a Fitbit, designed to track his daily exercise as well as tell the time. Danny always felt its smooth black face was judging him, taking careful note of his steps per day and raising a skeptical eyebrow at his evident sloth. "You'd better take my phone numbers." He read off the number of his landline and mobile and wished the two constables a good morning. The wind was coming up cold from the northeast, and he was damp from his run. All he wanted was a hot shower and even hotter coffee—and to get away from the thing in the water.

TADHG WAS unloading the dishwasher late that evening when his mobile rang. He recognised Danny's number and debated whether he should answer it or not. They'd parted on less than amiable terms after Tadhg had tried to tell Danny that what happened with his sister Sandra wasn't his fault and been rebuffed. Diplomatically rebuffed, but still. Danny wasn't interested in anything Tadhg had to say on the matter.

The house was empty except for Lily, upstairs in her bedroom. Tadhg had given Yvonne a couple of days off, considering how present and helpful she had been during Lily's recent crisis. He knew how close she and Lily were, and even though she tried to keep a professional distance, she was dismayed by Lily's most recent prognosis.

The phone rang and rang, and he ignored it. Fuck Danny anyway. Tadhg was willing to work to overcome past events that had torn them apart, but Danny seemed to want no part of it. After a moment or two, the ringing stopped—then started up again almost immediately. Tadhg continued to ignore it, stacking plates in the cupboard and filing away cutlery. Again the ringing stopped and again it started. "Leave a voicemail, you bastard," he said aloud.

The landline in his office began to ring. He clenched his fists and swore, then stomped into the room and picked up the receiver. "For the love of Christ, what?"

"Tadhg, is that you?" Danny sounded shaken.

"Yes, it's me." Tadhg wanted to shout at him, but not with Lily resting upstairs. He closed the door. "What's going on?" The unerring sense that something bad was about to happen lowered itself over him. He'd been feeling that way for the past several days but put it down to his worry over Lily.

Danny didn't waste words. "Llewellyn Single."

Every hair on the nape of Tadhg's neck stood straight up. "What?"

"His bones are on the beach in Kildevil Cove. He came in with the tide."

Tadhg felt for his chair and sat down. "Are you sure it's him?"

"It is." Danny didn't sound sure at all. "There's no one else it can be."

He had to be mistaken. If the bones had washed up somewhere in Ireland, he could see it. The way the ocean currents were, the bones could travel a long way over the course of many years, but even so…. "Danny, that was over thirty years ago." His heartbeat speeded up until it was hammering at his chest. "You can't seriously think it's… sure that could be anybody, bhoy." Danny was getting ahead of himself. Llewellyn Single was long gone.

"We should talk," Danny said. "Just in case."

There was nothing to talk about. "I'm going to have to let you go, Danny. It's time for one of Lily's medications." The graft-versus-host reaction had caused painful blisters to erupt over most of her body and required around-the-clock opioids.

"How is she?" Danny asked.

"The… it's gone into her bones now." He didn't know why he'd said it. Perhaps he wanted someone to share the burden with, someone to talk to. He had a great many acquaintances, drinking buddies, guys with whom he'd share a tee time at Clovelly or The Wilds, but no friends. Not now.

"Oh Christ, Tadhg. I'm so sorry."

"Yeah, so am I." His voice sounded flat and unemotional. He was used to making things happen, charming people and powering through business deals, making a path for himself everywhere he went. But Lily's illness he could do nothing about, and neither his money nor his most tender concern as a father could stop the fated progression of her cancer, and now this. A dead man's bones—a very particular dead man—taken from the sea in Kildevil Cove, some tiny fishing village barely big enough to register on Google maps.

"I should tell you the RCMP will be contacting you to ask questions."

"Was that your idea?" Tadhg asked bitterly.

"No. I wouldn't do that to you," Danny replied. *I'd do it to you,* Tadhg thought. He knew the type of man he was, knew he'd made himself that way, and wasted no shame on it. "Listen, is there anything you need? Anything I can help with?"

Tadhg ignored the question. "Are you involved in this investigation?"

"No. I'm not on active duty. I took a leave of absence."

Of course his absence from the constabulary had to do with Ireland. "What are you going to do if they ask?"

"Tadhg, you can stop worrying. I'm not going to fuck you over. I think the entire situation is a misunderstanding. Lord Christ, this was thirty years ago."

Tadhg wasn't convinced. "I told you. I told you it was going to come out, didn't I?" Don't panic, he told himself. This is nothing. Don't lose your mind over some little thing like this. You've got more important things to worry over. Think about Lily. "I have to go."

"Tadhg, we need to talk about this."

"We will. I promise. But right now I have to go."

He found Lily sitting up in bed, playing some complicated online video game involving trolls and flying pigs and giraffes with swords. "What in the name of Jesus is that you're playing?"

"The trolls come down from the mountains, trying to set the village on fire." She showed him on the screen where this was happening. "And the giraffes are very powerful against the trolls but you have to earn them."

"Eat them?" Tadhg asked, teasing her.

"*Earn* them," Lily said scornfully.

He rolled the small glass vial of medication between his palms to warm it. "And what about the flying pigs?" Tadhg stuck the needle into the gasket at the top of the vial and drew the liquid up into the syringe. He used insulin syringes, the smallest diameter possible, to avoid hurting Lily more than he had to.

"The pigs—" She grimaced briefly as the needle entered the skin of her upper arm. "Ouch, Dad! You get six pigs at the beginning of the game, but they can be killed, unlike the giraffes."

He rubbed the injection site gently with his hand. "Better?" He touched her forehead with the backs of his fingers. "Still a bit warm. Are you thirsty? Do you want a cold drink?"

She nodded. "Diet Coke?"

"Absolutely not. How about some fizzy water?"

"Okay. With lots of ice cubes." As he stood up to leave, she asked, "Who was that on the phone?"

"Danny."

Instantly her face lit up like a dozen sunrises. "Is he coming to Eigus? Can we go see him?"

How to tell a fourteen-year-old that he and Danny couldn't—wouldn't—see each other right now? "It's not a good time, love. Danny's really busy."

"Is he working on the old house too?" Now she was getting really excited. "Couldn't we go to Kildevil Cove and help him?"

"Danny's not able to have visitors right now," Tadhg said, hoping it would suffice. He should have known better.

"What did you do to him?" Lily asked with the innate suspicion of a teenaged girl. "Were you fucking with his head?"

"Lily!" He clenched his fists against the rising irritation. "What have I told you about that word?"

"There's nobody here but us."

Tadhg gestured around the room. "The walls are always listening," he said, trying for lightness.

She made a disapproving face at him. "How are you ever going to get back together if you keep driving him away?"

"Lily…." He pinched the skin between his eyebrows. "Danny and I aren't—"

"Oh, bull*shit* you aren't!" she said. "I've seen the way you look at each other." She huffed out a sigh. "Listen, Dad, you aren't getting any younger. It's time you found someone and settled down."

"It's not that simple." He didn't know if he could explain the elaborate nuances of adult relationships to her. "Danny isn't gay and—"

"For fuck sake, Dad!" There was that word again. "Don't be so twentieth century. Nobody cares about stuff like that anymore. Binary sexuality is old-school. Love the one you're with."

And now she was quoting songs that were before even his time. "I'll be back with your fizzy water," he said, hoping to evade any further questions. "Try not to kill any more giraffes."

"Pigs," she reminded him.

"All right, pigs."

He managed to make it to the landing before his vision blurred, and he had to lean against the wall. *All I do lately is cry like a little girl.* The reality of Lily's impending death pressed in on him then, as it did a thousand times a day, crushing him, stopping the breath in his lungs. Most of all he feared not being able to give her the kind of care she needed and failing her at a crucial time. Nothing in his business or personal life had prepared him for anything like this. Was anyone ever prepared to be told their child was dying? And Lily had been ill for most of her life, ever since she was three. True, there had been remissions in between the bouts, some lasting years, but the disease always returned.

"Cancer likes to come back," one of her oncologists had told Tadhg after her second remission failed. "All we can do is keep on top of it." They'd tried to beat back the hydra, but for every head the doctors lopped off with their powerful drugs, six more grew in its place, and with every hellish regeneration, Lily grew weaker.

I don't think I can do this on my own. He went down the stairs slowly, one hand on the wall, afraid of falling and not wanting to get up. A nonsensical children's rhyme that he'd learned in childhood kept repeating itself inside his head.

> *I had a little dog and his name was Tim.*
> *I put him in the bathtub to see if he could swim.*
> *He drank up all the water.*
> *He ate up all the soap.*
> *He died the next day with a bubble in his throat.*

He angrily willed it away. What a cruel and stupid rhyme, and why was he reciting it now? Why did people tell children such things, a poem about drowning a pet? And the stupid rock-a-bye-baby one, a child falling out of a tree and being hurled to the ground. Surely to God there was enough violence and cruelty in the world without inventing vicious rhymes for children.

He reached the bottom of the stairs and stopped for a moment. He felt dizzy and faintly nauseous, his head swimming as if it had been detached from his shoulders, and it was getting hard to breathe. He sat down on the last step and dropped his head into his hands. *You're all right. You're just tired. It will pass.* He wished savagely for Danny's presence and didn't bother to wonder why.

He made himself get up, went to the fridge, took out a litre-sized bottle of club soda for Lily, and got a clean tumbler out of the cupboard. A pile of dirty pots and pans that he hadn't yet put in the dishwasher filled both kitchen sinks. Dust bunnies floated under the dining room chairs. He looked around at the mess and felt even more defeated. The girl he'd initially hired to clean had quit suddenly and without notice, leaving him in the lurch. Yvonne would be back from visiting her family in a day or two, but he couldn't expect Yvonne, a registered nurse, to do housework. He'd have to call one of the housekeeping companies in the city, which would mean assigning someone to ferry the workers to Eigus and back again once the work was done.

I should take her back to Kildevil Cove. She'd like it there. What would be the point? He'd be bound to run into Danny, seeing how small the town was, and then what? If what Danny said was accurate, then Llew Single's body had been found. Both he and Danny would be the subject of gossip, and he didn't think he could stand that. He wouldn't subject Lily to that kind of stress, either, and he wasn't thrilled with the idea of other people's curiosity. They'd be bound to wonder what was wrong with her, and one or two of the more intelligent ones would eventually put it together. *Tadhg Heaney's little maid got cancer, poor thing.* Lily would absolutely hate being the object of their pity.

He dropped a few ice cubes into the tumbler and went upstairs, climbing slowly, his muscles protesting and his head feeling as if it were full of bees. The video game's tinny music reached him through the half-open door, full of electronic beeps and bells. He put the water and the glass on a small table inside the room. "I've got your water, love." But when he turned around, he saw that Lily had abandoned her laptop and was sound asleep, sitting up against the headboard.

"Hey, you sleep like that and you'll crack your neck off," he murmured softly, reaching out to guide her gently into a lying position. "D'ye want a cold drink?"

"No… thanks, Dad," she murmured, half-asleep. He closed the laptop and slid it under her bed, then pulled the duvet up around her shoulders.

It was past ten when he went downstairs. He couldn't remember the last time he'd eaten anything, but his appetite was nonexistent, and he knew if he ate anything it would probably come right back up. He went to the liquor cabinet and took out a half-empty bottle of Laphroaig. After fetching down a glass from the cupboard, he dropped two ice cubes in and poured four generous fingers. He was overdoing it, but what the hell. Maybe it would help him sleep, give him a few hours' worth of decent rest before the morning. He sat in his favourite chair, a reclining leather wingback he'd bought in Stuttgart and had shipped home. It warmed to the heat of his body and cradled him like a glove. He took a sip of Scotch and laid his head back, closing his tired, gritty eyes. He had never felt more alone or more powerless in his life. He fumbled for the remote and switched on the stereo, then sat back as the room filled with the silky-smooth sound of Stan Getz, "Sweet Rain." It swirled and drifted around him like smoke, and he sighed as his body relaxed. He knew he ought to get up and take a shower, maybe go to bed early with a book, but he couldn't make his muscles obey him. He dragged a throw blanket from an adjacent chair and moved over to the couch. *It will be all right. Everything will be all right. It has to be.*

Chapter Seven

Danny shielded his face as well as he could with the collar of his waterproof, but the driving winds slashed icy rain into his eyes. Two miles out from Portugal Cove and the small motor launch he'd hired was bucking and swaying like a randy animal.

"For the love of God, come in out of it!" Simmy Buchan, the fisherman Danny had hired to take him to Eigus, stuck his head out of the wheelhouse and shouted at him.

"I'd rather it out here," Danny replied. Simmy probably thought he was a bloody fool who deserved whatever he got. He couldn't help it. He loved being on deck, even in a storm, and the windier and rougher it got, the better he liked it. The men of his family were descended from hardy seafaring types who rode wooden schooners to Labrador to fish in summer, men for whom climbing a swaying mast in rough seas was no big affair. In later years these men and their descendants built skyscrapers in New York, thousands of feet in the air atop "high steel," balancing unsupported on beams no more than a foot wide.

"You'll catch your death out there."

Danny shrugged. "I'll die doing what I loved, won't I?"

"You're a fucking idiot." Simmy shook his head and went back inside. Eigus was becoming visible in the distance through a dense curtain of heavy fog, and Danny could make out the island's low, rounded bulk, looking like the back of a wet sheep. He closed his eyes reflexively as another wave struck the gunwale, slapping cold salt water in his face. At this rate he'd be soaked to the skin by the time they arrived, but he didn't really mind. The raw, damp air and pounding surf were invigorating, and he felt more awake than he had in ages.

Constables Thomas and Barnstable had kept in touch regarding the bones Danny had found on Kildevil Cove beach, but there was not much to report. The remains didn't match the description of anyone in their missing persons' database, and even modern investigative tools like DNA analysis couldn't do a whole lot with a handful of sea-bleached bones and a tuft of hair. The case had been turned over to one of their detectives, Moira Fraser, with whom Danny had something of a history. He'd worked with her some years before when a school girl had gone missing in the woods in Kilbride. The girl had never been found alive, although her corpse had turned up in a shallow brook in Bowring Park some weeks later, naked and badly decomposed. It had fallen to Danny to tell her parents, because he was supposedly more user-friendly than Moira. It was the one part of his job he hated the most.

Moira Fraser was a ball-buster and fiercely ambitious, but her skillful handling of any situation was beyond efficient. She drank too much coffee, swore like a longshoreman, and took her whisky neat and very expensive. Danny admired her despite her sometimes-caustic attitude, and by the time that particular case was done, they'd become lovers. She'd invited him to a cozy small hotel in Shoal Harbour, where they sat through a half-hearted dinner for the sake of appearances, then escaped to their room as soon as possible. She had torn off Danny's clothes with an animal fervour, her hands all over him, touching and teasing, and he embarrassed himself the first time by coming too fast. Moira didn't care. She knew what she wanted, and what she wanted was him.

He'd spoken to her briefly after Thomas's call, but she merely wanted to touch base with him; there was nothing new to report. "Let's meet soon for a drink," she said, before she rang off. "Just to see where we are." She did confirm that she would be visiting Tadhg Heaney in a couple of days, and it would be an official visit.

"You're going to question him?" Danny asked. He already knew the answer.

"I also intend to question you."

The prow of the boat bumped gently against the pier, and Danny ducked inside the wheelhouse to retrieve his bag. The heavy seas were lifting the boat and dropping it, making it hard for him to hang on to the wooden ladder, and twice he nearly went in the water. "I can only hold her here for so long," Simmy said. "You'd better get ashore." Danny clambered up the ladder, turning long enough to catch the bag when Simmy threw it to him. "When will I come back?" Simmy asked, shouting to be heard over the roar of the waves.

"I'll call ye," Danny said, "I can't say for sure just now." He waved his thanks and hurried on towards the house, eager to be out of the wet. He'd memorised the security code sequence from his last visit, making his entrance into the house with hardly a sound. It was very early in the morning, barely daylight. More than likely Lily would still be asleep, and Tadhg had never been an early riser. He shucked his wet coat and boots and left them in the foyer before stepping quietly into the living room.

Tadhg was lying on the couch, one hand folded across his middle and the other trailing on the floor, an empty glass lying inches from his slack fingertips. He was sound asleep. It was chilly in the room, so Danny turned up the furnace, then fetched a woollen blanket that had fallen on the floor and draped it over him. Tadhg looked like death warmed over, pale and thin, with dark shadows under his eyes. The indomitable Tadhg Heaney, playboy jetsetter, international businessman, gambler, and raconteur had finally burned through the last of his energy. Danny laid his palm against Tadhg's chest, over his heart. *You poor stupid bastard. Why in the name of God do you do this to yourself?* Tadhg didn't even stir.

Danny went into the kitchen and began to clear away the mess of dirty dishes, sticky glasses, and empty takeout containers. He ran the hot water in the sink and wiped down all the surfaces, then loaded the dishwasher. There was very little food in the fridge—a few eggs and some white bread—but it would have to do. He found coffee beans in the cupboard, so he dumped a handful into Tadhg's fancy grind-and-brew machine and turned it on. While the coffee drizzled into the carafe, he lit the gas and whipped some eggs into a froth, adding a little cream from a nearly full carton in the fridge. By the time the coffee was ready, the french toast only needed a quick flip. A sudden movement by the kitchen door caught his eye. He turned to see Tadhg, the blanket around his shoulders, bleary-eyed and half-asleep.

"Danny." He blinked. "What are you doing here?"

Danny suddenly felt immensely foolish. What the hell was he doing? Their most recent parting had been on uncertain terms. What made him think Tadhg even wanted him here? "I let myself in. I thought after our last phone conversation you could use a little help." He caught sight of himself in the reflective door of the microwave opposite. His hair was wet and sticking up, and he hadn't bothered to shave, so his jaw was covered in a film of silvery stubble. He was wearing a horrible old sweater his grandmother had knitted for him years ago and a pair of jeans that he really ought to have thrown out. *You stupid arsehole. You look like a fucking homeless person, you really do.* All at once he saw his good intentions as ridiculous and his presence in Tadhg's home as wrong, uncalled-for, indistinguishable from breaking and entering. Tadhg shuffled into the kitchen and slumped down on one of the mahogany bar stools next to the counter, his head in his hands.

"Didn't think you'd ever want to see me again," Tadhg said, his voice muffled by his palms, "especially after the way we left it last time." He yawned and rubbed his red-rimmed eyes.

Danny poured him a cup of coffee and set it down in front of him. "Drink this, and then have something to eat, and after that you should go take a shower. You stink of whisky."

Tadhg sipped the coffee and moaned appreciatively. "Why do I have to get a shower? Surely to God the smell of whisky doesn't bother you. Ye're practically a walking distillery yourself."

"Moira Fraser is coming later this morning to discuss some things." Danny tipped the french toast onto a plate and slid it across the counter to Tadhg.

"If she's coming to see me, why are you here?" Tadhg asked.

"Moral support," Danny replied. "I know her. I know what to expect. You don't."

"Could I have a knife and fork?" He watched Danny opening and closing drawers for a moment. "The big one next to the stove."

They ate mostly in silence, with brief snippets of conversation about the purpose of Moira Fraser's visit. "You're not a suspect," Danny said, "not yet." *And neither am I.*

"So why is she coming to question me?" Tadhg held up his empty cup, and Danny went to get the coffee pot. "You found the bones, not me." He waited while Danny refilled his mug. "Thanks." He took a healthy swallow of the fragrant brew. "I wasn't even in Kildevil Cove. Why does she think I've anything to do with it?"

"You were in Kildevil Cove for my grandfather's funeral," Danny said. "She wants to talk to you, rule you out as a suspect. There's no need to go to bits." He reached across and thumped Tadhg's shoulder with his closed fist. "I'll be right here the whole time."

"Mmm," Tadhg said, through a mouthful of french toast. "Right up until she takes me into another room and uses the thumbscrews on me."

"Don't be so dramatic," Danny said. Tadhg's clumsy attempt at humour showed he was at least a little cheered by Danny's presence. It pleased him, although he wasn't sure why.

"Should I take some breakfast up to Lily?" Danny asked. "Or would you rather I let her have a lie in?"

"She would love it," Tadhg said. "Just… don't get upset if she doesn't eat very much. She hasn't any appetite lately." He laid his fork down and pinched the skin between his eyebrows. "I'm going to ring the hospital later today about a feeding tube. It's not a big deal."

"It's a big deal to you," Danny said quietly.

Tadhg looked up and attempted a watery smile. "I'm glad you're here," he said. "Although fuck knows why."

Danny leaned over and gave him a rather awkward one-armed hug. Something deep within him reveled in the heat of Tadhg's body, his nearness. "I'll be here, Tadhg, my son. For as long as you need me."

MOIRA FRASER was about Tadhg's age, tall and trim and well kept. Obviously she maintained her body in good form by regular exercise, but her efforts couldn't quite mask the advancing years. He suspected she had been quite the athlete, but the broader hips and softer bosom showed that her youth, like his own, was long gone. She was plain-spoken, and her brisk manner indicated that she brooked no nonsense, but there was a warmth evident in her ready smile. She was also damned sexy, a buttoned-up type who probably cut loose at the slightest provocation. Tadhg had met her kind before. On an overseas trip to Hong Kong, he'd met an American businesswoman in the hotel bar. Tall, lean, leggy, with a lush figure that made his mouth water. She pretended to be outraged when Tadhg propositioned her, but half an hour later she was on all fours in the middle of his hotel bed while he pounded her through the mattress. If his instincts were right, Inspector Moira Fraser would probably tumble the same way. She nodded briskly when he said hello, and took a seat on the couch. "Do you mind?" she asked. She laid a small digital recorder on the table between them. "I prefer this to taking notes. It's more natural."

Better watch what you say now, boyo. This one will nail you to the wall. "Of course," he said. "Please, go ahead."

"Don't know if you've already seen this—the remains as they were discovered, in situ." She laid a photo on the coffee table. Some bones, arranged in a shape that suggested a human body. But it was an incomplete jigsaw puzzle with too many pieces missing.

"Is this everything?" Danny asked.

"Yes," Moira said. She sounded disappointed. "The currents disperse the smaller bones of the hands and feet and sometimes the teeth, although this one seems to have an almost full set." She indicated the skull's gaping grin. "The hair is suggestive."

"In what way?" Tadhg asked.

"Human hair tends to last in cold water. The hair on this corpse is a bright copper red." Moira indicated the skull. "Apparently there's only one family of redheads in Kildevil Cove. This narrows down the identity of our skeleton considerably." She reached into her briefcase and rooted around for a moment, swore quietly when she obviously hadn't found what she was looking for. "I told my assistant to make copies of the medical examiner's report, but obviously that flew right out of her skull altogether."

"Not good at her job, is she?" Danny asked.

"Oh, she's all right, usually," Moira said. "I can't help but think she's got something on her mind lately. She's been coming in to work late and leaving early, taking long coffee breaks. Her name's Nina. She seemed keen enough at the start but now I'm beginning to regret hiring her."

"Not Nina Single," Tadhg put in.

Moira glanced at him. "You know her, then."

"Everybody knows Nina Single," Danny said. "Short, fat, overly high opinion of herself?" He returned his attention to the photograph. "You're assuming it's from Kildevil Cove." He exchanged a look with Tadhg. "It could be from anywhere. You know how the currents run around here."

"Of course," Moira replied, "and we've taken that into account." She glanced at Danny, then back at Tadhg. "Listen, my team have been over the missing persons' records dating back forty years. Besides that, all the parish records are readily available." She looked pointedly into her empty cup. "Is there another coffee going?"

"I'll get it," Danny said. He seemed eager to escape.

"How long have you two been together?" Moira asked, once Danny had gone.

Tadhg stared at her, temporarily lost for words. "Danny and I? I mean… uh, we're not a couple." He thought back to the recent conversation with Lily. Obviously he and Danny were giving off some kind of vibe. "Just good friends. We were at school together. I've known him since we were boys."

"Oh. Sorry. I didn't mean to imply—" She was very pretty when she blushed. Probably a hellcat in the bedroom, Tadhg thought. He wouldn't mind finding out, either. "Because you seem very close… if you know what I mean."

"It's all right," Tadhg said. A lengthy and somewhat awkward silence followed.

"It's good that he has you for a friend," Moira said. She put her palms together, clasped and unclasped her fingers. It seemed an oddly anxious gesture for someone with her habitual composure. "I've known Danny since he first started with the constabulary. We had occasion to work together on some joint operations. He's a good man." She smiled. "Stubborn as your arse, wilful, opinionated…. We're not supposed to get emotionally involved with the victim in any way. We're expected to remain objective, but Danny… he always feels compelled to help. I often think he'd make a good priest, that one." She sighed. "Everything for him is personal, so what happened with that suspect last summer…." Her gaze was keen. "Do you know about it?"

"Yeah. He's never told me anything, but it was in the Irish and UK papers. Some kind of an armed standoff, wasn't it? And a suspect got shot?" The photographer on the scene had covered every aspect of the incident, from the police cordon at either end of the street to the snipers on a nearby rooftop, to Danny standing in the heavy rain, his clothes streaming with water. "I suppose if your own safety is threatened, you'd have to, wouldn't you?"

Moira blinked. "Danny didn't shoot him. He shot *himself*. Right there in front of Danny. He'd taken a hostage, but she was all right in the end."

"He did it? Himself?" Tadhg looked up as Danny stepped into the living room with a french press full of hot coffee.

"Who did what himself?" Danny glanced from one to the other as he put the coffee pot down. "Did I walk in on something embarrassing?"

"It's nothing." Moira held out her cup. "Me first, if nobody minds." She added cream and sugar in liberal doses and stirred vigorously. "There's one more thing." She reached for her briefcase and pulled out a brown envelope, which she passed across to Tadhg. "Your wallet. I think you must have dropped it."

Danny turned to gaze at Tadhg quizzically. "Dropped it where?" he asked.

"We discovered that on the beach," Moira said, "near where the bones were found." She sipped her coffee. "Which leads me to my next question. When were you last on the beach at Kildevil Cove, Mr. Heaney?"

Tadhg gripped his coffee cup so tight the tendons in his hand creaked. "Uh… I haven't been back to Kildevil Cove since the funeral."

"So your wallet has been missing since then?"

Tadhg struggled to appear nonchalant, but his guts were churning. "I guess that must be it, yeah."

"Why were you at the beach on the day of Mr. Quirke's funeral?" she asked.

Danny put out a warning hand. "Tadhg, you don't have to answer that without a lawyer." He narrowed his eyes at Moira. "He deserves to have a lawyer present if you're going to ask those kinds of questions."

"Don't remember you passing the bar exam," Moira said bitchily.

Tadhg shook his head. "Danny, it's all right. Yes," he said to Moira, "I think I must have been. I went down there for a stroll, to try to clear my head." *But you had your wallet with you in Amsterdam, so how the hell did it end up down the beach?*

"Clear your head?" She glanced at Danny. "Were you that close to Mr. Quirke, then? That you needed time out for… contemplation?"

"No, I wasn't…." Tadhg blinked rapidly, trying to centre himself. "I mean, I hadn't seen him for some time."

"Wait a minute," Danny interrupted. "This is starting to sound like a bloody coroner's inquest, Moira." He stood up, clearly agitated by her line of questioning. "You asked him if he went down to the beach. He told you he did."

"Of course," she said mildly. "And there's nothing to suggest the remains were there at the time… or that Mr. Heaney might have seen them." She was smug now, Tadhg saw. She'd scored a point. She shut off the tape recorder and put it in her purse, then folded up her laptop. "I'm curious," she said. Tadhg's stomach clenched. He'd assumed the inquisition was over. "You live here on Eigus by yourself, you and your daughter."

Danny's glance slid towards Tadhg and away again. "Yes," Tadhg said. "As far as I know, it's not illegal."

She stood up. "But don't you think it's a bit strange? You bought this entire island. Is there a particular reason why? Are you running from something? It's well known in Kildevil Cove that almost everyone there despises you."

"Moira," Danny said.

She persisted. "Are you a recluse, Mr. Heaney? Surely you'd have a good reason to hide yourself away, considering your personal history."

Tadhg refused to answer. He gazed over her shoulder, out the window at the sea.

"I will want to question you again," she told Tadhg. He wondered if this was the modern equivalent of the old noir movies' warning "Don't leave town." Moira gathered her things. "I'll be in touch."

"I'll see you out," Danny said. Tadhg heard their diminishing footsteps move away from him, and then the foyer door closed. He sank back down on the couch.

"Who was that, Dad?"

Tadhg glanced up to see Lily, still in her pajamas, the duvet from her bed wrapped around her shoulders. "Are you cold, love?" he asked. "I can put the heat up."

"No, I'm fine." She came and sat next to him, her head on his shoulder. When she was little, she'd do something the same, cuddle beside him until he stopped whatever he was doing and lifted her into his lap. But she was much too grown-up to sit in her father's lap anymore. "Was Danny here?"

"We had a visitor from the police. Danny's showing her out." Tadhg picked up his coffee, but it was stone cold. He grimaced and set it down again.

"Why?" she asked. "Is somebody dead?" She took up the remote control and aimed it at the flat-screen on the opposite wall. The television roared to life in the middle of some loud and tuneless music video. A line of girls not much older than Lily wiggled and gyrated, bending over so their bottoms were to the camera, their wispy underpants leaving absolutely nothing to the imagination.

"Disgusting," Tadhg muttered. He took the remote and switched to one of the news stations.

"Dad!" Lily exclaimed. "That was Kara Divinyl! She's top of the charts this week."

"Is this the sort of thing your generation listens to?" The music was absolute shite, and the video was little better than soft-core porn. Whatever happened to using your imagination, he wondered? Surely to God a song could be enjoyed on its own merits, without the addition of raunchy visuals.

"Better than the music you guys had."

"Oh come on now." Tadhg pretended to be wounded. "You can't get any better than 'Wake Me Up Before You Go-Go.' That's pure gold, that is." Tadhg heard Danny moving around in the kitchen. Then he appeared with another pot of coffee and clean cups on a tray. "Excellent," Tadhg enthused. "Just what I need."

Danny nodded over his shoulder in the direction of the foyer. "She's gone. I can guarantee you she'll be back. She's nothing if not tenacious."

Tadhg smiled thinly, an expression with no mirth in it. His head felt like it had been squeezed in a vise. "Thanks for… what you did for me there." He could swear Moira Fraser had it out for him. For whatever reason, she'd disliked him immediately. He was in her sights now, and she was bound and determined to pull the trigger. Like so many others, she'd decided he was a certain kind of person, one well beneath her personal contempt. "Lily," he said, forcing himself to sound light, "tell Danny about that rubbishy band you like. Go on. It was on the television just now."

"Is he giving you a hard time?" Danny asked Lily.

"Dad's telling me all about the crap music you had back in the eighties." She poured herself a cup of coffee and added cream and sugar. "Can we watch a movie?" When Tadhg agreed, she went to her bedroom and came back with a DVD of *The Ring*.

"Oh Christ," Tadhg moaned, "not that bloody girl in the well again." But he let her put it on the player and went to the kitchen to make a huge bowl of popcorn. "You and Danny start," he called, "and I'll be there in a minute."

"And Smarties, Dad!" Lily said. "Put Smarties in it."

He waited while the microwave hummed, only half listening to the occasional conversation from the other room. "…video tape that kills you when you watch it," Lily said.

"Why would you watch something that would kill you?" Danny asked. The microwave beeped, and Tadhg opened it, took out the puffy bag of exploded kernels and dumped the contents into a bowl. He nuked a half stick of butter and poured it over the popcorn, mixing the lot with his fingers. He'd tried to tell Moira Fraser the truth as he knew it, but he knew she didn't believe him. He'd have to check with Danny, see if Moira had said anything to him on her way to the door. She'd be more likely to tell Danny than him, considering their history.

He found a bag of Smarties, the ones in the little individual boxes, and spent a good five minutes dumping the chocolate candies into the hot popcorn. He knew not to stir them about too much, else the coating would melt, precipitating a third world war. At least Lily was eating. He licked most of the butter off his fingers, then rinsed his hands under the tap.

"Dad, what's taking so long?" Lily called from the living room. "It's already started."

"Be right there," he said. He took a six-pack of fizzy drinks from the fridge and carried the whole lot into the living room. "Here we are," he said, feigning cheerfulness. He glanced at the screen where a serious blond girl was walking slowly towards a snowy television. "Do televisions even do that anymore?" he asked. "I'd have thought it was all digital now."

"Dad!" Lily was indignant.

"Sorry," he said. Danny caught his eye as he put the popcorn and the drinks down on the coffee table.

"Just have to run upstairs for a bit," he said, ignoring Danny's quizzical look. He took the wallet and went up quickly into his bedroom. He usually kept it on a shelf above his shoetree, so he would always know where it was. As well to put it back there, he thought. The closet was the size of a spacious modern bathroom, and double-tiered clothing racks ran along all four walls. It might have been a fitting room in a stylish European department store. Tadhg stood on the lowest shelf and leaned into the upper compartment. He flipped open the wallet, checking to make sure everything was there that ought to be. A slip of paper fluttered onto the floor; he bent to pick it up and read it.

Remember, Remember.

CHAPTER EIGHT

DANNY WAS halfway around Quidi Vidi Lake one afternoon when he saw the bird, a starling or small crow, wedged between the branches of a naked willow tree. It hadn't been dead very long; the dark feathers were still glossy. It showed no signs of predation, hadn't been ripped up by an eagle or one of the ever-present skuas. Surely it hadn't died in the tree that way, which meant someone had picked it up and placed it there. It was a strange thing to do, and seeing it unsettled him. His romantic imagination, so at odds with his professional discipline, saw signs and symbols everywhere, some good and others bad. The dead bird was definitely bad.

A phone call early one morning from Jim Lynch had brought Danny back to St. John's. Jim had been Danny's immediate supervisor when he'd still been with the police force and was the only one who had denounced Danny's suspension. "Listen now," Jim had said, "this isn't the best of news. I tried to argue my way around it, but the bastards wouldn't listen." The constabulary had decided to conduct their own investigation into the incident in Dublin at the Clontarf sea wall, and Danny would be summoned to answer questions.

"I've already answered questions till I was black in the face," Danny said. The Gardaí had subjected him to a long and tedious interrogation, covering the same topics over and over until he was nearly weeping with exhaustion. *I've told you everything I know.* It had nothing to do with any investigation. It had to do with him. He'd embarrassed the constabulary in front of the Irish, and now he would have to pay. Never let it be said that his people didn't follow up. He was back in town now for an indefinite period, which he supposed could be counted a relief from what was going on in Kildevil Cove and Eigus, but he couldn't help worrying about Tadhg and Lily. Perhaps he'd call later, in the evening to check on Lily, see if Tadhg needed anything brought over from Portugal Cove.

He left the dead bird and started running again, easily breasting the low grade that circled the bottom of Quinn's Hill and then onto the wooden walkway, his feet thumping on the weathered boards, arms pumping easily at his sides. He emerged on the village road and followed the asphalt a short distance, passing the sail works and the chicken plant before merging back onto the gravel path.

He ought to have been paying attention, but as so often happened when he ran, his mind was elsewhere. He was practically treading on the man's heels before he realised it and managed to stop, barely escaping what would have been a painful collision. "I'm so sorry. Honest to God, I didn't—"

The man turned around. "Danny Quirke? My God, I heard you were back in town." He was about Danny's age, with grey hair cropped short and a craggy complexion that suggested he was often outdoors in all weather. Danny felt like he should know him, but he couldn't place who he was. Somebody he and Tadhg used to knock around with when they were boys? An old colleague from the constabulary? "You don't know me from Adam, do ye?" He laughed. "Rory Fraser." Danny must have still looked confused, for he added, "Moira Fraser's brother? We joined the constabulary about the same time, me and you. Right out of training."

"Oh my God, yes!" Danny's relief at finally recognising Fraser was overwhelming. "How have you been?" He stuck out his hand and Fraser shook it. "Seems like ages." These days there was a police cadet program at the university, but when Danny and Rory joined, training either meant a police academy on the mainland or on the job, learning as you go, or both since few came out of the academy truly ready for real-world policing. Luckily, they had both had a decent mentor in Frank Dowden, who was kind and competent, but who would also drop on you like a tonne of bricks if you screwed up. "Don't make me regret this, son," he'd often say when sending a new recruit out into the field. Danny had tried his hardest to never disappoint him, but he knew others weren't nearly as circumspect. He remembered one guy, Alan Hynes, whose misspent youth as a notorious city "corner boy" somehow never managed to lead to his arrest. Why Hynes had decided to join the constabulary, nobody knew, but he was a shirker and a troublemaker from the beginning. If anybody in the city was a bent cop, it was Hynes.

They made inconsequential small talk for a minute; then Fraser said, "Last I heard you were seconded to the Gardaí in… where was it?"

"Dublin," Danny said. Fraser's disingenuousness irritated him. Fraser knew damned well he'd been in Dublin; everybody knew. A cloud passed over the sun, briefly cloaking them in its shadow. The air was cold.

"Dublin. I hear it's a great city."

"It is." The conversation was leading him somewhere Danny didn't want to go. "Still with the constabulary yourself?"

"I'll be there till they cover me up with dirt, sure." He laughed, a cold noise with no mirth in it. "I made sergeant a couple months ago. Working on the drug squad now. You can imagine what that's like. This whole place is overrun with it these days. That and the oil—it's part and parcel of the same thing." Danny asked who he was partnered with. "Me and Hynes have been partners for a while now. He's a great one to get along with," Fraser said. "So you didn't bother to stay on in Ireland? Sounds like it would have been a great opportunity for a man like yourself." His gaze was cold and assessing. Danny felt like he was being cross-examined. And since when was Hynes "a great one to get along with"?

"I wanted to come home," Danny replied. "You know how it is." He didn't tell Fraser that Grandar had died; it would have meant nothing to him. The obituary had been printed in the Kildevil Cove *Register,* but neither of the city papers carried it. No one outside of Kildevil Cove knew or remembered Grandar.

Fraser gazed out across the lake. Three young women in a racing shell were struggling to get their oars in sync, the boat rocking violently. "You always were one to take advantage of an opportunity," he said. "Real Johnny-on-the-spot, you could say." His tone was bitter, accusatory. "Didn't your parents ever tell ye not to be greedy?"

"What?" Danny's fists clenched involuntarily. "What do ye mean by that?" Where was this coming from? He hadn't seen Fraser in years. Had he been nursing a grudge all that time?

"Oh, I'm sure you're smart enough to take my meaning." Fraser reached out and pushed Danny's shoulder, like a child would do, hoping to start a fight.

"Hey!" Danny stepped back. "What the hell is your problem?" This happenstance encounter with his old acquaintance had suddenly turned threatening and strange.

"No problem." Rory shrugged. "Just saying." He sneered. "Some people forget who their friends are. You wouldn't forget your friends now, would ye?"

"Whatever," Danny said. He pushed away from Fraser, his toes digging into the soft gravel of the path, lengthening his stride. The weird confrontation left him uneasy.

"See ye!" Fraser called from somewhere behind him. Danny pretended he hadn't heard. He rounded the top of the lake and continued on to the Rennie's Mill Road section of the trail, squeezing past young mothers with enormous strollers and older people picking their slow way along. Near the tennis club, a huge tree protruded from the centre of the trail, its six separate trunks leaning low enough to touch the chain-link fence that surrounded the soccer pitch. Danny ducked underneath it, then crossed the street to the uphill portion of the trail and the thirty steps to the top. His mind, usually pleasantly blank when he ran, kept returning to Rory Fraser. Last he'd heard, Fraser had taken a sabbatical to do some training courses in the States, a program of study that would have kept him away for at least a couple of years. So what was he doing on the island, and what were the odds he and Danny would meet up on the Quidi Vidi trail? There were lots of people he'd gone through training with, had worked with during his years with the constab, people who still lived in the city. He'd never met any of them on the trail.

"For the love of Jesus, Danny, don't be making up stories in your head. You'll drive yourself cracked." He could almost hear his grandfather's voice. Maybe meeting up with Rory Fraser was mere happenstance, but his detective's instinct suggested otherwise. Few things happened by accident; there was always some design behind what seemed like a casual event. Danny wasn't religious or even superstitious, but he suspected there was an unseen energy at work in the world, a native causality responsible for shifting things around.

Why was Rory Fraser so hostile to him? They hadn't seen each other for literally years, yet he acted like Danny had pissed all over him. And that remark about Hynes being—

Of course. Danny, Fraser, and Hynes had all joined the constabulary at the same time, but they each progressed in their careers at different rates. When a plum assignment came up on the job board, they all three applied, but Danny got it. Detective sergeant with the criminal investigation division. Christ, that was twenty years ago. Surely to God Fraser was over it by now.

He turned around and descended the stairs, heading back downtown. He took an extra lap around the waterfront, hoping to settle his churning mind, but he knew better. The added exercise was merely a diversionary tactic, a faint hope of delaying the inevitable. He would be awake until the small hours, wondering. As he ran past the stacked shipping containers, he thought of Tadhg, remembering the questions Moira Fraser had asked him. Why *was* Tadhg hanging around the beach in Kildevil Cove? Was he telling the truth about that, about any of it? Tadhg had never been the type to take long walks and contemplate life, so why would he linger on the beach?

An ocean-going RoRo was pulling in through the Narrows, navigating the small channel carefully, accompanied on either side by one of the harbour pilots. The pilot boats looked miniscule in comparison to the huge cargo ship, dwarfed by even the shadow of its immense bulk, but they were leading it, not the other way around. He stopped and watched for a while, stretching, enjoying the pull in his muscles. This was an unusually long run for him. He knew he'd be sore in the morning—and the constab, then, and their fucking internal investigation. Could they not leave anything alone? He'd given them everything he had, and they'd taken it. They'd taken all of it until he had nothing left.

He kept an apartment on Warbury Street, infamous for a 2009 murder when a man killed his girlfriend and dismembered her body. Police later found her head in the man's freezer. Since then, Warbury had had a bad reputation, but Danny liked the area, and his apartment windows overlooked the Martin's Meadow soccer pitch and the low hills of the Waterford Valley. Besides, the rent was cheap. Nobody wanted to live on a street that had once housed a murderer.

His apartment was the entire top floor of an old three-storey Victorian, built sometime after the second Great Fire. It was painted dark blue, a "heritage colour" approved of by the city council as being suitable for an area of historical importance. Considering the murdered woman's horribly sundered body, they ought to have painted it red. He checked the mailbox before climbing the stairs, surprised he didn't meet anyone else on the way. An elderly Scotsman, a World War II veteran, lived on the second floor. He was very old now, past ninety, and so frail he probably shouldn't be living alone. Danny was friendly with him, stopping by every three or four days to see if he was all right, if he needed anything from the shops. An avid reader of the newspapers, he often underlined passages of interest and talked with Danny about them, asking his opinion or supplying his own. Next door to him was Mr. Roberts, completely blind and somewhere past eighty. He'd moved into the house when his wife died and his daughters decided he belonged in a care home. He must have heard Danny on the stairs; he opened his door. "Is that you, Danny lad?"

"Tis indeed, Mr. Roberts." Danny stepped forward and shook his hand. The older man liked some kind of physical contact at the start of a conversation—a handshake, a touch on the shoulder, a brief grip of his elbow. It was a courtesy Danny was only too happy to provide. The air in Mr. Roberts's apartment was much too warm for him, though, and often smelled overpoweringly of liniment. He preferred to chat in the hallway and always declined the offer of a coffee inside—politely, of course. "Now tell me something," Mr. Roberts said. He came outside and stood with his back against the wall. "You're originally from around the bay, aren't you?"

"Yes," Danny said, wondering where this was going. Mrs. Picco came up the stairs, her arms laden with groceries, and nodded to them both. Why she nodded to Mr. Roberts, Danny didn't know. It wasn't like he could see the gesture.

"Out there around New Melbourne, isn't it?"

"Yes."

"When I was a younger man, I often went out that way in the winter, cutting wood. In those days it was hard to find a proper boarding house, so I ended up staying with a man I think might have been your grandfather."

The declaration unsettled him. "Oh?"

"Karen Swyers, her daughter, Kelly, put me on to him. So I rented out their upstairs bedroom and took my meals with the family." He shook his head sadly. "Shame what happened with your mother and father." Danny was used to people saying such things, and it no longer bothered him when someone referenced his parents. Or at least it didn't bother him as much as it once had.

"Yes," Danny agreed. "I miss them very much."

"You were only a youngster when it happened."

"I was."

"See, there was no need for any of that." He shook his head. "He always had a temper, your grandfather. There was no need of it."

Danny's memories of that night were faint and jumbled, vague impressions of voices and places, someone shouting. His grandparents' kitchen was much too hot, but he was afraid to leave and go elsewhere in the house. He took a chair and put it beside the old Philco refrigerator with the handle you had to pull down to open the door. He laid his cheek against the cool metal and listened to the humming of the motor. It seemed to make the time go by, gave him something to focus his attention on.

"But you weren't still living with Grandar then," Danny said.

"No, this was years after, but we kept in touch, Mrs. Swyers and me. She said she never seen the like—the old man turning the two of them out on a night like that, practically driving them away with the shotgun."

A surge of apprehension stabbed him to the heart. "Shotgun?"

"Oh yes, he got the gun and drove the two of them out."

Grandar had driven his parents away at the point of a gun? How had Danny not known this?

The old man sighed. "I better go get a shave. My daughter is coming over with the youngsters."

"Of course," Danny said. "Always best to make a good impression. I'll talk to you later." He stepped away and heard the door close. What had Mr. Roberts meant when he said there was no need for it? "No need for any of it," he'd said. A shotgun? Had his grandfather threatened Danny's parents, somehow forced them from the house? If so, this was the first he'd heard of it. Then again, it wasn't the sort of story that got passed down in family folklore. What else was there about Grandar that Danny didn't know?

His landline was ringing when he unlocked the door. He strode into the kitchen and picked up the receiver but heard only dial tone. He figured if it was important, they would call back. He went into the bathroom, stripped, and took a long, luxurious shower. His thoughts kept going back to Tadhg and Lily. Maybe that had been Tadhg on the phone. He ought to call back in that case, should probably call Tadhg anyway. There were no messages on the landline when he got out of the shower, but when he checked his phone, he saw he had an email from Sandra. Instead of calling her back, he logged on to his laptop and opened his email program.

Just wondering, did you get the flowers I sent for the funeral?
Sandra

He hit Reply and wrote

The flowers were gorgeous. I clipped some of the Oriental lilies to take home. The whole place smells like spice.
Danny

He clicked Send and imagined the note winging its way across oceans and continents, finding his sister in Portugal.

A FEELING of profound emptiness, not unlike the way he'd felt before Grandar's funeral, hollowed out the pit of his stomach and bulged up into his chest and throat. The inquiry would begin in the morning. He was expected to show up at constabulary headquarters at nine and explain all over again to a room full of people how he'd fucked up at the Clontarf sea wall in Dublin. The chief would be there, he thought. McAuley was chief now, a transplant from the mainland, and Danny knew him only slightly. McAuley had been in charge of the last case Danny worked before he left for Dublin. Oddly enough it had been on his recommendation that Danny had gone—strange, because he and McAuley couldn't stand each other. To say they were a bad fit was an understatement. McAuley believed in guiding an investigation according to his own procedures and didn't care for officers with differing ideas. He decided how an investigation was to proceed, which lines of enquiry officers were to follow, and discouraged independent thought. Danny, used to following his own instincts, was a persistent thorn in McAuley's arse. He'd rather cut his own balls off with a rusty knife than have to be in a room with the man. More than likely McAuley would have some difficult questions for him in the morning. He'd enjoy seeing Danny squirm.

The landline rang again, jarring him out of his reverie, and he reached for the receiver, irritated. "Hello?"

Nothing. Not even the sound of someone breathing on the other end, only dead air and a faint crackling, like lightning in the distance. "Who is this?"

No answer, so he hung up.

He took some fresh salmon out of the fridge and drizzled it with olive oil, then heated the frying pan. The vegetables were already prepared; he'd bought one of those ready-made side dishes where all you had to do was warm the whole thing through. His stomach was jumping so badly he wondered if he would be able to eat, but when he sat down, he realised he was hungry after all and polished off the salmon and the veg along with two glasses of white wine. He almost never drank wine. With Danny it was scotch or beer. Tadhg was the oenophile, not him, collecting rare and expensive vintages like the Richebourg Grand Cru he'd picked up on eBay, or the Chateau Lafitte stacked in neat rows down in his basement. Well, that was fine for Tadhg. He could afford it. Wealth wasn't a novel concept to him. He'd been born with the proverbial silver spoon in his mouth. No, a silver hook, Danny amended. The first Heaney ancestor to land in Kildevil Cove hailed from County Wicklow, a member of the landless gentry who figured he'd be better off on some other island. He'd come across in the late eighteenth century with the clothes on his back and his pockets full of gold he'd won at gambling. By combining several businesses (bought on credit and good will, with accompanying promissory notes to secure the loans), he was able to set himself up as a fish merchant, purchasing boats and fishing gear. At the end of the first year, he was arguably the richest man on the island, and by the mid-1950s, the Heaneys owned practically everything in Kildevil Cove, and beyond.

The Heaneys built a big house on the point of land at the opposite end of Kildevil Cove from where Danny had grown up, a Queen Anne revival with turrets and cupolas, or whatever they were. In an era of postwar frugality, this marked them out for scorn, but of a muted sort. Practically everyone in Kildevil Cove owed their living to the Heaneys, from the clerks and managers in their stores to the fishermen who brought the day's catch ashore. Danny's father had driven an oil truck for them, and his mother accepted seasonal work in the fish processing plant. Even the town's small boys managed to make some pocket money by cutting out cod tongues at the Heaney wharf and selling them to the plant in bulk.

By all rights, Danny and Tadhg should have been mortal enemies, but he and Tadhg were at school together from kindergarten straight through. The economic differences that ought to have set them far apart didn't figure in their friendship at all. Tadhg shared his lunch when money was tight for Danny's family and Danny, naturally tall and stocky, shielded Tadhg from the western-shore bullies who resented him and his family's wealth. When Harvey Squire blackened Tadhg's eye one day in grade nine, Danny caught up with him and gave him a bloody nose, then took Tadhg home with him.

"Just hold the ice cubes on it. Don't touch it." Danny'd raided his grandmother's medicine chest and found an ancient ice bag. They snagged a half-full flask of whisky from his grandfather's stash and sat in the stable doorway drinking it.

"Thank you for what you did," Tadhg said. "He's a big bastard. I'm not afraid of him, but he's big. And he's fast too."

"Stay the hell away from him," Danny said. He leaned over and looked at Tadhg, pushing the ice bag out of the way so he could see the injury. "He got you good."

The swelling bruise marred the pale landscape of Tadhg's face. He flinched when Danny touched it. "Jesus, that hurts."

"You knows yourself, sure it got to hurt." Danny had experienced a curious tenderness that day, a desire to help Tadhg and keep him safe, to care for him. It would be all too easy to fall back into that dynamic: him being the helper and Tadhg being eternally helped—and grateful.

He'd just gotten up to bring his dishes to the sink when his mobile rang. It was Tadhg. "What is it?" Danny asked. "Is anything wrong? It's not Lily, is it?"

"No, Lily's fine. We're getting her feeding tube fitted day after tomorrow," Tadhg said. "Hopefully it'll help her take in a few more calories. She needs all the nutrition she can get."

"How are you?" Danny went through to the living room and sat down on the couch with the phone pressed against his ear.

"That's why I'm calling." Silence, then Tadhg drew a shaky breath. "There's something I have to tell you."

"Something to tell me." A thrill of unease slid between Danny's shoulder blades like icy water. His mouth was suddenly dry, and he knew what Tadhg was going to say before he said it.

"It's about my wallet."

There was a long silence. Danny waited.

"I…. Jesus, Danny, look…."

Danny would wait as long as it took. It was something he did during interrogations. It usually unnerved the suspect, and they rushed to fill the silence, often telling him what he wanted to know.

"I know how my wallet ended up on the beach."

"You do."

"But you already knew that."

"Yes," Danny replied, "I did." His unease widened, flattened into disappointment. But he'd been foolish to believe in Tadhg Heaney in the first place. He knew that now. Some part of him had always known it. "You were down there, weren't ye? More recently than Grandar's funeral." His heartbeat thudded in his chest.

"Yes." Tadhg sounded wretched, broken.

"So you lied to me."

"Danny, I never—"

He was suddenly, viciously angry. "You did! By omission, you lied! When I told you Llew Single's bones had washed up, you said nothing, Tadhg. Not one *fucking* word. You realise I've got to tell Moira Fraser about this." She would be furious, and that was putting it mildly.

For a long time, Tadhg said nothing. Then, "But you've never lied in your life, have ye, Danny?" His voice was low and venomous. "Not you. Not Danny Quirke."

"What?" Danny's anger—and his confidence—faltered. "What are you talking about?"

"That business at the Clontarf sea wall in Dublin. Did ye think no one would find out the truth?"

CHAPTER NINE

IN THE end, and in blatant disregard of protocol, he'd gone to Eamonn Nolan's funeral. Most funerals, in Danny's experience, were desperately sad, but this was beyond grim. The recent spell of rainy weather had seen fit to continue uninterrupted, and it was so cold the mourners' breaths formed clouds of mist in front of their faces as they huddled into heavy coats and scarves. Danny had stood some distance away from the gravesite that day in Glasnevin Cemetery, near the round tower marking Daniel O'Connell's tomb. Oddly, Eamonn's family hadn't opted for cremation, which was the done thing nowadays, or maybe they couldn't bear the thought of his final mortal remains vanishing in a puff of smoke.

He had little memory of his parents' funeral; he and Sandra were very young children at the time. He remembered school had been closed for the day so his and Sandra's teachers could attend, and after the long church service, there were sandwiches and cookies at the Orange Lodge, where trestle tables had been set up across wooden sawhorses loaned out for the occasion from local families. The hall was full of people he knew, and some he didn't, and he went around being hugged and kissed by adults in their Sunday best even though it was a Thursday morning. The whole thing was queerly unrealistic, as if he were standing outside an open door and watching people as they passed by, holding cups of tea or coffee or a plate of sandwiches.

"There's going to be cake," Sandra told him later. "Nan said. A huge cake with blue-and-white icing."

Danny had scoffed at this. "Sure it's not a wedding. Don't be so foolish." But there was a cake, a huge chocolate sheet cake with blue-and-white icing and the words "Forever Loved" written on the top in flowing script. It was the kind of cake you'd see at a birthday party, but there was nothing convivial about this gathering, and the sight of people his parents knew walking around with cake and tea upset him so, he was compelled to hide away. He crawled in behind the stage, a small raised platform at one end of the hall, and curled up in a storage cupboard, his head on his knees. He wasn't missed until much later in the day when his grandmother sent Sandra to look for him. She knew immediately where he was. "How'd you find me so quick?" he asked her.

"I know you like small spaces, Dan. You always did."

He remembered this remark, standing in the endless goddamn rain at Glasnevin cemetery, and suppressed a smile. Sandra never knew him as well as she thought she did. He hated small spaces, was claustrophobic in the extreme… but that one day, a small space had felt like a comfort to him.

He managed to escape the crush of mourners at the cemetery's main gate as the graveside service concluded but ran full-on into a mob of reporters and press photographers outside.

"Inspector Quirke, what have you got to say about Eamonn Noble's murder?"

"Did the family invite you to the funeral?"

"Have you anything to say to the mother of the man you killed?"

"Inspector Quirke, are you the worst policeman in Ireland?"

They followed him along the pavements to where he'd left his car and surrounded him, pushing in like a mob of football hooligans. He reached into his coat pockets but couldn't find his keys. A mounting sense of panicked hysteria drew hot colour into his face. They were too close to him now; he couldn't breathe.

"Will you stand trial for killing Eamonn Noble?"

He found the keys in his trouser pocket and pressed the fob. The door didn't open.

"Inspector Quirke, do you expect to be struck off for your actions at the Clontarf sea wall?"

He pressed it again. Nothing. He was beginning to sweat now, his hand cramping around the key fob that he held in a death grip.

"Have you always carried a gun?" This from a young woman with a helmet of startling pink hair and metal barbells in her eyebrows. "Would you use it to kill again?"

A hot rush of anger surged up into his chest and throat. "I killed no one!" he said, turning to face her as the rest of the vultures clustered round him. "He shot himself. I had nothing to—"

The door clicked open, and he fell gratefully into the driver's seat. He closed his eyes and forced himself to take slow, deep breaths. Then, hands trembling, he started his Volvo, grateful for the reassuring purr of the motor. He signaled to turn onto the roadway, nosing the car past two or three photographers who tried to prevent him leaving by standing in his way. After some aggressive posturing and rude gestures they stepped back, allowing him to leave.

He drove blindly, with no idea of where he was going. He took exits onto supplementary roads he'd never seen before, went the wrong way down one-way streets, was stopped by cul-de-sacs that appeared, unexpected, at the last minute. He ended up in a narrow laneway running parallel to Clontarf, lined with storage sheds and garages. "I know you like small spaces, Dan. You always did."

But he didn't like this one. Stout stone and concrete walls loomed up either side of him, and once a ginger cat ran out in front of his car, startling him so he had to stand on the brakes. He put the car into park and sat for a moment, his elbows on the steering wheel, his head in his hands, while an immense trembling rose up from deep inside his belly and rattled his bones. No, Sandra was wrong. He didn't like small spaces at all. He wanted to be out in the open with empty land all around him, the sea and the sky, some other island than this. He engaged the engine and drove slowly out to where the lane met up with a major road—Clontarf Road. Of course he'd end up here, a stone's throw from the Wooden Bridge, where the straight street opened out into a swath of green on one side, then stretched itself across the sea on the other.

A makeshift memorial of sorts had sprung up in the days since Eamonn Nolan's death, with bouquets of flowers and religious candles placed near a Slí ne Sláinte sign at one end of the bridge. This was, he knew, only the beginning. There would be further tributes laid there in the coming weeks and months: teddy bears and spare pieces of someone's football kit (Eamonn had played in a neighbourhood league), handwritten notes full of sentiment and wishes for the repose of Eamonn's soul. No doubt masses were being said even now. If things had been different—if Danny had been the one shot dead on this spot—would anybody bother leaving tributes? Probably not. No tributes for a killer cop, and many of the locals had little enough sentiment where the Gardaí were concerned.

They'd both been at the corner where the Wooden Bridge gave onto Clontarf Road. Danny, accompanied by two marked patrol cars, had pursued Eamonn from the Temple Bar, up through North Strand. Just before they emerged onto Clontarf Road, Eamonn's battered car gave up the ghost. He ditched it in the parking lot of a Thai restaurant and took off on foot. Danny followed. It was a short run, but Eamonn was fast, and twice Danny nearly lost him when Eamonn decided to abandon his route and swerve in and out of traffic. "You're nicked, Eamonn! Ye might as well stop now," Danny called. A young woman had halted her bicycle before the bridge and leaned it up against the stone wall. She was fumbling in her knapsack for something when Eamonn reached out and grabbed her by the shoulder, spun her around so her back was against his chest.

"Fuck off," Eamonn shouted as Danny drew closer, "or I'll blow her fucking brains out." He pressed an automatic against the girl's temple. "I will."

A gun. He has a gun. The idea was a mere abstraction—the girl, terrified and crying, occupied an even smaller part of his attention. *And I have a gun as well.* Nolan whispered something to his hostage, but the words were blown away by the wind. He stepped backwards onto the wall and dragged her up after him. The two marked patrol cars stopped when Danny waved them back.

"Eamonn, you don't want to do that." The standard phrases anyone would utter in such a situation, but they sounded hollow and ridiculous to him now. "Let the wee girl go. She's done nothing to you."

"What's it to you, ye gobshite?" Nolan laughed as if he'd heard the best joke in the world. "You don't even know her." He tightened his hold. "You don't even know me."

I do, Danny thought but didn't say. *I know you and every other bastard like ye. You probably had a shit childhood, and your old man was a violent drunk. He got your mother pregnant while they were both still at school and spent years knocking her around. You grew up to beat your girlfriend because it makes you feel like a hard man.*

"I've got Donna on the phone," he said. He held up his mobile so Eamonn could see it. "She wants to talk to you. All's forgiven. She wants you to come home."

Nolan wasn't about to fall for that. He was a repeat offender; he knew how the system worked. "That slut doesn't want me anywhere near her!" he spat. "She's been whoring herself, so she has. Fucking anything that moves."

"It's the truth." Danny held up the phone again. "She's willing to talk it over if you are." It started to rain, huge drops splattering down. "Come on, bhoy. We're all going to catch a death of cold out here, sure." He was aware of his own gun nudging his hip and sending a tremor down deep into the bones. If he drew his sidearm, then he and Nolan would both have a weapon. *Go on then,* an inner voice urged, *even up the odds, why don't you? It's him or you.* "What about if we bring Donna here? She's not far away, ye know. I can have them get her if that would help."

"Why the fuck would I want to see her?" Nolan screamed then, a hoarse, animal sound that raised the hair on Danny's forearms. He pressed the gun harder into the side of the girl's head. "She's nothing to me!"

The rain intensified, a heavy curtain of falling water that soaked Danny's hair and his clothes, pooling on the road at his feet. It was hard to see Nolan through the downpour gushing like a waterfall. Danny sensed movement behind him as two Gardaí moved forward. "No," he said, without taking his gaze from Nolan, "don't. He'll shoot her." There were three people present in Nolan's sights—Danny, the girl, and Nolan himself. He would almost certainly shoot one of them.

"Somebody's got to pay," Nolan shrieked. He bared his teeth at them, laughing. He was fucked up on something—heroin or meth or fentanyl—and it was making him reckless and insane. "I'm not going back inside. I'm not."

"No one's said anything about that," Danny said.

"I know you." Nolan waved the gun at him. The girl tried to twist out of his hold, but he caught her and pulled her back against him. "You fuckers say one thing and do another. You'll have me inside again, and I'm not going!"

Danny's radio chirped. He kept his eyes on Nolan, always on Nolan. He filled the whole of Danny's vision now. "Yes?"

"Gregson's gone to get the girl." It was Ronan Fraser, a young detective sergeant Danny had worked with once or twice before. "Two minutes. She's just round the corner." Danny liked Ronan; he was sensible and reliable. When Danny mentioned he was from Newfoundland, Ronan had claimed relatives there. "Lovely spot. I've got cousins in St. John's, sure."

"Where are you?" Danny didn't dare look around. He couldn't afford to take his attention from Eamonn Nolan for a fraction of a second.

"Just behind you, blue Ford." The younger man sounded confident that the situation could be peacefully resolved. "He'll talk to her. Maybe she can get him to let the girl go."

"Right." Danny ended the call. A crowd of spectators had gathered in the street, where they were being kept well behind the barricade by several Gardaí. From the corner of his eye, Danny could see their inquisitive faces, their bodies pressed against the blue-and-white tape like runners at the end of a marathon. Clontarf Road had been barricaded either side, and the traffic rerouted. The Wooden Bridge had been likewise closed off. It was high tide, the water lapping at the girders. That and the falling rain, coupled with the subtle noise of his own breathing, was all he could hear. The girl was sobbing silently, her chest rising and falling in a hectic rhythm that matched Danny's own breathing. Nolan's hand never wavered; his arm never tired. He held the girl in place, the barrel of his gun at her temple, and he and Danny stared at each other, both trapped in this hellish tableau. She was somebody's sister, that girl, somebody's well-loved niece or girlfriend. She was expected home, and when she did not arrive, her family would worry. They would worry and wonder where she was. *Where is she? Where's…?* But Danny didn't know her name. Maybe he would never know it.

A car pulled up behind him. A door opened and slammed shut. This would be Donna, Eamonn's common-law wife. Danny's radio twittered. Fraser again. "What is it?"

"Bad news, boss." He sighed heavily. "She's brought the youngsters with her."

"Look at me, Eamonn!" Donna started forward at the edge of Danny's vision. She was carrying a young toddler in her arms, a little girl, and holding the hand of a boy perhaps a year or two older. "Ye got to come home now. That's enough."

Fraser moved into Danny's line of sight, holding on to Donna's free arm, escorting her as he might escort a woman onto a dance floor. Danny shook his head, but they kept coming until she was standing at Danny's side. She was about twenty-five but aged beyond her years and with sharp lines carved into the sides of her mouth and under her eyes—eyes circled with dark smudges that might have been bruises or fatigue, Danny couldn't tell. Her hair was dyed a silvery grey, a current fad among the younger folk, who thought it fashionable to look like their grandparents, and her lips were daubed with thick purple lipstick. She wore jeans with strategically ripped holes, and a tight Mickey Mouse T-shirt. *God love her.* She looked like every poor trashy girl he had ever seen.

"Eamonn," Donna said, "are you listening to m—"

For a long time afterwards, the incident and its aftermath had the quality of a half-remembered dream. He remembered unholstering his weapon and raising it to sight along the barrel. He remembered watching as Nolan released his grip on the girl, positioned the gun against his own head, and…

…fired.

Everything around him froze. Later he would recall that even the rain seemed to stop where it was, halted in the middle of its rush downwards. He stared at the place where Nolan had been standing, his gaze coming to rest on the empty expanse of air. The girl screamed, and time started again, jolting into its customary motion with an almost audible click. She screamed and screamed, a hoarse animal sound, her hands spread at her sides, her arms working up and down like pistons. Her blond hair was plastered to her head with Nolan's blood, and there was a dark, viscous stain all down one side of her blouse. A young female Guard came forward and took her by the hand to lead her to the waiting patrol car. An ambulance, Danny thought, someone needed to call an ambulance, and then there came the sound of a siren, as he had wished it.

"Sir." Fraser stood in front of him, gazing intently into Danny's eyes. "Are you all right, sir?" He gently pushed Danny's gun hand down. "It's over with now." Somewhere behind him a woman said, "Oh my God" and kept saying it, "Oh my God oh my God oh my God," each successive repetition rising in volume and intonation. People stopped their cars on Clontarf Road and got out to look, and those bystanders already present surged forward against the blue-and-white tape, murmuring to themselves and each other. "What's after happening? Somebody killed, bhoy. The Guards shot him. The Guards shot him? Sure the Guards haven't got guns, have they?"

For a long time Danny sat in one of the patrol cars, watching as the ambulance arrived and two young men scrambled over the wall to retrieve Nolan's body, strapping it to a board and levering it up and over. It was covered with a sheet, but a dark stain marked an emptiness on one side of the head, the fabric falling over a visible absence. He turned to watch as the corpse went by, but he felt nothing. The police negotiator, delayed by heavy traffic, had arrived too late. She stood by her car and watched as the ambulance pulled away, her face as blank and empty as everyone else's. Later he sat in Superintendent Adrian Halsey's office, numb in his soaking wet clothes, the shed rainwater making a pool around his feet.

"Ye're getting my floor wet, I suppose you know that." Halsey placed a hot cup of tea in front of Danny and sat down. "D'ye want to tell me what happened? In your own words, of course."

Danny told him. Halsey listened without interrupting. "And your firearm?" he asked, after Danny finished talking.

"It's… uh…." He felt at his side but the gun wasn't there. "I think I left it in my coat. It's probably still in Gerry O'Roarke's patrol car." In any other circumstances it would have sounded flippant, even cheeky. "I'll go down to the garage and retrieve it immediately." He reached out for the cup of tea but didn't pick it up. His fingers traced the handle and the rim while some small part of his mind made note of the smoothness of the texture, the miniscule chips and dents. *They ought to buy new cups.* He nodded to himself. There was blood under his fingernails. Where had it come from? Not Nolan's blood. His own, then. He'd cut himself that morning while shaving in the bathroom of his rented flat on Parnell Square, squinting into the steam-streaked mirror, his razor cutting swaths through the foam.

"We think Nolan was involved with some of the big gang boys up north," Halsey said, "and we've had our eye on him for a while." He sat down. "Someone had to stop him. It was only a matter of time. Luck of the draw that it happened to be you." He nodded at Danny's cup of tea. "Drink up. We're keeping the girl for questioning. I figured you might want to get a look-in."

"All right," Danny said. He followed Halsey to an observation room where they watched two Gardaí—a young female officer and a man about thirty—interviewing Donna. She wasn't particularly forthcoming, sitting in silence, gnawing at a thumbnail. Twice she asked where her children were; twice the young female Guard told her that her sister was on the way.

"What do you remember about when you were on the bridge with Eamonn?" the male officer asked. He was almost ridiculously handsome, with curly dark hair and big brown eyes. Like a goddamn baby doll, Danny thought sourly. "Can you tell us?"

"I've told you like fifty times already." She shifted in her chair. "He fucking shot Eamonn. Eamonn didn't shoot. He never had time."

The two Gardaí exchanged a look. "You're sure about this," the woman said. "Inspector Quirke fired on Eamonn? You saw it?"

"Do you believe her?" Danny asked.

Halsey shrugged. "Hard to tell. It's early days yet."

"Sir, I didn't—"

"Let's leave it for now, hmm?" The older man held the door open, and Danny followed him back to the office. He waited until they were both seated again before speaking. "Now listen here, son. You know as well as I do there's little credence in what that girl is saying. She's got a police record as long as my arm. But we're duty-bound to investigate. If we don't follow proper protocol—"

"Yes," Danny interrupted. "I know you have to. It's just…."

"Something to add?" Halsey waited patiently, one big hand wrapped around his mug of tea. He took a sip, eyes on Danny.

"I didn't fire my weapon." He couldn't have. Nolan shot himself.

"You'll put that in your report, then."

Danny looked up. "Of course, sir." They sat there, gazing at each other, the moments between them stretching into eternity.

"And we will require your firearm," Halsey reminded him.

"Right." It was a new one. When he'd started here, some months before, Halsey had personally taken Danny down to the armoury to choose his weapon, a Glock automatic. "We don't normally carry guns here," he'd said. "We leave that to the firearms officers, but you're a special case."

"And we'll want to swab your hands for trace residue." Halsey said this almost casually, as if he were suggesting they take a stroll around the parking lot.

"Nolan shot himself," Danny said.

Halsey nodded slowly. "He did. But your weapon was drawn—"

"That was for my own protection."

"Of course it was." There was something about Halsey's tone of voice that Danny didn't like. Obviously his displeasure showed on his face, for Halsey continued, "You're not being singled out, Danny. Never think that. It's procedure, that's all. In a situation like this, we've got to cover our arses." He made as if to say something further but changed his mind. "That's all. You can go now. Stop by the lab on your way and get the swab done."

Danny avoided the elevators—and his colleagues—and took the back stairs down to street level. He didn't go to the lab or the garage, as he'd told Halsey he would, but took a taxi back to his flat off Parnell Square. Then he stripped and showered, taking care to scrub his hands. Later, he would burn the clothes he was wearing in the basement incinerator. He made himself strong coffee and a sandwich, then sat down on the sitting room floor and switched out the barrel of his Glock for a new, unfired one. He'd get rid of the old barrel later that night.

It was fear that made him do it, and what did it matter now, anyway? Either way, Nolan was dead, and maybe that was for the best. He'd seen the bruises the bastard had left on the girl.

You can't be taking justice into your own hands, Danny. Was that what he'd done? This wasn't who he was, this duplicitous man. This wasn't who he was at all.

CHAPTER TEN

LYING CAME easily to some. Danny had seen it so many times in his work, people caught flat-footed and red-handed with the evidence laid out in front of them who nonetheless protested, "I didn't do it." They could stand in front of a magistrate and swear on the Bible they were innocent, all the while looking like butter wouldn't melt in their mouths. It astonished him.

The constabulary's inquiry—or, as Danny liked to think of it, the inquisition—had lasted two and a half days, but to him it had felt like twenty years. Two senior officers had taken him into one of the newly refurbished conference rooms at the rear of the building, offered him a seat at an unsettlingly shiny table, poured him a glass of water from a big glass jug. The room smelled like fresh latex paint and new carpet, and someone had recently cleaned the table's mirrored surface with something lemon scented. The smells all got together to create a sickening miasma that burned his throat and nostrils.

At one end there was a huge video screen—that was how the constabulary did things now—and computer tablets were set into the table at each place, configured to display the contents of the Smart Board at the other end of the room. You had no choice but to pay attention. The interview, of course, was taped on an old-style cassette deck, which seemed strange, except audio cassettes were cheap, easy to use, transportable, and hard to erase, unlike the newer memory cards or thumb drives. Each place also had a thin blue folder, containing the details of Danny's encounter at the Dublin seawall.

"Have a seat, Inspector Quirke." The taller of the two senior officers was Vincent Arsenault, a transplant from the Montreal police force, a quietly thoughtful man who only ever spoke when he had something significant to say. With him was Hugh Maher, an old-school copper from Shea Heights who believed the best way to secure a confession was with a baseball bat. He and Danny had gone through training at the same time, but there was no love lost between them. They had been assigned together on a routine drug investigation, a quick search and seizure of a suspected crack house up the back of Linegar Avenue. Maher had charged in like he was going over the top at Beaumont-Hamel while Danny was left scrambling to keep up. In the end, the suspects had all fled out various windows and disappeared into the woods. Danny wondered if maybe that hadn't been Maher's intention in the first place.

"Didn't think we'd ever see you in here," Maher said, smirking. "Not been keeping your nose clean, eh?"

Danny didn't bother answering him. If anyone had reason to make him look bad, it was Maher, and he'd be damned if he allowed him that much leeway. The third member of the tribunal was Police Chief Bryan McAuley. It would have gone easier for Danny if it had been Satan himself.

They kept at it all throughout the morning. At eleven a constable wheeled in a tray of Tim's coffee and a selection of donuts. The group broke for lunch at one and reconvened an hour later. By five o'clock that afternoon, Danny was exhausted. The process continued for another day and late into the morning of the third, the three investigators asking him the same questions over and over, waiting to see if he'd break, or change his story.

"So you encountered the deceased at the Clontarf seawall in Dublin."

"Yes. We had attempted arrest earlier that day at his residence."

"And the accused resisted?"

"Yes. He then fled the dwelling on foot. Some of our officers gave chase but were unsuccessful." They'd given him several young Gardaí, all fit men and fast on their feet, but Eamonn Nolan had a car waiting for him at the end of the block. "A short time afterwards, we received a report that he had been spotted in the area of the seawall. I went there with several constables to try and apprehend him."

"And you failed."

"Normally there's a police negotiator, but she got held up in traffic." Nolan's finger had tightened on the trigger, and his agitated expression had smoothed out into something more accepting, and much more chilling. "There was heavy traffic in the area. The negotiator was delayed. That's what they told me."

"Didn't bother trying to help—you yourself I mean." McAuley fixed his unblinking stare on Danny, peering at him like a reptile. "You figured it was just as good to sit there on your arse and—"

"Respectfully, Chief," Arsenault said quietly, "I think we're being led away from the primary purpose of this hearing." He glanced round the table. "Inspector Quirke is not qualified to negotiate in such a situation.

In my opinion he acted appropriately." His nod was so very slight Danny might have imagined it. At least someone here was on his side. "I don't believe there was anything else you could have done."

But he'd failed, standing in the pouring rain and shaking with cold. Nolan had had a young girl up there with him, and he would have shot her, would have probably shot Danny as well.

"I tried to make the suspect surrender his hostage, but he refused."

One step forward was all it took. Danny's foot had barely touched the ground, but he was miles and years too late, and then Eamonn Nolan was dead.

When the inquiry finally adjourned, it was almost noon, and Danny felt like he'd run a thousand miles. He went back to his apartment on Warbury Street and stripped off the clothes he'd spent hours sweating through. A throbbing ache had started at the back of his head some time before, and now it felt like metal claws were digging into his skull and pulling. He stood under a hot shower for half an hour, letting the pounding water knead the tightness from his muscles, and then he dressed in clean jeans and a heavy wool sweater, hiking boots, and a waterproof, and drove the one hundred miles to Kildevil Cove. The journey back to his childhood home made absolutely no sense whatsoever. There was nothing there for him apart from bad memories and the bitterness of recent loss, yet he went anyway. He had no idea what was driving him.

He wanted to talk to Tadhg, yet they had hardly parted on the best of terms. "Did ye think no one would find out the truth?" Tadhg had asked. Danny still wasn't sure what Tadhg meant by that. No one, none of the other Gardaí, not even Halsey, knew what Danny had done that day in Dublin. No one could have known. That whole business with the gun, switching out the barrel, that was done in the privacy of his living room. He'd thrown the evidence in the Liffey late one night. No one had seen him. There was no one there to see. So what the hell was Tadhg talking about? Maybe he'd be better off to keep his own counsel. Deal with the fallout on his own. Lock himself in the house and quaff a few jars until the pain went away, like he did after Alison died. People said it wasn't possible to die of loneliness, but Danny knew that was bullshit. Loneliness was like water dropping on stone: it wore at you. He took out his phone, scrolled through his contacts until he found Tadhg's number, asked him to come.

"I realise it's a bit of a drive. Sorry to be such a pain in the arse."

Tadhg had replied immediately and without question. "I'm in Kildevil Cove myself. Just tell me when." He arrived at Danny's rented house mere moments later.

"Jesus," he'd exclaimed, stepping out of his car. Danny was waiting in the driveway. "You look like shite." He reached into the front seat and brought out something bottle-shaped. "Macallan," he said. "Think you're worth it?" But his attempted levity fell flat. Danny turned wordlessly and went into the house. Tadhg followed him. In the kitchen, Danny fetched down two thick glass tumblers and held out his hand for the bottle. Tadhg gave it to him, and he poured them each a generous measure.

"For the love of Christ, will ye talk to me!" Tadhg said sharply.

Danny sank into a chair and took a healthy swallow of the whisky. It burned agreeably on the way down, and then the fire subsided into a soothing glow that warmed the pit of his stomach. "I didn't shoot him," he said after a moment. He raised his eyes slowly to look at Tadhg. "I swear to God." Tadhg looked at him blankly, and Danny continued, "Eamonn Nolan. He shot himself."

Tadhg nodded, tasting his whisky. "I know," he said.

Danny didn't pursue it. "They kept me there for almost three days, the bastards." He gazed into his glass. "Asking the same fucking things over and over and over. Jesus." He swiped a hand across his forehead. "It's what they do, you know, to fuck with your head. Ask ye the same questions and hope you'll trip yourself up."

"Did you?" Tadhg asked. Danny noticed Tadhg was sipping his whisky, taking his time with it, but Tadhg had never been much of a drinker. Likely he'd just have the one, whereas Danny, in his current frame of mind, could possibly finish the bottle.

"Don't think so."

"So you've nothing to worry about." Tadhg's expression was sardonic. "But ye will. Worry, I mean. Because that's you all over, isn't it? You worry yourself half-sick about things that happened forever ago, and which have absolutely no bearing—"

Danny's head snapped up. "I'm not talking about Llewellyn Single."

"Aren't ye?" Tadhg's green-eyed gaze bored into him, hollowing him out. "Sure, a police inquiry's bad enough, but now there's this."

"Tadhg, we didn't—"

"I know." Tadhg glanced away, for a moment, out the window, and Danny followed his gaze. The gathering late-afternoon darkness seemed to press against the panes. He shivered and looked away. "It's what they can prove, Danny," Tadhg said. "You know that. Sure you're a cop."

"If ye came here to make me feel better," Danny said, "you're doing a piss-poor job of it." He stood and went into the kitchen. The wind was rising, the sea whipped to a froth. He braced his hands against the sink and stood staring at nothing in particular. He hadn't even been thinking about Llewellyn Single until Tadhg brought it up.

"I'm sorry." Tadhg came into the kitchen quietly and stood near him. "I shouldn't have said anything."

Danny shook his head but didn't turn around. "Not your fault, bhoy. It is what it is."

Tadhg's hand rested for a moment on his shoulder. "When's the last time you ate something half-decent?" he asked, and, "What have you got in the fridge?"

DANNY SAT at the counter and watched Tadhg sprinkle fresh cod fillets with sea salt and minced garlic before searing them in hot olive oil. He pricked a pound of small Yukon Gold potatoes with a sharp knife and cooked them in the microwave before tossing them with pepper and flour and frying them in pork fat. Two baby bok choy Danny had purchased and forgotten about were rescued from the crisper, deftly sliced through the middle, and steamed in a colander.

"Got anything to drink?" Tadhg asked. His silvery hair was standing up in tufts, and he'd rolled his sleeves up, revealing surprisingly muscular forearms. "What?" he asked, when he saw Danny staring. "I don't just supervise, you know. I'm the hands-on type."

Danny scoffed. "You, with a hammer and saw? Yes, my son. I'll believe that, I will so."

"Oh, is that right?" Tadhg slung the tea towel he'd been holding over his shoulder and came close to Danny, holding out his arm. "Feel that," he said, flexing a bicep.

"Go 'way with ye," Danny said, embarrassed.

"No, seriously, feel it."

Danny did. Tadhg's arm was hard as steel, blood-warm. He curled his fingers around the muscle and squeezed gently. "I believe you," he said. Tadhg smelled like pine and cypress, like sea salt and cold northern air. His chest rose and fell gently with each breath. He felt like something

Danny remembered, or ought to remember—solidity, familiarity—and for which he longed desperately. It wasn't possible to die of loneliness, and anyway, he wasn't lonely. "Promise me," Alison had said, that last terrible day, "that you won't be lonely."

"Now, see?" Tadhg nodded and took the towel from his shoulder before moving back to the stove. He turned off the heat under the cod and the potatoes and lifted the cover from the bok choy. "Almost done."

Danny set the table and fetched out a bottle of Yellowtail Chardonnay he'd brought from town with him. It wasn't quite cold enough, but the crisp tang of it would go well with the fresh codfish.

"Do you want some help?" he asked, but Tadhg declined, then ushered him into a chair. He served Danny a generous portion of the cod with a side of fried potatoes and fork-tender bok choy drizzled with olive oil. Danny tried the fish. It all but melted in his mouth.

"Well?" Tadhg asked.

Danny feigned disinterest in the meal. "It's all right," he said.

Tadhg's eyebrows rose. "You're full of shite."

"No, bhoy, I'm just taking the piss. It's really good," Danny amended. He was curious. "Where'd you learn to cook?"

Tadhg shrugged. "It's always been Lily and myself," he replied. "I wanted to make sure she was eating properly. I took some cooking classes. Basic stuff."

"This isn't 'basic,'" Danny chided. "Jesus, Tadhg, this is world-class."

He had never seen Tadhg blush. Danny smirked as a faint roseate glow heated Tadhg's pale cheeks. "Thank you," Tadhg murmured. They finished the meal in a companionable silence, then retired to the living room with hot cups of coffee and slices of store-bought chocolate cake Tadhg had unearthed from the freezer. Outside the windows it was growing dark, and the night was closing around them, folding in on itself.

"Game of cards?" Danny asked.

"Sure."

They pulled the coffee table closer to the couch, and Danny dealt them each a hand. Tadhg picked up his cards and examined them. "What game are we playing?"

"Fucked if I know," Danny said. The warm conviviality of their shared supper had vanished, replaced by a sense of bleakness, a flat inevitability that never seemed to leave him nowadays. He threw the cards down. He needed to talk about it—all of it—but had no idea where to start.

"Say the first thing that comes into your mind," Tadhg said quietly, as if Danny had spoken aloud. He tossed his own cards down. "I'll listen." They were close enough to touch each other, and Tadhg did. He reached across and laid his palm on Danny's shoulder. "I will."

"You should go," Danny said. "It's getting late. I... I don't want to be keeping you here past time."

"Okay." Tadhg nodded, then rose slowly, picking up his coffee cup. "If you're sure that's what you want."

"I'll be fine," Danny said. He waited while Tadhg put his coat on, then walked him to the door. "Listen, thanks for coming. I appreciate it."

Tadhg glanced away for a moment, a sardonic smile curving his mouth. "Not going to let on, are ye?" he said, turning back to Danny. "You'll die first."

"Tadhg, I—"

"Ye can always talk to me, Danny." Tadhg lingered near him, one hand in the middle of Danny's back, his palm spreading warmth, soothing him. There should have been something to say, Danny thought. But he had no platitudes left. "I'm going back to Eigus," Tadhg said. He stepped away, let his hand drop. "Text or call if you need me."

Danny nodded. "Yes."

"Goodbye." Tadhg hurried to his car and slipped inside. Danny stood watching him until Tadhg's taillights disappeared around a bend, and he was gone.

He went back into the house and tried to occupy himself. For a while he sat and attempted to read, but his mind kept wandering all over the place, hopping from Tadhg to Lily to Moira Fraser. The wind continued to howl, the waves groaning in the distance, and tiny feathers of snow twirled in the maelstrom. Danny stood at the living room's large window and looked out across the harbour, straining to see in the thickening darkness. The beam of Kildevil Cove's lighthouse, automated since the 1980s, shone and disappeared at regular intervals. Shine and go, they used to call it when they were kids. Shine and go, shine and go. Where it went, of course, was nowhere. Like the sun, its beacon drew away from them for a time and then returned, always right on schedule.

Being alone in the house was giving him the creeps. There was absolutely nothing to fear from the house itself. As far as he knew no one had ever died there or been attacked. Violent crime in Kildevil Cove was nonexistent. The house was located on a headland, a narrow spit of rock reaching out into the sea. Its wood-frame construction was solid enough, but it creaked and groaned like a wrecked schooner whenever the wind blew. Darkness lay about its corners in the early evening and pushed away available light. No matter how much wood Danny piled into the stove, it was often cold, and the ever-present gale blew through tiny gaps in the structure.

He shivered and went upstairs to his bedroom to get a heavy sweater. The wooden stair treads were cold under his stockinged feet. He pulled on a thick Icelandic wool jumper he'd brought back from a trip to Reykjavik and a pair of merino socks. He couldn't seem to get warm. He was descending the stairs when his phone rang. "Hello?"

"Is that you, Danny?"

The female voice with its thick Scots brogue brought him up short, heart pounding, and for a moment he thought it was his nan. "It's Dora Belbin, over on Southside. I've just been for a walk with Taffy."

"Oh yes, Mrs. Belbin, hello." Dora Belbin was his grandmother's best friend, a doughty transplant from Aviemore; Taffy was her Airedale. "How are you?"

"Oh, fine. You know how it is. I'm grateful to be topside of the grave."

Well that was cheerful. "Good."

"I was in by your grandfather's house. Did you go by there earlier today?"

"No. I've been here for ages."

"Well, you should go and have a look. All the windows are open, and the doors too. I didnae go too close, just in case."

He hadn't been to his grandfather's house in a while, not since the day he'd cleaned up the mess. It had taken hours for him to gather everything into bin bags and drag it to the end of the road for pickup. Who would have reason to destroy his grandparents' house? There was absolutely no one left in Kildevil Cove who had anything against them. It made no sense. "Thanks. I'll go have a look right now."

He stuck his feet into his hiking boots and pulled a parka on over his sweater. The flurries had stopped, but the wind was viciously cold from the north. The moon was a thin fingernail slice, obscured by a ragged strip of cloud. They would probably have snow before morning.

He pulled his car up close to his grandfather's house and got out. At first glance the house looked the same as it always had, but as he drew closer, he saw several of the windows were open, their curtains streaming in the wind. No, not open. Broken. He drew closer and saw that every window in the place had been smashed. When he went round to the side, he found the kitchen door in the same condition. The porch was full of trash: chocolate wrappers and empty potato chip bags, old newspapers. Why would anyone break in, he wondered. There was nothing there to steal. His grandfather had owned little of value. If anybody wanted something, they'd have to strip the wallpaper from the walls or pull up the kitchen tiles, and even that was worth less than nothing.

He checked all the rooms methodically, moving from the kitchen to the small downstairs bathroom, then the living room, the upstairs landing, and the bedrooms. A lot of the old furnishings he remembered had been discarded and replaced with newer models, some of them quite expensive. The old iron bedstead that had stood in his grandparents' bedroom since the year dot was gone, replaced by a sleek, modular shelf holding a thick memory-foam mattress. The ancient chesterfield and chairs from the sitting room had been replaced by a leather sofa and recliner, and the lamps were of an expensive Scandinavian design. Oddly, these new accoutrements were left undamaged by whoever had broken into the house, but why? Why scatter rubbish from arse to altitude and leave the furnishings untouched?

Whoever had been in the house had left a continuous stream of rubbish from the kitchen door all the way upstairs. They must have brought several large bin bags with them and emptied the contents throughout the house. Danny pulled his phone out of his back pocket and dialled Tadhg's number. "It's happened again," he said when Tadhg answered. "They've been in and trashed the house. All the windows are broken, and they kicked in the door."

"What do they want?" Tadhg asked.

"I don't know what they want. I don't even know who would do such a thing. My grandfather had no enemies. Everybody in Kildevil Cove loved him. It makes no sense at all."

There was a pause, during which Danny could hear Tadhg's television set on the other end, murmuring away quietly in the background. "Do you want me to come?" Tadhg asked.

"No, you stay where you are. There's not much I can do here now." Danny glanced around. "I'm going to find some boards to nail over the broken windows and then, I don't know, get someone to do some repairs in the morning."

"Are you all right?" Again, there was that tenderness in Tadhg's voice that Danny had heard when last they'd been together, sharing a simple meal.

"I'm fine. I'm… I'll call you." He rang off before Tadhg could say anything else.

He went upstairs to check the damage, found all the windows on the second floor broken out as well. At least the fuckers were consistent, he thought. The mattresses had been overturned, the bedding thrown onto the floor. Someone had ripped a feather pillow apart, with predictable results. Had they taken any of his grandfather's things, or were they only interested in general destruction? He climbed onto his grandparents' old chest of drawers—the thing must have been at least five feet tall, an ancient highboy with a huge oval mirror—and tapped a few of the ceiling tiles. He knew his memory wasn't reliable, especially for something as ephemeral as this, but Grandar had always stored his important papers up here. He tapped his way across the swath of ceiling he could reach and back towards the wall. None of the tiles gave way. He climbed back down and went into the adjoining smaller bedroom. The window in here had been smashed as well, and when he peered over the shattered sill, he could clearly make out a discarded brick on the ground below. The window had been shattered from the inside, then. The net curtains blew wildly in the wind.

He hoisted himself up onto the top of the antique wardrobe in the corner. There was a lot less space than he remembered, but the last time he'd been up here, he was twelve years old. He started in the corner, methodically pushing up on the tiles one at a time. The third tile gave way, and he was able to reach a hand up into the attic space. The box was there. It had to be. He pushed forward, scrabbling with his fingertips. The wardrobe rocked beneath him, and he reached out reflexively to catch himself, holding on to an adjoining ceiling tile, which broke in his hand.

Jesus. A huge space loomed above, an entire hidden section of the house built into the attic. Someone—his grandfather, probably, since he'd built the house—had managed to lower the ceiling of the room enough to create the area. He stood on tiptoe and pushed his head and shoulders into the opening. Nothing but cobwebs and the sawdust leavings of whatever bugs had burrowed into the wood—but the tin box was there. He caught hold of a corner and drew it towards him, holding it securely as he climbed back down.

The box held remnants of Danny's childhood, including a straight razor that once belonged to his grandfather and a collection of old papers: the property deed to the house and land, some bank receipts, a portion of torn newspaper folded in four. Danny unfolded it carefully, mindful of the paper's fragility and age. It was an old advertisement for a Raleigh bicycle, "available in red, blue, or green," with extravagant whitewall tires and a wicker basket on the front. Nice. Danny had never had a bicycle like this, although Tadhg had had one. Old man Heaney insisted on nothing but the best. Clipped to this was a photograph of Tadhg and Danny standing with their arms around each other, grinning like loons. It must have been taken in the summer, sometime in the late seventies, him and Tadhg wearing swimming trunks and squinting into the sun. They would have been, what? Eleven? Twelve? Roaming the expansive Kildevil Cove summer together, feasting on sun and cold salt water, together from daylight to dark, living like kings in exile on molasses bread and his nan's strong dark tea. Tadhg spent as much time at Danny's house in those days as he did his own. They were inseparable; they loved each other. Even his love for Alison, as powerful and beautiful as it was, bore no comparison for what he'd felt for Tadhg.

Underneath the papers and ad was a stack of much older black-and-white photographs, some of them so ancient they had started to chip at the corners. He sat down on the bed to look at them. They were the usual thing. Brides in lacy gowns posed with their staid-looking grooms, most of whom had large moustaches or beards and whose faces reflected the gravity of the situation. There was a picture of Heaney's fish plant, taken on the day it first opened, but whoever took it had been positioned a long way off, standing on a hill, perhaps. The details of the photograph were blurry, smudged. He suspected the photo had been taken in a hurry and on the sly, as if the photographer were afraid of being caught. The next picture showed a young couple, arms around each other's shoulders, squinting into the camera. He didn't recognise the woman, but the man with her was most definitely his grandfather. It had been taken in the mid to late 1960s, judging by the clothing and hairstyles.

Danny turned the picture over, hoping for some clue in the inscription, if there was one, but there was only the name Margot, written in light-coloured pencil. He laid it aside and looked through the others. About five photos in, he found something that stopped him cold: a picture of a naked woman reclining on a couch, her arms behind her head. She was also identified as Margot. Who was Margot? Why did his grandfather have pictures of her? It had to be Grandar. Danny didn't think his grandmother knew anyone named Margot, doubted she would have saved the photos so lovingly, certainly not the nude one. No, these had been deliberately hidden, stashed in the tin box and stuffed into the ceiling, like a shameful secret.

A shuffling noise downstairs caused him to turn from what he was doing, and he stiffened, frozen in place, straining to hear. Maybe whoever had done the damage was back, had seen him come in and intended to confront him face to face. He climbed down as quietly as possible and slid behind the door, waiting. The stairs creaked. Whoever had come in was making their way upstairs. Danny's fists clenched, and his body thrummed from the sudden squirt of adrenaline suffusing his blood. He had no weapon, and there was nothing to hand, not even so much as a sturdy broomstick. The familiar feeling of dread descended, smothering him, and he struggled to draw breath. Nausea clawed at his insides, and he swallowed desperately.

"Danny?"

Tadhg. *Jesus.* Danny blinked. It was only Tadhg.

"Here." It came out as a croak, and he cleared his throat. "I'm right here," he said, and stepped out from behind the door.

"Christ, they made a bloody mess of the place, didn't they?" Tadhg gazed around him at the devastation, the shattered window. "Although I suppose we're lucky they didn't shit on the carpets and smear it around. They do that, you know. It's the thing nowadays, or so I've heard. They shit on the floor and—"

"Tadhg!" It came out much louder than Danny intended. "Nobody shat on anything."

Tadhg moved his shoulders up and down, then stuck his hands in his pockets. "Well, that's good, then." He glanced at Danny and then away, and there was something shifty in it. "Who do you think did this?"

Danny wanted to ask, "Did you do it?" But he kept silent. No sense in stirring that particular hornets' nest. "No idea," he replied, after a moment. "Fuck," he said quietly, and again, "fuck."

Tadhg nodded. "It's all bad enough," he said. His gaze went to the hole in the ceiling. "Did they do that, as well?"

Danny's gut tightened. "Yeah," he lied, "I think so. Bastards."

"Bastards," Tadhg agreed. "Do you want me to help clean up?"

"I wouldn't say no to it," Danny replied. He was suddenly glad Tadhg had turned up after all.

CHAPTER ELEVEN

TADHG ARRIVED back on Eigus refreshed from seeing Danny again and feeling wonderfully sure of himself, despite the damage to old man Quirke's house. He found Yvonne finalising the week's medications schedule at the kitchen counter. "Hiya," he said cheerfully. "Where's young madam?"

"She said she was tired and went back to bed. I expect the treatment is taking it out of her," Yvonne replied. "She's been up there a couple of hours." She looked him over. "You look like shite. Where've you been?"

"Went to Kildevil Cove. The property I'm buying got vandalised again." He shook his head. "What are the odds, eh? Just my bloody luck." He opened the fridge and took out the bag of coffee beans and turned to fetch a mug down from a shelf. Yvonne was right; not only did he look like shite, but he felt like it too. The boat ride across from Portugal Cove had been rough, fighting the whole way against a vicious November gale. Tadhg didn't often get seasick, but he was nauseous when he stepped ashore. All he wanted was a cup of hot, strong coffee and a rest.

"What's his face from Amsterdam called looking for you," Yvonne said. "He didn't bother to leave a message."

Tadhg dumped beans into the grinder. No doubt Rutger had tried his luck with other investors and been turned down flat. The only reason he was looking for Tadhg was to try to recoup some of the money he'd wasted on his luxury condo scheme. Naxco, Rutger's company, had secured some prime real estate right along the Amstel. By sheer happenstance, a block of seventeenth century houses had burned to the ground. Once the remains were razed and hauled away, the empty lots went up for sale. Rutger had gambled on the international tourist trade being willing to spend their euros on luxury holiday accommodations—but the millennials and backpackers who frequented the city were more interested in hostels and other types of cheap accommodation. Inevitably they departed in a day or two for the countryside, where they would see the windmills and great wheels of cheese and buy wooden clogs to bring back home. To make matters worse, city officials refused to grant Rutger a building permit. Something about unpaid taxes. Tadhg had gone over to try to persuade him to look elsewhere.

In recent years Newfoundland had become wildly popular, thanks to a series of gorgeous tourism ads and a hit Broadway musical about the 9/11 attacks. Wealthy Europeans were coming to the island in droves, with lots of money to spend, and they expected top-notch accommodations. "It's a virtual gold mine," Tadhg had said. "You'd recoup your initial investment in no time, guaranteed."

The coffee beans clacked and rumbled in the plastic hopper before they were decanted into the brewing chamber. "Will you have one?" Tadhg asked Yvonne.

"Yes." She took out a mug for herself. "Are you sure you're all right?"

He waved her concern away. "Just a bit quarmish. The crossing was rough this morning."

"I sent Gary over to get some cinnamon buns from Georgetown Bakery." She took them out of the fridge. "They're some good. You want one?"

Just the idea of a soft, sticky cinnamon bun made Tadhg's stomach roil. He shook his head. "No, thanks," he said quickly. "Maybe later."

He took his coffee and headed upstairs. The house was built so that each upstairs room was located on its own landing. Lily's room was one floor below his, so he stopped and rapped lightly on her door with his fingertips. "Lily? It's Dad." The door was ajar, so he pushed it open. "Are you awake?"

Her bed was empty, the duvet pulled up and her stuffed animals arranged on top. She had left her laptop open, so maybe she'd gone to the washroom and would be back in a minute. "Lily?" He crossed the room and tapped on the door of her en suite. "Have you got a minute?" When he tried the knob, it turned easily. The bathroom was empty as well.

Her laptop was left open on her desk, but she'd erased her recent browsing history, and when he navigated to her email account, she'd changed the password. His heart began to pound against his ribs. He suddenly remembered all the stories he'd heard of terminally sick animals going somewhere else to die. *Don't be such a fucking idiot. She's got to be around here somewhere.* Only what if she was tired of being prodded and poked with needles, subjected to painful tests and poisonous chemicals? What if she had decided enough was enough? *She's fourteen years old. She doesn't know her own mind.*

"Lily?" he called—louder now, shouting. "Where are you?" But there was no sound besides the roar and tremblor of the ever-present wind. He raced downstairs, startling Yvonne in the kitchen. "Where's Lily?"

"She's asleep, isn't she?" Yvonne read the look his face. "Oh dear God, no."

"I checked in her room. She's not there. The bed's not even been slept in."

"Let me ring Darren down at the boat shed," Yvonne said. "She might be down there." She picked up the landline and called Tadhg's maintenance man, but he'd been busy preparing the boat for winter and hadn't seen Lily in days. Tadhg reached over and took the phone from Yvonne.

"Has anyone been around the wharf at all today?" Tadhg asked. He forced himself to take deep breaths and not give in to panic. Lily had to be around somewhere. She couldn't have left the island under her own power, and Tadhg knew it was more than Darren's job was worth to take her somewhere without Tadhg's express permission. There was a lengthy pause while Darren went to confer with some of Tadhg's other staff members. Then he came back on. "Jesper says there was a longliner idling near the wharf when he came on this morning, 'long about six o'clock. He didn't bother with it. Figured it was someone from Portugal Cove out after mackerel."

"So nobody bothered to find out?" Tadhg's blood pressure rose like a steady tide.

"He was only there for a couple minutes, Jesper said. Couldn't have been any more than that. He powered up then and headed for Portugal Cove."

She can't possibly have gone far, Tadhg thought. Then, *Six o'clock this morning she could have gone anywhere without being seen.* Lily could pilot a small boat with an inboard motor, but he seriously doubted she'd take off on an ill-advised excursion to the mainland. "I'm coming down there," Tadhg said and rang off. He shrugged into his heavy down jacket and shoved his feet into his winter boots.

"Do you think she's there?" Yvonne asked.

Tadhg shook his head. "Still and all, I have to look." A pair of icy hands wrapped around his heart. "What if she's gone and done something stupid?" It hadn't been that long ago Lily had told him, "No more treatment. You have to stop. You have to stop now. Please. I'm tired." Her voice as she told him was still the voice of a little girl, but her eyes were the eyes of a woman, old before her time.

"She wouldn't do that." Yvonne patted his arm. "I'll start calling around to some of her friends. You know what young girls are like. Maybe they decided to have a sleepover and didn't think to tell anyone."

"Of course." He nodded, not entirely sure what he was agreeing to. "Yes, she'll have done that. Call Gemma. Her number's in the phone. She might have gone there." He stepped out into the chilly morning air, dangerously close to tears. He couldn't lose her. Goddammit, he wouldn't. He'd talk to whoever might have seen her last, including Jesper, who'd seen the fishing boat that morning. And he'd call the one person he knew for certain could help.

He snatched his mobile phone out of his pocket and dialled. The call was picked up after only two rings. "Lily's gone," he said. Her name stuck in his throat. "I got home this morning, and Yvonne... we thought... I mean, Lily was in her room asleep, but I checked and"—he forced himself calm—"she's not there."

"Gone? So she sneaked out and did a runner."

"Yeah, I mean, where the hell could she go?" He drew a breath that sounded like a sob. "This is an island."

"All right, hold on." Scrabbling noises on the other end of the line and the sound of something dropping... a pen, probably. "Can your man meet me at Portugal Cove to bring me across?"

"Yes." He reached the boathouse and pulled the door open. "You'll be here?"

"I will." A pause. "I promise."

DANNY QUIRKE clambered up the narrow wooden ladder and onto Tadhg Heaney's private island. He was red-cheeked and windblown, but right then he was the best thing Tadhg had seen all morning; he reached down to give Danny a hand up the ladder. "You're freezing," he observed. "Do you not own any gloves?"

"Left them behind," Danny said. "I was in a bit of a hurry to get here." He shivered, hunched into his wool coat. "Tell me what you know so far." Tadhg did. "And the only people who might have seen her were at the wharf this morning?"

"Yes. Darren and Jesper. They work for me."

Danny drew his brows together. "I didn't think they were bloody Hobbits," he snapped. "Doesn't everybody work for you?"

"Everybody on Eigus does," Tadhg said bitchily. *And that pisses you off, doesn't it?* His family's wealth had never sat well with Danny. There were times Tadhg could have sworn Danny resented him for being well off, even as he resented himself and his own family for their modest means.

"I'll want to talk to Darren and… what's his name? Jesper?"

"Jesper." Tadhg led Danny towards the boat shed, pushing against the wind.

"What kind of a name is Jesper?" Danny asked. "I've called Moira Fraser. She's agreed to send a patrol by. I don't know how much good that'll do, but the extra bodies can help in the search." He pulled out his phone and punched the dial pad. "When did you see her last? I mean, physically lay eyes on her?"

"Before I went to Kildevil Cove."

"Alex." Danny was speaking to someone on the phone. "Didn't get you out of bed, did I? Listen now, my friend's daughter is missing. Chances are she's run off somewhere with a pal to spend the night, but he's tearing his hair out in the meantime." He listened for a moment, nodding, even though whoever was on the other end couldn't see him. "Could you? Ah, that'd be grand. God love ye. We'll send the boat across to Portugal Cove." He hung up and turned to Tadhg. "Young cop I've worked with now and again, a detective sergeant with the constabulary. He's real good at finding people. Can you get your man to send the boat across to him?"

Tadhg was warmed by Danny's efforts, made on his behalf, to help find Lily. Danny owed him nothing—quite the opposite, really—and he was suddenly foolishly grateful for his assistance. "Of course."

They reached the boat shed and went inside. An elderly man with a heavily wrinkled face looked up from a laptop computer. A spreadsheet was displayed on the screen, the modern equivalent of a mariner's logbook. He nodded at Tadhg. "Good morning, skipper. What can I do for ye?" He listened while Danny explained that he was to pick up Alex at Portugal Cove and bring him directly to Eigus, and why.

"That lovely girl is gone?" he asked. "Mr. Heaney here was asking if myself or Jesper seen her, but I never did." He frowned, the expression pulling his face into dozens of deep lines. "She's a sweet girl. I hope she's not gone too far. I'll get the boat ready. Jesper can go across."

Tadhg and Danny went back to the house to wait for Alex. Tadhg made coffee while Danny phoned around to the various law enforcement types he knew. Tadhg texted him a recent photograph of Lily, which Danny then passed on. A mass email to his professional contacts ensured they would know what Lily looked like and encouraged them to keep an eye out for her.

"We will find her," Danny said, with a certain authority that was probably part of his cop persona. He accepted a cup of coffee from Tadhg and added cream and sugar liberally. Tadhg smiled. "What?" Danny asked.

"I remember you from school," Tadhg said. "Every dinner time you'd sit with the same bunch at that table in the corner, and you'd take out your homemade sandwiches wrapped up in wax paper and a thermos full of tea. I can see ye now, dabbing in a bit of milk." He laughed. "The rest of us were drinking Coke or Pepsi and stuffing our faces with chips." Too late it occurred to him that Danny's grandparents probably couldn't afford to give him dinner money like the rest of them had. Even Danny's parents, when they were alive, worked at the Heaney's fish processing plant in season; during the winter months, his father did finish carpentry indoors, putting in kitchens and renovating bathrooms. Danny and his sister never went without, but there was never any extra either.

Something passed over Danny's face, something that struck Tadhg's heart like an icicle. As quick as that, it was gone again. "Alex won't be long getting here from Portugal Cove," he said. "I'll go down and meet him."

"I-I'm sorry," Tadhg stuttered, but Danny was already heading for the door. Tadhg followed. "I am… look, it was stupid. I don't think sometimes, and I—"

"Soon as Alex gets here we'll start searching," Danny said, cutting him off. He nodded at the iPhone in Tadhg's hand. "I'll text you." Then he was gone.

You really fucked that up. Can ye not keep your mouth closed now and again? And here was Danny trying to help him. He made a mental note to apologise properly later on. Lately he was all mops and brooms, especially around Danny, which didn't make sense—or perhaps he wasn't used to seeing this Danny, older now by many years, no longer the awkward orphan boy, the misfit who never really seemed to fit. This was Danny the adult, Danny the cop, who walked into a situation, assessed it with a glance, and knew immediately what to do and how to go about it.

About an hour later, Danny reappeared with a younger man in tow whom he introduced to Tadhg as Alex Ryall. "Alex is going to set up a perimeter and map out the search area." Tadhg had gathered his entire staff to help look for Lily; they stood now in his living room like soldiers waiting for their marching orders. "I'd like five or six of you to go across to Portugal Cove in case she hitched a ride on somebody's boat. She might be on her way to town, you never know."

"I very much doubt she's gone far," Alex said with a reassuring smile at Tadhg. He was dark-haired and pale, with brilliant blue eyes like Danny's. Idly, Tadhg wondered if maybe he was Danny's natural son, born of a dark-haired mother, some woman Danny had met in passing years before. He knew so little of Danny's life now. Until his grandfather's death, they hadn't spoken in a very long time. What slight intimacy they might have shared in childhood had irrevocably vanished.

"What can I do?" Tadhg asked. Alex looked up from his iPhone, then glanced across at Danny. Tadhg saw something pass between them, but he wasn't sure what—a look, a gesture, a subtle wink—and his gut burned with anger.

"It's best if you stay here," Danny said, "in case Lily comes home." To Tadhg it sounded as if Danny was putting him off. He didn't like it.

"She's my daughter. For fucksake, I have a right to look for her!" He started forward, was stopped by Danny's palm in the middle of his chest.

"Alex, you can take everyone outside now. We'll start the first sweep towards the south," Danny said. "The terrain gets a little rough after a while, but try to be as thorough as you can." He waited until everyone had gone before turning to Tadhg. "I'm sorry," he said, "but I think your place is here."

Tadhg looked pointedly at Danny's hand, still pressed against the front of his sweater. "Do ye?"

"Tadhg, I promise you, we will find her, but it's important to maximise the time we've got. You know how little daylight there is this time of year. It'll start getting duckish around three, and forget seeing anything in the woods by then. It's cold. We don't know if she's taken a coat or a sweater, or how far away she is." He dropped his hand. "Sorry," he said. "I don't mean anything." He looked at his hand, turned it over and gazed at the palm. "I apologise for putting hands on ye. It won't happen again." He picked his coat off the back of the couch and shrugged into it. "Stay here. When she comes home—and she will come home—you need to be here."

"Is there nothing I can do?" He heard the desperation in his own voice, but he didn't care.

"Yes. Go through her room. Search everything. I mean everything. Tear up the bed, flip the mattress, go through the bureau drawers, tip out the rubbish bin."

"What am I looking for?" He couldn't imagine violating Lily's privacy that way.

"Anything pointing to some outside contact, a boyfriend or a girlfriend, someone she'd leave home for," Danny said. "You might keep an eye out for a notebook or diary, letters…. Of course nowadays this is as likely to be on her computer, so check her laptop. Did she take her phone with her?"

"I don't know." He thought for a moment. "I don't think so."

"If you find anything"—Danny held up his phone—"text me."

Tadhg nodded. "Okay."

Danny turned to go but stopped, one hand on the doorknob. "I will find her."

"Thank you."

Then Danny was out the door and gone.

Tadhg went upstairs to Lily's room and opened the door. He disliked intruding in her absence, feeling that her bedroom ought to be her sanctuary, a place to think her own thoughts, fool around with makeup, and moon over pimply-faced boy bands like other girls her age. The space was simply decorated in shades of purple, Lily's favourite colour. Three of the walls were pale mauve while the fourth was a deep lilac. She'd always wanted a skylight, so Tadhg had built one into the roof right over her bed; in the summertime, and with the benefit of the dark sky on Eigus, she could peer up at the stars and wish herself to sleep. The bedcover was a thick purple duvet with tiny flowers handstitched on its surface. Tadhg had ordered it from England, and the damn thing had cost the earth.

He knelt by the side of her bed and ran a hand between the mattress and box spring. When he was a lad, it was where he hid everything he didn't want his mam to see: bad report cards, dirty magazines (when he could get them), and the few spare condoms he kept just in case. There was nothing under Lily's mattress. For good measure he lifted it and made a visual search of the gap and the underside, but it was empty. He laid it back down and smoothed the sheets. At the head of the bed behind the pale mauve bed curtains was a bookshelf, mostly open but with one or two sliding doors that parted to reveal a small compartment. He found a pack of gum, three hair elastics, an earring, and a tattered copy of *Tiger Beat*—Christ, were they still publishing that magazine? He'd bought the damn thing as a boy for the pictures of Lynda Carter in her Wonder Woman outfit. Living in Kildevil Cove and without reliable access to porn, it was either Lynda or the women posing in their underwear in the Sears catalogue. Not a whole hell of a lot to beat off to.

In the drawers of Lily's bureau, he found tops and jeans and all her other clothes but no hidden diary. He even dropped down onto his knees and swept a hand underneath it, coming up with a bobby pin and dust. Why did Danny think she kept a physical diary? Sure none of them did that nowadays. It was all online, password protected, locked on to a thumb drive or a memory card, and hidden away. What good was he doing, crawling around here on his hands and knees? He debated ringing Danny up and telling him to hell with it, but what if there really was something, and he missed it? Danny or one of Danny's volunteers would find it. That Alex character would find it. Oh, never you mind, that fucker would find a fart down a well. Some boy, he was.

Tadhg spent two hours weeding through the contents of the room, examining and discarding clothes and books, rereading some of Lily's homework assignments and looking at old school pictures. He even picked up each of the snow globes in Lily's extensive collection and shook it, wondering if she'd hidden anything inside. Nothing. He sat on the floor next to Lily's desk and picked through the rubbish, tipping the entire bin out on the carpet. He found a chocolate wrapper, an empty drink box, and some crumpled balls of paper that he carefully unfolded, smoothing out the wrinkles.

> *Why can't you let me*
> *Not fair*
> *Gemma said her mam is going to*

A note, written in purple ballpoint pen and then discarded. Lily was uncomfortable discussing things with him in person, preferring the anonymity of text messages or the telephone's imposed aural distance. He'd once told her she could talk to him about anything, but that wasn't true, and they both knew it. Yvonne had given her the necessary information about boys, sex, and her period, not him. Tadhg couldn't imagine how he'd even begin to broach the subject. When she was little, it was so much easier—when she asked about why the sky was blue and how did birds know where to go when it got cold in autumn.

He got up and sat in Lily's chair. The desk was scaled for a young girl, the chair so absurdly low his knees were almost dragging on the floor. She'd left her laptop on, the cover not quite closed. Her desktop wallpaper was a photo she took herself, the year before when they'd gone to Gros Morne, a selfie of him and Lily with the mountains at their back. They had driven up to Norstead, the recreated Viking village at the very tip of the peninsula. Lily wasn't interested in the wooden church or the longhouse, or the knarr *Snorri*, meticulously handcrafted by a master boat builder. Instead she'd wandered down to the beach alone, watching as the evening sky darkened to the wan glow of the blue hour. "You go away, Dad," she said, waving him off. But he stayed close enough to see her silhouette as the day bled into the Atlantic, and then...

"Dad. Oh my God, *Dad*! You have to... come and see this!" And she'd hauled him by both hands down to the beach, heedless of the darkness and the rocks, intent on one thing. "Look up."

The Northern Lights. Yes, he'd seen them before, but Lily never had, so he held his tongue while the aurora unfurled itself, hissing and snapping above their heads. Some of the Norstead actors, still in Viking costume, came down to the beach in little groups. No one spoke above a murmur. The band of light undulated lazily in the night sky, changing through green to red and purple, vanishing and reappearing, seeming almost to move towards them. She backed herself into him, and they stood for a long time together, his hands on her shoulders while the aurora consumed the sky.

"Is it real, Dad?" Lily had asked. "How can it be so real?"

Tadhg clicked through the various document and photo folders, finding the usual stuff—pictures with her friends, school assignments, music she downloaded off the internet. He found one subfolder labeled 'Recipes' and clicked on it out of curiosity. If Lily had developed any sudden fascination with cooking, this was the first he'd heard of it. Even before the cancer, she had little interest in food, subsisting on the bare minimum, feeding herself with tiny bits of things like carrot sticks and wands of stringy celery dipped in thick Icelandic yogurt. Tadhg wondered why she couldn't sit down and eat a meal instead of roaming about the place, grazing on vegetables.

He opened the folder and realised almost immediately what it was—Lily's diary. She'd set it up on a template downloaded from the internet, separate pages with dates starting from several years back. He took the laptop with him when he went down to the kitchen to put the kettle on, and browsed the entries while his tea steeped. Mostly she had written about school, and boys, and him. *Dad won't let me do anything. Dad is going to take away my phone. I think Caden likes Lori and not me.*

Later entries were more mature and had been conceived as structured essays, her thoughts on the state of the world, her friends, her cancer.

Maybe this is it, as far as I'm going to go, and I'm all right with it. No, seriously, I am. I guess I figured all my life that nothing bad was going to happen to me until it did.

Another round of chemo. Bad dreams! The stuff always gives me nightmares. I'm too old to call out for Dad at night.

He stopped reading for a moment. Lily had written it when she was twelve, two years previous, all the things she couldn't or wouldn't tell him. Tadhg got up and went to look out the window. From up here, he could see Danny's team of searchers fanning out across the island, looking for her. Maybe they were calling out her name, but Tadhg couldn't hear them. The wind rattled the casements in their frames, blew spindrift off the eaves. He couldn't hear them calling. Maybe they weren't calling at all. He squeezed the teabag with his fingers and reached into the fridge for milk. How much more could he stand to read, he wondered. Not only because it violated her privacy, but did he really want to know about the things she'd written?

He paged forward in the document, stopping in August of this year. Here the diary entries took on the furtive tone of a young girl who was getting away with something.

I've only told Gemma, nobody else. She figured it was her he was interested in! What a nerve!

I got a text from him last night. He said probably we should go for a coffee!!! I got nothing to wear. Ugh. FML!

Tadhg paged through the rest of August and stopped in the middle of September. 'He' still didn't have a name, but Lily's diary was all about him and little else. *Stayed up past two last night texting. He wants me to send more pictures. OMG!*

Tadhg's jaw tightened as he clenched his teeth. Pictures? Oh, but that was the done thing now, wasn't it? Young girls exposing themselves in the privacy of their bedrooms, snapping quick pictures on their mobile phones, sending the photos to other interested parties. He was going to have a serious talk with Lily when he found her, his own embarrassment be damned. Maybe that was the problem in the first place—he hadn't sat her down for a proper explanation of what was what between men and women. That part of her education he'd neglected, letting Yvonne do it and supposing that she'd tell Lily whatever needed to be said. Maybe Yvonne hadn't felt comfortable saying such things as "Your body is your own and no one else's. You choose to share it with someone or not, but it is always your choice. Don't cheapen yourself because it's what everybody else is doing."

The entries for October were pretty much what he'd expect from a teenager, except Lily's often dealt with her illness and the effects of the chemotherapy.

Another round of Red Devil. Glad I shaved my fucking head. This shit makes me sick as a pig. Dad went all the way to town to get some ice cream. I ate a little bit. Gemma said smoking pot makes the stomach sickness go away. Yeah, I can just imagine Dad letting me do that.

Dad gone to Kildevil Cove to buy the house. Can't wait to go there next summer.

Met Dad's friend Danny, who used to be a cop. OMG cute! He's old like Dad but sooooo sexy! Yeah I'd hit that LOL.

Couldn't sleep last night so I stayed up 2 play WoW online with this guy from Romania. He said his name was Vlad, like Dracula. Bullshit! His profile pic looks like he's a goth. No big surprise.

At the end of November, her diary took a different turn.

Glenn said he can get a loan of his uncle's boat. I acted like I didn't know what he was talking about. He's not sure when. He said maybe some time before Christmas. Gemma is going to DIE when I tell her!

Tadhg remembered Gemma's phone number. He'd dialed it often enough on Lily's behalf. "Where is she?" he asked when Gemma answered. "Who's Glenn?"

BY NOON the search party had scoured the entire island, finding no trace of Lily. At half past twelve most of the volunteers (apart from a couple of stragglers) gathered in the boat shed for hot tea and sandwiches Yvonne had sent down. It had been snowing intermittently all morning, the brief, intense "dwai" typical of the season, and everyone was cold and weary.

"I don't think she's even on the island," Alex told him. "What do you want to do now?"

"There's no point in keeping anybody here," Danny said. He sipped his tea, grateful for the pool of heat it made in his stomach. "When they've finished lunch, you can take them back across to Portugal Cove." He sighed. "I'd hoped we'd find her, but I think you're right. She's not here."

"Where is she, then?"

"My bet is she's gone to town. Probably to visit someone, a relative maybe." He leaned against the wall. "I'll make some calls."

"The girl's unwell, isn't she?" Alex sipped his tea.

"Yes," Danny replied, surprised. "She's got cancer. How did you know?"

"I went to take a piss before we'd gone out. There's feeding tube buttons in the cupboard under the sink, and syringes and stuff."

"Do you always poke around in other people's bathrooms?" Danny asked, amused. Outside, the unmistakable sound of an outboard motor seemed to be coming closer. Probably the searchers who'd gone to Portugal Cove, on their way back now. "Ye nosy bugger."

"Don't you?" Alex shrugged. "My cousin had a gastrostomy button. She had a digestive disorder and couldn't swallow properly. I've seen the whole thing before."

Danny was suddenly very sad. "She's all he's got," he confided. "I honestly don't know what's going to happen to him when—" He stopped himself. A boat bumped up against the wharf.

"So it's terminal, then." The younger police officer shook his head. "Damn shame. It's always the innocent." He turned around to put his cup on the workbench. "Well, I'm off."

Before he could leave, the shed door opened, and Bert, one of the stragglers, stepped through. His clothes were soaked, and there were ice pellets clinging to his wool cap and his beard. He went immediately to Danny. "It's bad," he said. "You'd better come and see."

Danny put down his cup. "What is it?"

"We just got back from Portugal Cove."

Danny knew what he was going to say next.

"There's… we found a body."

CHAPTER TWELVE

THE DETECTIVE sergeant in charge was young, probably not even forty yet. He stood to one side, huddled into his waterproof, which was doing him no good at all. The earlier snow showers had thickened into fat, wet flakes, pouring from the sky like confetti being dispensed out of a bucket. "Sergeant Cillian Riley, sir. The body's this way." Without waiting for Danny to introduce himself—all business, this one—he splashed through the twenty feet of bog separating them from the corpse. "Didn't touch her, sir. Didn't even turn her over." Riley's big dark eyes were fastened on Danny like he expected Danny to congratulate him. "Just covered her up," he said. His accent wasn't purely of the island; there was a subtle hint of something else riding underneath his words. It reminded Danny of certain British police dramas he'd seen on television, an English soap opera his grandmother liked.

"Know anything about her?" Danny asked. He crouched beside the shrouded bundle and pulled back the tarpaulin. The figure was lying face down, and the midafternoon light wasn't the best, but he could see at once it wasn't Lily Heaney. This girl had a full head of long, dark hair, now clotted with blood at the back and soaked to her scalp by the endless snow. "Riley," Danny said, "help me turn her, would you?" They flipped the girl gently onto her back. "She's not dressed for the weather," Danny murmured. The girl's thin capri pants and denim jacket wouldn't have protected her against the cold. She wore horn-rimmed glasses of a style popular when Danny was in high school. The lenses were thin, so the glasses were probably a fashion choice rather than a corrective device. Her blouse might have been white once but had been stained a peaty brown by the bog. A thin gold chain around her neck bore what looked like a religious medal. Saint Someone, protector of dead girls who somehow find their way into Newfoundland bogs. He estimated she was about twenty-five, a young woman rather than a girl, and all at once he recognised her. Her disappearance had been all over the news. Her family organised almost daily searches in their efforts to find her, but until now, the location of her body had been a mystery.

Riley got there first. "Good Christ, that's—"

"Yeah." Danny stood up. "She's been gone a while. Her mam reported her missing last April." Part of him was glad they'd found the girl's body. At least now her family had something to bury. "The bog's preserved her somewhat." He sighed. "Okay."

"Sir?"

"You don't have to call me sir," Danny told him gently. "I'm no longer with the force."

Riley nodded. "I know," he said. "I… it was in the papers." He glanced over the terrain. "I'm thinking we should get the search and rescue people in with a helicopter. No way anybody's getting in here with an ambulance."

"I agree," Danny replied. "Has anyone been over the ground yet?" Whoever had dumped the girl's body had almost certainly left something behind. His phone beeped; he pulled it out and looked at the screen.

Tadhg: *Did you find her?*

Found a body, he typed, *BODY IS NOT LILY. Will contact soon.* He thought for a moment and added, *Stay where you are.*

"We've had a look." Riley indicated the uniformed constables nearby. "Getting too dim to see anything now. Be black dark by four o'clock." He squinted at the sky, which was still sending down buckets of wet snow with ominous regularity. "I'd best be getting back." He held out his hand for Danny to shake. "I hope you find her soon," he said. "It's no weather for a young girl." He shivered. "No weather for anybody, really."

"Could you…?" Danny hesitated. He hardly had any right to ask.

"Sir?" The cold was getting to Sergeant Riley. His lower lip was trembling.

"Can you let me know what happens? I'm… interested."

Riley drew out his phone and passed it across to Danny. "Just punch your number in there," he said, "before your hands freeze." He grinned. Christ, he was pretty, all big wide eyes and curly dark hair, mouth like a sensual promise. "I can give you mine if you like."

Danny blinked, momentarily surprised. "Oh. Yes, please do." He handed over his phone. "I suppose everything goes both ways, doesn't it?"

Riley grinned. "I should hope so."

"Give it a rest," Danny growled. "I've got underwear older than you."

"That mean we can't have a beer sometime?" Riley gave him back his phone.

Was the little bastard actually asking him out? Times had changed since Danny's last go-round in the dating scene. Maybe things moved a lot faster nowadays. "We'll see."

He left Riley in the bog and splashed his way back to the narrow dirt road linking this portion of Portugal Cove to the government-built wharf at the lower edge of the land. What was left of the late afternoon light was fading rapidly, and the sun was setting unseen behind the bank of heavy cloud. When he reached the wharf, Tadhg's motor launch was idling there, unmoored, waiting for something. Obviously Tadhg had sent it back across to pick him up. He pulled out his phone and dialed Tadhg's number. "You sent the boat for me."

"I'm on the boat," Tadhg said. "Waiting for the car to arrive so I can go into town." He leaned out of the wheelhouse and saw Danny, waved him over. "Come into the warm," he said, as Danny stepped down onto the deck. "It's cold enough to kill ye."

"It's not her," Danny said quickly. He followed Tadhg into the wheelhouse and pulled the sliding door shut behind him. It was a welcome respite from the cold. "Oh," he said, as Tadhg passed him a cup of tea, "God love ye." It wasn't just tea in the cup, but Danny didn't care. Right then he was grateful for the burn the whisky made as it slid down inside him.

"I know it's not," Tadhg said. "I've been talking to Gemma, Lily's friend. She's in the city."

"Oh she is, is she?" Danny took another slug of the tea. God love the Chinese, he thought, for coming up with this stuff. "Where?"

She had a boyfriend, Tadhg told him, who'd come across to Eigus for her in his uncle's boat earlier that morning. The two of them planned to rent a hotel room. "She's underage," Tadhg said. "I'm going to kill him. I'm going to find the little fucker and pull his arms off. And that bloody Gemma…." A car horn sounded outside. "That's our ride. Come on."

They left the boat and climbed aboard the waiting SUV, a glossy Range Rover that looked like it had never seen the outdoors. The driver was a young man from the southwest coast, whose impenetrable accent made conversation nearly impossible. It took Danny a good half hour of tortuous dialogue to understand that he worked for Tadhg.

"Do you know where she is?" Danny asked. "There are a lot of hotels in the city." He imagined a long and arduous trek of several hours, going from hotel to hotel, needing to see the register and arguing with the desk clerks when they wouldn't give it. He couldn't force anyone to give him information. He wasn't a cop anymore.

"Holiday Inn," Tadhg replied. "Apparently she's texted Gemma." His face shifted from its usual amiability to something much darker. "I am going to have a long talk with Gemma's parents as soon as we get back."

Danny smirked. "Should I alert your lawyers?"

Tadhg's murderous expression deepened. "It's not funny."

"No, you're right," Danny replied. "I shouldn't have said it. Did anyone else know she was planning this? Yvonne?"

"She's fired if she did," Tadhg said.

They both got out at the main door. Tadhg told his driver to keep the car running. "This will only take a minute," he said. The reception area was busy, clogged with out-of-town bargain hunters who came from the more remote villages to do their holiday shopping. There were the usual business types wearing expensive suits and sipping their designer coffees out of paper cups while they shouted into their cellphones and a few Icelanders sitting in little groups, conversing quietly. Every year before the holidays, chartered planes arrived from Reykjavik, filled with people who came south to buy jeans and mp3 players, laptop computers—Christmas gifts—because such items were much cheaper here.

As expected, the girl at the reception desk refused to tell Tadhg whether or not Lily had been there. "I'm sorry, sir. I can't give out that information. We value the privacy of all our guests—"

"I'm her father," Tadhg said. He leaned over the desk, trying to see the clerk's computer screen.

"Sir, I couldn't possibly give out that information." She angled the screen away from him.

"I don't think you understand," Danny said. "This girl is fourteen years old. She's in fragile health. It's very important that we find her and take her home."

The clerk glanced from Danny to Tadhg. "Are you two married?"

Under any other circumstances, the question would have been ludicrous, even hilarious. "Yes," Tadhg said. He didn't even blink. "And I'm her father." Beside him, Danny stiffened like a spaniel before a covey of grouse, but said nothing.

"I do sympathise, but I'm afraid—"

Danny delved into his pocket and laid his badge on the desk. "I insist."

The room was on the third floor at the back, overlooking a small pond and an enormous condominium complex. Tadhg wasn't much interested in the view, and he didn't even bother to knock. He inserted the key card into the slot, and as soon as the light flashed green, he went in.

Lily was sitting up on the bed, her legs crossed beneath her. She was fully dressed. Lounging next to her was a man of about twenty-five with greasy brown curls, a spotty face, and the sleepy-eyed expression of the habitual drug user. Tadhg went to the bed and gently took hold of Lily's upper arm. "Come on, time to go."

"Dad!" Lily tried in vain to pull away from him. "What are you doing?"

"Hey." The man struggled to sit upright. "What's going on here?" He rummaged in the bed and brought up a video game console. "You got some nerve."

"Get up, I said." Tadhg didn't let go of Lily's arm but used it to pull her off the bed. "Put your coat and shoes on. We're leaving." She did as he asked. "Are you Glenn?" Tadhg asked. He didn't wait for the answer. "She's fourteen years old. By my reckoning you're at least twenty-five. I could have you arrested and charged."

Glenn stared at him blankly.

"Did you touch her?" Danny asked. "If you prefer not to answer, I'll just assume you did and you'll go out of here in handcuffs."

"Awww, fuck," Glenn said. It sounded like the moan of a dying animal. "That's just my fucking luck, that is."

"He didn't touch me," Lily said, clearly embarrassed. "We were playing video games."

"You can't play video games in your own house?" Tadhg was vicious, beyond anger now. "You have to sneak out at the crack of dawn with this scumbag and worry me half to death?"

"You don't need to worry! I'm old enough—"

"Like fuck you are." He fixed Glenn with a basilisk stare. "I could rip your fucking head off right now. Did she tell you she's sick?"

"Dad!" Lily started forward, but Tadhg held her back.

"She's got cancer. Did she tell you that?"

"She didn't say anything." Glenn looked at Lily, then back at Tadhg. "I never knew she was sick. I never knew she had… that." He laid the game console aside and stood up. "She said her old man was loaded, that we could order in and use the minibar. I wasn't going to do nothing to her, I swear to God. Look…." He delved into his jeans pocket and rummaged around, brought out a small slip of paper. He also brought out, purely by accident, Danny thought, a handful of condoms. They dropped onto the carpet with a gentle slap. Danny watched in fascination as Tadhg's face flushed a deep, curiously vibrant shade of purple.

"You little cunt."

There was a sudden blur of motion, and Tadhg was holding a knife against Glenn's throat—no, not a knife. A straight razor. *Where the fuck did he get a straight razor*? The sight of it shocked Danny nearly speechless.

"Tadhg," he said, "come on, now. Don't be at that. Little fucker's not worth it." He couldn't take his eyes off the blade. He fervently hoped Tadhg's hand was as steady as it looked. "Give me that."

"All I would have to do is draw my hand back," Tadhg said. "And that's the end of you, boyo." He might have been conversing about the weather.

Lily crouched against the door, crying quietly, her hands over her mouth.

"Tadhg." Danny could almost hear Alison's voice in his head: *if you're going to make a move, now's the time.* "Don't do this. Trust me, you don't want to do this." He held out his hand. "Give me the razor."

"Please, Dad." Lily sounded very young, like the little girl she had once been. "Can't we please just go home?"

Danny moved forward until he was standing directly behind Tadhg, shadowing him. "Come on, now. Let's take Lily home."

Tadhg took the razor from Glenn's throat and folded it. He did this with one hand. *He's like fucking Sweeney Todd.* Danny reached over Tadhg's shoulder, took the razor from him, and dropped it very carefully into his own pocket. Nobody breathed.

"Come on." Danny pressed his hand against Tadhg's back, on that flat spot between his shoulder blades. "Time to go." Tadhg's body trembled under Danny's palm. "Let's get you and Lily home." He began slowly to walk Tadhg backwards. "Come on now. Let's go home."

"You ever come near her again… you ever contact her, call her, text her…." Tadhg drew a shuddering breath. "I'll gut you like a codfish."

LILY DIDN'T say a word during the drive to Portugal Cove, nor did she speak when they boarded Tadhg's motor launch but sat to one side of them, her arms crossed over her chest, her mouth a thin line. She was probably dying of embarrassment, Danny thought. He would be. Still for all, it was brainless, what she did. Where in God's name did teenaged girls get such ideas? Romance novels, he supposed—romance novels and television soap operas and internet chat rooms and Reddit and Facebook and all the rest of it. And never mind Lily. What the fuck was Tadhg at?

"Just what did you think you were doing?" Danny leaned close, his voice pitched low so that only Tadhg could hear him. "A straight razor, Tadhg? Where did you get it?"

Tadhg turned to gaze at him. "I found it in your grandfather's house. We were in there clearing up, remember? It was in that tin box."

"What tin box?" Oh right, he thought, *that* tin box. The one in the ceiling. "How the hell did you know it was there?"

"I climbed up to take a look at the hole in the tiles," Tadhg said. "Nothing much in there but a bunch of old papers. It's a rare make, that razor. A Frederick Reynolds, from Sheffield. They stopped making them in the 1940s." He returned Danny's gaze without a trace of embarrassment. "Do you know how much those things sell for on eBay?"

"You don't strike me as being short of cash," Danny said sourly. "So you just… stole it?"

"Well…." Tadhg blew out a breath. "What were you going at with it?"

"You know, you're just lucky I'm not a cop anymore." Danny shook his head. "I would arrest you, you stupid bastard."

Tadhg was incredulous. "For stealing a dirty old razor?"

"For holding it against that boy's throat!" Danny clenched his jaw. "What were ye doing fiddling with that old box, anyway? It's nothing to do with you."

"I didn't think," Tadhg said. His voice was little more than a whisper.

"Ye knew the box was there."

Tadhg nodded. "I did."

For a moment he looked haunted, and Danny wondered how much Tadhg knew about the other contents of the box. Of course Tadhg knew it was there. He'd practically lived at Danny's house when they were young, was just as prone to picking and poking around—'reenjin,' his Scottish nan used to call it—as Danny was.

"That's your trouble," Danny said bitterly, "you never do think." Tadhg had been the same way when they were boys, always impetuous, always ready to do what the others wouldn't because they were scared.

Tadhg didn't speak to Lily until they were inside the front door of the house. "You are grounded until further notice," he said. "No phone, no computer, no internet. You won't see or speak to Gemma. I'll call her father in the morning."

"Why don't you just call him now?" Lily asked. "Get it over with."

"Go to your room."

She rolled her eyes. "Whatever."

"By the Jesus, you'll get whatever." Tadhg started after her, but she was already halfway upstairs. He stood watching her for a moment, then sank down onto one of the treads, his head in his hands.

"Are you okay?" Danny asked. Despite his anger towards Tadhg, he felt like a real tool, stood in the foyer with his hands stuffed into his coat pockets, wondering if there was anything he should do or say. Maybe Tadhg wanted him to leave now that Lily had been safely found.

"Yes, bhoy, I'm just grand," Tadhg retorted. He sighed. "Sorry. I'm sorry. It's not… you've been real good. I shouldn't have said that."

"When's the last time you ate anything?" Danny shrugged out of his coat and hung it on the newel post.

"God only knows." Tadhg stood up wearily, moving like an old man.

"Come on." Danny started towards the kitchen. "It mightn't be cordon bleu, but I'll make something, anyway." He gestured to Tadhg that he should get up. "Let me feed ye. Ye looks like the wrath of God."

He cooked scrambled eggs and crisp bacon for himself and Tadhg, while Tadhg brewed a fresh pot of coffee. "Would Lily eat something if I brought it up to her?" Danny asked.

"She might," Tadhg allowed, "but don't be surprised if she doesn't." He grinned. "Maybe she'll eat for you."

He found some fresh fruit in the fridge and added that to the plate, arranged a slice of toast cut into points around the edges, then climbed the stairs to her room. He tapped on the door lightly. "Lily? It's me."

"Come in." Her voice was teenage-girl surly, and he grinned. He well remembered his sister Sandra at this age.

Lily brightened when she saw him. "Inspector Quirke. You cooked?"

"I thought you might be hungry." Danny held the plate towards her. "And you can call me Danny. Do ye mind if I sit?" He waited for her nod and, when it came, pulled a wingback chair up beside her bed and sat down in it. It was pink velvet, deeply upholstered, and made him feel like he was being devoured by a sentient lump of chewed bubblegum. "You scared your dad quite a bit," he said. "I've known him all my life, and I've never seen him that scared." Not even what happened with Llewellyn Single had frightened Tadhg so badly.

Danny had brought a cup of tea for himself, and he sipped it, watching her covertly over the rim. Yes, she knew she'd done wrong. He was pretty sure she was sorry for how she'd treated Tadhg. "D'ye often strike out on your own like that?"

She shrugged, stirring the eggs around the plate. "Dad treats me like a baby."

"Oh." Danny nodded. "But you are his baby. You always will be, no matter how old you get. Did ye not realise?"

"Do you have kids?" Lily asked.

"No."

"Why not?"

She was a proper genius at asking the hard questions. "Never got around to it, I guess. My wife… passed away." This wasn't exactly the truth. He and Alison had decided early on that children weren't really in the cards for them. They both had careers they loved, and the life they'd made together was important to them. Neither he nor Alison had felt the need to disrupt that by bringing a child into the world.

"Was she sick?" Lily laid the plate on her nightstand. She'd barely touched the food.

"Yes." Danny's throat tightened, a palpable lump expanding to press against his vocal cords. "She was very ill for a while."

"Did she have cancer like me?" Suddenly, she reached out and laid her hand on his wrist. "It's okay. You can say it."

"No. She didn't have cancer." It had been much, much worse, a disease he hadn't even known existed. "It was a prion disease. She couldn't fall asleep. That's how it started."

"Do you miss her?"

He nodded mutely. It had been long enough now that the pain ought to have dulled. Sometimes he could even speak Alison's name out loud without weeping. On good days, he remembered the happiness they'd had together, and how deeply he had loved her.

"Dad will miss me when I'm gone." Lily said this frankly and clearly, without a trace of self-pity. "He's going to need you."

Christ. Danny drew a slow breath. "You're not going anywhere," he said.

She carried on as if he hadn't spoken. "That's why I want to do things. Because there's not much time left."

Danny took a sip of his tea. "Is that why you went to that hotel?"

"I wanted…." She reddened. "I wanted to know what it was like."

For a moment, Danny didn't know what she meant. "What what was like?" Then it clicked. "Oh."

"Don't tell Dad," she whispered, not looking at him. "There was a boy at school. I really liked him. If I was going to do it with anybody, it'd be him. But then I had to stop going for a while. I guess he lost interest." She lifted her face, and the blatant misery etched on her features took his breath away. She was so like Tadhg. "Gemma texted me and said he's going out with Kelsey now."

"Who's Kelsey?"

"Just some girl in my class. She thinks she's shit hot."

Danny hid his smirk in the rim of his cup. "Is she?"

"No!" Lily made a disgusted noise. "She's all tits."

He couldn't help himself; he laughed out loud at this. Yes, she was Tadhg's daughter all right.

"Do you think it hurts to die?"

"I hope not," he said, and it came out much too flippant, the wrong answer. He wasn't thinking of Alison then. He was remembering Eamonn Nolan, a gun to his temple, screaming obscenities in the pouring rain.

"I really liked him." She picked at the stitching on her duvet with bone-thin fingers. She was so pale her skin was nearly translucent. "That boy at school. No odds, though. Dad would never let me go out with him."

She was going to miss so much, if the cancer won. She'd never have a boyfriend, never experience her first kiss or the flush of new love. She would never know the feeling of overwhelming safety you could get from someone who loved and understood you absolutely.

A feeling he and Tadhg had had, many years ago.

Danny rose to go. "Don't tell Dad," Lily said again. "I told him we only went to the hotel to play video games."

"I won't say a word." He indicated the untouched plate of food. "Sure you don't want to eat?"

"I'm sure." She watched him pick up the plate. "Thanks anyway."

"You're welcome." He should do something—touch her shoulder, offer some words of reassurance—but he couldn't think of anything. In the end, he took the plate and went downstairs.

Tadhg was waiting in the living room with two glasses of Scotch. "Did she eat anything?" he asked.

"No," Danny said. "Sorry. I did try."

"She never was much of an eater," Tadhg said, "even before she got sick. Now… she almost never gets hungry." His face darkened with his ever-present grief and worry. "You could think she's any regular teenager. She doesn't look that sick." He took a sip of whisky.

"She looks pretty good," Danny said. "You have to admit, running off with her boyfriend like that took some energy and initiative. That's got to be encouraging."

"Encouraging? You're off your fucking head."

"No, that's not what I meant." Backpedaling furiously, Danny continued, "She's a good girl. You've done well with her."

Tadhg made a small noise that Danny took to be agreement. "It's not easy, let me tell you, bringing up a youngster on your own. Always wondering if you're doing the right thing or fucking them up for good."

"You're not fucking her up." *Like was done to you*, he thought, but he didn't say this out loud.

Tadhg said nothing.

"Anyway." Danny stood up and laid his glass on the coffee table. "I think I'll push on."

"You're not going out there," Tadhg said, getting up. "Sure it's blowing a storm. You'll end up over a cliff."

Danny stared at him. "You don't need me. I've got to get home."

"You can go home tomorrow." He picked Danny's glass up and poured two more fingers of whisky into it. "There you are. Get that down ye."

Danny gazed into the glass. "Getting bossy in your old age, are ye?"

"I'd feel bad, sending you out into the weather. It's not fit. There's plenty of room." He nodded at the glass. "I'm hoping you'll be too drunk to drive."

"Okay." Danny nodded. "Okay." He sat back down. The hockey game had gone into overtime, and they spent the extra two periods swearing at the goalie.

"What the fuck is he doing?" Tadhg gestured at the set. "They'll be scoring on an empty net."

"He can't keep nothing out," Danny said. "I don't know why they bother putting him in goal. He's a liability." He watched as the other team's slap shot slid between the goalie's legs and into the net.

"That's it," Tadhg said, getting up. "I can't stand any more of this."

"Don't blame ye," Danny said. He gathered both their glasses as he stood up. "I'll put these in the dishwasher."

"You don't always have to be cleaning up my messes, Danny." Tadhg sounded apologetic and a little ashamed. Danny knew immediately what he was referring to.

"That was forever ago," he said quietly.

"Oh, there's some in Kildevil Cove that still hate me." Tadhg's uneasy smile hovered for a moment, then disappeared.

"I don't hate you."

A log shifted in the fireplace. The wind roared around the side of the house, shaking the windows in their frames.

"Maybe you should." Tadhg turned abruptly. "The guest bedroom is right next to mine, off the landing." Danny followed him upstairs, and Tadhg stopped in front of a half-open door. "I just had the crowd in to clean the place. This is your lucky day." He pushed the door open with his fingertips and flicked on a light. A king-sized bed dominated the centre of the room, which was decorated in multiple shades of green—even the carpet was green, darker than the walls and luxuriously thick. One wall was entirely made of glass and overlooked the dark waters of Conception Bay. Danny could see the lights of Portugal Cove in the far distance.

"Wow."

"The decorator did a good job," Tadhg said. "I wanted a nice guest bedroom so somebody—a friend—could spend the night." He shrugged. "I don't see very many people outside of business. No point staying in touch with anyone in Kildevil Cove." His smile was self-deprecating. "Except you, of course."

"Am I a friend?" Danny asked.

Tadhg laughed. "Christ, I hope so. Not going to murder me in my sleep, are ye?"

Danny laid a hand on his shoulder, squeezed gently. "Haven't got the energy," he said.

"I'll get ye something to sleep in," Tadhg said. "You can borrow mine." He went next door and returned with a pair of flannel lounging pants and a T-shirt. "Hope this is okay."

"That's perfect," Danny said. "Thanks."

"I appreciate what you've done for me. It's good to have her home." Tadhg patted him on the back. "Good night."

Danny didn't think he'd be able to sleep in a strange bed, but he slipped into a profound slumber in minutes. He awoke several hours later to the sound of someone retching. Thinking it might be Lily and wanting to help her, he climbed out of bed and started up the stairs to her room, then realised the noise was much closer. He went into Tadhg's bedroom and saw the bathroom light on. Tadhg was on his knees in front of the toilet.

"Are you all right?"

Tadhg looked around. His face was bone white, his eyes rimmed with red. "I'm fine," he croaked.

"You don't bloody well look fine."

"It's nothing—" He bent forward and vomited. "Always happens." He reached out to flush the toilet. "Just like fucking clockwork."

Danny found a washcloth and wet it under the cold-water tap. "Here." He handed it to Tadhg and helped him up off his knees. "Wipe your face with that. Make you feel better."

Tadhg wiped his face, then went to the sink and rinsed his mouth. "Been like that since we were youngsters," he said. "Any kind of a shock or startle and up she comes."

"I remember." Danny stood to one side. "Come on, back to bed."

Tadhg grinned weakly. It seemed to require enormous effort on his part. "Are you coming on to me?"

Danny lingered near him for a moment, a slight smile playing about his lips. "When I'm coming on to you, my son, you'll know it."

He reached out and laid his palm against the centre of Tadhg's chest. His voice thrummed with emotion. "Trust me. You'll know."

Tadhg looked at him as if seeing him for the first time. "Here I thought you were arrow straight."

"Maybe you thought wrong." Danny shrugged. "It's always been about the person to me, never their gender. And I hate labels anyway."

"Aren't you the man of the world." Tadhg's habitual grin came and went, and he was suddenly shy with Danny in a way he hadn't been before. "I've been around myself, you know."

"That surprises no one." Danny clasped a hand on the back of his neck and drew Tadhg closer. "You should sleep," he said quietly. "You're tired."

They went into the bedroom, and Danny pulled back the covers. "In you go." The clock by Tadhg's bed read 2:27 a.m. "You need your sleep, a growing lad like you."

Tadhg got into bed and propped the pillows behind his back. "She scared the hell out of me, you know."

"I know."

"It was easier when she was little. You do all the regular things: baths at bedtime, getting her ready for school." He scrubbed a hand across his face. "Then she turned thirteen, and all hell broke loose."

There was silence between them, except for the sound of the wind tossing handfuls of sleet at the windows. "Will you stay for a bit?" Tadhg asked.

"If you like." Danny pulled a wingback chair close to the bed and sat down in it. "Who hates you in Kildevil Cove?" he asked, after several moments had passed.

Tadhg shook his head. "It's not important."

"I think it is," Danny said. "I think whoever it is might have vandalised the house. They knew you were buying it."

"Maybe." Tadhg lay down, bringing the pillows with him. "Looking for money or something."

A sudden chill ghosted into the room, and Danny shivered.

"Come and lie down." Tadhg patted the bed. "Sitting there freezing. At least it's warmer over here."

"I thought this house had the best of everything," Danny said. He abandoned the chair and lay down on the bed. It was incredibly soft, cradling his tired body like the gentle hand of God. "You'd be better off with an old wood stove like my nan had." He remembered frigid winter mornings, shivering between the sheets while his grandfather lit the fire and his grandmother got the kettle boiling. That first hot cup of tea was usually enough to get him up and moving.

"Here." Tadhg threw the duvet over him. "Might as well see what's on television." He picked up the remote and switched on the set. Danny watched for a while, but Tadhg's choice of program—a business analyst's opinion on Chinese imports—bored him to death. The last he remembered, Tadhg was saying something about fireworks and gunpowder.

WHEN NEXT he woke, it was daylight. For a moment he didn't know where he was. Then the sound of Tadhg's soft, steady breaths filtered into his awareness. Right. He'd spent the night with Tadhg after they found Lily. He turned to look at Tadhg, sprawled on his back, dead to the world. His face was turned away from Danny, half-hidden in the folds of his feather pillow, one hand curled loosely against his cheek. He looked the same as he had in years past, when he and Danny would clamber up into the hills behind Kildevil Cove to make bough houses out of the spruce and fir they cut with their pocketknives. They were going to live off the land like Daniel Boone and Davy Crockett, two heroes they'd only recently learned about from the American films the teacher showed downstairs in the school library. At Christmas time and before the Easter holidays, the school ordered movies that arrived at the local post office on huge rolls sealed inside metal cans. Disney films, usually, although they were shown an educational one now and again, usually about things they already understood, like seabirds, cutting hay, and the fishery. A film about culling wolves by shooting their pups in the ears scarred him forever. *No room on earth for anything but humans*, Danny thought bitterly. He remembered something he'd been told in church once—that people came first and animals came after because they had no souls. He'd always thought that was a load of shite. In his long police career, he'd arrested plenty of murderers and rapists, child molesters, people who killed and destroyed for the fun of it and because they didn't give a damn about the ones they hurt. He'd yet to meet an animal like that. "It's not all black and white, Danny my son." His first supervisor after he graduated training had said that to him. "You can't divide people up like sheep or goats." It struck him funny at the time. "I'd rather the sheep and goats," he'd said, "if it's all the same to you."

He took a shower in Tadhg's en suite and washed his hair with some pine-smelling shampoo that apparently came from Scotland. He stepped out, dried himself off, and dressed, but the house was still silent as the grave. He went downstairs and left a note for Tadhg propped up against the toaster. *Thanks for letting me stay.* He paused, wondering what to say next. *Call me later, okay?* Then he stepped out into the morning air. The relentless snow showers of the night before had frozen into solid ridges of pure ice, treacherous underfoot. Twice he skidded and lost his footing, and once he nearly fell. The trip to the boathouse took much longer than usual, and he was glad to exchange slippery ground for the heaving but solid deck. He declined Jesper's offer to shelter in the cuddy, enjoying the brisk wind and the pallid winter sky. The waters of the bay sparkled, illuminated by the first shafts of morning light. It looked the way it had when he was a boy and climbed to the top of Robber's Hill in Kildevil Cove in the summertime. From there he had an unimpeded view of the town all the way to New Melbourne, six miles away. It was the first place he'd taken Alison when he brought her home to meet his grandparents.

They'd been together six years at that point, but right up until he brought her to Kildevil Cove, Danny's grandparents had no idea Alison even existed. He didn't visit often, and when he did, fobbed off questions about his work in favour of other subjects. His grandmother, already afflicted with the stomach cancer that would eventually kill her, was forever at him about when he was going to settle down, get married, have children. He didn't particularly like children, found them whiny and tiresome; the one time he went along with a high school girlfriend to a babysitting job, he was both bored and irritated by the banal and repetitive nature of the children's questions and their relentless noise. *Guess what kind of animal I am. Do you know what Matthew and Jason said to me at school yesterday? No, guess what kind of animal! Guess what kind! You have to guess.* His feelings about marriage were similar to others of his generation: you didn't need a piece of paper to legitimise your union.

He and Alison hadn't started out intending to fall in love; it simply happened. He'd encountered her at several crime scenes when she'd arrived first or had been sent as backup. She'd been the constable assigned to him after he'd passed his inspector's exam. They found a commonality and a kinship in each other that felt like it had existed for years. Their first big case together was the murder of a prostitute whose body was dumped in a remote area bordering the city. A man walking his dog had found her and called it in. It didn't take long to track down the john who'd killed her. After that, the two of them worked almost exclusively together, becoming inseparable off duty as well as on. Of course he was attracted to her sexually. Alison was lovely. But that was only one small part of their equation. More important than any of this, she understood him. She knew what made him tick, was able to coax him out of the deep depression that often gripped him later in his career.

They never did get married, Danny mused, gazing down at the water rushing past the bows. They bought a house together in the Waterford Valley, an Arts and Crafts bungalow built in 1906. That it was haunted by the ghosts of WWI soldiers, Alison had no doubt. Things moved around, she claimed, of their own accord. Cupboard doors slammed open and shut, and window sashes were raised and lowered as if by invisible hands. Items got lost in the house and then reappeared somewhere else. On quiet weekend afternoons, she swore someone was reading aloud in one of the back bedrooms. Danny neither saw nor heard any of these things, so they laughed about it, each blaming the other. Then Alison began roaming around at night, floating up and down the halls in her nightgown, as silent as a spectre.

"What are you doing, love?"

"I left my reading glasses in the living room."

"They're on your nightstand. Alison, come back to bed."

"In a minute. I have to make sure."

The diagnosis, when it came, was no surprise. He'd expected something like this. Some part of him had known it all along.

His cell phone rang, interrupting his musings, as the boat pulled into the wharf. "Deiniol Quirke."

The caller was Riley. "I've found something I think you should see. Immediately. Right now, in fact."

Chapter Thirteen

Danny found Cillian Riley standing in the kitchen of Danny's grandparents' old house, a pen and notepad in his hand. All the doors were open, and the boards covering the broken windows until they could be fixed had been torn down. The chill December wind blew through, mixing with drifting papers and occasional snowflakes. Riley greeted him sombrely. "One of the constables was driving by early this morning and saw something amiss. I figured you would want to know."

Danny took a long, careful look around the room, noting the damage. "It's worse than last time," he said. "They've even stripped the friggin' wallpaper off." High up where the walls met the ceiling, someone had torn away the white-and-orange paper decorated with images of teapots and kitchen canisters, a standard choice in 1970s décor. The wooden shelf for his grandfather's old radio had been wrenched from its moorings and lay splintered at Danny's feet, along with various knickknacks from the shelves beside the window. "And they left the doors open?"

Riley nodded. "All of it. Even the root cellar"—he nodded towards the outside—"was left open." Danny started towards the door, but Riley stopped him. "There's nothing there, sir. We've already looked."

Danny resisted correcting Riley's use of 'sir.' "Is there any other damage?" he asked.

"Come with me." Riley led him first into the small bathroom off the kitchen, which looked as if a bomb had gone off. Someone had taken what must have been a sledgehammer to the bathtub, chipping off the porcelain and exposing the cast iron underneath. The same instrument had been used to make huge gouges in the tile floor. The sink was ripped from the wall and lay shattered in chunks on the floor. "That's not the worst of it," Riley said. He and Danny went through the living room and upstairs. "Best brace yourself," Riley said. "They got a bit creative up here."

The first bedroom off the landing—his childhood bedroom—was relatively untouched, but the other two were in spectacular states of disarray. The intruder or intruders had kicked the doors nearly off their hinges, leaving the wooden frame of each and the doorjamb splintered and broken. Dressers had been overturned, mattresses tossed awry, and pillows ripped open. The floor of his grandparents' bedroom was a blizzard of shed feathers. The graffiti Lying Cunts was spray-painted on the wall above the bed.

"Have a look at this." Riley directed his attention to a section of baseboard behind a toppled bureau. "Someone's been poking and picking around." Danny got down on his knees and looked. The board had been prised away from the wall, revealing a ten-inch gap that was perhaps six inches deep. It extended into the space between the wall joists and had been deliberately made. "Do you know what it is?" Riley asked. He sat back on his heels and scratched his curly dark hair with the end of his pen. "Obviously made to conceal something. Did your granddad not believe in using banks? Some of the older folk liked to hide their money in the house."

Danny shook his head. "I've never seen this before." He gazed at Riley. There were fine wrinkles fanning out from the corners of the younger man's eyes and a bracket of lines around his mouth. Not as young as Danny had originally thought, then. His eyes weren't brown, but a dark green, the sort of eyes that would seem to change colour with the light. When he spoke, a single dimple came and went in his right cheek.

"Well...." Riley got up. "Whatever was there is gone now. Either they got what they came for or went away very unhappy." There was a commotion downstairs. Riley called, "All right there, constable?"

"There's a man here," the constable replied, "who wants to come up. Says he's a friend of the family."

"Danny?" Tadhg's unmistakable voice floated up to them. "Are you there?"

Riley leaned over the banister. "Come on up, Mr. Heaney."

It had taken Tadhg no time at all to figure out where Danny had gone. He crested the top of the stairs, slightly out of breath. "Got your note," he said. He nodded at Riley. "Sergeant." His gaze took in the damage all at once. "Christ," he breathed, "they've been here again."

"They?" Riley asked. "So you know who did this?"

"No," Tadhg said quickly. He shook his head. "No idea. But I assume there was more than one." He glanced at Danny. "How'd you know about it?"

"Sergeant Riley called me," Danny said. "I still own the house."

"Right." Surprisingly, there was no rancour in Tadhg's tone. "There is that, yeah."

One of the constables called up the stairs for Riley. "Excuse me, gents," he said. "I'll be wanting to talk to you both in a minute." He clattered downstairs.

Danny turned to Tadhg. "I didn't feel like waking you," he said. "I figured you had enough to be getting on with."

Tadhg lifted one corner of his mouth in a half smile. "I wasn't asleep."

"Oh," Danny said. "Like that time in summer camp when you were 'talking in your sleep'"—he made finger quotes—"only you were awake?" They had both spent a week at church camp in Mackinsons when they were boys, in a rickety wooden building set in a forest of fir trees with nowhere to swim and drinking water that smelled like rotten eggs. Their days were structured around Bible classes, outdoor sports, and "quiet time" spent lying in their bunks and pondering spiritual matters.

"I was bored," Tadhg replied. "All that lying around in the dark thinking about God. I figured—"

"You'd better come down here."

Riley's voice. He was speaking calmly, the way people spoke to small children during some tragedy or crisis, but he might as well have been shouting. Danny and Tadhg found him in the living room. Riley was standing over two constables who were kneeling on the floor, holding something wrapped in cloth. They passed the bundle to Riley, who turned it so Danny and Tadhg could see.

"Good Christ," Tadhg breathed.

The bundle was a stack of money, fifties and hundreds, the odd twenty-dollar bill. Impossible to tell at a glance how much there was. It would have to be counted. It was a good eight inches thick, packed tightly together like the pages of a Bible. Danny reached out, and Riley placed the money in his hand. "Didn't trust banks, your granddad?"

Danny shook his head. "No. I mean, he did. They had an account at the bank in Heart's Desire, up the shore." He'd gone with them on what his grandar called 'grocery getting days,' first to the bank to withdraw some money and then to the supermarket. He'd help steer the shopping trolley around the narrow aisles, reading labels for his grandfather, deciphering sodium and calories in keeping with the old man's doctor-appointed diet. He was a big man, Danny's grandar, tall and burly, running to fat later in his life as the powerful muscles succumbed to age and the pull of gravity. He developed painful arthritis in his back and legs, which made him unsteady on his feet, and his hands became gnarled and twisted like old ropes. He began to forget things, tell long, meandering stories with no discernible meaning and no end. "That money he give me… I was out in boat with 'un that day, I was so… saving up fer to buy a bicycle…."

Riley was looking at Danny as if he didn't believe him. "Why hide money in the wall, then?"

"His mind was going," Tadhg said. "Poor old soul didn't know what he was doing, did he?" He glanced at Danny briefly, before his gaze skidded away.

"This money has been here for quite a while," Riley said. "We'll check the serial numbers of course, but I doubt it's stolen. Thieves usually come back for the takings. This has been in the wall for a good twenty years at least."

"Thank you," Danny said. "I really appreciate you coming out like this. Mr. Heaney and I can take it from here."

Riley nodded. "Best get some security system in place," he advised. "You've got repeat customers. I've no doubt they'll be back." He called to the constables, who obediently cleared out, then gestured that he wanted a private word with Danny. They went into the front porch, and Riley closed the door behind them. "I'm a little concerned about Mr. Heaney," he said.

"Why?" Danny could see Tadhg through the glass window of the inner door. He was standing in the kitchen, pretending to examine a brass etching of Robbie Burns hanging over the stove. Danny wasn't sure how much Tadhg could hear, if indeed he could hear anything. He was obviously very interested in what the young sergeant and Danny were talking about.

"How well do you know him?"

"Well enough." The question irritated him, although he couldn't say why. "We grew up here and went to school together. So?"

Riley nodded. "It's rumoured some of his business dealings aren't quite above board. I'm sure you're well aware of his reputation." He glanced past Danny into the kitchen. "Just watch him, is all I'm saying. Sometimes illegal activity isn't immediately apparent. I wouldn't want—" He broke off as a constable came up the front steps and into the porch. "What is it?"

"Martin found a bicycle out back of the old stable up there." The officer pointed up the hill. "Buried, it was. We managed to pull it out of the ground, but it was put in there pretty deep."

Tadhg hovered near the porch door, waiting until Riley and the constable had gone. Then he pulled open the door. "What did he want?"

"He says they found a bicycle, buried up the top of the garden," Danny told him.

"A bicycle?" Danny knew by the tone of Tadhg's voice that this wasn't the first he'd heard of it. Tadhg wasn't as good a liar as he thought he was. "Who'd bury a bicycle?"

"I don't know," Danny said. "Maybe the same kind of person who'd put several thousand dollars in a wall."

IT TOOK a couple of hours to put the house to rights, but they managed it between them. Danny pulled down the torn wallpaper and stuffed it into bin bags while Tadhg unearthed the ancient Hoover from the linen closet and did the floors upstairs and down. Despite the damage to its shelf, the kitchen radio still worked, and they listened to a local call-in show while they cleared away the mess. An hour or so into it, Danny put the kettle on and unearthed a bottle of instant coffee from the cupboard under the sink. "Have one?"

Tadhg regarded the jar with disdain. "That rubbish? Wouldn't miss it." While Danny waited for the kettle to boil, Tadhg took down two mugs and a canister of non-dairy creamer. "You left a lot of stuff," he said offhandedly. "Groceries and such. You weren't planning on staying, though."

The kettle came to a boil, whistling shrilly, and Danny reached across to take it off the hob. "No," he said. "I was not staying. That's what Grandar had. I was going to throw it away once I got a chance."

"Couldn't bear to part with it?" Tadhg spooned coffee crystals into each of their cups. His half smile said he was kidding, but the expression in his eyes refuted it. It was the face he wore for business, the glad-handing sleveen who'd promise the moon to get what he wanted. He was just like his old man, Danny thought. He'd tell anything to anyone.

"So tell me about the bicycle," Danny said, stirring sugar into his coffee.

"It's an old bike, Danny." Tadhg tasted his coffee, grimaced, and reached across Danny to add sugar. "Could have been there for donkey's ages, I don't know."

A rising gust baffled down the chimney, shaking the stovepipe like an invisible hand. Danny put down his cup and lifted the damper, shoved another thick log of birch into the fire. Nothing he did seemed able to dispel the chill in the house, the cold that seeped into the walls and tapped at the window glass with icy fingers.

"But you see, I think you do know, Tadhg."

Tadhg didn't meet his gaze. "Going all cop on me, are ye?" His grin lasted no more than a second or two.

Danny said nothing.

"Look." Tadhg sighed and rubbed a hand across his eyes. "It was a long time ago, right? We said we weren't going to bring it up again. What's done is done, you said." He gulped some of his coffee and grimaced. "You did say that."

Danny was confused. "I don't know what—" And then he did know. The event they'd both sworn to forget. He put his cup down on the counter. "Look, I should be getting back to town. I've hung round here long enough as it is." He turned to go, but Tadhg caught his arm, holding him in place.

"We said we wouldn't remember." Tadhg's voice was very quiet. No longer trying to evade the truth. "What kind of life would he have had, Danny? Huh?" He shook Danny by the arms. "The damage was already done. And it's not like we pushed him, is it?"

No, they hadn't pushed him, Danny thought. He fell. Of his own accord and by accident of course, but he fell. They tried to save him but there was nothing they could have done, no outside help they could have roused that would have arrived in time.

"I should get back to town before dark." He was finished with this conversation. "I think we're going to have weather."

DANNY ARRIVED back in the city mid-afternoon, with the December light already fading and a band of snow sliding in over the Southside hills. He let himself into his apartment and took a quick look around, subconsciously inventorying the contents and where he'd left things. Ever since the break-ins at his grandfather's place, he'd been expecting similar activity here at home, but nothing had been touched. A pile of mail was sitting on the floor inside the front door, but it was mostly bills and such, a leaflet from some local evangelical group inviting him to find himself with Jesus. Danny laid the bills on the kitchen counter and threw the rest in the bin.

He went into the bathroom and turned on the shower, running the water until it was blood-warm. He stripped and tossed his clothes into the hamper, mindful of the mess he and Tadhg had cleaned up and wanting to be rid of it, at least on a subconscious level. He ought to go out for a run, but the weather was foul, and the lazy part of him said it was better to stay where he was. But he was restless. He'd missed the city, and he wondered what he could do, where he could go, to ease the itch inside of him.

He found his cell phone on the kitchen counter and picked it up, paging idly through the list of contacts until he found Cillian Riley's number. What would be the harm in it, going out for a beer or maybe a meal? He could use a distraction.

Riley picked up on the first ring. "Yeah?" He sounded as if he'd been sleeping, and Danny wondered if maybe he shouldn't have called. Riley might have done the night shift and was catching up on his sleep. Instantly his mind flooded with images of Cillian Riley, stark naked and tangled in the sheets, and he almost groaned aloud. *Do you know what you're getting into, I wonder.* His inner voice was mocking, sarcastic. *'Tis your funeral, I suppose.*

"It's Danny Quirke," he said. "I wondered if—"

"Absolutely," Riley said through a yawn. "Yellowbelly, seven o'clock or so?"

"Good God," Danny said, "you're easy." Not to mention being a mind reader.

"Yeah," Riley agreed through another yawn, "but I'm not cheap."

RILEY WASN'T yawning when he slid into the seat opposite Danny at the Yellowbelly Brewery. He looked pretty spruce in a leather jacket, jeans, and a dark green henley that showed off his impressive chest muscles. Not a few female heads turned to look as he went by, and several of the men. Danny wondered how much time you had to spend in the gym to get pecs like that, pushing and pulling complicated machines, pumping iron. Naked, the bastard must look like a Greek god, all sleek muscle under silk-smooth skin. He probably had a lot of stamina, too, could go all night. *Why am I thinking this?*

No doubt Riley was someone who got up at four in the morning to go and work out for two hours before reporting for duty. Men like him made Danny feel old and tired. "Beer?" he asked.

"If ye please," Riley replied. He glanced around at the crowd, ebullient by anybody's standards and unusual for a weeknight. "So you and Inspector Fraser go back a ways, is that right?"

It was an odd opening to their conversation, and Danny was taken aback by the abruptness of it. "I knew her when I was with the constabulary, yes. She was my supervisor." He didn't think it was necessary to divulge that he and Moira had had a fling back in the day, even though he suspected it was more than common knowledge.

"She's been keeping an eye on you ever since your grandfather's funeral," Riley said. He glanced up as the waitress appeared with two foaming pints of Harp. He nodded at the girl, "Ta, my love," and dropped some coins on her tray.

"I know," Danny said. "No big surprise there." Moira tended to keep tabs on everyone with whom she had any kind of connection. If she ever tired of ordinary police work, she could make a good living working for Interpol.

"Not too keen on that Tadhg Heaney, though." Riley took a healthy swig, paused to wipe the foam off his upper lip. "She'd skin him for the fun of it."

Danny nodded. Tadhg had that effect on a lot of people. "He's an acquired taste," he said. "What's she got against Tadhg?"

Riley drew a slow, meditative breath and rubbed his forehead with the tips of his fingers. "I've been meaning to talk to you about it, but between this and that there's been no time." He paused, then for some reason, changed tack. "Did ye get the mess cleaned up? At your grandfather's house, I mean."

"Yes." Danny took a healthy slug of beer. "I suppose I should be glad nobody shat on the carpets or pissed in the kitchen sink... although I've seen that in my time, and worse."

"Bet you could tell some stories." Riley grinned, a flash of white teeth. "Senior police officer like yourself." The not-quite-local accent Danny had noticed the first time they'd met was even stronger now—probably because of the alcohol, or maybe Riley was in a more relaxed setting. Danny often found himself smoothing out his own accent when he was in a professional situation—softening the strong rhotic *r* sounds and fully pronouncing the usually slack dental fricatives, slowing down the rapid-fire pace of his speech. It annoyed him when those not from the island urged him to 'say something in Newfoundland talk,' as if he were a performing parrot. His internal response usually ran along the lines of a not-very-polite *Go fuck yourself.* Riley's accent reminded him of certain actors on *Coronation Street*, his grandmother's favourite show. She never missed it.

"Former police officer," Danny corrected. He had to raise his voice to be heard above the increasing din. A group of young women, probably out on a hen night pub crawl, stood by the hostess station, giggling and pushing each other. He assumed the one wearing the dollar-store veil was the bride. The others had pink plastic tiaras. They all wore T-shirts emblazoned with the slogan Who Let the Hens Out? Riley smirked as one of the women, no more than twenty, tripped over someone else's leg and went down on her arse. The other girls all rushed to help her back up.

"There's good money in that," he said, nodding at the group.

"What? Hen nights?"

"They hire strippers for the party. Usually in a hotel or some place. The pay's crap, but you can pick up a lot in tips." He tilted the pint glass to his lips and winked at Danny. "'Course, the best money's the big conventions when they're in town. Some of the exhibitors like the delegates to have a good time, and there's often private parties in the bigger hotels."

"Are you fucking kidding me?" The idea of Riley as an exotic dancer made him roar with laughter. "You do it on the side or what?"

"No, not anymore," Riley said. "It's not exactly compatible with the job I'm in now." Across the room, the hostess arrived and escorted the hen party to a large table in the back. "Before I joined up, I used to. Made a fair bit too."

"So…." Danny couldn't stop laughing. "On a pole and everything?"

Riley grinned like a naughty schoolboy. "On a pole and everything."

"Would ye ever go back to it?"

"Probably not. It's all body and no brains, know what I mean? I've got a good brain, and I like using it." The younger detective laughed.

And ye've got a fantastic body, that's for damn well sure. Danny moved to change the subject. "You were saying something about Tadhg Heaney." He hoped he didn't sound brusque, but he needed to know.

"Yes." Riley took another swig of beer and set the pint glass down with a decisive thump. "We've been keeping tabs on him ever since he got back from Amsterdam. Well, before that really." He tipped the last of his beer into his mouth and signaled the waitress. "He's been a person of interest for a while."

"What do you mean?" Danny asked.

"He's got businesses registered in various places. Now, there's nothing strange in that." Riley paused as the waitress came and took their empty glasses. "But when we looked into it, we found that very few of those businesses actually operate. They have no assets, no staff, nothing."

"He's set up shell companies?" Danny was more than a little surprised. He knew Tadhg could justify cutting corners, but it didn't seem likely he would erect a nonexistent company to move money or drugs in and out of the country.

"Technically they're shell companies, yeah. But he's done nothing with them. They're all legally registered, but there's been no activity. It's like they were set up for show." A loud sizzling sound came from the kitchen, and the smell of frying beef wafted on the air. Danny was suddenly famished. Their waitress appeared and laid down two more pints of Harp.

"Ye two looks like ye're starving to death over here," she said. She was a pretty redhead, about thirty, with generous curves and a complexion like milk. "Gonna eat something?" She dropped two copies of the menu down on the table. "Corey's just frying up a fresh batch of hamburgers. Best in the city."

"Homemade chips on the side?" Riley asked.

"As if I'd serve ye supermarket chips," she scoffed, grinning.

"That sounds about right," Danny said. He looked over at Riley. "Two?"

"Are ye going to eat both of them yourself or can I have one?" The beer was making Riley as merry as a lord, Danny thought. Maybe he ought to encourage the younger man to ease up a bit. The waitress jotted their order on her pad and went away again.

Danny jerked his chin at Riley's pint glass. "Sure you're going to be all right?" he asked. "That's strong beer you're drinking."

Riley's amiable expression changed so quickly it was like pulling down a shutter. "Is that right? You're my fucking mother, now, are ye?"

Danny was stunned into momentary silence. "What?"

Riley took a long pull off his pint—rather deliberately, Danny thought—and turned away to gaze at something across the room. He was behaving like a disgruntled toddler. The sudden change from the amiable, smiling man of a few moments before was unsettling. He waited for Riley to say something, but the silence stretched into several long moments. Finally Danny said, "You were talking about Tadhg Heaney."

Riley turned around and laid both hands flat on the table. "Right."

Danny waited.

"Mr. Heaney's business influence doesn't extend as far as you might think." Riley's voice was cold now, professional. "He's only got the one company that's for real, Heaney Construction. It's a real estate development firm, one of these jobbies that builds all the new subdivisions you see around. The rest is all bullshit. There was no earthly need for him to go to Amsterdam."

"What?" Danny was gobsmacked. "I'm finding that hard to believe. Surely to God he wouldn't up and fly to the Netherlands on a whim." Would he? Tadhg could be capricious in the extreme.

"He's borrowed heavily against his own property: the house and the island, his boat, the whole works. Tadhg Heaney is mortgaged up to his eyeballs. He owns sweet fuck all." Riley toyed with a cardboard coaster on the tabletop. "And that's not the worst of it."

Danny's scalp prickled. "What's the worst of it?"

"Until very recently, he was paying large sums of money to an unknown party." Riley took a gulp of his pint and licked his lips. "Thousands, every single month."

"You said 'recently.'" Danny couldn't imagine Tadhg paying blackmail money to anyone. For what? Tadhg had no big secrets. He wasn't part of any clandestine group that Danny knew about. "So when did the payments stop?"

"The day your grandfather died."

THE FIRST time Tadhg Heaney ever saw Danny Quirke, they were twelve years old, in grade six. He didn't know Danny, which was strange, because Tadhg and his family knew everybody. Danny was by himself at the edge of the schoolyard one day during recess with his hands in the pockets of his standard-issue 1970s corduroys, gazing around at the other children like he was much older than they were and fatally amused by it all. Like most days, Tadhg was standing to one side of the front steps, a treacherous scaffolding of ancient, rotting wood held together with iron nails so old they might have come from Christ's cross. He was fiddling with his birthday gift, an electronic game called Merlin, replete with flashing lights and automated noises like the robots in *Star Wars*. Almost nobody in Kildevil Cove had even seen *Star Wars*, but there were commercials for it all the time on television, and the steel soft-drink cans they bought their ginger ale and Pepsi in had games printed on the inside. If you matched certain symbols, you could win tickets to the cinema. This wasn't much use in Kildevil Cove because there was no cinema. There was the school auditorium, used by local church groups for youth group movie nights and wedding receptions, and the lodge, where certain men of the community went to enact strange and arcane dramas in costumes that the Pentecostals said were satanic. If you were bored some evening, you could play soldiers in among the furniture for sale in the dry goods store next to the fish plant, but the Heaneys owned it, and there would be hell to pay if Fraser Heaney caught you. He had big fists, and he was free with them, had grown up bossing the Heaney Company fishing crews that went each summer up to Labrador. Fraser Heaney could lay you out solid on the wharf and barely twitch a muscle. He was a cruel and cunning bastard of a man and Tadhg Heaney's father. There was no love lost between him and Tadhg, either. Danny had been in their shop once with his grandmother, and Tadhg was working to one side of the till, arranging packets of chewing gum in a cardboard display. He didn't spare Danny so much as a passing glance.

Fraser Heaney came out of a back room, his arms loaded down with cardboard boxes, which he dropped onto the floor next to where Tadhg was working. "Put them up when you're finished," he said. "If you're ever fucking finished."

Tadhg murmured, "Working as fast as I can."

He never saw the blow coming. His father's hard hand caught him on the right temple. His head snapped back as he fell, upsetting the display and scattering packets of gum on the floor. "Go on, you makes me fucking sick," his father hissed. "Should send you back where you fucking came from." He raised his hand again, but Tadhg scrabbled backwards on his heels, skittering across the floor like a crab. Not for the first time, Tadhg wondered if his father would kill him. He glanced at Danny, glad for once he had a witness despite his embarrassment.

WHEN THE bell rang to signal the end of recess. Tadhg hung back in the shadows until most of the other children had gone into the building, but three boys—the same three tormentors who shadowed him for all of his childhood—waited for him.

"What's that ye got?" Trevor Neeley, two years older and held back for being so bloody stupid, swiped at Tadhg's game. "Something fancy yer old man bought for yer, is it?"

Tadhg neatly sidestepped him, holding the game out of his reach. "Leave me alone. I'm not bothering you."

"Let me see it." Roger Palmer was tall and skinny, with beady black eyes and the uncertain stubble of a moustache already starting under his nose. "Let me fucking see it, I said!"

Tadhg started for the stairs, but the others were too quick. Darryl Stone, the third of their group, grabbed for Tadhg's legs and yanked them out from under him so that he fell face first, hitting hard and bloodying his nose. Unexpectedly, Danny Quirke appeared and stepped between Tadhg and his tormentors. "Leave him alone."

Roger laughed, a harsh noise like the cawing of a crow. "What are you gonna do? Make me?"

"He wasn't bothering you," Danny said. He held out a hand to Tadhg. "We're gonna be late for geography," he said. "Mr. Squires might get mad."

None of the others moved to intercept them, something that astonished Tadhg. Even back then, Danny had an authority about him, a maturity of manner that swayed people to behave as he suggested.

When they were inside, Danny steered Tadhg to the boys' bathroom and helped him clean the blood off his face. "It's not broken, is it?"

Tadhg palpated his nose gently, looking into the mirror. "I don't think so." He caught Danny's gaze in the reflection. "Thanks," he said, somewhat shamefaced.

"Don't let them fuckers pester ye," Danny instructed. "Give 'em a good poke in the gob."

But Roger and the others saw no reason to stop tormenting Tadhg. They were just careful to do it when Danny wasn't around. Tadhg showed up in class with a black eye, then scratches on his face, and another time serious scrapes on his hands and knees from where the bullies had pushed him down. Tadhg wasn't a coward. He tried to fight back, but there were three of them, all older and bigger than he was. They cornered him at recess time and stole his money. They waited for him after school and chased him home to the big house on the point, a Gothic monstrosity with cupolas and a widow's walk. On rainy days the teachers let them play ball hockey in the gym, and Roger and his friends lined their shots up, calculated them carefully to hit Tadhg's shins and his knees. Once, when he had the audacity to steal the ball away from Trevor, Darryl swung his hard plastic hockey stick into Tadhg's forehead. A bruise the width of a jam jar puffed itself to grotesque proportions, pulsing and dark purple. Danny cornered Darryl after gym class, catching him alone in the locker room, and threatened him while Tadhg waited.

"Thinks ye're a hard man, do ye?"

"Fuck off!" Darryl struggled in Danny's grip. "I'll tell me father on ye!"

"Your old man works for Fraser Heaney," Danny said. "Makes a good wage too." He glanced at Tadhg. "He makes a good wage from your old man, don't he?"

Tadhg nodded. "He does so."

"I wonder what if we told Fraser how Darryl and them are always after ye," Danny said. "What would he do then?"

"I expect he'd have to fire him," Tadhg said. "Make an example out of him."

"I suppose you'd be on the welfare then," Danny said. "Ye'd lose your house for certain. They'd have to put you in a home, I daresay."

Darryl, even stupid as he was, understood immediately. He pulled away from Danny's grip and ran.

"He won't bother you no more now."

"I don't know," Tadhg said. "I don't trust that one." Privately he thought Danny should have given Darryl and the others a good shit-knocking to drive the lesson home. "What if he tells someone?"

"He won't tell no one." Danny slung an arm around Tadhg's shoulders, something he would have never done in the presence of other boys. Danny enjoyed no special status among his schoolmates, was neither hated nor ignored but somewhere in the middle. But he was usually careful not to draw unwanted attention to himself. And Tadhg knew well if any of the others saw Danny being friendly with him, Danny would likely get a damn good hiding some afternoon out behind the school.

"Ye got to use your brains, bhoy, not your fists." Danny punched Tadhg on the arm. "You're smarter than that crowd."

Except I'm not, Tadhg thought now. *I'm lying to everyone. I'm lying to my daughter and to my best friend. I'm lying about that bike up behind the stable.*

He always thought they would be thicker than blood, him and Danny. They would have been, if only Tadhg had been man enough to admit his part in the whole bloody mess. But nothing was ever his fault. He'd lie to the Pope if it meant getting away with something… if it meant someone else would take the blame.

Except for that one particular time in his life when he took the blame willingly, Tadhg was an accomplished liar.

A hot July afternoon, so incredibly rare, and he and Danny at the swimming hole in Kildevil Cove. It wasn't a proper swimming pool, only the wide end of a brook that someone had dammed with a makeshift wall of salvaged beach rocks worn smooth by the continual ingress of the tide, but every child in Kildevil Cove swam there. They'd taken turns jumping off the bank into the sun-warmed water, heads bent over their clasped knees, allowing themselves to sink like stones. The bottom was sprinkled with small, smooth pebbles, and near the shore wide bands of esoteric sea grass waved lazily over the dappled sediment.

Llewellyn Single was sitting on a wide, smooth rock near the water's edge, pretending to fish with his usual blue plastic rod. Someone called to him, asked if he was fishing for whales, and a chorus of jeers rose up from the assembled crowd. Roger Palmer spent a sharp-edged stone spinning into the air. It connected with Llewellyn's thigh muscle, and he let out a yelp of pain. "Going in swimming, Llew?" Roger shouted.

"You're not supposed to touch me!" Llewellyn said. Two bigger boys rose up from their place on the bank and caught him under the arms, dragging him forward. He struggled and fought, screaming for them to let him go, but they hauled him into the water, forcing him to his knees.

Tadhg surfaced too close to Nina Single, the postmaster's daughter and local teacher's pet, spraying her with water. When she objected, he did it again, to listen to her ridiculously girly shrieks and because it pleased him to do so. This attracted the ire of Niall Pelley, a ninth-grade behemoth with frizzled hair and the flat, expressionless eyes of a gargoyle. He grabbed Tadhg by the nape of his neck and held him under water until his breath failed and the world turned red. "That'll fucking learn ye," he said, when he finally let Tadhg up. Tadhg staggered into the shallows and fell down, while the shock of his near death rattled him down to the bone.

"What did he want?" Danny hadn't seen this particular exchange; he'd been giving the girls piggyback rides, diving under the water and then surfacing, tossing them into the air to land safely some distance away, soaking wet and giggling. His keen gaze took in Tadhg's expression, his blood-veined eyes. "Did that fucker do something to you?" But Tadhg didn't need to say anything. The marks of Niall's enormous thumbs were clearly visible on the sides of his neck. Tadhg looked to where Nina was sitting on the bank with some of her friends, lolling on her towel and applying lip gloss. "It was her, wasn't it?"

"You can't blame her," Tadhg said. "Sure she's only a girl." He felt his throat. It was hard to swallow. "He just came barging over." He didn't tell Danny what he knew to be the truth; Niall could have killed him quite easily. Perhaps it was what he intended. Or maybe he would have stopped in time. Niall Pelley's father worked for the Heaney family, like everybody else in Kildevil Cove. He depended on his job as plant foreman to feed his family through the winter months when the seasonal fishery was dormant and local people made do with unemployment insurance payments from the government.

"Sure he did," Danny said. "And I bet she was screaming like a stuck pig, wasn't she?"

"It's no odds," Tadhg said. But later, when he and Danny were lying on the living room carpet eating macaroni and watching *The Price is Right*, he had a thought. "We should do something."

Danny was immediately suspicious. "Like what?"

"We should send her a message."

They found a sympathy card they liked in Tadhg's father's shop, and doctored the interior so that what began as a poem of condolence turned into the most perfect vitriol. "We can't sign our own names to it," Tadhg said, so he wrote *The Lone Ranger* and Danny added *Batman*. In retrospect, it wasn't the brightest idea they'd ever had. Someone would have remembered them buying the card, and when it later showed up on Nina's doorstep, she immediately intuited who had sent it. Tadhg's father confronted him that night at supper, but he denied everything.

"I had nothing to do with it," he said. "It was Danny's idea. He did it. He even dropped it off. It wasn't me."

Within a day, the whole town knew what Danny had supposedly done. Nina's father showed up at his grandparents' house, threatening jail time, and Danny, ashamed of his own small part in the transgression, offered an apology.

"I don't accept it," Nina told him primly. "You shouldn't have done it." From then on until he left Kildevil Cove for good at eighteen, he was the local outcast, derided as mentally unstable and universally despised.

The clock on his mantelpiece chimed, and Tadhg looked up. It was after two in the morning. He'd fallen into sleep, or something very like it, with a book on his lap: Fitzgerald's *The Great Gatsby*. He'd read it before, maybe as many as a dozen times altogether, and he would read it again, he knew. Jay Gatsby was a man extraordinarily good at kidding himself, denying until the very last that the world was anything besides his own personal oyster. Tadhg rubbed his eyes and laid his head back against the chair. He was so bloody tired, but he knew he should get up and go to bed. He'd fallen asleep down here before and woke in the morning full of aches and pains. *Ye're not a little lad no more, Tadhg my son.* Groaning, he levered himself upright and moved to put the book back on the shelf.

"Dad?" Lily stood in the doorway. "What are you doing, still up?" She was wearing a pair of grey flannel sweatpants and a pink shirt with a picture of Lady Gaga. He could tell by the way she was blinking that she'd been asleep.

"What's wrong, my love?" He pushed *Gatsby* back in its usual place. "Did I wake you up?"

"No, it wasn't you." She had a set of earbuds slung around her neck. "I fell asleep listening to some music. I thought I heard something."

"I suppose you heard music," he said. He gathered her into his arms and hugged her. "Did ye have a bad dream?"

At first she wouldn't tell him, so he made them both a cup of tea and got out the biscuit tin. He sat at the table with her, sipping tea and watching her covertly.

"Dad," she began, "what does it mean to have someone under surveillance?"

Tadhg started. "That's an odd question." He dunked his biscuit into his tea and put the soggy fragments into his mouth. "Where'd you hear that to?"

"The other day, when I"—she blushed furiously, her cheeks turning a brilliant pink—"when I got lost. One of the men who came to help said it."

Tadhg ran a mental inventory of everyone who'd shown up to help that day. "Who said it, my love?"

"I don't remember his name. Alex something. That one with the dark hair who came to help Danny… I mean, Inspector Quirke."

The hair on Tadhg's forearms lifted. "He said I was under surveillance?"

Lily hesitated, breaking her biscuit into tiny pieces and arranging them around the edge of her plate. "I don't know if he said it was you or not. I didn't hear all of it."

"And he was here helping Inspector Quirke look for you."

"Yeah."

"I wouldn't worry about it," Tadhg lied. "It's probably nothing." He nodded at her cup. "Drink that, now, and go on to bed." When she'd finished he put the dirty dishes in the sink and went about turning off the lights. "Come on. Help your old man up the stairs. He's that weak he can barely move." He put a hand on her shoulder and pretended to lean on her.

"Dad, when is Danny coming back?" she asked, as Tadhg leaned down to kiss her good night after she'd settled in bed. The full moon shone outside her window, lending the surrounding landscape a curious illumination. "Can he come for Christmas?"

"You want him to spend Christmas with us?" Tadhg drew back, astonished. "He might have plans of his own, my love."

"He's got nobody," she said. "Nobody except us."

"Don't you want to go to Florida like we usually do?" Tadhg had a condo near Tampa, and even after Lily's diagnosis, they'd always spent the holidays there.

"No," she said. "I'd rather stay here. I want Christmas with you and Yvonne and Danny. I want to stay up late on Christmas Eve drinking eggnog and then get up early in the morning—"

"Not too bloody early," Tadhg said ruefully. "I'm an old man." He reached out and cupped her cheek in his hand. She was so beautiful. "What do you want for Christmas?" he asked. "That charm bracelet you showed me last week? The one with all the little horsey things on it?" Maybe he would buy her a pony. Yes, that was a good idea. They'd offer to rehome a rescued Newfoundland pony, and he'd build a beautiful stable for it and a paddock, and it could be Lily's horse, her very own. There was a little pony over on Bell Island looking for a home, he remembered now, a sweet young mare named Raisin Bun. He'd call about her in the morning, and maybe he and Danny could go over there to see her. She would make a lovely surprise for Lily on Christmas morning.

"I don't need anything," she said. There was a maturity—and a finality—in her voice that scared him. "You've always been so good to me, Dad."

"So you noticed." His voice cracked and he turned away.

Lily sat up and threw her arms around him, resting her cheek against the flat space between his shoulder blades. "Go to bed, Dad," she said, and he could feel her laughter vibrating through the bones of his back. "You're a tired old man."

Tadhg went to bed but he didn't sleep—not at first. When slumber finally overtook him, his dreams were filled with bizarre and disturbing imagery that made no sense: an empty beach lashed by waves, a bicycle driven inshore and stranded between the rocks, driftwood that resembled a floating corpse. He woke just after eight feeling shaky and unrefreshed and went down to the kitchen to make a pot of coffee. Part of the dream had been about Lily's mother, Gwen, which probably accounted for his emotional discomfort.

He wasn't in the habit of thinking about Gwen. Since he'd assumed custody of Lily, there had been perhaps half a dozen emails and one phone call. But nothing in recent years. Gwen had severed ties completely. There were no birthday cards, no Christmas gifts, no offers for Lily to come and stay for a week or two in the summer. The year before, Lily had managed to track Gwen down on Facebook, against Tadhg's wishes and his better judgement. She'd wanted to add Gwen as a friend, but the request had gone unanswered and unacknowledged. Tadhg had tried to comfort her, but Lily was inconsolable.

"She's not worth bothering about, love."

"She's my mother."

It would be better for everybody if Tadhg had found Lily in a patch of heather.

His phone rang as he was on his second cup of coffee. It was Danny. "We need to talk," he said without preamble. "Can you come into the city?"

TADHG WASN'T sure about parking his Land Rover on Warbury Street. Like everyone else, he'd heard about the girl's murder, about her torso in a suitcase and her severed head in her former boyfriend's freezer. It was one of these smaller streets below LeMarchant Road, an older part of the city known for a certain degree of lawlessness, petty thievery, and a thriving drug culture. In the end he left his car on adjoining Leslie Street, locked all the doors, and set the alarm.

Danny's apartment was on the top floor of a massive old Victorian house. Tadhg exercised regularly and considered himself in reasonably good shape for a man his age, but he was winded by the time he reached Danny's door. He paused to get his breath back before ringing the doorbell.

"Could you not live in a building with an elevator?" he asked as Danny swung the door open. "Good Christ, I just about had a heart attack climbing those stairs."

Danny didn't smile. "Come in," he said. "Have a seat. I've put the kettle on." He gestured at a large overstuffed sofa. "Or take the chair. It's up to you."

Tadhg chose the chair, a huge leather recliner near the window. The view looked out on Martin's Meadow and the Waterford Valley beyond; the Southside hills were faint rounded shapes in the distance. "Nice spot ye got here. I suppose this costs the earth." The apartment was almost aggressively masculine, decorated in rich earth tones with a lot of wood and leather. A Christopher Pratt print of a white clapboard house hung over the fireplace, against the dark blue chimney breast. The walls were lined with built-in bookshelves. Tadhg recognised the classics they'd had to read in school—*Oliver Twist* and the various Shakespeare plays—as well as several forensic volumes, including many of Elliott Leyton's books.

"Here."

Tadhg glanced up as Danny handed him a cup of tea. He took a seat opposite Tadhg, the coffee table between them. He had a notebook and a pen. *Obviously not a friendly chat, then.* "Do you ever stop being a policeman?" he asked a little sharply. He tried to soften it with a smile, but the idea of being summoned here for an interrogation irritated him.

"I'm not a policeman," Danny replied evenly. "Not anymore."

"Sure you are." A bubble of resentment welled up in Tadhg's chest. "You're probably a cop when you're on the fucking toilet." He sipped at the still-hot tea, burning his tongue.

"Why did you set up shell companies, Tadhg? There's a number of them. They have no assets and aren't publicly traded. As far as I can tell, they don't do anything at all." Danny reached for an open laptop on the coffee table, turned it so Tadhg could see the screen.

"Why would you be looking into my business affairs, Danny?" Tadhg's voice sounded hollow to his own ears. "I don't see how that's anything to do with you."

Danny carried on as if Tadhg hadn't even spoken. "You said you were in Amsterdam when your wallet was stolen."

"I *was* in bloody Amsterdam! For fuck's sake, what's this about?" He slammed the cup down so hard that some of the hot liquid slopped over the side onto Danny's immaculate coffee table. "Am I under investigation now? Is that it? Is this something you and that fucking Moira woman have cooked up?"

"So how did your wallet travel all the way from Amsterdam to Kildevil Cove on its own?"

Tadhg laughed, a strangled sound. "I can't fucking believe you. Obviously I only thought I lost it in Amsterdam. It was… it was probably in my checked luggage, and I didn't notice."

Danny said nothing, merely gazed at him with the steady look Tadhg remembered from childhood. There was very little in this world or the next, he thought, that could rattle Danny Quirke. He didn't respond to Tadhg's outburst, simply sat and waited, and something in Tadhg strained towards him, wanting to fulfill Danny's expectations, to get it off his chest. Confession was good for the soul, wasn't it? Danny should have been a fucking priest.

He took out his handkerchief—Lily made fun of him for being resolutely "old-school," but Tadhg hated to be without one—and mopped up the spilled tea. "I'm sorry if I ruined your table," he said grudgingly. "I'll pay to replace it."

Danny was silent.

Tadhg finished cleaning up and left the crumpled handkerchief on the corner of the table. "I've gone from arse to altitude looking for the right treatment for Lily," he said. "But you know that already. It's so fucking expensive in the States, but we've tried everything here." He felt the press of tears against his lids, blinked them away. Crying would only make his head ache, and he'd had enough pain lately to last him for a good long while. "She's going to die, Danny. There's not a fucking thing I can do about it. No matter which way I turn, the disease is always there. Always there."

"That doesn't explain these shell corporations," Danny said. His voice was very gentle. No doubt that was another cop technique to encourage someone to talk—pretend you care; make believe you give a sweet fuck what the other person is going through.

"I needed money for her treatment." He blinked, but the tears were gone. He was calm and dry-eyed. "Rutger van der Heide from Naxco offered me a deal."

"Why would he need to offer you a deal?"

"I owed him money. A lot of money. The year before I'd taken Lily to Russia… there's a treatment where they heat up the body and use magnets." He'd made it into a holiday for her, visiting historical sites like the Winter Palace and the Hermitage in St. Petersburg. She'd insisted on visiting the village of Dargavs, the so-called City of the Dead, even though it was a five-hour flight and Tadhg thought it morbid in the extreme. "I realise it sounds like quackery, but it's a genuine treatment."

"You couldn't pay for Lily's treatment yourself?" Danny had flipped open the notebook, but so far hadn't written anything in it. Tadhg took that as a good sign.

"I'm broke, Danny." For some reason this made him laugh. "Can you credit that? The only thing that's mine is that bloody island. I bought it for cash outright." He pressed the heels of his hands into his eyes until he saw cascading lights around the edges of his vision. "I'm that broke I can't even pay the grocery bills. I was counting on your grandfather's house, developing that and making some money off it. You know, keep the wolf from the door. I had to try. She's all I've got, Danny. Surely you can understand—"

"What was the deal with Rutger?"

"That I set up empty corporations in my name for him to use."

"For him to use." Danny jotted something in the notebook. "So he was, what? Laundering money?"

"Christ no!" Tadhg's heart thudded in his chest. "I would never be involved in something like that."

"What was it, then?"

"He was cheating on his taxes," Tadhg said sheepishly. "He had all this undeclared income, work he'd done in other countries. He was planning to hide some of it in the companies I had set up for him." Tadhg saw Danny's expression and raised his hands. "That's it."

Danny closed the notebook and tossed the pen onto the table. "You're a fucking idiot," he said quietly. "You're just lucky there's been no activity, no money in and out of these companies, or you'd be in shite up to your eyeballs." He gazed at Tadhg. "You know what you've got to do, don't you?"

Tadhg nodded.

"Close the whole works down," Danny said. "There's been no illegal activity, so you've nothing to fear. Shut it down."

"Yes," Tadhg agreed, and it sounded like a promise. "The sooner the better."

Tadhg rose to go. "Just tell me one thing," he said.

"What?"

"Who told you? About the companies, I mean." It was unlikely Rutger would make any such confession himself, which meant that somebody had been doing some digging around in Tadhg's interests. He was hardly a big enough fish to warrant that kind of attention.

"Cillian Riley."

The detective sergeant seemed to be ever-present these days. "Wouldn't think this was part of his purview."

Danny shrugged. "Sometimes the police come across bits of information that might be useful. If not to us, then to somebody else."

Tadhg picked his coat out of the closet by the door and put it on. "Interesting what you did there," he said. He buttoned his coat and felt around in the pockets for his gloves.

"What I did?"

"When you were talking about the police." Tadhg tried not to smirk, and failed. "You didn't say 'them.' You said 'us.'"

Danny shrugged. "Some habits are hard to break."

"You're a cop, Danny." Tadhg felt a sudden rush of gratitude for Danny's tactful handling of the situation, and his graciousness. "You'll always be a cop. It's in your blood."

He went downstairs and out into the pale winter sunlight, crossed onto Leslie Street, a certain lightness blooming in his chest. It would be all right now. He'd confessed to Danny; he'd come clean. To hell with Rutger and his shady dealings. Tadhg would find some way to pay him back the money he owed, but it would be legal and above board.

He'd just pressed the button on his key fob to open the Land Rover's door when a sudden rush of air made him turn around. It was too late by half and then some.

The other car came barreling around the corner and hit him at full speed, sending him hurtling into the air, his body turning slowly end over end until he fell into darkness.

CHAPTER FOURTEEN

DANNY HAD heard the screech of tires but dismissed it as the usual overhyped meth heads roaring around the neighbourhood in their tricked-out muscle cars. He pondered what Tadhg had said as he went into the kitchen to put the kettle on. Maybe he really was telling the truth; maybe he was innocent and his only crime was making dangerous deals with the devil to save his daughter's life. Family, it all came down to that in the end. Keep the ones you love close.

The sound of an ambulance siren swelled to fill the street outside. He put down his teacup and went to look. A man lay spreadeagled in the centre of the intersection, his head flung back, a dark halo of blood growing inexorably around him.

Danny wouldn't remember how he got downstairs so quickly; he only knew that he was kneeling in the street beside Tadhg, touching him with gentle fingers, listening intently for his breath. The sirens came nearer and stopped abruptly. A young blond woman in an EMT uniform got between him and Tadhg. "What happened?" she asked.

"I didn't see it," Danny replied. "I heard a car." Someone else must have seen the accident, and called it in.

"Do you know this man?"

"He's my… yes, I know him. He's a friend. He left my flat a few minutes before this happened." *I should have made him stay longer. If I made him stay, he'd be all right now.* This was nonsense. For all he knew, Tadhg might have been targeted. Maybe someone saw him go into Danny's flat and waited for him, some business associate who took exception to Tadhg's irresponsible wheeling and dealing and wanted payback.

"You need to step back now, sir." The blond EMT had been joined by a tall, ginger-haired man, who took Danny by the arm and moved him out of the way. He watched as they loaded Tadhg onto a gurney and lifted him into the ambulance.

"Is he going to be all right?" Danny asked. Tadhg's face was grey, his silvery hair matted with dark blood. Danny had never seen him so still.

"Are you his next of kin?" the blond woman asked.

"No, I'm—"

"I'm afraid we can't give out that information to a member of the public." She climbed into the ambulance, the doors were shut, and Tadhg was driven away. Danny followed in his own car, cursing the traffic and inevitable red lights that separated him from the other vehicle. He had almost arrived at the hospital when his phone rang. He pulled over to answer it. "Danny Quirke."

"Danny? It's Lily. Some lady called and said Dad was hurt."

Oh Christ. Danny squeezed his eyes shut. "He's on his way to hospital, love. I'm going with him."

"Are you in the ambulance?"

"No, I'm in my own car. Listen, Lily—"

"Is Dad going to die?"

He didn't hesitate, even though later he would curse himself for the lie. "No, my darling, that he's not. Listen, now. You stay where you're to and I'll call you as soon as I know what's on the go." His tone was half concerned relative, half police officer. "Have you got anyone to stay with you?"

"Yvonne's here. Do you want to talk to her?"

"No," he replied hastily. The last thing he wanted was having to explain the situation to Tadhg's employee. She'd find out soon enough; they all would. "I'll call you as soon as I know something." He ended the call before she could say anything else and keyed in Cillian Riley's number.

The young detective answered on the first ring. "Riley."

"Tadhg Heaney has been attacked," Danny told him. "He was coming out of my flat when he was struck by a car. I'm pretty sure it was deliberate."

"Where are you?" Riley asked. "What hospital?"

"St. Clare's." It was the closest. Tadhg would get excellent care there. "I'll meet you there," Riley said.

"Thanks." Danny huffed out a breath. "Bring your badge."

DANNY KNEW that barging into the emergency department and demanding to know where Tadhg was would get him exactly nowhere. He no longer had any jurisdiction, but he hoped Riley's badge might help. "You do realise this isn't done," Riley said. He'd arrived ten minutes after Danny's call, still dressed in his workday shirt and tie, his cheeks and nose red from the cold. "I'm considering this a favour, and don't think I won't call it in someday."

Danny found Riley's presence strangely reassuring. "They took him straight in," he said. "Right out of the ambulance. I guess he's being examined before they decide what to do."

Riley nodded. "You wait here, and I'll see what I can find out."

"What are you going to tell them?"

"That he's part of an ongoing investigation." He grinned. "I'm sure you've used that one a time or two." He clapped Danny on the shoulder.

Danny took a seat in the waiting area. Time seemed to crawl. He took a shabby *National Geographic* from a pile of ancient magazines and paged through it, looking for the naked-breasted native women he and Tadhg used to giggle over when they were boys. He remembered being fourteen and finding a yellow-backed erotic novel, *School for Courtesans*, in his grandfather's sock drawer. He'd smuggled it to school the next day, and they hid behind the stage in the auditorium, laughing themselves sick at the improbable sex acts it depicted. In the end, he deliberately lost it, throwing it over the precipice of Robber's Hill on his way home one afternoon. He watched as it sailed out into the unknown and bounced off an outcropping of rock before falling at last into the sea. If his grandfather noticed its loss, he never mentioned it.

"Do you think people really do that?" Tadhg had asked, the next day. "What was in that book. Do you think they do it?" They were sitting on the low concrete wall in front of the school, basking in the late-May sun and pretending the warm weather would last, that June wouldn't degenerate into the cold drizzle, the fog and rain typical of the annual "capelin scull." Danny had always hated the month with a passion, resented the endless dreariness necessary to ensure that millions of tiny silver fish made it safely to the island's beaches to lay their eggs. He asked his grandfather why the fish couldn't lay their eggs in sunshine. "Because they'll burn up, bhoy. If there's no capelin there's no cod, no whales, no seals, nothing." They'd gone together, he and Tadhg, in rubber boots and waterproof coats, scouring the coastline, gathering the slippery silver fish into plastic pails to use as fertiliser on Grandar's potato ground. Some people didn't even wait until the capelin came ashore but went after them with rod and reel, hauling them in one at a time like trout.

Llewellyn Single had been fishing for capelin that day, perched on an outcropping of rock over the mouth of Kildevil Cove harbour. He was standing dangerously close to the edge, despite the posted warnings, and despite the advice of everyone who knew the vagaries of the sea. It was windy that day. It was often windy on the island; a strong and sudden gust could sweep you off your feet.

Riley returned after about half an hour, grim-faced and reticent. "It's not good," he said. "The doctor suspects some kind of"—he gestured at his head—"traumatic brain injury. He wasn't responsive when they brought him in." He sat down beside Danny. "You want a coffee or something?" He grinned. "I can ask missus to put t'kettle on."

Danny laughed in spite of himself. "Your accent's not the usual St. John's Irish, is it?"

"Newcastle," Riley said. "My dad relocated here for work when I was fourteen. I guess all the salt water in the world can't shake the Geordie out of my voice completely."

A moment of companionable silence and Danny said, "Do you think they'll let me see him?"

"Nope." Riley shook his head. "Next of kin only, and even they'll have a hard time getting in." He turned in his chair so he was facing Danny. "He's in a coma. Not medically induced, either—a real coma. They've got to wait and see if he'll come out of it or no." His phone buzzed. He pulled it out of his pocket and looked at it. "I've got to take this. Sure I can't get you a coffee on my way back? Christ knows, I need one." His expression said he desperately wanted to do something to help.

"Yeah, all right," Danny said. "Go on, then."

Riley swiped the screen to accept his call and walked away. It was nearly another half an hour later before he returned, carrying two cardboard containers of coffee and a carton of Tim Horton's donut holes. "Didn't know they even had a Timmie's here," Danny said, lifting a chocolate glazed off the pile. "Thanks, by the way. What do I owe you?"

Riley waved it away. "Nothing. You can get the next one." They were quiet for a few moments, each man lost in his own thoughts. The public address system bleated endless announcements, paging various doctors and other medical personnel, reminding visitors that no smoking was permitted on hospital property. "You're close with him, aren't you?" Riley asked. The question affected Danny curiously; it sounded almost like an accusation.

"What do you mean?" he asked—too late he realised he'd been more brusque than he intended.

"I… no offence," Riley said. "It's just that… you don't seem like the sort of man who's got a lot of close friends." He shrugged. "I'm just saying." His dark-eyed gaze was incisive but not unkind.

"I've been away," Danny hedged. He peeled the plastic lid off his coffee and dropped it in a nearby bin. "In Ireland, working for a while." He took a sip of the coffee. It was hot and delicious, sweetened just right. "This coffee's perfect," he said, an effort to change the subject. "How'd you know the way I take it?"

"I don't know… you look like a one sugar, two cream, flat white kind of man." Riley's grin came and went. "You never answered me, though."

"I don't keep an active social calendar."

"Nice answer. Reminds me of an uptight Edwardian just back from the Somme, employing every euphemism he can find to avoid bandage-rolling parties with the local girls. 'Mother, I fear I shan't be well enough this afternoon.'"

Danny suspected he was being mocked, and he didn't like it. "I don't have time." He hoped that would put an end to it. "I'm going up to talk to the doctor," he said, rising from his seat. "Thanks again for the coffee."

"Can I call you later?" Riley stood up as well. "As soon as I know something I'll give you a ring."

"Thanks." Danny nodded and turned towards the bank of elevators across from the nurses' station. He didn't go up to the ICU to talk to Tadhg's doctor. He knew it was a pointless errand. The doctor was unlikely to tell him anything. Instead he left the hospital, got into his car, and drove. It was still very early, the sun just climbing above the tops of the hills, its wan winter glow now and then occluded by passing snow bands. He left the city, heading west towards some of the outlying towns—Topsail, Manuels, Upper Gullies. When he reached Holyrood he pulled into a gas station to refill his car, then turned back towards the city. At Topsail he turned off, took the narrow road leading past the bluffs and down to the beach. The snow squalls had blown away to the south, and the air was clear, with a sharp wintery bite that enlivened him. He parked and went down to the water, stood for a while with his hands in his pockets, his body hunched against the cold. He gazed out over the bay towards Bell Island and Eigus, wondering how Lily was doing, wondering if he should call her and see if she needed anything or leave well enough alone. She wasn't his daughter. She was Tadhg's daughter, Tadhg and this faceless Gwen woman, who might as well be some Highland dryad for all Danny knew about her. What sort of mother, even a non-custodial one, had no contact with her own flesh and blood?

An old man with a blue plastic carrier bag passed to his left and behind him. Danny turned and nodded to him. The plastic sack was filled with empty fizzy drink tins, beer and liquor bottles; the contents clanked quietly as the man went by. He and Danny were the only two people on the beach; it was polite to acknowledge him.

Danny knew this beach well. He'd come here with Alison all those years ago when they were first together. She liked to bring a picnic lunch and eat it sitting at one of the small wooden tables or leaning against a boulder on the rough shingle of the seashore. Afterwards, they'd follow the forest trail along the cleft between the Topsail bluffs, stopping periodically to gaze out at the sea. Alison never tired of seeing it. He'd made love to her there, her back pressed against a rock, her naked legs around his waist, their bodies clinging together. She always got a kick out of having sex in the wilderness—"doing it wild," she called it—although Danny was usually terrified of being caught. She encouraged him to go against his natural caution, to make love outdoors in all weather, to swim naked, to eat foods he'd never in his life considered, such as sushi. "But it's raw fish," he protested. "Raw fish is bait, not food." She fed it to him sitting on the floor in their living room, tiny pieces between chopsticks, slipping it into his mouth like he was an infant. Her insistence that they try new things pleased him, brought him out of himself in a way only she had ever been able to do.

He kept all these happy memories as images, a set of still frames tucked inside his mind. The fleeting sensory impressions of happier times and places kept him going after Alison got sick and during the long and painful months of her illness. There were days when the sedatives finally took hold long enough to let her sleep, and he'd make a pot of tea and sit on the window seat, gazing over the bay while the snow and sleet buffeted the glass and the north wind roared, screaming down the chimney flue. Now and then he'd kid himself that he had everything quite well in hand, that he could care for Alison better than anyone else. Of course she didn't need to go anywhere else—at first they suggested a hospital, the long-term care centre, then hospice. Danny refused them all. He would care for her himself. He'd keep her at home. She was an ideal patient; she almost never complained.

"Danny, my head hurts something shocking." This meant she wanted morphine, what they jokingly called "the hard stuff." It was supposed to make her sleep, but because of her illness, it had the opposite effect. In the beginning he administered it as tiny white tablets, taken with a glass of water or a cup of tea. Later, when it became impossible for her to swallow, a public health nurse came to show him how to inject the drug directly into her IV line. *Why the hell did you leave me?* Her leaving made him angry, and for a long time he convinced himself that all he felt was rage—not grief, not sorrow or any of the so-called gentler emotions. The notion amused him. What gentleness was there in grief, that sudden blow that cut deeper than the bone? Or the grinding sameness of sorrow, worrying away at the back of his mind like a psychic toothache?

The old man was coming back, bag in hand. He approached a metal bin and pried the lid off, dipping one hand inside, rummaging around. He glanced up to see Danny watching him. "Not bothering you, am I?"

"No sir," Danny said, "that you're not." It didn't matter. The peace was broken anyhow, if ever there was any to begin with. This was something his grandfather would often say, even as he knew otherwise: "Not bothering you, am I? I wouldn't want to pester you too much."

Danny remembered, with a sickening lurch, that sometimes he despised him.

It was different before his grandmother died. She and Danny were allies, best pals. He helped her with the garden, making up the beds that would receive the seed potatoes, carefully quartered and set into the soil. Then later in the summer, he would weed and take the old wooden wheelbarrow down to the beach to gather kelp for fertiliser, raking it over the new potato plants while mosquitoes and black flies made a proper meal of him. "Ye're a good lad," his nan would say. "Them bitches have got you barbarised, just luh!" She'd bathe his fly bites with cool water and apply chamomile lotion to soothe the itch. She was kind to him, behaved as though she needed him to help her around the house. Even when he was very young, she gave him little tasks—sweeping up the floor or emptying the rubbish bins so they could burn the contents in the woodstove. He'd tell her stories about things at school, or he'd make up fantastic tales about sea monsters to make her laugh. Her round belly would shake, and sometimes she'd laugh so hard she had to wipe her eyes with her apron. "Oh Danny, ye're so full of shite. I just dies at ye."

His grandfather was a different sort: quiet, morose, a man of few words and little sentiment. He acknowledged Danny's being insofar as Danny existed in the same space as himself. The boy was a physical fact, born of an alliance he didn't condone or approve of. Unlike Danny's grandmother, he took no interest in Danny's tales from school or the antics of his friends. While most of Kildevil Cove worked for or were beholden to the Heaney family in one way or another, Grandar never had and would never be, and he loathed them.

Danny left the beach and headed back to the city through a grey sleet that slapped and tore at his car's windshield. He was unlocking his apartment door when the landline rang. It was Moira Fraser. "Tadhg Heaney was deliberately run down," she said.

"I see." Danny unwound his scarf and tossed it over the back of the couch, then unbuttoned his coat one-handed. "So it was payback for something."

"Almost certainly," she said. "Listen, I'm in town for the day. I'd like to discuss this but not over the phone. Are you going to be home in the next little while?"

Danny glanced at the wall clock in the kitchen. It was just past eleven. "Too early for a drink, I suppose."

"Never too early, my son. Think of it as medicinal. I'll see you in a few minutes, then?"

"I'll be here."

Danny went to his laptop and pulled up his instant message program. What time was it in Portugal? Sandra might be sound asleep or out on the town, clubbing with the Australian, dancing the night away. Always the party girl, their Sandra. He typed a quick message about Tadhg's accident, hit Send, waited. But Sandra's avatar didn't pop up in the reply panel. Not online, then. He shut the lid and made a mental note to check in a few hours' time.

Moira was at the door mere moments later. Danny tugged on a heavy wool sweater and went to greet her. Besides her usual purse and laptop, she had two large grocery bags. "Here." She handed him the bags. "God knows you can't even feed yourself."

"I think you've underestimating my capabilities," Danny said. He took her coat and steered her to the sofa. "Kettle on?" The bags contained a loaf of home-baked bread, a jar of cloudberry jam, some butter, a box of Typhoo tea bags, and a bottle of Glenfiddich whisky.

"Please." She dragged the throw blanket off the back of the couch and wrapped it around her. "Aunt Sarah Maidment baked the bread. She gave me three loaves, so count yourself lucky I never kept them all for myself." Aunt Sarah wasn't related to Moira in any way; the appellation was a custom on the island, a form of showing respect to elder members of the community, and did not imply kinship. "So you and Cillian are getting on?"

Her tone struck an odd chord with him. "What d'ye mean?" He leaned out of the kitchen.

"He said you'd gone out for a beer." She turned on the sofa to look at him. "It's all right, Danny. You're allowed to have friends, you know. And he's good to get on with." She gazed at him in silence, then said, "Danny, you have to let her go sometime. She wouldn't want—"

"You don't know what she would or wouldn't want." He fought to keep his voice level. "Stop talking like you knew her. You never knew her."

"She knew about me though, didn't she?" Moira spoke quietly, but the insinuation stabbed him to the heart. "Still took you back."

"She did."

They'd discussed it in the kitchen: Alison sitting at the table, Danny standing by the island, one hand on the granite worktop, like figures in a postmodernist tableau. She'd made them both cups of tea, which neither she nor Danny drank. "I don't understand why you did it. Am I not enough for you? Is that it?"

"I don't know why I did it." This was a lie. He did it because he wanted to, because he and Moira had been sniffing around each other for months, and when she presented herself, he saw no reason to refuse her. "It was just the one time." This, too, was a lie. They made assignations at all hours of the working day, meeting in hotels or quaint Victorian B&Bs downtown. He made up excuses to go out of town. He met her in her condo overlooking the lake. They went to policing conferences together, had sex in elevators and, once, the back of a taxi. Alison didn't need to know about it, and he and Moira weren't hurting anybody. "What the eyes don't see, the heart don't feel," his grandmother used to say—but Alison had her bags packed and a taxi waiting when he pleaded with her to stay. "I think we should try again. Please, Alison, this was one mistake." It was one mistake that went on for months, and he loathed himself because of it.

"So who ran him down?" Danny asked. The image of Tadhg, lying bloodied and broken in the street, would never leave his inner vision. He hated being stuck here with Moira. He ought to be at the hospital, waiting to see if Tadhg was going to be all right. "One of his business cronies?"

"No." Moira nodded at the kettle. "That's boiled."

"It's not snapped off yet."

"You're boiling all the oxygen out of the water."

Danny poured the tea and brought both cups into the living room. He set out a jug of milk and a tray of bourbon creams. "Who, then?"

"A useless shite named Roger Palmer. He turned himself in. Bragged about it, he did, the stun fucker." She picked up her tea and took a long sip of the boiling-hot drink. "You know him?"

"Yes. He used to pester Tadhg and me when we were boys." He'd heard Palmer was doing time for assaulting his former girlfriend—hauling her by the hair around their apartment and bashing her face against the bathroom sink. It was typical behaviour. Palmer enjoyed making what he saw as lesser creatures submit.

"Llewellyn Single's cousin, as it turns out." Moira helped herself to a bourbon cream. "But you already knew that."

Yes. Llewellyn Single, who'd died fishing for capelin more than thirty years ago. Llewellyn Single, whose bones had washed ashore in Kildevil Cove. He was a year or two older than Danny and Tadhg, not particularly bright—he'd been kept back more than once at school—but seemingly normal. Until his twelfth birthday. He attacked the gym teacher during a game of floor hockey for no particular reason, pinning the man to the floor with his body and slamming his forehead into the teacher's face until his nose was broken and bloodied. He didn't seem to feel pain the way other people did, exhibited no discomfort at the cottage hospital where the doctor stitched up his forehead, cut by the gym teacher's front teeth. Llew was absent from school for a long time, and when he came back, he was never the same. He behaved like a much younger child, was prey to tantrums and sudden outbursts, and spent long periods alone, wandering through Kildevil Cove.

"Why would Llewellyn Single's cousin run Tadhg down with a car?" Danny asked. "Lord Christ, Moira, that was thirty years ago that Llewellyn died, and everybody knows it was an accident." You don't wait thirty years for revenge, Danny thought. If Roger had wanted to get back at Tadhg for what he and Danny had done, he'd had plenty of time and opportunity. "I want to see him," he said. "I want to talk to Roger Palmer."

THE PROVINCIAL lockup was located in the lower portion of the main courthouse. Palmer was in a cell by himself when Danny arrived, seated on his bunk and reading a newspaper. "The fuck do you want?"

"Mind now, Roger." Danny leaned against the bars and peered in at him. "You might frighten me."

"Yeah, ye can fly to fuck with that other fucking faggot." Palmer flicked through the pages of the newspaper peevishly, not really reading it. That was interesting, Danny thought. He was obviously ill at ease and not well pleased that Danny had shown up to see him.

"Got a good lawyer, I hope." Danny ignored the "faggot" remark. It was and always had been Palmer's epithet of choice. "They got quite a list of charges on you, my son."

Since Danny had last seen him, thirty years before, Palmer had been busily making himself a general nuisance and a pain in everybody's arse. His doting mother, Marjorie, wanted him to find useful employment and paid for him to travel elsewhere looking for it. A brief flirtation with the Alberta oil fields ended in disaster; he was similarly unsuited for mining work in Sudbury and eventually ended up back home, living with his parents. While living in Kildevil Cove, he found himself bored and at loose ends, so he stole Viney Single's postal delivery van and ran it into the front of Clive Bailey's shop. He then reversed violently, taking out most of Martin Thomas's fence before seeing Vera Belbin's little dog Toby and deliberately running him down. Palmer was the same bully Danny had always known, only with long, greasy hair and a bushy beard reaching to the middle of his chest. His neck and both arms were heavily tattooed, much of the latter readily visible below the hem of his T-shirt sleeves. He also had the usual three-dot triangular pattern on his right hand, in the web between his thumb and forefinger, a prison tattoo declaring he'd done federal time.

"Go fuck yourself," Palmer replied. "I done my time."

"Why'd you do it?" Danny asked. "Sure, what's Tadhg Heaney to you?"

"You knows fucking well." Palmer tossed aside his newspaper and rose. He was taller than Danny—he must have been about six foot six—bristling all over with a surfeit of boiling rage. "He seen Llew that day up in the cove. He knew Llew was in trouble. He could have done something, but he did sweet fuck all, that's what he did." Palmer stuck his face through the bars so his nose was inches from Danny's. "And you did fuck all as well."

"But you didn't come after me." Danny took a step back from the stench of Palmer's tobacco-laden breath.

"You were gone. Over to Ireland." Palmer turned aside and spat on the floor. "Over being the big man, weren't ye? I heard that didn't work out so well." He laughed. "Ye're the same fuck-up you always were. Some detective."

"So ye ran Tadhg down because of what happened to Llew, only you waited thirty years to do it. What took ye so long?"

"I was inside," Palmer said.

"Come on, now, Roger. There's got to be more to it than that." Danny fought to keep his voice calm, but there was anger in him. Anger that a piece of shite like Roger Palmer could run someone down in the road like it meant nothing to him. Like they were nothing. "Been sitting down in Her Majesty's all this time, dreaming of what you were going to do when you got out? Making plans, I suppose."

"You knows sweet fuck all," Palmer said. "I just got out. I never had a cent to me name. Somebody offers me a bit of work, and I'm going to take it."

"What kind of work?"

Palmer shrugged. "Now see, that would be telling. They paid me a few bucks extra to keep me mouth shut." His skeevy grin made Danny itch to punch him in the mouth.

"Who paid you?" he asked. "Let me guess—he had someone else contact you. You never learned his name. It was all done over the internet. You met in a café. He was the blind man smoking two pipes?"

"That was always your trouble, Dan, my son." Palmer laughed explosively. "Ye reads too many fuckin' books, ye do."

Danny bristled. No one ever called him 'Dan.' "Who paid you?"

"Some fella from Clarke's Beach, Bareneed, out that way."

"Did he have a foreign accent?"

"Yes, bhoy, he talked like he was from Clarke's Beach." Palmer rattled the bars experimentally. "Listen, tell the cops they can let me out now. I'm after learning me lesson." He laughed again, the guttural bark Danny remembered so well from childhood. "Is he dead, Tadhg Heaney?"

"No. He's not dead." Danny's hands clenched into fists. In his pocket, his cell phone buzzed, but he ignored it. "Is that what you were supposed to do? Kill him?" His phone buzzed again. He took it out of his pocket. Cillian Riley. Danny swiped the screen to accept the call and walked away from Palmer's cell. "What is it?"

"You better come back to St. Clare's," Riley said. "He's after throwing a clot. It's not looking good."

"What do you mean?" Danny struggled to comprehend what Riley was saying.

"He's not going to last much longer. Father Kelly is here. You better come."

CHAPTER FIFTEEN

IT WAS a hot day. That entire summer had been punishingly hot, breaking century-old records. The days were particularly windless, and the feeble breeze that sometimes sprang up after sunset was unable to cool their houses enough for people to sleep. The fishermen rose early, sometimes before their usual 4:00 a.m., seeking the cooler air lying over the water. Tadhg often woke to hear them as they left the harbour, listening to the slow thump of their inboard motors and their murmured conversations. It was the same summer Elihu Bungay beat his teenaged daughter Eunice nearly to death, enraged that she'd fallen pregnant for Harry Tuck's young fellow, that he caught them copulating in the school bus shelter down on Belgium Road. His rage put Eunice in the hospital with a broken collarbone and drove the unwanted baby from her. People shook their heads and made tutting noises. *That's 'Lihu for ye.* Elihu was cracked, sure; all the Bungays had a filthy temper, every single one.

Tadhg had a summer job working in his father's shop, Heaney's Dry Goods, unpacking shipments upstairs in the attic, a physical job he liked because it worked his muscles, hauling up boxes and bales of sewing fabric through the loading hole, using only his grandfather's ancient block and tackle. He'd been saving whatever money he made, hoping to have enough to buy a ring for Danny Quirke's sister Sandra. He was going to ask her to marry him, hopefully by the end of the summer, but more likely he would propose to her at Christmas. That's how things were done in Kildevil Cove. Everyone got engaged at Christmas. But this one particular day in late July, an expected shipment of goods hadn't arrived from Spaniard's Bay. Tadhg's father, in one of his rare good moods, gave him the afternoon off. Tadhg went looking for Danny.

He found him idling around the front steps of Clive Bailey's shop with Rayfield Barrett and some other boys. Like most days that summer, they were stood around gatching, making bloody fools of themselves, flicking rocks at the few seagulls brave enough or hungry enough to try for the half-rotted hotdog wiener left lying in the road. Danny pushed away from the railing when he saw Tadhg, came forward to meet him. "What are ye at, my son? Queer thing to see you around this end of town."

"Some hot," Tadhg replied. "Enough to burn a hole in ye." It was the kind of meaningless chatter they usually engaged in, having nothing of greater seriousness to say. Danny jerked his chin at the other boys, and he and Tadhg headed for the Point. The heat rose in waves off the asphalt, forming a shimmering haze in the near distance. "You going swimming?" Danny asked. "It's hot enough." He wore his swimming trunks underneath his clothes in the summertime. It was easier than having to run home to change, Tadhg supposed.

"No," Tadhg replied. "Mam said there's a stomach flu going around and not to go in the water." He shook his head. "Lord Jesus, bhoy, I had that last summer and I was on the toilet for a week. Had it coming out both ends, I did."

"I always knew ye were full of shite," Danny said mildly. They had reached the end of the pavement, where the road narrowed to a dusty gravel path.

"Where's Sandra to?" Tadhg asked suddenly. "We should see if she wants to go swimming." If Sandra went, Tadhg would go in. He'd have to go in.

"Oh, for fuck sake," Danny said. "That's all I wants now I know, her hanging around. She got me fucking drove, her and Debbie Rogers over to the house all the time, doing each other's hair and putting on makeup."

Tadhg fell silent, wounded by Danny's vehemence. Then he said, "She never goes swimming anyway. I haven't seen her in the brook, not once this summer."

"She's sick," Danny said. "She told Nan she was all the time throwing up. I suppose she got a stomach bug, I don't know." Something up ahead caught his attention; he caught hold of Tadhg's arm. "What the Jesus is he at, atall?"

Right at the spot where the land jutted out into the sea, a boy was fishing with a rod and reel. He was wearing a pair of cutoff jean shorts, and his feet were bare.

"Capelin are right late this year," Tadhg observed. They watched as the boy flicked his line out with practiced ease and reeled it back in.

"He'd be better off picking them up in a bucket down to Melbourne Beach," Danny said. "The stun fucker is going to be killed if he keeps that up."

Llewellyn Single balanced on his toes, leaning far forward over the water. He overbalanced, stumbled, caught himself. Even from this distance they could see his bare toes gripping the naked rock.

"Llew, my son, get in out of it!" Danny called. "You'll fall and break your neck." But he wouldn't break his neck, Tadhg thought. He'd drown in the roiling waves that rushed and foamed around the base of the cliff.

Llew shouted some words, but he was too far away for them to hear him plainly. He might have said anything at all. "Come in out of it, bhoy!" Tadhg shouted. He turned to Danny and laughed, called to Llew again. "Come in out of it. Sure your mother got buns in the oven."

"We'll go sit on the government wharf," Danny said, "keep an eye on him." They scrambled down over the bank, heels and hands skidding on loose rocks. From here they could see him, reeling in his line, picking the small, silvery fish off the end, dropping them into the empty salt-beef bucket at his side.

The wind freshened from the east, ruffling the branches of the alder trees, turning the grass in Barrett's meadow into an undulating carpet of the deepest green. They grew bored, watching the small white dories rocking gently at anchor. Tadhg plucked dandelions from the grass and blew on them, dispersing the seeds. Dandelion clocks, they'd always called them. You could tell the hour by how many breaths it took to blow away the seeds. Tadhg remembered his grandmother telling him when he was just a little boy—how to do it, and how to find the wind's direction, to know whether a storm was imminent by how high the seagulls flew. Useless knowledge. He knew that now. All of his knowledge was little better than useless. They ought to teach children more useful things, like how to apologise when you hurt someone, or what to say to God after you died.

He glanced behind him, back towards the town, but the group of boys had deserted the front steps of the shop. Someone on a bike was turning slow circles at the far end of the road where it met the main highway: a tall, skinny figure with wild hair and dark sunglasses, still too far away to see clearly. The road was otherwise deserted.

Tadhg turned around in time to see Llewellyn Single fall to his death.

It was like a scene from a cartoon, the boy stepping out into empty space, his arms cartwheeling violently as he fought to regain his balance. "Oh my God." Danny was on his feet. "We might be able to help him." They both dropped directly into the shallow water at the landward end of the wharf, splashing towards the point of land where Llewellyn fell. They waded as far as they could, the icy water quickly saturating them. Tadhg stopped when it reached his chin, looking down into the chilly depths. The water calmed, smoothing itself out into a mirrored surface, and he could see himself reflected there. His face and Llew's. Yes, it was definitely there, the resemblance. But it would be all right. Nobody knew. No one in Kildevil Cove knew the truth except Tadhg... and Danny's grandfather. "I can't go any farther," he gasped. He stumbled, struck out blindly, grabbing for Danny's sleeve while the current swirled and sucked at them, threatening to pull them under.

And then Tadhg was on dry land again, standing on the road in front of Harvey Matthews's twine loft, and the figure on the bicycle was coming closer, riding straight for him with enraged ferocity, striking him, running him down.

He sat up with a gasp. "You're not awake," a voice said. "You're not really awake now." The room around him was familiar: not his own bedroom on Eigus, but the room he'd slept in as a boy, with his model battleships on a shelf above his head and the rock star posters on the wall. If he turned a little to his left, he'd see the closed door with the Kiss poster taped to it, ruining the pale blue paint his mother had sent to the mainland for, a particular shade between turquoise and robin's egg, not quite the blue of an early summer sky. It was not much after dawn and already hot. The day would be a scorcher, hot enough to split the rocks. If his father didn't need him in the shop he'd go fetch Deiniol Quirke, and the two of them would ride their bikes down to Melbourne beach. He got out of bed, yawned and stretched, ignored the morning's piss erection, pulled his clothes on. He was of an age to shave now, had been for several years, but today he wouldn't bother. He opened his bedroom door. Everything had changed.

"Dad?" Lily's voice reached him from a long ways off. "It's me, it's Lily."

You're not awake. "Lily." He tried to speak but couldn't make a sound. "I'm right here. Dad loves you, Lily." Then he and Danny were boys again, throwing snowballs in the road when school let out for Christmas holidays, building complicated igloos with long tunnels leading to adjoining rooms and a spyhole at the top. It was summer, and they were deep in the woods behind Danny's house, nailing together bits of plywood and discarded lumber to make a camp. They hid from Sandra there, ignored her calls when Danny's twin came looking for them. They told each other lies about girls, smoked stolen cigarettes together, and lay on still summer nights looking up at the stars. "I'm going to be an astronaut," Danny told him. He never did, though. Danny was a cop. He'd always been a cop. It was autumn, with icy wind and the cold sound of chainsaws cutting logs, and he and Danny stacked loads of firewood, getting it laid in for the winter. "Your old man don't bother with the woodstove," Danny had said, bitterly. "I suppose the Heaneys can afford to have the electric on. Ye crowd got money to burn."

"Tadhg."

He forced his eyes open. Danny's face was so close, Tadhg could have counted every hair in his eyebrows. Then Danny went away and someone was shining a bright light, peering into him. "Can ye hear me, Mr. Heaney?" A woman's voice, unnecessarily loud and strident. "Don't try to talk. You've still got a tube in your throat."

Danny was here, Tadhg thought as his awareness faded. *I know he was. What'd he come here for?*

He was elsewhere now, in an empty twine loft near Barrett's meadow. It was a mauzy day in midsummer, and the sea was a leaden cloak slopping listlessly over the rocks. Flies rose in clouds from the dead capelin littering the shore. "Of course I'll marry ye," Tadhg said. The air, abnormally still, felt dead. He'd given the answer already, before the question was even asked.

Sandra stood in the doorway, her arms crossed on her chest. "I s'pose Danny told ye," she said bitterly. "He can't keep his fucking mouth shut for love nor money." She wore a Mickey Mouse T-shirt and a pair of cutoff jean shorts. Her bare feet were shoved into a pair of canvas sneakers. Her knees were dirty. "I knows it was you," she said. "There wasn't no one else except for you."

Some part of him knew this was a lie. In this curious in-between place, things made sense to him. He wasn't confused anymore. *It wasn't me. It wasn't me and you know it.* He could only think the words; he couldn't say them. *You lied.*

"You haven't got to marry me," Sandra told him. "I'm going to stay with Aunt Pearl for a while. It'll all be over when I gets back."

"Tadhg." Danny's voice again. Tadhg forced his eyelids open like he was lifting the lid of a coffin, and it was so difficult. It was the hardest thing he'd ever had to do.

"It wasn't me," Tadhg said. It was little more than a harsh whisper, but perhaps Danny had heard him. Perhaps Danny understood.

TADHG'S ROOM was dark, quiet except for the beeping of monitors. He'd been placed in a special unit for traumatic brain injury patients and was sequestered in a room by himself. Danny had been given five minutes with him, but so far all he'd done was sit by Tadhg's bed looking at him.

"Imagine," Danny said at last, "me and you in here. Queer old business, what?" He reached out to smooth the blanket over the tangle of wires and leads at Tadhg's chest. "Some queer. I suppose Sandra would be laughing her arse off if she could see ye." Tadhg was paler and more still than Danny had ever seen him, and it wasn't right. This wasn't the Tadhg he knew. He'd been in touch with Yvonne and had sent regular texts to keep her updated about Tadhg's condition. Lily hadn't been told the entire extent of her father's injuries, only that Tadhg had been in a traffic accident and was recovering in hospital. He'd also emailed his sister Sandra with the news, certain she would want to know. She'd emailed back immediately.

Do you want me to come over? I can be there in a day.

But he'd demurred, put her off as gently as possible. *There's no need. I'll let you know when he wakes up.*

"Listen now." Danny reached out and took hold of Tadhg's hand, squeezing lightly. "Sandra was asking for ye. She said she's sending good energy." Danny laughed. "She's right into that stuff, if ye can believe it." He thought about Sandra as a young girl, the Sandra he and Tadhg knew who despised anything spiritual or religious, who'd shocked their grandfather nearly into his grave when she told him the Bible was "a load of old shite." His memory suddenly held two images of Sandra, before and after…. Sandra the day she told him she was pregnant, sitting on his bed in her Bay City Rollers T-shirt and cutoffs, rigid and white-faced… then Sandra walking in the road from the school bus stop, a dark stain spreading on her jeans, her books clutched against her chest. The thing he could never forgive Tadhg Heaney for, getting his sister pregnant. He remembered Sandra sobbing behind the bathroom door while their grandmother murmured useless words of comfort. "It's for the best," she said later, when Sandra had bathed and gone to bed with a hot water bottle. She had lost the baby. "Some of the hardest things are for the best."

Weeks later, Danny had gone into the stable at the top of his grandparents' property, looking for some prosaic thing, a tool to fix his bicycle with, perhaps. There was a heavy wooden chest under the workbench, a crate that once held soft-drink bottles. He dragged it out with some difficulty and rummaged through it, choosing and discarding wrenches and chisels, laying each one on the wooden floor beside him. When he came upon it, he didn't know what it was at first: a scrap of nylon rolled into a bundle and tied with butcher's twine. He worked the knot until it came loose, unrolled the fabric, and stared, repulsed. It was a woman's nightgown, a diaphanous thing of netting and lace, with satin ribbons down the front arranged in little bows—a negligee, the sort of thing a bride would wear on her wedding night. It was stiff with dried blood.

He dropped it on the floor and sat back on his heels, looking at it. It was late afternoon on a warm, early-September day. The air smelled of clover and drying hay. Nothing could ever be wrong in a place like this. But there it was, a bloodstained nightgown, rolled into a ball and hidden under a pile of tools in a wooden box too heavy for almost anyone to lift. He remembered telling Tadhg what he'd found and Tadhg looking at him like he couldn't believe it. "Maybe the night she lost the baby, she bled all over it," Tadhg had said.

Danny had countered by asking who would wear a filmy negligee to lose their baby? Wouldn't a woman in such physical and emotional distress crave comfort? "She'd wear a flannel nightie," Danny said, "but not something like this. Never something like this."

A shadow fell across the doorway, snapping Danny abruptly back to the present. It was the priest someone—surely not Tadhg—had summoned, to administer the last rites.

"Not yet," Danny snapped. "He's not dead just yet. Ye can wait a few more minutes." The shadow receded. "She said you got to stop this bloody foolishness and get out of this bed, right now." He pleated an edge of the blanket between his fingertips. "She said that herself."

Tadhg's head moved on the pillow, only a little at first, a downward, sideways motion like he was trying to scratch his cheek. It was uncannily like Danny's own unconscious gesture for weeks after the incident at the Clontarf seawall, when he'd been splattered by Eamonn Nolan's blood. Tadhg's shoulders rose off the bed, and an expression of unease flickered on his features. His eyes flew open. He was lucid, gazing at Danny with recognition. "It wasn't me, Deiniol."

"You don't need to talk," Danny said. "Just rest. I'll get the nurse—"

Tadhg caught hold of his wrist. His grip was surprisingly strong. "No. You got to listen, Danny." He was as insistent as Danny had ever seen him. "I didn't get Sandra pregnant. Sandra and I never... we never did that."

Danny was absolutely gobsmacked. He'd taken it as gospel that Sandra and Tadhg were going at it like rabbits and that's how she'd gotten pregnant. "But you were planning to get married to her."

"She wanted to wait." Tadhg closed his eyes and took a deep breath. Danny assumed he was tired, and rose to go. "It wasn't me," he repeated. "He sent me letters, you know."

"Who sent you letters?" Danny asked. He should go. He should let Tadhg rest, but the policeman in him needed to know the facts. He glanced at the doorway, but no one was watching.

"The old man," Tadhg whispered. His face was ashen, and he looked terrified. "We'd made a pact, ye see. He knew about Mam and what she did. He said he'd tell everybody." He sighed and let go of Danny's wrist. "I'll tell you all of it the once, when I'm out of here. But it wasn't me. It was your grandfather."

"My grandfather...." It took a moment before Danny managed to put it all together. "You mean Grandar and Sandra...?" He knew he shouldn't be pushing Tadhg to talk, but he had to know. He had to know if what Tadhg had told him was the truth.

"He was at her for years," Tadhg murmured. "I sent him money, so much every month."

"He was blackmailing you?"

Tadhg nodded. It seemed to take the last of his strength.

"I… didn't know." Danny looked up as the doctor came in. "I'm going," he said. "I am." He touched Tadhg's shoulder. "I'll be back soon." He forced a smile on his face, even though he was still reeling from what Tadhg had told him. "Bring ye a fizzy drink and a shop bun." He wanted to ask what his grandfather had been blackmailing Tadhg about, but not now. There would be time for deeper investigation later.

"Listen, now." Tadhg caught Danny's sleeve. "Give Lily a call, will you? Tell her you've seen me, and I'm all right."

"Of course." Danny paused. "She'll want to see you. I can fetch her if you like."

Tadhg nodded. "Give it a day or so. I don't want her to see me like this."

"Okay." Danny hovered for a moment, shoulders hunched, hands shoved into his pockets. "I'll call her first thing in the morning." There was more he wanted to say, but now wasn't the time.

"Bring her to Kildevil Cove," Tadhg murmured. He seemed to be slipping back into sleep. "She'll like that."

Danny laid his palm against Tadhg's cheek. *Christ, I love you. I've loved your sorry arse for years.*

ALL THESE years and the blackmail letters found Tadhg no matter where he was in the world. He could be in Malaysia or Outer Mongolia, and the same plain white envelope always managed to track him down. He was being watched. Someone always knew where he was. It was far too precise to be merely luck.

Finding out that it was Danny Quirke's grandfather didn't surprise him. The old man held an almighty grudge. He'd expected Tadhg would go quietly all those years ago, take the blame the old man had so eagerly foisted upon him, and he was outraged to be proven wrong. They'd almost come to blows one night in the kitchen when Tadhg had gone to ask him what he planned to do about Sandra. She told me, Tadhg said. "She told me everything about you, what you did, what you've been doing all these years." The old man grabbed him by the throat and shoved him back against the woodstove. There was strength in those gnarled old fingers even at his age, his hands made powerful by many years of hauling nets and chopping firewood. He held Tadhg there until Tadhg was seeing stars. "You mind who you're talking to. I'll fuckin' gut you."

The nightgown was another matter—or maybe it was the only matter. He'd given it to Sandra for her to wear on their wedding night. "Maybe I'll try it out beforehand," she said, laughing at his shocked expression. "No, bhoy, not like that. Ye're not getting near me till you puts a ring on my finger. You needn't think it." She was going to wear it to bed that night, she said, to see how it looked. "I'll give ye a full report."

"You're a friggin' cock-tease, you are," Tadhg said. But he didn't really mind. Their wedding night wouldn't be his first time, but it would be hers.

Or so he'd thought. The illusion was shattered the next time he saw her, red-faced and crying, standing at his mother's front door. She'd brought the nightgown with her in a brown paper bag. The first thing Tadhg asked her was "Does Deiniol know?"

No one knew, she told him. The old man swore her to secrecy. He said if she ever told anyone, he'd kill her. He'd kill her pet cat, Sam. He killed the cat anyway—gave him a hundred aspirins and shut him in the garage with the car running. It was the single cruellest thing he had ever done, but he defended it by saying the cat was old and sick, and it was time he was gone anyway.

"I can forgive a lot," Sandra said, "but not that. There was no need of that."

Deiniol didn't know. As soon as high school ended, Danny was gone, off to university and then to the police academy on Prince Edward Island, a world away as far as Sandra was concerned. It angered Tadhg that Danny had left her. Surely to God he must have known something was going on, seeing as how he lived in the same house as his sister.

"What didn't he know?" Tadhg asked her. "What was he aware of, anything or nothing?"

He'd known she was pregnant, Sandra said, but she let him think it was Tadhg who did it. "I didn't want anyone to know what the old man did. It's all bad enough." The knowledge of it, in a town as small as

Kildevil Cove, would shame her. She'd be talked about. She'd be stared at in the shops. Tadhg wouldn't put her through that.

"Tell Deiniol it was me." Anything to spare her. Of course Danny took this as licence to find Tadhg one afternoon, working in his dad's warehouse, and pound the living daylights out of him. Tadhg took the beating—willingly—and didn't bother fighting back.

"That's how much of a fucking coward you are," Danny had said, standing over him while Tadhg wiped the blood from his mouth with the tail of his shirt. "Ye're a fucking liar, that's what you are. Stay away from my sister." And so his and Danny's friendship ended; Danny despised him.

The doctor's head and shoulders blocked out the ambient light. He leaned over Tadhg and flashed a light in his eyes. "I guess it worked," he said. "We gave you a drop of the good stuff." He grinned. "It's a drug that breaks up the clot, dissolves it harmlessly. You're lucky. You could have died. How do you feel?"

"When can I leave?" Tadhg asked.

"Ye're not going nowhere yet, bhoy." The doctor made some notes on Tadhg's chart. "You cracked a couple of your ribs, and you're bruised from top to bottom. Ye've got a while yet, my son."

Tadhg didn't bother protesting. He was much too tired. He lay back on his pillows and let sleep take him for a while.

IT WAS after midnight when Danny let himself into his flat. He didn't bother to turn on any lights, but the tiny bulb over the stove gave sufficient illumination. He planned a short stop, just long enough to pack an overnight bag before he made his way back to Kildevil Cove. The things Tadhg had told him, the truths he'd willingly unearthed—Danny needed to be there.

There was a small snowdrift of mail waiting inside the door. He bent and picked it up, arranging the envelopes into a small stack. Light bill, phone bill, letter from the city council advising of a planned water shutoff in the area. At the bottom was a pale yellow envelope with an Irish stamp and a Dublin postmark. Danny's heart stuttered, paused, started up again with a godawful thump. The return address was the headquarters of An Garda Síochána.

He groped his way to the living room and sank down on the couch, reaching for the small lamp on the end table. It couldn't be anything good. There was no way in God's green earth it was good news. He stuck his index finger under the flap and tore it open, drew out a single sheet of paper.

Further to the recent inquiry into the incident at the Clontarf sea wall—

Danny couldn't breathe. He skipped to the end of the sentence: *You have been cleared of all wrongdoing, and any charges pending against you have been dismissed.*

"Fuck," he said. It echoed hollowly in the empty apartment. "Fuck." He pressed the heels of his hands into his eyes and listened to himself breathe. It was over. He looked at the paper again, reread the letter. He wasn't responsible for what had happened. An inquiry had proven it.

It was over. Surely now his life could go back to being normal.

He went into the bathroom and ran the tub. Every muscle in his body ached, and all he wanted to do was sink into a hot bath and relax. He fetched a bottle of Glenfiddich and a glass from the kitchen and laid them on top of the laundry hamper in easy reach of the tub. He put his phone there too, just in case. Then he sank into the water with a luxurious sigh. He was still there forty minutes later, the Glenfiddich having pleasantly anaesthetised him into a half-dozing state where he wasn't quite dreaming.

His phone rang, but he ignored it and poured himself another two fingers of Scotch. He'd told Tadhg he would call Lily, but it was too late for that now. He doubted it was her calling, but he opened one eye to check the screen, just in case.

Rory Fraser.

Danny opened both eyes, blinking in confusion. Why would Rory Fraser be calling him, and especially at this hour? He was the last person Danny wanted to talk to, especially after their unpleasant meeting down at the lake. He set the ringer to mute and laid the phone face up on the laundry hamper. Four more times it lit up blue while Danny lay in the tub watching it. Every single time the caller was Rory Fraser.

Chapter Sixteen

He smelled the fire before he saw it—a gust of smoke and ash riding the wind. By the time Danny had crested Robber's Hill, he could also see it. His grandfather's house was burning. A late-night long-distance phone call from the village had woken him out of a sound sleep. Harve Tuck, a neighbour, apologised for waking him. "Your grandfather's house is on fire," he said. "I looked out the window just now and seen it. I would have called earlier, but I only seen it just now."

Danny had stumbled out of bed, still groggy, and dragged his clothes on. He'd driven to Kildevil Cove the moment he got the call, and the hundred-mile journey had tired him more than he expected.

It was very early in the morning, or it was the middle of the night, he wasn't sure. His sense of time was distorted, pulled out of shape. He parked at the bottom of the lane, far enough away that the fire was no danger, and got out of his car. He could go no farther than the front gate before the heat of the lingering blaze forced him back. A small group of locals had gathered to one side of the fire, huddled up against the cold with their hands in their pockets. He was too late. The house was gone. If he'd had more time, he would have been able to save it, but he hadn't and there *was* no time, not anymore. He went to stand next to Stan Pynn, who'd served in the same British Army unit as Danny's grandar.

"It's shocking, what's after happening," Stan said. He nodded at what remained of the house. "Break your heart, it would." He shook his head slowly. "Alan English and them are on the way down with the truck and hoses, but I don't think it's going to make much difference."

"No," Danny said, agreeing with him. "I think the damage is done." The night was bitterly cold, the sky a bolt of dark velvet, stippled with stars. There were so many stars, he thought, as many as the night his parents left, as many as the night his grandmother passed. Sandra had called him at his apartment in the city. "Nan's gone." He'd stepped out onto the fire escape and looked up at the sky, and there they were, millions upon millions of them, all the stars that ever were. He could see the outstretched arm of the galaxy, its edges dappled with variegated points of light, all of it so far away now, so far from him. The night sky, the sight of the stars, that enormous swath of darkest blue—it awed him beyond the power of words.

The night his parents had left Grandar's house for the last time, there had been a vicious argument. Danny and Sandra were little, four years old, and they crouched together on the stairs, listening to the adults fighting. It seemed to go on forever. A sudden gust of wind blew the front door open, rattling the windows and the closed doors of all the upstairs rooms. That had been a clear night, too, with all the stars spread out across the sky and a meteor that fell into the atmosphere, passing close overhead before burning itself to ash and dying in the sea. Danny knew this because he'd left the stairs and Sandra and ran outdoors in his pyjamas, calling after his mam and dad. "Come back for me. Don't go without me."

His grandfather was angry; he had a long stick in his hand. "You talk to me like that in my own fucking house, will ye?" In his child's innocence, he assumed his parents were going on a trip. He figured they'd be back. But his father was too angry; he shouldn't have tried to drive, and when they ran into a moose just outside Cavendish, no one survived.

The ululating blare of the fire truck's siren dragged him back into the present. The crowd moved aside to make room as several firefighters—all local, all volunteers—jumped down and dragged their hoses into the yard.

"It's no sense, bhoy." Danny shook his head. No one could hear him over the cacophony, but he was talking mostly to himself anyway. "The whole thing's gone." Already several men were hacking at the structure with axes, revealing great swaths of the living room as the walls fell away. The front of the house, directly in the path of the prevailing wind, had already burned to the foundation. In moments there would be nothing left. He took out his cell phone, thinking to call Tadhg, then remembered that he was still in hospital, and what was the use, anyway? There was nothing Tadhg could do. There was nothing anyone could do. The firefighters managed to knock the blaze down to a pile of smouldering embers within the hour. The house, crafted of dry ancient timbers, burned incredibly hot and incredibly fast. In the end, nothing was left beyond the concrete foundation. When the firefighters and the last of the spectators had gone, Danny moved closer, wanting to get a last look at the remains of his childhood home.

There would be an investigation, he thought, as the stench of burned timber rose into his nostrils. They'd find out how the fire happened, whether it was started deliberately or if there had been a fault in the wiring. Blame would be either laid or lifted, according to the investigation's outcome. It didn't matter either way. The house was irrevocably destroyed. Danny remembered the wad of cash Cillian Riley had found in the wall, wondered if there was more. What else was hidden in the ruins of the house? Apart from the family photos and his grandfather's few belongings, some of his and Sandra's childhood toys, what was left of the lives they'd led there? Nothing of consequence.

"I know what he is," Sandra had said, when Danny had called to tell her about the old man's death. He hadn't expected her to attend the funeral and had torn a strip off her about it, but now he understood. That would have been too much for anyone who'd suffered at the old man's hands the way she had. All those years, Danny mused, and nobody noticed. Instead, they blamed Tadhg Heaney, and Tadhg had taken it, willingly, and never told a soul—taken it, and stood for the old man's blackmail, his insistence that Tadhg vouchsafe the agreement they'd made. If anybody asked, Sandra was pregnant by Tadhg and nobody else. It didn't make sense, Danny thought. The old man was to blame, so why was Tadhg giving him money? Shouldn't it have been the other way around? Shouldn't Danny's grandar have paid Tadhg to ensure his silence?

He walked around to what had been the rear of the house, the side facing the stable on the hill. The fire had burned so hot that the nearby fir and spruce trees were singed, their branches black and twisted, and the stable's white clapboard was dark with soot. Danny opened the door and went inside, holding his cell phone out in front of him, using it as a flashlight. Nothing had changed. The lower floor was scattered sawdust, and the walls were stacked with the firewood his grandfather had stored away for winter. The small room smelled of brined codfish, and in the corner he saw the overturned puncheon tub Grandar used to soak the fillets before drying them outdoors on the wooden racks called flakes. It had been Danny's job to watch the fish as it dried, and also to watch the sky, because if it rained and the fish got wet, it was ruined.

He had taken this responsibility very seriously. On summer afternoons he'd take a book and sat just inside the stable door, in close view of the flakes, keeping careful watch. He could see the front door of the house from there, watching Sandra or his grandmother going back and forth, bringing vegetables up from the cellar, letting the cat out. His grandmother was extraordinarily solicitous to Sandra, more so than him, but he always supposed that was because she was a girl. He didn't need the extra attention that his nan lavished on his sister; being doted on that way would embarrass him.

Sometimes on lazy summer afternoons, he'd tip his chair back against the wall and doze, listening to the hum of bees in the meadowsweet and yarrow that grew along the fence. He passed hours this way, the heat of the sun making him drowsy to the point of drunkenness, while the little world of Kildevil Cove went on about its business. Often his grandfather would return early from the fishing grounds, with three or four fat codfish strung up on a length of twine or a bucket of fresh mussels or an errant lobster he'd found lounging in the rocks along the shoreline. "He's a big bugger, ent he? Never even seen me coming."

He was sitting this way one afternoon when Tadhg approached, walking slowly down the lane, wheeling a bicycle in front of him. It wasn't his—it was much too small for him, and besides, Tadhg's father wouldn't let him be seen on such a shabby-looking thing—and Danny couldn't figure out what he was doing with it. "Where'd you find that?" he asked. "Been hanging around the dump, have ye?"

"Keep this for me, will ye?" Tadhg asked. "Just put it in the stable, and don't say nothing." He wouldn't tell Danny where he got it or what he intended to do with it.

"Did you steal it?"

"Nah. Just borrowing it, that's all."

"Who owns it?" Danny asked—and Tadhg had given him the usual grin and said, "Never you mind."

It was Llew Single's bike, ill-used and rusted to its spokes, the ragged seat patched with duct tape.

Maybe it was better that the house was gone. All of his bad memories were tied up in it. Maybe the house being gone was for the best. He'd sell Tadhg the land if he still wanted it, and Tadhg could build whatever he liked. It was no odds to Danny.

Why had he even come back here? Because Grandar had died, and it fell to Danny to take care of things. There was no one else. His nan was dead, and Sandra was in Portugal, not inclined to come back here for love nor money. He couldn't blame her. He sighed, drawing in the scent of smoke and sending it back out, thinking suddenly of Alison. *I wish you were here. I wish I had you to talk to.* He wished Tadhg were here, because he needed to tell him about the house, but it could wait. He didn't even know the cause of the fire yet, whether it was faulty wiring or arson or something else entirely—and Tadhg needed to rest and recover. He wasn't up to taking a late-night phone call from Danny or from anyone else.

He got into his car and drove the short distance back to his rented house on the point. It was bitterly cold, and the wind had freshened from the east. He shivered as he fit the key into the lock and pushed open his door.

Someone had been in the house. He wasn't sure how he knew this, but he did. Absolutely nothing was out of place, but in the past hour or so, someone had passed through, leaving a trace of their scent behind. It couldn't have been more than an hour, else the lingering hint of perfume… aftershave… whatever it was, would have long since vanished. For a fleeting moment, Danny thought of his service weapon and how he no longer had it—and how he wished it were as easily to hand as it had once been. There was nothing nearby that he could use for a weapon, except for perhaps the antique lamp on the end table, and he didn't think his landlady would appreciate that.

"Hello?" he called, edging along the living room wall to the kitchen. "Is somebody here?" He felt for the light switch and turned it on, but the only person he saw was himself, reflected in the window opposite.

He strained to listen in the silence, but there was nothing except the rhythmic dripping of the bathroom tap. "If you're in here, come out. I just want to talk to you." His mind's eye provided an image of the Clontarf sea wall in Dublin, him stood there calling out to something he couldn't see. Not Eamonn Nolan, but the dark thing that haunted him, that hung from his shoulders like a ceremonial cloak. The logical, police-trained part of him said this was nonsense; he was imagining things. But Danny could feel it, a palpable presence that sat between them—watching, waiting. He'd wondered if anyone else at the scene was aware of it, but he was afraid such a question would make him seem a fool, so he said nothing.

He reached out for the light switch and snapped it on. The sudden wash of brightness illuminated the kitchen. There was no one there. Everything was exactly as he'd left it. Even the dishtowel he'd slung over the back of a chair and the empty teacup in the sink. He'd left a stack of advertising flyers on the kitchen table, the usual junk mail that got pushed under the door, and there was a grubby white envelope next to it. "You're losing your wits," he muttered.

He sat down at the table and opened the envelope, expecting a nasty message from an irate neighbour—maybe he wasn't putting his recycling close enough to the curb on pickup day, or he played his radio too loud. This seemed to be the pattern of his life lately, receiving envelopes, letters, and messages containing secrets or the answers to old questions he hadn't known to ask. There was a folded slip of paper inside, studded with dirty fingerprints.

Remember, Remember.

The hair on the nape of his neck prickled; he had the keenest sense of being watched, but when he looked around there was no one else there, no other face besides his reflection in the window opposite. He had a sudden image of himself, Tadhg, and Lily at Tadhg's house on Eigus, Bonfire Night. *Remember, remember the fifth of November.* Someone wanted him to remember Bonfire Night? To remember what Guy Fawkes had tried to do? It made no sense.

Leaving the kitchen light on, he climbed the stairs to the second floor and checked the bathroom and both bedrooms. He opened and closed the door to the small storage room, but it too was empty. "You're off your nut, my son," he said aloud. "You're after losing your marbles." He went downstairs and checked both the front and back doors. It felt like a strange thing to do, since nobody in Kildevil Cove ever locked their doors. There was no need. People didn't even bother to knock, they simply walked in and called out, "Is ye home? Where's yer to?"

Danny turned on the kitchen radio. It was late, but he knew he wouldn't sleep, at least not yet. Every time he closed his eyes he could smell smoke, see the remnants of his grandparents' house crumble into ash and dust as a shout went up from the assembled crowd. The radio was playing "Zoot Suit Riot," a leftover from several years ago when swing music had enjoyed a brief but intense renaissance. It reminded him of his grandmother, who'd danced through the Great Depression and World War Two, cavorting well past curfew in underground dance halls and volunteer-run canteens. She'd met his grandfather in a canteen. He'd come in with several other soldiers, all eager to spend their carefully rationed leave in the company of pretty girls. The function of the canteen was to give young enlisted men somewhere to go to relax and enjoy themselves, an alternative to some of the shadier—fleshier—establishments. It was wholesome, "good fun," and gave young women the opportunity to do something for the boys by offering hot meals and home-baked goods, a spin or two around the dance floor.

"He told his friend he wanted to dance with me." Danny's nan had told the story more than once, but he never tired of hearing it. "His friend—this big ginger fellow from Sheffield with an accent as thick as paste—said 'that Newfie over there wants you to dance with him.'" His grandmother always burst into laughter at this point in the story. "I said, 'does he not have a tongue in his head? Can't he ask me himself?'" She danced with no one else the rest of the night, in direct contradiction to established protocol. The volunteer girls were supposed to dance with any of the men who wished it. What had she seen in him? Danny often wondered. Pictures of them together showed a matinee-idol handsome young man in a leather bomber jacket, with a sombre expression and troubled eyes. He'd gone everywhere by the war's end, done and seen everything. In one of his rare loquacious moods he told Danny how he'd been in Holland at the liberation and hoped to see the vast fields of waving tulips, hyacinths, and daffodils. But there were no flowers. The Dutch people had eaten all the tulip bulbs, grating the dry, desiccated husks into something resembling flour, which was baked into bread. There had been a bad famine that year, his grandfather said. "They called it Hongerwinter…. The Hunger Winter…."

He took up the envelope and turned it over. There was nothing written on either it or the unsealed flap. "Jesus," he murmured, even though there was no one to hear. He tucked the envelope and its contents into his hip pocket. He needed to think.

HE WOKE much later to find himself lying on his stomach on the couch, drooling onto his arm, with murky daylight beyond the windows. The radio was broadcasting the news as he hauled himself up and went to look outside. The sky was a dim grey, the sea whipped into whitecaps by a persistent wind from the east. To the side of the house, a single mourning dove was fighting to retain its perch on an electrical wire. Assuming the fire had been deliberately set, why would anyone burn down his grandfather's house? Was there something significant hidden inside? A brief snippet of memory surfaced: Tadhg and the straight razor. The day they'd gone to the hotel to retrieve Lily, Danny had asked Tadhg where he got it.

"I found it in your grandfather's house. We were in there clearing up, remember? It was in that tin box," Tadhg had explained, and it had made perfect sense.

The fire had completely died away when Danny pulled up to the gate of his grandfather's house later than morning, even the stubborn embers remaining after the firefighters had doused the collapsed structure with water. It had begun to rain, a thin lancing drizzle that struck his skin like hailstones, and the wind was freezing. He'd brought thick gloves for searching through the burned remnants of the house, but he wasn't sure he'd need them. It must have rained during the night because the ground all around the structure was soaking wet. He stepped warily over the section of concrete where the front door had been and tried to mentally recreate the house's internal arrangement. The bedroom where he'd found the metal box was to the right, roughly, and at the back of the house overlooking the garden. So if the box was still there, it ought to have fallen into the ash and burned timbers. He put his gloves on and bent down to sift through the detritus. He found several of his grandmother's silver coffee spoons, now horribly charred, and a half-melted plastic button that might have come from her winter overcoat. He found an old metal dustpan and shoveled away ash as he went, clearing a path in front of him. His left foot collided with his grandmother's old Singer sewing machine, a 1940s relic if he'd ever seen one, and an empty tobacco tin…

…and then the metal box. Finally.

He crouched on his heels and levered it open with an old butter knife. It took some effort, but he managed, with much swearing and grunting, to get it open.

Amazingly, the envelope containing the pictures was intact, probably protected by the thick metal of the old box. He eased it open carefully and flipped through the photos. The pictures of Margot were gone, as were a couple of his grandfather in his younger days. Someone had been here before the fire, found what he wanted, and took it.

He needed to see Tadhg, ask him about it. But Tadhg was still in hospital, too badly injured to move and drugged into dreaming by heavy sedatives. Danny would have to wait.

TADHG OPENED the door at the first chime of the bell. The doctors had sent him home, but he still looked like he'd been run over by a herd of caribou.

"Come in," he said to Danny. He leaned on the doorframe, clearly less than steady on his feet. "Will you have a cup of something? Coffee? Tea?"

"Why did you take the pictures?" Danny asked. He was tired and foul-tempered; the crossing to Eigus had been rough, and he had the beginnings of a sore throat. He couldn't seem to get warm.

Tadhg stared at him as if he'd just materialised from the ethers. "Danny, what are you talking about?"

"The house in Kildevil Cove was set on fire. It's burned to the ground."

"It can't be. I was just there the other day!" Tadhg turned towards a slight sound from the interior of the house, then back to Danny. "I was just there."

"So you admit it."

"Admit *what*?" Tadhg shook his head. "For Christ's sake, Danny, you're not making any sense. You're talking like you're mad, sure."

"The house is gone. It's—" He stuttered into silence. Saying it out loud suddenly made it true.

"I truly didn't know, my son. I've just gotten home, and I've seen no one but Yvonne and Lily. Haven't even watched the news. I've been sleeping most of the time. It's helping. I think."

They stood looking at each other. Music swelled from somewhere in the house, loud modern techno pop with a driving beat. Danny leaned against the wall, one hand on the doorframe. "It's probably arson, but they don't know for sure, not yet." The cold crept in on him, a subtle chill staining his bones. He was getting sick; he knew it. Probably some damned virus going around that would sideline him for weeks. *Fuck.* "The pictures in my grandfather's house. Why did you take them?"

Danny drew himself up. "Please don't deny it. I know it was you. There's no reason for anyone else to have them, except you. You're the only other person who knew they were even there."

He waited for Tadhg to utter his usual denials and excuses, but the other man was silent. "I wanted them," he said.

"For what?"

Tadhg sighed. "Danny, look, can you come into the living room and sit down? It's not civilised, us stood up here, you hanging off the door. You're letting all the cold air in."

Danny did as he was asked. He sat down on the couch in front of the fireplace, where three stout birch logs were crackling merrily. The house was silent, except for the quiet ticking of a clock on the mantelpiece. He unbuttoned his coat but didn't take it off. "You lied to me."

Tadhg sat across from him in a large wingback chair. He didn't look well. He was pale, and he'd lost weight in hospital; there were dark half-moons underneath his eyes. "Not deliberately."

"By omission, you did." Danny took the envelope out of his inside pocket and laid it down on the coffee table that lay between them. "Here's what was left from the fire. Not all the photos are there. Where's the pictures of the woman called Margot? And my grandfather, when he was young?"

Tadhg stood up and took a book down off the shelf opposite. He sat down, drew out an envelope, and laid it on the table. His face was expressionless, deliberately blank. He had a good poker face, Tadhg did. "The rest are here." He tapped the envelope with his fingertips.

"Why did you take the pictures?" Danny leaned forward. The envelope lay between them on the table.

"I wanted them." Tadhg's voice was barely a whisper.

"Why?" Danny asked. "Who is she? What's this Margot person to you?"

Tadhg didn't look up. "Margot Single. She was me mam's best friend. Poor old Margot. She never got over it."

"Margot Single," Danny repeated. Light dawned. "Llewellyn Single's mother. The woman who drowned herself."

"That's right."

Danny peered more closely at the photo. He could see the faint tracing of resemblance in the shape of the jaw, the angle of the nose. "Is she related to your crowd?"

Tadhg glanced at the picture, then shook his head. "No, bhoy." He laughed, but it seemed somehow forced. "Sure I'm not related to the Singles."

"Must be," Danny replied. He held the photo at arm's length, aligned with Tadhg's face. "Ye got the same nose."

Tadhg reached for the picture, but Danny tugged it away from him. "You're cracked," he said. His smile hovered briefly, and was gone.

"Where did you find them?" Danny asked. "In the tin box in my grandfather's house, the tin box hid away up in the ceiling, where you got the straight razor. You must have known it was there." Tadhg looked up suddenly, and Danny saw his pupils contract. Fear, he thought. He's afraid. "Who is Margot Single to you?" he asked.

Tadhg didn't hesitate. "She was my mother."

It fell like a hammer blow between them. "Your mother. So Llew Single was your—"

"Half-brother," Tadhg said quietly. "He was my half-brother."

"Did anyone know about this?" Danny asked. It seemed inconceivable that something so huge had remained a secret for so long, especially in a place like Kildevil Cove.

Tadhg laughed humorlessly. "My mother did. I can't imagine the scene when the old fucker brought me home to her." He shook his head. "I heard them arguing once. She was saying something about him bringing home 'his leavings' and expecting her…." He stuttered into silence, and Danny's heart ached for him.

"I'm so sorry."

"The illustrious Heaneys," Tadhg said. "Biggest goddamn soap opera in town. I found out when I was in high school. Grade eleven. About a year before Llew died." He drew a slow breath and rubbed his forehead. "Margot told me. She made me promise to keep it a secret. There were a handful of people in Kildevil Cove who knew, though. Your grandfather, I know for certain. Him and Margot's husband were drinking buddies. Your grandmother, I'm not sure. I can't think why he'd tell her. My father and Margot were carrying on for a while before I was born. Afterwards, well, I don't know. I wouldn't put it past him."

"So the bike you had… that was Llew's bike," Danny said. "Why did you take Llew's bike?"

"It was a joke," Tadhg snapped. "I was playing a joke on him. For Christ's sake, he never left me alone, always fucking following me around. "'Let's go down the beach, Tadhg, come on. Let's go up the cove, Tadhg, come on, me and you.' Like we were brothers, him and me, like I wanted anything to do with him." He pressed his hand against the side of his head, clearly in pain. "I wanted him to… leave me alone."

Danny reached out and laid his hand on Tadhg's wrist. "All right?"

Tadhg nodded. "I… it's about time for another dose. Can you fetch my pills from the kitchen? On the counter next to the toaster." He grimaced. "Listen, don't ever crack your skull, will ye? It hurts like a cunt."

Danny brought Tadhg his pills and a glass of water, sat down next to him on the sofa. "I should leave you alone."

"No, stay." Tadhg twisted the top off a bottle of Vicodin and swallowed two of the pills with a sip of water. "You deserve to know." He patted Danny's knee. "I really need a coffee. Do you want one?"

Danny shrugged. "Yeah, go on then." They wandered into the kitchen, and he watched Tadhg's hands as he spooned coffee beans into the hopper, reached to take cups down from the cupboard, fetched sugar and cream. His hands were slender, almost delicate, with tapered fingers—so different from Danny's own. But there was a strength existing there in the deceptively fragile-looking bones, an inborn stubbornness in the curve of Tadhg's thumb. He had a sudden urge to take hold of it, draw it into his mouth, suck and bite it, and this impulse disturbed him. What would Tadhg do? Indeed, what would Tadhg do if Danny caught his arm, turned him around, pushed him back against the worktop or the table, pressed his mouth to Tadhg's? What would happen then?

It had been a very long time since he'd kissed anybody or been kissed. He couldn't remember when last he'd spent the night in someone else's arms, or their bed.

"Why are you looking at me like that?" Tadhg had finished with the coffee maker and was staring at him strangely. Danny reached out, as across a vast distance and caught hold of his hand. "Danny?"

"Come here," he murmured. As soon as Tadhg was close enough, he wrapped a hand around the nape of his neck and pulled him tight against him, reaching to kiss him. Tadhg resisted—*Christ, I've made a horrible mistake*—but only for a second, and then he kissed Danny back, holding him tight. Tadhg's body was firm and solid, warm in his embrace, and the caress of his mouth set up a frenzied throbbing in the base of Danny's belly. When he finally drew away, Danny was breathless, drunk with desire.

"Oh, *gross!* Do you guys have to do that here?"

They jumped apart like they'd been scalded. Lily stood in the doorway, wearing flannel pajamas and a huge, baggy cardigan.

"I thought you were in bed," Tadhg said weakly. "Until I heard your godawful music."

"Obviously." She scoffed. "So you finally made a move. It's about damn time."

Danny reddened. "Lily, this is…."

There was an ominous silence; then Tadhg said, "Exactly what it looks like." Danny opened his mouth to speak, closed it again. He ran the tip of his tongue over his lower lip, bruised and hot from the intensity of Tadhg's kisses. "I know you always thought I was one hundred percent straight." What did this make him, he wondered. He'd been with his share of women. Danny had been married to Alison. Was it even that simple?

Lily rolled her eyes. "Dad, nobody cares about that anymore. Love who you love." Her scornful expression softened. "I want you to be happy." She came to him, wrapped her arms around his waist, and laid her head on his shoulder. "You come and hug too, Danny." She extended a hand to him, and he took it, folding himself against her and Tadhg, holding on. It felt… not exactly uncomfortable, but unusual. He thought he might get used to it. "Now we can be a proper family." Lily sighed with happiness.

Tadhg's mobile phone rang. He muttered a quiet curse and reached to retrieve it from the kitchen counter. Danny took over the coffee maker, closing the lid of the hopper and starting the machine. Lily pulled out one of the barstools and sat down, elbows on the counter.

"Are you going to hurt him?" she asked. Her gaze was clear and direct. There was no point in lying to this girl, he realised. She'd long since found him out. "Because if you are, you might as well leave now. He's already been fucked around plenty."

"Your father doesn't like you using that word," Danny said. He shot her a grin. "You know how uptight he gets."

She refused to be sidetracked. "I'm serious, Danny. Don't hurt him." She glanced over her shoulder. Tadhg had gone into the den with his phone and could be heard talking quietly to whomever was on the other end of the call. "He acts like a total badass, but that's all it is, an act."

"Lily, I don't—"

"I worry about him." She got up and edged closer to him, caught hold of his sleeve. "When I'm gone, he'll be alone. He's got no one else in the world but me." She held his gaze, making him promise. "I know you've got history. I know there's more going on than what he says. My dad's not strong, Danny, not like you are."

She was wise beyond her years, this one. He wondered how much she intuitively understood, how much she had deduced on her own. Maybe his and Tadhg's history clung to the two of them, an almost-visible penumbra.

"I'll do my best for him," he said. "I want to. I really do." He was surprised to realise he meant it.

Tadhg came back into the kitchen. He was white as paper, the dark circles under his eyes looking like gouges.

"What is it?" Danny went to him, took the mobile phone from his hand, and laid it on the countertop. "Come and sit down. You've gone all pale." It was as if he hadn't spoken at all. Tadhg went to the sink and leaned on it, staring out the window, sunk deep in his own thoughts.

The coffee maker burbled to a stop. Lily reached for it and filled their cups. "Who was that on the phone, Dad?"

Tadhg stared at her like he was seeing her for the first time. "That was Gwendolyn," he said. He looked from Lily to Danny, his expression glazed and uncomprehending. "That was your mother. She wants to see you."

CHAPTER SEVENTEEN

CILLIAN RILEY had called Danny late the night before and asked if he wanted to meet for coffee. Since it was a Wednesday and Riley was working, Danny figured the invitation wasn't a social call. He was tired, having just returned from Eigus, but he agreed to meet Riley at the Rocket Bakery on Water Street around eleven. He wasted ten minutes looking for a viable parking spot within decent walking distance of the café. It was a cold, wet morning, and the walk had been a misery, with sleety snow blowing into his face on a chilly northeast wind. By the time he arrived, his clothes and hair were covered in a fine coating of ice.

"Christ, you look like a fucking snowman." Riley got up from where he was sitting and helped Danny off with his coat. "I'll sling this over here so it can dry out." He spread the coat over an empty chair. "Did you walk the whole way?"

"No, you know what it's like." Danny shivered as the building's interior heat began to soak into his skin. "I had to park down on Harbour Drive, that new parking garage across from the piss boy." The "piss boy," a replica of the famous Manneken Pis statue in Brussels, was mounted on the upper storey of a Bier Markt restaurant and had caused much controversy among those who felt a naked child pissing was akin to pornography. He ordered coffee and a piece of carrot cake, while Riley asked for cherry pie.

"You're freezing," Riley remarked. He laid a warm hand on Danny's back, rubbing circles between his shoulder blades. "You want warming up."

Danny canted a sly look in his direction. "Are you offering?" He remembered the kiss he'd shared with Tadhg and wondered whether he should be ashamed of himself. In his head he could hear Lily asking, *Are you going to hurt him?*

Riley grinned. "Well, I didn't get you out in this weather for nothing."

"Oh?" Danny looked up with a smile as the waitress, a young woman with flaming red hair, reappeared with his coffee and cake. His skin tingled under his clothes where Riley had touched him.

"The fire at your grandfather's house was deliberately set." Riley added sugar to his coffee and stirred in a healthy measure of cream. "I heard from the fire investigator yesterday morning."

"They investigated the fire?" Danny sank his fork into the carrot cake and tasted it. It was moist, delicious, and good. Outside, the sleety snow beat against the windows, and a siren sounded somewhere farther up the street. Business as usual. "I'd hardly think…." Why would the RCMP bother investigating a fire in Kildevil Cove? It wasn't exactly a hotbed of criminal activity. Unless Riley and his superiors thought there was reason.

"I wouldn't usually tell tales out of school, but I trust you'll keep this between us." Riley plunged his fork into his cherry pie. "We found traces of accelerant in the ruins and a blowtorch."

"A blowtorch?" Danny sipped his coffee carefully. It was burning hot. "And what was the accelerant used?"

"Gasoline," Riley said. "The cheap kind you'd use in an outboard motor. Small-boat fuel." He answered Danny's question before he'd even asked it. "Someone with access to a boat shed most likely set the fire." He grinned. "Pissed off any fishermen lately?"

Danny shook his head. "So I'm guessing nobody drove the hundred miles from the city strictly to burn my grandfather's house down." Of course the arsonist was someone local, probably with a long-standing grudge against the family, maybe Roger Palmer or one of his cronies… someone who knew the secrets Grandar had fought so hard to keep, the hidden truths long buried. The crime had probably been perpetrated by the same person or persons who broke the windows, trashed the house, and spray-painted insults on the walls.

"You look like you've got a suspect in mind." Riley reached out and tapped Danny on the knuckles with the handle of his fork. "You were a thousand miles away there." Danny told him what he assumed, and Riley nodded. "You're probably right. Do you think…?" He dragged the tines of his fork through the filling of his cherry pie. "Do you think Tadhg Heaney might have been involved?"

The supposition hit Danny like a slap. "Why would Tadhg burn down my grandfather's house?"

Riley shrugged. "Why wouldn't he?"

Danny shook his head, unwilling to accept this theory. "No. He wanted to buy it, restore it to period, turn the whole property into holiday cottages. I don't see him setting fire to it. Do you?" Then he remembered an earlier conversation with Tadhg, right after he'd returned from Amsterdam.

"I'm broke, Danny," Tadhg had said. "Can you credit that? The only thing that's mine is that bloody island. I bought it for cash outright."

"Burning it would depreciate the property value considerably," Riley said. "Christ, it would bring it down to practically zero, apart from the land, and he probably figured he could get that for a song." He signaled the waitress as she passed by with a fresh pot of coffee. "There's no hard proof, not yet. But we're looking."

"I don't think Tadhg would do something like that. Anyway, he was in hospital a hundred miles away when the fire broke out, remember?"

"He could have hired somebody," Riley said.

Danny suppressed a flash of anger. "I doubt that."

"Look, I know you and Heaney are tight." Riley glanced around the café, slowly filling up with workers from downtown government offices, there for an extended coffee break or early lunch. He pitched his voice low and leaned close across the table. "But until we know for certain, we're not ruling him out. Heaney's got connections everywhere. It's easily within his scope to engineer something like this." He considered Danny's lack of response. "You think I'm reaching."

Danny pushed his plate away. "I don't know what to think," he said. He had lost his appetite for the conversation and the cake.

"A fire of this type, we normally wouldn't bother with it. There's a lot of old wood-frame houses in small towns like Kildevil Cove. Dry as tinder, they are. One spark and they're gone." The table they were sitting at was small, and as he shifted in his seat, Riley's knee pressed against Danny's. The sensation was electric, a shaft of pure lust that shot straight to his groin. What would that be like, he wondered. They could leave here and go somewhere. They could get a hotel room, spend the day and the night together, if Riley was willing. "Moira wanted to go the extra mile and make sure. Now that we now it's arson, we can lay charges."

"Surely to God you aren't going to charge Tadhg." Danny's stomach clenched. "He's innocent. For Christ's sake, what is this, a fishing expedition?"

Riley stared at him in open disbelief. "Don't you want to find out who did it?"

"Of course I do!" Danny pushed his chair back from the table, leaving his coffee and uneaten cake. "But you and Moira Fraser are bound and determined to pin something on Tadhg Heaney." He stood up and reached across to retrieve his coat, shrugging into it. It was still wet, and the heavy wool hung like chainmail on his shoulders. "I can't listen to any more of this. Clearly there's some vendetta you're pursuing." He took out his wallet, dropped twenty dollars on the table. "Do you even have another suspect? Or did your inquiries stop at him?"

"Danny, if you would just let me explain." Riley started to rise from the table, but Danny was already at the front door, pulling it open, head down and shoulders hunched against the biting wind.

RILEY CAUGHT up with him inside the parking garage. Danny had stopped his car at the glass booth near the exit and was paying the attendant. He frowned as he saw Riley.

"I'm sorry." Riley stopped beside the driver's side and held up both hands in a conciliatory gesture. He waited while Danny rolled down the window. "I'm sorry," he said again, now that Danny could hear him.

"Are you parked here too?" Danny asked.

"No, I walked," Riley replied, a little amazed that Danny's anger had faded so quickly. "Can we talk about things?"

"Get in." Danny received his change back from the parking attendant and tossed the coins into a well in the centre console of his car. "I'm afraid I went off on you," he said, as they emerged into the drifting sleet of Harbour Drive. "I shouldn't have said what I did. I understand you're just doing your job." He turned right onto Water Street at the next set of lights and waited while a laden beer truck lumbered through the intersection. Even though it was nearly noon, the grey skies made it seem darker, much later in the day.

"I understand." Riley turned to look out the passenger side window, watching Water Street slide by. "I know what I'm like sometimes. All about the work. I forget that people have actual human connections." He shrugged, turned to look at Danny. "Bit of tunnel vision." He tried to smile but feared it came off as a twisted smirk. "I understand he's your friend," he said after a moment, "but I thought you would want to know."

"I do," Danny said. "I'm glad you told me."

"You've been away from it too long," Riley observed. "I expect Ireland made you want to take a step back, but now you have, you don't know what to do with yourself." He was good at reading people; it had become an asset to his profession. He knew men like Danny Quirke, career officers who felt responsible for everything and everybody in their purview or outside it. In ten years or fifteen, Danny's overweening sense of responsibility would break him, and he'd be fit for nothing. Riley would hate for that to happen, but it seemed inevitable.

"Sorry I walked out on our coffee date." Danny stopped at the next red light, turned to look at Riley. His smile was embarrassed, sheepish. "I've got a bit of a temper, as you could probably tell."

"We could always have another date." Riley bit his lip. Maybe that was a bit too forward. "If you want."

Danny seemed to be mulling it over. He said "All right. When?"

"What about now?"

Danny stared at him. The light turned green, and the cars behind them started blowing their horns. "Now?"

"Why not?" Riley nodded at the steering wheel. "You should probably move. They're getting angry back there."

Danny turned left onto Prescott Street, then right again on Duckworth. "What would we do?" he asked. "I don't think I could drink any more coffee."

He was so goddamn cute. Riley reached across and cupped Danny's cheek in his palm. "See that big cream building up ahead there? That's a hotel, that is."

Riley showed his badge at the reception desk, told the clerk they needed a quiet room to interview a suspect. They rode up together in the elevator, hardly daring to look at each other. Anticipation churned Riley's insides. Oh, he wanted this. He'd wanted Danny ever since he'd first laid eyes on him. As far as he was concerned, this hookup was long past due for the both of them. He forced himself to wait until Danny had closed the door before he pushed him up against it, claiming his mouth in a bruising kiss, running his hands up under Danny's heavy woolen sweater.

"D'ye fancy it?" he murmured, and he had to lean close to hear Danny's whispered "yes."

RILEY CAME to himself slowly, after what seemed like a very long time, his body heavy, his limbs entirely liquid. "Sorry," he murmured, after a moment, "I must be crushing you." He made to move away but Danny snaked out and arm and looped it around his waist.

"No, stay where you are." Danny's face was close to his own, so close that Riley could see each individual eyelash and the gleam of silvery stubble on his chin. Outside, the day darkened, and the wind blew hard so that the windows rattled, but here, inside this room, it was warm and cozy. Riley's body was pulling him inexorably towards sleep, but he couldn't stay.

"I have to go," he said. "This was a lot of fun." It was always best to keep things light. He'd learned the hard way not to get in too deep. It was better to take your fun and have done with it. No hurt feelings, no lingering regret. "We should do this again sometime."

Danny's eyes widened in what was probably surprise. Riley elected to ignore it. "Right," Danny said. He recovered quickly from this shock and sat up, gathering the sheets into his lap. "You can have the shower first."

When they had both showered and dressed and were ready to leave, Riley said, laughing, "Wonder if we can slip out the back way?"

"Yeah." Danny, clearly distracted, pulled his coat on and buttoned it, lingering near the door. "So… should I wait for your call, then?" He looked like someone who'd lost his way in an unfamiliar neighbourhood and was wondering what to do.

Riley's gut tightened. This was the point at which he usually offered some facile excuse and got the hell out of there. "Look, Danny… this was great fun but—"

Danny's face closed up. "Right on. See you around." He pulled open the door.

"No, wait, it's not like you think." Riley rushed to explain. "I'd rather—"

But he was speaking to empty air. Danny was gone.

DANNY SAT in his parked car at the top of Signal Hill, looking out over the broad expanse of water before him. A thin, sleety drizzle pattered against the windshield, interrupted by the occasional sway of the wipers. His gaze was fixed on the middle distance, watching the fall and swell of the sea. He felt drugged, like someone coming out of a coma or waking from a long sleep, and his head ached endlessly. What the hell was he doing going to bed with Riley in the middle of a workday? Was he that desperate for sex? No—he amended the thought almost immediately— it wasn't sex so much as human touch. He wanted to be held, wanted the sweetness of someone else's mouth on his, their hands holding him. Only it wasn't Riley he wanted.

Who, then?

He remembered Tadhg's long, slender hands cupping his face, the taste of Tadhg's mouth, the press of his body.

No, it wasn't Riley he wanted at all.

He sighed. What a clusterfuck this was turning out to be. He wished there was someone he could talk to, who'd give him a sympathetic ear and not judge, but he had no close friends. In the past, there were work colleagues, of course, who'd gladly go for a drink and let him bend their ears, but all that was behind him now. If he rejoined the constabulary—if he ever went back to being a police officer—the perceived disgrace of what had happened in Ireland would follow him around like a bad smell. He might as well forget the whole bloody works of it, get a job on a deep-sea trawler or as a roughneck on one of the rigs.

Feeling sorry for yourself won't help. He could almost hear Alison's voice in his head. It made him smile. Wish fulfilment, he thought. He was imagining her saying all the things to him that he most wanted to hear.

What do you recommend? God, he wished he really could talk to her. He imagined she would understand what he was going through. The truth of his sexuality was never an issue with Alison. She too had had her share of girl crushes and same-sex affairs in the past. She'd fallen hard for her roommate at the University of Edinburgh, a lithe Latvian beauty named Katja who had ultimately broken her heart.

Tell the sad bastard how you really feel. He could imagine her smiling when she said this. *At least then you'll have it out in the open.* For some reason, he thought of the Dutch painter he'd known in Maastricht. The memory bloomed in his mind like the blossoms of the artist's wild irises. That man would have no problem telling anyone anything, Danny realised. He'd simply come out with it, consequences notwithstanding.

Had he feared Danny would reject him that night in Maastricht? "Come upstairs to my flat. Come on, we'll fuck and have a good time. You seem like a great fucker." The idea of saying such a thing to Tadhg made him laugh out loud. But he suspected the Dutchman was right. Life wouldn't wait for him to get his shit together. He needed to sit down with Tadhg, tell him the whole, unvarnished truth.

TADHG WAITED at the bottom of the stairs in the arrivals area at half past one in the afternoon, only partially listening to the various announcements over the somewhat scratchy public address system. For some reason he found himself thinking about Danny, that kiss.

Lily had begged to come with him, but he'd made her stay at home. He hadn't seen Gwen himself for more than fourteen years, and he wanted the chance to assess her before allowing her to meet Lily.

The Gwen he remembered was impetuous and young, beautiful and headstrong, with very firm ideas about the path and progress of her own life. He'd met her unexpectedly, in the endless sunlight of a Highland summer, and before the week was out, he'd taken her to bed. She was camping with a company of Travellers very near the house where he was staying, living in a caravan and subsisting on the basics, washing her underthings in a nearby burn. His initial sight of her was that very thing, in fact, on her knees beside a narrow stream, slapping her tights against a rock, humming to herself. She was so unexpected; he might have slipped through a rift in time and found himself in another era or even a parallel existence, and her kneeling there, her long flame-coloured hair rippling over her naked back—she'd taken her top off in the afternoon heat. He was walking with Jock, his friend's border terrier, and as soon as he saw her, he veered away, wary of intruding on her privacy. He still had that decency in him then. But she saw him and waved him over: "It's fine, it's only me, the others are all sleeping." An odd greeting. Maybe she really was a changeling.

They stood and talked while Jock sniffed around, exploring, trying in vain to coax mice out of their holes. Tadhg forced himself to look at her eyes and mouth, but no lower, conscious of her uncovered torso between them, the risen peaks of her small breasts. After a while she asked, "Are you a homosexual?"

The question took him aback. "Why?"

"You aren't looking at my tits at all. They're very nice tits. You should look at them." She raised her arms over her head, revealing unshaven armpits furred with light red hair.

"You're not very subtle, are you?"

"What's the point?" she'd countered. "It's just a waste of time." She was, he decided, a strange kind of animal, not really a woman at all but a changeling, a chimera. Later, when she discovered she was pregnant, he did what he thought was the proper thing and asked her to marry him. The notion amused her. "Why would I want to marry you?" And, with regards to their child: "You take it. When it's born, you have it. I don't want it." He was surprised she didn't have a termination, but seemingly the idea didn't occur to her. She was a mass of contradictions. He didn't love her. He enjoyed fucking her, and they fucked everywhere: in his bed, outdoors on the heather, up against the bathroom wall in his borrowed house. If he tried to initiate conversation after a bout of lovemaking, she shut him down.

He saw her now at the top of the stairs, and his heartbeat stuttered. She looked so different, but that was to be expected, he supposed, and fourteen years was a long time in anybody's estimation. She wore her lustrous red hair cropped short, standing up in spikes all over her head, some of it dyed blue. She had aged rather more than he'd expected, and not well. Her clothes were bohemian, a long loose skirt with a baggy shirt on top, a scarf around her waist. Her neck and wrists were laden with strings of wooden beads and lanyards strung with sea glass. There were sharply indented lines in her face, under her red-rimmed eyes and running from the sides of her nose to the corners of her mouth.

"I wasn't sure you'd meet me," she said, once she'd reached the bottom of the stairs. She had brought only one bag, a brocaded satchel in deep peacock blue, the colour a favourite of hers that always made him think of swimming in some tropical ocean. Tadhg had never swum in tropical waters; the only ocean he'd ever submerged himself in was the freezing North Atlantic.

"I said I would." He reached to take her bag, but she yanked it away from him.

"Where's the girl?" Her eyes scanned the arrivals terminal. "Why isn't she here?" She turned as a man came down the stairs. He was a fair bit older than Gwen, tall and cadaverously thin, with sparse hair arranged in a disastrous comb-over. His eyes were small and blue, the keen eyes of an inquisitive potato. His accent was Yorkshire, or somewhere close to it. Tadhg disliked him on sight.

"Girl not 'ere?" he asked. He glanced at Tadhg for no longer than it took to register his presence, then away again, his small blue eyes eagerly scanning the terminal. "Ah thought girl were gon't be 'ere." He had a set of wheeled Samsonite luggage in bright green—"snot green," Lily would have called it—and a man purse of woven hemp over one shoulder. He dragged both large suitcases to where Tadhg was standing and left them there as if expecting Tadhg to porter his belongings to the car.

"This is Tom," Gwen said, "Tom Farrage." She offered nothing further in the way of explanation—who this Tom person was, whether they were married, what he did for a job, or where she'd found him.

"Nice to meet you, Tom." Tadhg offered his hand and was ignored. After a moment he withdrew it, pretended to be patting his pockets for his keys.

They won't stay long. They just want to meet Lily, that's all. They'll be gone again in a day or two. "Lily is back at the house. She wasn't feeling up to the trip." He nodded towards the exit. "My car's outside. This way."

Gwen and her man friend dropped their bags on the ground beside his Range Rover and waited expectantly for him to unlock the doors. "There's room in the back for those," Tadhg said, gesturing at the luggage. They exchanged a look, then bent grudgingly to their things and tossed the bags into the cargo space with ill grace and rather more violence than was necessary.

"Where's this place you live to, then?" Gwen asked. In their years apart, her accent had changed—deliberately, he thought, as if she were putting on airs. She sounded like Camilla Parker Bowles. "Out in the sticks, is it?"

"It's on an island not far from here," Tadhg replied, "called Eigus." He waited while they both settled themselves into the back seat, then got in and slipped the seat belt around him. "Buckle up," he said, attempting cheer. "It's the law around here, I'm afraid."

"Oh, excuse me!" Gwen said. In the rear-view mirror, Tadhg saw her raise her eyebrows at Tom, who smirked. Tadhg's hands clenched on the steering wheel. She took out a cigarette case and offered it to Tom, who accepted.

"Can't smoke in the car," Tadhg said. "I'm sorry." He wasn't.

Gwen shrugged and put the cigarettes away. "No skin off my arse," she said breezily, but Tom looked like a baby whose dummy had been eaten by the family dog.

"Can't do nothin' nowadays," he complained. "Folk are too uptight if you ask me."

Nobody bloody asked you. Tadhg's head was pounding. He ought to have taken a Vicodin before leaving for the airport, but obviously short-term memory loss was a side effect of his concussion. "So," he said after a few moments had elapsed, "how long have you two been married?"

"Eleven—" Gwen started to say, before Tom interrupted her.

"Thirteen years."

Tadhg forced a laugh. "Missing a couple of years there in between, are you?"

"Listen, Tadhg." Gwen delved into her bag for her cigarettes, remembered she couldn't smoke in Tadhg's car, then drew her hand back. "Tom and I have every intention of taking Lily back to the UK with us."

Her words felt like hammer blows to his heart. He met her eyes in the mirror. "I don't think so," he said. "Lily is my daughter—"

"She is also my daughter."

Tadhg pulled up at a red light and stopped. He turned around in his seat. "You are not taking my daughter anywhere."

"I have as much right—"

"You've got no right!" he roared. Tom jumped like he'd been electrocuted. "For fourteen years you've not laid eyes on her. I raised her—I did, myself! She is my daughter. I adopted her. You abandoned her so you could go and be a dancing dolly with the circus or whatever the hell it was." His shouting made the pain worse, and he leaned forward, resting his head against the steering wheel. "You gave up any right you had to her two days after she was born, you bitch."

"'Ere!" Tom started up in his seat. "That's no language to use with a lady."

"Piss off," Tadhg hissed, "or I'll leave you by the side of the fucking road."

An immediate chorus of car horns indicated the light had turned green. Tadhg turned back around and stamped savagely on the gas. His heart was in his mouth, and it was hard to breathe. He wondered if he were actually having a stroke or a coronary. Perhaps it was better in that case that the car should be in motion. If he died en route, he'd most likely take these two with him.

BY THE time they finally reached the house on Eigus, he'd had enough of Gwen and Tom to last him twenty lifetimes. The trip to Portugal Cove had been a litany of complaints and allegations. They were horrified when he explained they would have to take a boat for the last leg of the trip, with Tom protesting over and over that he had no stomach for open water, while Gwen announced that she was going to walk.

"No, you're not," Tadhg said grimly, "unless you're Jesus Christ. I've told you already it's an island." He herded them and their baggage aboard the motor launch. Jesper came out of the cuddy to introduce himself; Tadhg told him not to bother. "I'll explain later," he said, punching him lightly on the upper arm. "We're in the company of savages, my son," he whispered. Jesper nodded sagely and went back inside while Tadhg ushered his visitors into the lounge, offering tea and biscuits, lingonberry jam, and fresh-baked bread.

"What I'd really like is to smoke a cigarette," Gwen snipped. "But I suppose I'll have to clamber out on deck like a fisherman to do that." She pushed back the sleeve of her shirt and looked pointedly at her watch. "How much longer is this interminable journey going to take?"

"Twenty minutes across," Tadhg said briskly. "And by all means, please make use of the deck area to smoke." He'd ceased to care about their personal comforts. Given half a chance and an appropriate list to starboard, he'd cheerfully push the two of them into the Atlantic. He lingered nearby while they smoked, eavesdropping on their conversation. Gwen seemed to think their taking Lily back with them was a forgone conclusion, telling Tom, "She's a beautiful girl, and I think having her along on our holiday might be nice." Tadhg wondered how Gwen even knew what Lily looked like but supposed she could have searched her whereabouts online. "I know just what to say to make her come with us," Gwen said. "She'll be a great friend for Siobhan, and that'll put you in

good with Andrew. He'll be falling all over himself to give you the job."
Who the hell were Siobhan and Andrew? "And she's at about the right
age for Gareth. Mind you, he's got a couple years on her, but girls mature
so much faster than boys."

"Yes, but Gareth's a queer sort," Tom said. He drew on his cigarette
and expelled the smoke in one long plume. "Got sent 'ome from that
fancy school, you know. Couldn't stop 'im lookin' up under the girls'
kilts!" He roared with laughter, seeming to think this sort of deviant
behaviour was uproariously funny.

"Would be worse if they couldn't stop him wearing them," Gwen
commented dryly. "No, it will be all right. A month in Marbella, and
we'll all be friends. Lily can be Gareth's little girlfriend, and Andrew
will be so grateful."

Tadhg clenched his jaw so hard the bones of his skull creaked. He
moved towards them, intending to interrupt their little tête-à-tête, when
Jesper called that they were nearing shore.

"Must be the house up ahead there," Gwen commented. "Nice little
shack."

"It is that and all," Tom replied. He took a last drag on his cigarette
and tossed the butt overboard. "This bloke's got money."

LILY STAYED in her room while Tadhg showed Gwen and Tom to theirs.
He could hear the distant murmur of her beloved techno pop from behind
her closed door. Gwen made for the doorknob, but Tadhg stopped her.
"Not now." The look she gave him in response was pure hatred. He
settled Tom and Gwen in a guest suite at the other end of the house, as far
away from Lily as possible. When he'd shown them where everything
was, he sat down on the end of the bed and waited.

"Well, er, thanks," Tom said, glancing at Gwen. "Right comfortable
'ere. I expect we'll sleep like babies."

"I overheard you on the boat." Tadhg's voice was like flint.
"Discussing your plans for my daughter."

Gwen uttered a short, incredulous bark of laughter. "Nothing like
eavesdropping on folk's private conversations!"

Tadhg waited, borrowing a page from Danny's book. He looked
from one to the other, while a portentous silence stretched between them.

"Er, well, it's like this." Tom passed a shaking hand over his nearly bald pate, dislodging a few glued-down strands. It hung down alongside his face like a girl's hair ribbon. "My boss, Andrew MacFarlane, Andy Mac we call him, I expect you've heard of him, he runs these—"

"Betting shops," Gwen put in quickly. "A chain of betting shops."

"So he's a bookie."

"Not… as such," Tom said. "It's a bit more sophisticated than that. See, he's got a number of international properties, a real goin' concern, 'e is. You're a property man yourself, so I expect you can understand how he's always trying to expand his business."

"Look," Gwen said, clearly irritated at having to explain, "Tom's in line for a big promotion. Andrew has invited us to spend a month with his family in Marbella so we can get to know each other. He's got a young son, Gareth, and we thought—"

"You thought you'd use Lily to seal the deal." Tadhg would have laughed, except he suspected it would make his head hurt more. "That's why you wanted to meet her. You haven't got any interest in getting to know the daughter you gave birth to." He stood up. "Tell you what. You can stay the night, and then tomorrow you're on the first flight back to the UK."

"But we came to meet Lily!" Gwen cried.

"You'll meet her at dinner tonight," Tadhg said. "And that's the end of it."

"She is my daughter too." Anger twisted Gwen's face into a grotesque mask. "I have every right—"

"To prostitute her in Marbella, in exchange for a job promotion?" Tadhg started for the door, stopped. "You do realise human trafficking is as illegal here as it is there. I mean, you do realise that, don't you? That you could be arrested for even suggesting such a thing to me."

"There might not even be any commercial flights out tomorrow," Tom pointed out. "We could be stuck here for days, us. What are you going to do about it?"

Tadhg smiled grimly. "Then you'll fly freight," he said. "I really don't give a shit. Either way, you are out of this house tomorrow." He yanked the door open. "Dinner is at seven."

He stopped at Lily's door and tapped on it lightly. "It's Dad," he said. "Can I come in?" She was lying on her bed, working at something on her iPad. She jumped up excitedly when he told her that Gwen had arrived. "Can I see her? I'll go see her right now."

"Wait." He sat her down beside him. "Lily, your mam's not what you might think she is." Christ. Was there any good or easy way to tell her the truth about Gwen? In the end, he gave it to her whole and unvarnished.

"So they were going to use me." Lily was making a valiant effort not to cry, but Tadhg could see it was costing her, the trembling of her lower lip making it difficult for her to talk. "She doesn't want me. She never wanted me."

Tadhg gathered her into his lap and held her. "Oh my darling baby," he said. "I'm so sorry." He hugged her, and the press of her too-thin body against his own felt like the fragile skeleton of a baby bird. "I love you," he murmured.

"I know." She pressed her face into the curve of his neck. "Dad, can you make them go away?"

"I can and I will." He took his mobile phone out of his pocket, tapped in the number he had recently come to know by heart, and waited. It rang four times before the call was picked up. "Come to dinner tonight?" Tadhg asked. "There's people I want you to meet." He paused, listening. "Perfect. I'll see you then."

CHAPTER EIGHTEEN

AS FAR as Danny could make out, the woman named Gwen—Lily's biological mother—was married to the weedy-looking fellow with the *Coronation Street* accent. He knew Gwen had ceded all parental rights to Tadhg soon after Lily was born; even though Tadhg had explained the entire sordid mess to him, he still couldn't understand what she and her husband were doing on Eigus. Did she think she could simply take the girl and go? They were standing near the big window in Tadhg's living room, watching the wind-driven sea as it foamed against the rocks. Tadhg had hired a chef from the Mallard Cottage restaurant in Quidi Vidi, a young woman dressed all in black who was preparing a seafood feast in Tadhg's gourmet kitchen. Danny had been present when the van, ferried across to Eigus on Tadhg's enormous boat, had pulled up to the door earlier that afternoon, disgorging a quartet of delivery men carrying crates of fresh mussels, cod, halibut, scallops, crab, lobster, and oysters. He couldn't imagine where Tadhg was getting the money for it all, but figured it was none of his business. They'd managed a moment alone before anyone else appeared—Gwen and Tom were "resting" in their suite while Lily had gone down to the rec room to play video games on the large-screen TV.

"Not interested in meeting her mother?" Danny asked, sitting in Tadhg's study with a cold beer in his hand. Tadhg sat behind a large mahogany desk, rocking back in his leather chair, a scotch in front of him.

He shook his head in response to Danny's question. "Not after I told her the truth." He rubbed at his forehead with his fingertips. "I'm hoping you'll be able to help me there."

"With Lily?"

"With…." Tadhg tilted his head towards the rest of the house. "With her and him." He nodded in the approximate direction of Danny's lap. "Did you bring it?"

Danny raised his eyebrows and started to laugh. "By 'it' I assume you mean my badge. Because your eyes were pointing"—he gestured—"elsewhere."

"Well, I hope you brought that with you too." Tadhg caught and held his gaze, then blushed a deep florid pink. "But yes, I meant your badge."

"Oh yes." Danny took a long pull on his beer. "That I did, my son. That I did." He paused, started to say something, thought better of it, and stopped. He reconsidered and started again. Better to plunge right in and get it over with. "Tadhg, I think you should know how I feel about you."

Tadhg blinked. "Oh?"

"I've spent thirty years thinking you were a certain kind of man. Unethical, without morals, no conscience." Danny set his beer on the floor next to his chair and went to lean against Tadhg's desk. He couldn't stop himself from touching him, his hands going to Tadhg's shoulders, squeezing gently. "Ye know the lies I was told, the lies we were both told." He seized a small wooden chair from where it stood against the wall and dragged it close, sat down so he was facing Tadhg and could look into his eyes.

Tadhg turned and shimmied nearer, so their knees were touching. "Danny, none of that was your fault." He smiled, but it didn't reach his eyes. "You know, I did try… over the years, I did try to get in touch with you. I managed to track Sandra down, but she wouldn't give me any of your contact information."

Danny said nothing. He hadn't bothered looking for Tadhg, assuming everything he'd been told was true. *Thirty wasted years*, he thought bitterly—but he couldn't regret his time with Alison. "You are…." He drew a shaking breath. "You are the dearest soul in the world to me."

He wasn't sure how he ended up pressed against the wall of Tadhg's study, or when Tadhg had tilted his chin just so and captured Danny's mouth with his own as Tadhg's deft hands slid underneath his sweater, hard fingers all but crushing his waist. "Ye came back to this fucking island for a reason," he murmured as he pulled away, his voice husky with desire. "Ye came back for me." He leaned in and kissed him again. "And I'll be damned if I'll let ye go."

A light tap at the door pulled them out of their reverie. "Dad?"

"Christ." Tadhg shook his head at Danny. "Leave it to her. She's got a wonderful sense of timing, that one." Danny moved to sit behind the desk, and Tadhg opened the door. "Won't be but a minute, my love," he said to Lily.

"She wants to know when dinner will be ready," Lily said. She glanced between him and Danny. "What are you guys up to in here?" She rolled her eyes. "Never mind. It's probably something gross."

"Couple more minutes," Tadhg said. "I'm just showing Danny—"

"Your etchings," she said sourly. She closed the door and left them alone.

"How does she know that reference?" Danny asked. "Christ, that's even before our time."

"She reads," Tadhg said. "Too much."

They made awkward small talk with Gwen and Tom until Dayna called them all to the table. Tadhg made sure their guests were seated directly opposite Danny for maximum dramatic effect.

"So, the two of you would like Lily to accompany you to Marbella on holiday," Danny said, once they'd all been served a starter of pan-fried cod tongues and steamed fresh mussels in garlic butter. "That's a very generous offer. Can I come?" He laughed loudly. "That's the chance of a lifetime, that is. Now where is Marbella? In Spain, isn't it?"

Tom looked up from his plate and frowned. "Course it is," he said. "Everybody knows that, don't they?" He took a swig of wine. "What are these round things?" he wanted to know.

"Oh, those are cod tongues," Tadhg replied airily. "Local delicacy. They're delicious."

"Tongues?" Gwen looked appropriately appalled. "Are you telling me these were cut out of a fish's mouth?"

"Didn't all come from the one fish," Tadhg said, "if that's what you're asking." He pointed at her plate with his fork. "Come on, don't let 'em get cold."

Tom pointedly pushed his cod tongues to one side of his plate. "Don't want them?" Tadhg asked. "Oh well, more for me, then." He reached over the table and forked the unwanted items off Tom's plate and onto his own.

"Marbella." Danny drank some of his own wine, a delicious sauvignon blanc, icy cold. "Didn't they have some trouble there a year ago?"

"Trouble?" Gwen's eyes flicked to Danny, then back down to her plate. "What kind of trouble?"

"Yes, there was a big thing about it in the papers and on the news," Tadhg said. He caught Danny's gaze and smirked.

"Right, yes." Danny smiled as the young man Tadhg had hired to serve appeared from the kitchen, bearing a platter laden with pan-fried codfish drizzled with the rendered pork fat cubes known elsewhere as lardons but that locals knew as scruncheons.

"I heard about that," Lily said. She was dressed in a pair of baggy flannel pajamas and another huge cardigan that Danny was certain belonged to Tadhg, and her eyes were painted with several lurid shades of what looked like clown makeup. She certainly shared her father's sense of the dramatic. "The police shut down this huge trafficking ring, didn't they? All these young girls held in sexual slavery."

Gwen jerked upright in her chair and made a tutting noise. "I hardly think this suitable conversation for the dinner table."

"Disgusting," Tom said. "What some folk don't get up to."

"What do you think of Marbella, Lily?" Tadhg served Gwen and Tom a large portion of the cod, then passed the platter across to Danny.

"I'm not sure the docs will let me go," she said, not quite smirking. She'd come downstairs before dinner to meet Gwen and Tom, and their reaction to her physical condition was enlightening. Danny heard them whispering together over pre-dinner drinks, talking about how *the girl's a walking skeleton* and *why didn't he tell us she was sick?* She fingered the feeding tube port in her upper chest, visible above the low scoop neckline of her pajama top. "It's a lot to manage," she told Gwen. "I can't do the feedings myself, so you'd have to help me. Oh, and there's medication, isn't there, Dad?" Tadhg nodded. "Can either of you do intramuscular injections?"

"Injections?" Tom looked distinctly queasy. He poked one of the small cubes of pork fat with his knife. "Wouldn't know where to begin."

"Anyway," Gwen put in, "we were hoping you'd want to meet a young man we know. Gareth, his name is."

Danny had to give her credit for her tenacity. Even knowing what they now did, she seemed prepared to go ahead with the plan. Most criminals—the really stupid ones—were impossible to dissuade once they had something in their minds.

"Oh riiiiight," Tadhg drawled. "The one you're planning to inflict on my daughter." His affable manner had vanished as quickly as a summer fog. "The same boy who's been kicked out of school for sexual assault." He sat back, wine glass cradled in his palm. "He's had… let's see if I can remember… one hundred and twenty-five behavioural 'incidents' this past year, twenty-seven of which were reported to police, resulting in his arrest."

"Rubbish," Tom said. "Lad was misrepresented."

"Is that so?" Tadhg looked at Danny. "The judge who tried the case said he was 'out of control, violent and manipulative.' Is that someone you'd want my daughter—" Tadhg paused. "—*our* daughter spending time with?"

Her mouth opened and closed. She looked at Tom, probably hoping he'd help, but he was silent as well.

Danny reached into his trouser pocket and pulled out his badge. He laid it on the table. "What you are suggesting is—" He glanced around the table. "—so incredibly illegal it's not even funny. I could have you both in custody for even suggesting it."

"It's not like that—" Tom started to say.

"You shut up," Tadhg said viciously.

"I should arrest the two of you and have done with it," Danny said. "I don't think you'd enjoy the cells, though. The building's very old. Nineteenth century, in fact. Haunted as fuck."

Lily giggled.

"But I'm prepared to let you go with a warning," Danny continued, "as long as you stow your worthless arses on the next plane out of here and get back across the pond." He smiled. "Otherwise it might get a bit messy. We'd have to charge you here, then extradite you back to the UK. You'd be in an unfortunate state."

Gwen looked at Tadhg. "Are you going to let this man talk to me this way? Who's he to you anyway?"

Tadhg caught and held Danny's gaze. "He's my best friend, Gwen." He reached for Danny's hand and held it. "I love him."

A profound silence fell over the table. Tom dropped his fork with an audible clink. "Christ," he said. "Thought you were straight and all."

"You should never make assumptions, Tom." Danny patted Tadhg's hand before letting go of it. "That's the sort of thing that gets you in a lot of trouble."

The rest of the dinner passed with awkward conversation. Gwen picked at her plate while Tom shoveled his dinner in like a machine. The pan-fried cod and scruncheons was followed by a light shrimp bisque and then lobster tails in lemon and garlic. There was coffee and cloudberry cheesecake to finish, after which Gwen and Tom fled to their suite to pack. "Let me know which flight you've booked," Tadhg said, "and I'll have Jesper take you to the airport."

He and Danny sat with Lily for a while in the rec room downstairs, watching a local film about mummering. "Be Christmas soon," Tadhg observed, reaching to tweak Danny's earlobe. They were sitting on the large leather sofa together, Danny half-reclining in the circle of Tadhg's arms while Lily stretched on the floor in front of the TV, her chin in her hands. She rolled onto her back as soon as Tadhg said this, then up into a sitting position.

"Danny, you'll have Christmas with us, won't you?"

Tadhg felt Danny's body tighten. "We'll have to see how your dad feels about that, my darling."

"But you haven't got anybody to have Christmas with," Lily said. She appealed to her father. "You want him to come for Christmas, don't you?"

Tadhg jostled Danny's elbow. "You'll break her heart if you say no."

"I feel like I'm being ganged up on." Danny laughed. "Yes, I'd love to."

"It's on Tuesday this year," Tadhg said. "Why not come on Sunday night and spend Christmas Eve as well?"

Danny turned until he could see Tadhg's face. "You're sure that won't be an imposition?"

"It's no imposition at all," Tadhg replied quietly. He wrapped an arm around Danny's waist and pulled him backwards so he was lying against Tadhg's chest. "We'd love it if you had Christmas with us."

Once the film had ended, Tadhg saw Lily to bed, then returned to the rec room with a bottle of chardonnay and two glasses. Danny was still sitting where Tadhg had left him. He poured the glasses and handed one to Danny. "Deep thoughts?"

Danny shook his head and sat his glass down on the coffee table. "Come here," he murmured. He pulled Tadhg close and kissed him long and deep. "Maybe we don't need the wine," he said, when he at last drew away.

"I want you to stay." There was a naked vulnerability in Tadhg's eyes, as though even now he feared Danny's rejection. "I want you to stay the night. With me."

And then they were in Tadhg's bedroom, gazing at one another, suddenly shy, both of them lost for words. *Maybe words are beside the point,* Danny thought. He reached to cradle Tadhg's face in his hands and kiss him—long and deep and wet, an aching caress full of the desire of years. It was so entirely fitting that finally it had come to this, and nothing else.

Danny must have slept, for suddenly a light was in his eyes, and the corridor outside Tadhg's bedroom was full of sounds and voices. He sat up, acutely aware of his nakedness, holding the duvet close to him. The bedroom door opened and Tadhg was there. Oddly enough, he was fully dressed for outdoors in a heavy coat and boots. "What is it?" Danny asked. "What's happened?"

"She's sick," Tadhg said tersely. "Lily's had another hemorrhage. It's… it's bad this time."

It went through him like a spear. *It's punishment. We're being punished.* He wondered at his sudden superstition, his apparent belief in a God who saw fit to avenge himself on an innocent young girl. He forced the thought away from him. "What can I do?"

"A helicopter's on the way from Universal. Luckily there was one coming back from the rigs. Will you come with me?"

Danny got up and dressed as quickly as possible. Even though it was warm in the room, he was shaking, his hands fumbling with his buttons and zippers. "Where's Gwen and her fancy man?"

"Downstairs." Tadhg, anticipating Danny's response, had brought his coat and boots along. He glanced up at the insistent noise of approaching helicopter blades. "Here they are."

"Right behind ye."

Yvonne, Lily's nurse, was waiting at the foot of the stairs with Lily, who was wrapped in several layers of blankets, a bloodstained bath towel pressed against her face. She sought Danny's gaze as he neared, and he reached out a hand to her, squeezing her thin shoulder. "Won't be long now, love." The front door flew open and two paramedics stepped inside, bearing a stretcher between them. Danny followed Tadhg outside and into the waiting helicopter.

THE HOSPITAL chapel was small and plain, representative of no particular denomination. A stained-glass window behind the altar bore an abstract illustration of a white dove surmounted by a rainbow, but there were no hymnals or holy pictures, no agonal Christ writhing on his cross. Besides himself and Danny, the room was empty, and Tadhg was glad, even though he doubted anyone would expect civil conversation.

"I don't know what's going to happen to me." His own voice sounded unnaturally loud in the little room. "We've been fighting this thing for years, Lily and me. Surely to God it can't be over." He turned to Danny, who was sitting beside him in the narrow pew. "Can it?"

"Do ye want to say a prayer?" Danny asked. Tadhg knew Danny didn't believe in God—couldn't believe in God, not after some of the things he'd seen in his life. "If it would help, I mean."

"I'm going to lose her, aren't I?" It was hollowing him out inside, this horrible expectation. "What am I going to do?"

"Wait until we've heard from the doctor," Danny said. He reached for Tadhg's hand, lacing their fingers together. "Let's not get ahead of ourselves. There's a lot we don't know yet."

They left the chapel and made their way back to the family waiting room outside the ICU. Moira Fraser stood up and hugged Tadhg as he approached. "Danny told me what happened," she said. "I wanted to be here." Tadhg saw Cillian Riley returning from the coffee shop with a laden tray.

"Mr. Heaney." He laid the tray down on a nearby cabinet. "I hope you don't mind." He glanced at Danny for a second, and in that brief moment, something passed between them, a recognition and a realization that struck Tadhg between the eyes. "Inspector Quirke and I are… well, we've become friends. When I heard about the young miss…." He drew what sounded like a nervous breath. "I thought to add my prayers to your own."

Inspector Quirke and I. Riley had been careful to call Danny by his title, rather than his Christian name—like he was hiding something, or trying to conceal a truth he figured nobody else need know about. Oh, it was easy to understand what Danny saw in him. He was younger than Tadhg, well built and gorgeous… and available. Tadhg imagined Riley made himself quite available to senior officers whenever the situation warranted. He'd almost certainly made himself available to Danny. Probably they'd ducked out in the middle of a shift, Tadhg thought, found themselves a little hideaway where they could fuck undetected. He should have known. Here he was making a fool of himself with Danny, when all along Danny's attention was focused elsewhere. And Danny then lying in Tadhg's bed with him, exchanging kisses and caresses interspersed with murmured declarations of affection. What a bloody cheek.

"I don't need your prayers," Tadhg said bitterly, "and neither does my daughter." He sat down on one of the hard plastic chairs outside the unit and waited, rubbing his tired eyes and trying not to look at his watch. He ought to be in there with Lily, holding her hand, talking to her even if she couldn't hear him. He was her father, for Christ's sake. It ought to count for something. He clenched his fists so hard the bones in his hands creaked. Danny reached over and touched his wrist, nodded towards the other end of the corridor. Tadhg got up and went with him.

"I can't imagine how hard this is for you," Danny said when they stood together near an exit door. It wasn't fitted properly and leaked cold air that swirled around the back of Tadhg's neck and lifted the hairs on his arms. "I wish there was more I could do." He rested his hands on Tadhg's shoulders.

"Well, at least your young fancy man turned up." As soon as he'd said it, Tadhg realised he'd made a grave error, but there was no going back now.

"What?" Danny asked, puzzled.

"Young Riley down there." Tadhg deliberately kept his gaze fixed on a nearby window, where his and Danny's reflections gleamed back at him, surrounded by the winter darkness. "I should have figured it out before now, but I guess I'm stupider than you give me credit for." He shrugged Danny's hands off his shoulders. "I knew as soon as I saw the two of ye together. I'm not stupid, ye know. I do understand what that looks like." He laughed, a bitter sound without any humour in it. "That just-fucked look, isn't that what they call it?"

Danny stared at him, pupils wide with shock. "What…?" Tadhg turned away. "Wait." Danny started after him. "What the hell are you talking about?"

"Was he good in bed?" Tadhg hissed. "Looking like that, he could hardly be anything other."

"We weren't together then." Danny narrowed his eyes. "Me and you weren't together when I—"

"When you fucked the boy wonder?"

"Tadhg, I swear to you—" He paused, decided to rephrase it. "I love you, Tadhg," he said quietly. "You know that."

"I know nothing of the sort. Now if you'll please fuck off, there's somewhere else I have to be. My daughter is dying."

Danny recoiled as if he'd been physically slapped. Now there was a thought. Maybe if he clocked him a good one round the face, Danny might get the message that his misplaced sympathy was neither wanted nor required. "Fine." He nodded. "Right." He turned and walked away, pushing open the exit door and clattering noisily down the stairs to the ground floor.

"Good riddance," Tadhg murmured. He knew his petulance was childish but he couldn't help himself. He needed to hurt someone, make someone else suffer as much as he was suffering right now. Was he keeping score? Was that how it worked? Whenever Danny hurt him, he'd return the favour, matching every flick of the lash?

Yet Danny had said he loved him.

Tadhg walked back to where the others were waiting and sat down. He dropped his head into his hands, wishing he could summon enough tears to relieve the horrible weight resting on his heart, but his eyes were as dry as the Sahara.

DANNY DROVE around town, going nowhere. It was very late, past three in the morning, and bitterly cold. He could have gone home, but he didn't see the point, and besides, he intended to return to the hospital as soon as his anger had lost its ragged edge. He parked for a while on the waterfront, but the swirls of blowing snow obscured any view he might have had. He should have told Tadhg about Riley, should have made certain Tadhg knew before they even went to bed together. Had he deliberately held back the truth, fearing Tadhg would react exactly as he'd reacted tonight?

He pulled into the small car park bordering Bannerman Park. There were other parks in the city, other places he might have gone, but this one had always been his favourite. It was small, tucked tidily into a corner of the historic district, bordered by stately Queen Anne Revival mansions and venerable old churches, the Presentation Convent and School. There was an ice-skating loop, a bandstand dating back to the Second World War, and benches sprinkled between the stately oaks and maples. Danny pulled his coat tight around him as a gust of wind dashed icy spindrift into his face. It was well below zero, bitterly cold, the kind of night that always had him worrying about the city's homeless, the vagrants who drifted here and there among the ancient streets and empty laneways. In years gone by, when he was still new to the constabulary, he'd chanced now and then to find some poor soul expired on a bench or huddled beneath a picnic table. One freezing January night, he and Alison had come upon a boy of about fourteen, curled against the side of a restaurant, his skinny knees drawn up to his chin. He'd been dead for several hours, his skin icy to the touch when Danny bent to check him for a pulse. Danny had wept for him, waiting for the ambulance with Alison. "D'ye know him?" she asked.

Danny did. "He was a rent boy," he told her. "I see him down here every night." You couldn't always tell. Sometimes they looked like your usual young lads out for devilment, hats on backwards, pants bagging down around their arses, skateboards under their arms. They didn't stand about on street corners soliciting, although some of them frequented Church Hill, where the nightly parade of curb-crawling older men never let up.

Despite the cold and the late hour, several people were gliding around the skating loop to the Pogues' "Fairytale of New York." No lie, it was Danny's favourite Christmas song. The canteen was still open, perfuming the air with the smell of coffee and baked pastries, hand-cut chips hot from the deep fryer and served in greasy brown paper bags. Maybe when Lily was better, he and Tadhg could take her skating some night, buy hot chocolate and sip it underneath the coloured Christmas lights. She would be well again. She had to be. Danny couldn't imagine Tadhg existing without her. If Lily died, Tadhg would waste away and perish.

He left the park, driving home through the nearly empty streets to the lonely void of his apartment, where he waited in the dark. The hours crawled by like years while he sat in his habitual armchair by the window and looked out at the Southside hills. He watched the lights of other people's cars going up into Shea Heights and coming down again, and then the slow crawl of false dawn spilling through the Narrows. It was cold, and he ought to have put the heat on, but he'd lost all impetus and couldn't move. He held his cell phone in one hand, bending his head to gaze at it now and then. What was happening in the hospital? Where was Tadhg? He ought to call someone, perhaps Moira Fraser, find out what was going on. Tadhg would think he didn't care.

When he woke the next morning, it was full daylight outside, and snowing. The sky was a soft dove grey, and the snow fell straight down from it in large, feathery flakes. He felt cramped, contorted in the chair as he was, and it was very cold in the flat, so cold that he could see his own breath. His mobile phone was lit up blue and vibrating in his hand. "Hello?"

"Danny." It was Tadhg. "Where did you go?"

"I went home." He sat up straighter, wincing as his back cracked. "What's after happening?"

"That's why I'm calling." He heard something in Tadhg's voice that had long been absent: a cautious optimism. "She's going to be all right. The transplant worked after all. It just took a while longer. She might still have nosebleeds. They said it's not always an exact science." Tadhg drew a long, quivering breath. "The doctor came in, and she's— you have to come—you have to come and see her, Danny. She's asking for you."

Chapter Nineteen

Danny had stopped back home after seeing Lily to change clothes and have some breakfast. He was jubilant—that was the only word for it—on seeing her profound transition from sickness to health. He didn't believe in so-called Christmas miracles, but what had happened to Lily was perhaps evidence of some kind of providential angels.

"They're right resilient, the young people," Tadhg had said, standing with him in Lily's room. "She's just grand, she is so." He reached out and smoothed Danny's stubbled cheek with the backs of his knuckles. "You're pretty grand yourself." They'd tacitly agreed not to mention Cillian Riley, at least not then. He was a topic for another time, when things had settled down and returned to something approaching normal. And Tadhg had even kissed him before he left, full on the mouth and right in front of the doctors and nurses. "Will I see you later?"

"I hope so," Danny replied. He glanced to where Lily was peacefully sleeping. "D'ye want me to bring ye anything? Coffee, breakfast?" He grinned. "Bottle of Glenfiddich?"

"I wouldn't mind a bit of breakfast," Tadhg said. "Something sustaining."

"Full breakfast from Ches's," Danny said. The local fish-and-chip shop was a perennial favourite for more than just their deep-fried cod. They did a mean breakfast fry-up too.

"With toutons," Tadhg said, referring to the lumps of fried bread dough drizzled with molasses. "I'm famished."

"I won't be long," Danny had promised. He intended to keep that promise. He shucked last night's clothes and stepped into clean jeans and a woolly sweater, layering a thick scarf around his neck before slipping on his jacket. There was a distinct taste of snow in the air as he stepped outside. They'd have heavy weather before long, no doubt about it.

"Are you Danny Quirke?"

The summons came from across the street. A well-dressed man about Danny's age stood leaning on the hood of a late-model BMW, smoking a cigarette. "Joe Ellis," he said as Danny approached. He held out his hand. "I daresay you don't know me from Adam. I'm Nina Single's husband."

Danny blinked, jarred by the sound of her name. "Nina Single?"

Ellis took a last draw on his cigarette and flicked the butt into the street, where it died in a shower of sparks. "We're getting divorced," he said, "me and Nina. About bloody time too." He pulled back his coat to examine his wristwatch. "They're probably arresting her right now."

"Arresting her?" Danny was confused. "Ye've lost me."

"You and that other fellow, Tadhg Heaney." Ellis paused long enough to light a second cigarette. Good Christ, Danny thought, the man was eating them for breakfast. "You pissed her off once when the three of you were youngsters."

"Right. The card we sent her." It was a typical kids' prank—not very nice and certainly not kind, but it hardly warranted mention in the adult world.

"She likes to hold grudges, Nina does."

Danny was starting to get impatient. "If there's a point, Mr. Ellis, I wish ye'd make it. There's somewhere I've got to be." He still needed to pick up breakfast for Tadhg and get back to the hospital.

"I'll be as quick as I can. Nina hired Roger Palmer to run Tadhg Heaney down. She's still pissed off about the nasty letter you sent her back in school. She's been fucking with the two of ye, sending notes telling ye to remember. Always dramatic, that one. She got hold of Heaney's wallet from the evidence locker at the RCMP. She works there—or she did. I don't think she'll be working anywhere, not after today." He laughed with genuine relish. "You can't imagine the bloody torment that woman has been to me from day one." He shook his head. "I'll be glad to get rid of her. I'd have dumped her in the fucking harbour if I thought I could get away with it."

"You wouldn't," Danny told him. "Get away with it, I mean."

"Anyway." Ellis moved to open his car door. "She won't be bothering either one of ye no more. I just thought you should know." He lowered himself into the seat, then rolled the window down and waved at Danny. "Merry Christmas." With that, he put the car in gear and drove away. Danny watched the BMW vanish down Leslie Street, pausing at the corner before turning onto Water Street, heading west.

A little while later, Danny checked his email messages while he was waiting for his breakfast order at Ches's. There was the usual spam and garbage, adverts for penis enhancers and lonely Russian women looking for husbands, but one particular message caught his attention. It was from the constabulary, a terse little paragraph informing him that the internal inquiry had ruled in his favour and he could be reinstated at his earliest convenience. They made no mention of paying him back wages, though, the cheap bastards. He grimaced, wondering if he should let loose and tell the whole bloody lot of them what he thought, but in the end decided to exercise restraint. He thanked them for the information, told them his career plans were on hold until after the holidays, and he would certainly let them know.

He took himself and the hot bag of food back to the hospital. Tadhg met Danny at the elevator, drew him close and kissed him. "She's sitting up on her own." He couldn't stop smiling. "Asking for breakfast and all. She's actually hungry, Danny. For the first time in ages." Danny passed him the bag, and he peered inside. "God, that smells heavenly. We can eat in her room if you want. The doctor said it's fine."

Lily was sitting propped up against her pillows, doing something on her iPad, when Danny and Tadhg arrived. She dropped the tablet immediately and held out her arms to Danny, wanting to be hugged. He squeezed her gently, afraid of hurting her. "I'm not made of glass," she scoffed. "Anyway, if you're going to be my stepfather, you'll have to give good hugs. It's part of the deal."

Danny looked at Tadhg, suddenly bewildered. "Stepfather?" he asked. "Deal?"

"Lily, we talked about this." Tadhg glared at her. "Stop getting ahead of yourself." He sat down on the end of her bed and pulled the small rolling table towards him. "Danny, get that other chair."

"Family breakfast." Lily sighed with exaggerated happiness. "All three of us together." She accepted the touton Tadhg passed her and doused it in molasses. "God, I've been dreaming of these," she said before taking a bite. "It's fucking ambrosia, this is."

"What have I told you about that word?" Tadhg said. He was trying for sternness and failing miserably. It was cute. "Here." He portioned the breakfast out between two paper plates and handed Danny some plastic cutlery. "Tuck in. You must be hungry."

"Where's Gwen?" Danny asked after he'd downed the first few bites of egg and sausage. "Didn't come to say goodbye?"

"I've had a text from her." Tadhg pried the lid off his cardboard container of tea and took a sip. "They're on their way across the ocean."

"Good riddance to bad rubbish," Danny said. "I mean, did they actually think we were going to let them take Lily to Spain?"

"I don't think *we* will let Lily go anywhere for a while," Tadhg said, smiling. "I think *we* have to make sure she stays safe at home for as long as possible."

"I couldn't really arrest them," Danny said. "I hope you know that. The badge was just for show. Officially I was on 'administrative leave.'" He made air quotes with his fingers. "I'd no jurisdiction whatsoever." All at once he twigged to what Tadhg had said. "We?" he asked quietly. Danny was anything but bashful, but at that moment he was feeling an overwhelming wash of shyness. It wouldn't do to misread the situation, presume Tadhg was offering him something.

"We," Tadhg confirmed. "If you're up for that." He sipped some more tea and made a face. "This tea's horrible. I swear to God it tastes like sweaty socks." He snagged another touton and drizzled it with molasses. "Listen now," he said to Danny, "I've been thinking."

"Oh?" Danny caught Lily's eye and winked at her. "Stepfather" indeed. Had she and Tadhg been discussing him while he was gone?

"About your grandfather's house."

"It burned down," Danny reminded him. "Nothing left but ashes. I bet the blueberries will grow some good there next summer, though." Fire purified the earth, burning away old growth and encouraging the emergence of new plants. You burned your pasture land once every couple of years so the grass would come in. It paved the way for new life and a fresh start.

"I know that," Tadhg retorted. "I was thinking about a reconstruction. You know, rebuild on that same spot, using the original house plans. I want something from that era...." He smiled, his eyes alight with possibility. Danny liked seeing him this way, alert and engaged with life. "And I was thinking up the back, redo the old stable, and then put a row of beach huts to one side of the house. What do you think?"

"For holidays," Danny said. "Is that what you mean?" Something occurred to him. "How are you going to have beach huts if there's no beach? Sure the beach is a quarter mile away."

Tadhg shook his head impatiently. "Details," he said, "mere details. Now, I want to build the house again, restored to period—"

"You can't restore something that's not there," Danny pointed out.

Tadhg huffed out an irritated breath. "Would you shut up, for the love of Jesus?"

"Way to go, Dad." Lily speared a slice of bacon from his plate. "The two of ye sound married already."

"Beach huts," Tadhg went on, "and a saltbox house, original nineteenth century design, heritage paint colours. All original or restoration furniture inside, wooden table and chairs, one of those old oil stoves. The grounds are beautiful, but I might put in a swimming pool. A family-friendly, pet-friendly holiday rental where people can come to get away from it all. What do you think?"

A new house on his grandfather's land, rising out of the ashes. People coming from far and wide to enjoy the property, hike and pick berries on the hills, swim and picnic with their children and their pets. "It sounds ideal," Danny replied. "It sounds wonderful." It would serve to lay a lot of ghosts and put to rest the pain of several generations. "You'll be looking for investors?" This was a polite way of asking where Tadhg intended to get the money for this project.

"Already lined up," Tadhg said. He turned to drop his empty plate into the bin and wiped his mouth with a paper napkin.

"Please tell me it's nobody from Amsterdam," Danny pleaded. The last thing Tadhg needed was to get tangled up again with Rutger What's-his-face.

"It's nobody from Amsterdam," Tadhg reassured him. "He's Australian, in fact. A real nice fellow with more money than God." He grinned. "Your sister knows him. She put me on to him. They're coming back for a visit in the spring to look at the site. I've been talking to him on Skype. He's into hotels all over Europe. I think it'll be a good fit."

Danny started to laugh. He laughed and laughed until tears ran out of his eyes. "God Almighty," he gasped, "there's no flies on you, my son." He pushed his empty plate away and stood up to take his leave, leaning in to give Lily a hug.

Tadhg walked to the elevator with him. "What are your plans for today?" he asked.

"Christmas shopping," Danny said. "Sure it's only a few days now. What do you think Lily would like?"

"She'll love anything you give her," Tadhg told him. "She thinks you hung the moon." He reached out and pulled Danny into his arms, hugging him tight and holding on. "So do I," he murmured. He drew back so he could gaze into Danny's eyes. "I love you." Danny grinned at him, but said nothing. "Well, d'ye love me or not?" Tadhg asked, huffily.

Danny shrugged. "A bit, I suppose." He laughed aloud at Tadhg's expression, then leaned in to kiss him. "You know I do."

"Call me later on," Tadhg said, as the elevator arrived and Danny stepped inside.

Danny shrugged again. "I might," he teased, "I might not." He kissed Tadhg again. The taste of Tadhg, the feel of him, tingled in his belly and his scalp and the soles of his feet. It would be difficult to concentrate on anything else for the rest of the day. "Bye." The doors slid shut, and Tadhg disappeared from view.

DANNY HAD been thinking of Moira Fraser when she suddenly appeared over a rack of ties. He'd been perusing the items on offer at William L. Chafe and Son, a venerable haberdashery responsible for outfitting "the quality" since the year dot, in the hope of finding something suitable for Tadhg. He'd about decided to buy him a bottle of Scotch instead when he spotted a handsome dark grey tie with a paisley pattern… and Moira Fraser. She rushed towards him smiling, and for a moment he was afraid she might embrace him.

"Danny. I've been hoping to run into you." She glanced at the tie he was holding. "Are you going to buy that? Listen now, we should go for a coffee. I have something to tell you, and I think you'll want to hear it." She waited while he paid for the present and had it wrapped, then held the door open for him to step out onto Water Street. "Come on, then."

They took a corner table in a small café and ordered hot coffee and pastries. Danny was still full from breakfast, so a fresh-baked scone was an extravagance he didn't really need, but he reasoned he could work it off later, maybe go for a run or something. In bed with Tadhg or something. The idea produced a thrilling frisson of pleasure.

"You're busting to tell me, so get it over with," Danny said.

But Moira took her time, warming her hands around the coffee mug. Finally she said, "You turned down an offer of reinstatement from the constabulary."

Danny looked up from buttering his scone. "How the hell did you know that? I only just gave them my decision."

"Unofficial channels." She smirked. "You know nothing's a secret in this place."

He allowed that this was true. Hard to believe a city of 100,000 or so people had a gossip network to rival an old wives' weekday knitting club, though. "And?" Danny prompted. He bit into his scone, which was warm and buttery and dripping with cloudberry jam.

"I've been trying for ages to float this idea past my bosses. They finally agreed." She stirred sugar into her coffee. "Danny, I'm wondering if you'd come and work for us."

"What?" A blob of jam clung to his lower lip; he swiped at it with a napkin. "Work for the RCMP?"

Moira nodded. "The Harbour Grace detachment wants to increase police presence in places like Kildevil Cove, but the federal government is dragging its heels. With the increase of rural drug trafficking, we're seeing a lot more serious crimes committed in these little tiny places where you'd think nothing ever happens."

"I'm listening," Danny prompted.

"We initially hoped to set up a separate detachment, but I'm afraid that's not going to happen. No funding, lack of proper administration available, blah blah blah. But"—her eyes sparkled with pleasure—"we'd like to set up a small substation in Kildevil Cove or New Melbourne, somewhere on the Avalon Peninsula outside of St. John's, responsible for the entire area. It's to be a joint task force, us and the RNC. I want you to run it."

Someone dropped something in the kitchen; it fell with a noisy clatter like the clanging of an out-of-tune bell. Danny stared at Moira. "Are you taking the piss right now?"

"I'm quite serious. You'd have the rank of inspector, same as before, but you'd answer directly to me." She bit into her croissant.

"You're giving me my own patch?"

"Your own patch, your own station, a handful of staff—nothing too extravagant, mind you. There's no funding for it. But we could give you three or four people to start with, and we'll go from there."

He sat back, stunned into momentary silence. "Inspector," he said. "Detective. Homicide?"

"Yes. CID, same as when you worked with the constabulary." She pushed her plate aside and laid her hands flat on the table. "Danny, I need you. A strong and visible police presence in that area is becoming more and more necessary. You'd be doing me a favour if you said yes."

He didn't hesitate. "Yes. Good Christ, *yes*!" He laughed. "I guess it won't be for a while. I mean, you'd need to find a space and get it outfitted."

"Already done," Moira said crisply.

He stared at her. "You were that sure I'd agree?"

"I hoped you would."

"Right." Moira wasn't one to let grass grow under her feet.

"So you'll start January 2. I'm eager to get this thing up and running." She drew her plate towards her and polished off the rest of her croissant in several huge bites. "Being a pig," she said, "but I'm starved. Think I'll have another one." She waved at the waiter as he went by. The young man reversed course and came back to their table. "I've got news about your grandfather's house, by the way." Moira smiled at the waiter. "Another one of these croissants, please."

The young man offered the coffee pot, and Danny held out his cup for a refill. "So you know who burned it down."

"It's a simple enough story. A longtime Heaney's employee was fired for stealing. When he heard Tadhg was buying your grandfather's house, he went in and tore the place up. Apparently that didn't satisfy his need for vengeance. He went back, doused it in gasoline, and dropped a match."

"But there's no crime in rural Newfoundland," Danny said sarcastically. He stirred cream into his coffee.

"And I must apologise for Rory." The waiter returned with Moira's second croissant; she accepted it with murmured thanks. "Our cousin Ronin was at the sea wall in Dublin the day Eamonn Nolan died. He's tight with Rory. The two of them talk all the time. His description of events managed to cross the Atlantic before the official version. Tadhg Heaney was building a house for Rory and his fiancée. He must have overheard Rory on the phone."

"Why didn't he tell me?" Danny said. "Tadhg, I mean. He could have told me." He supposed Tadhg had told him, in his own way.

"I'm sorry Rory caused you so much trouble." Moira reached out and placed a hand over his. "He's been disciplined and placed on administrative leave."

"So that's that." Danny gazed down into his cup. "You know, these past few months I've had enough excitement to last me for the next ten years. I hope it's quiet in the new year."

"Don't count on it, Danny Boy. You're the sort of man things happen to." Moira grinned at him over the rim of her cup. "Welcome aboard."

Epilogue

December 25

DANNY ROLLED over in bed and smiled as his outstretched hand connected with Tadhg's warm shoulder. "Merry Christmas," he murmured. Tadhg opened his arms, and Danny went into his embrace, sighing happily. "As far as Christmas presents go, this is pretty friggin' good," he said.

"It is, isn't it?" Tadhg's eyes were a little red-rimmed and bleary—probably from the large amount of celebratory Scotch they'd drunk the night before—but he was smiling. "Do you think Roger Palmer cares that his cousin's death has finally been ruled accidental?" he asked Danny. One of Moira's contacts in the RCMP had gotten in touch with Danny late on Christmas Eve to relay the news.

Danny frowned. "I don't think Roger Palmer gives a Jesus about anything," he said.

"I'll never forget it," Tadhg said. His voice was hushed. "I still think we could have saved him."

"Tadhg—"

"No." Tadhg moved so that he was looking down at Danny. "It was my fault. I got scared in the water. I should have pushed forward. We could have reached him. I know we could have. He'd be alive now."

Danny cupped Tadhg's cheek in his palm and smoothed his thumb over Tadhg's lower lip. "Is that what you've thought all these years?" he asked quietly. When Tadhg didn't answer, he went on. "They think it's likely he had a seizure, Tadhg."

"What?"

"Llew had epilepsy. Remember all those times he missed school because he was sick? He'd been having grand mal seizures for years, some so severe they nearly killed him." Llewellyn had been in and out of hospital for much of his childhood, prey to violent convulsions that often left him bedridden for days. "Moira's team checked the medical records, and they confirmed it. Even if we could have reached him in time, it's likely he still would have died."

Tadhg shook his head. "He was my brother. I should have tried harder."

Danny sighed. "My darling, you can't be crucifying yourself with guilt. Let it go." He kissed Tadhg gently. "There's no point in trying to turn back the clock. It's sad the way he died, but you had nothing to do with it."

"He should have a proper funeral," Tadhg said. "After all these years. A decent burial, for Christ's sake. He deserves that much."

"Do you want me to talk to Father Kelly?" Danny asked. The local parish priest had known them both since they were boys, had known Llewellyn too.

"Thought you had no time for religion," Tadhg teased.

Danny sighed. "Sometimes ye have to make concessions," he allowed. "At least a funeral will let you lay his memory to rest," he said, "and that's the right thing."

They were quiet for a moment. Tadhg rested back onto his pillow, facing Danny. "Did it help you?" he asked.

Danny was confused. "Did what help me?"

"Having a funeral… for Alison." He gazed sombrely at Danny. "You never did tell me how… how she died."

"It was horrible." He could never allow himself to forget it, nor would he ever will the memories away. She'd been the world to him. "It took ages for the doctors to figure out what it was," he said. "Months of tests, day after day being hooked up to machines." They'd taken MRI scans, PET scans, run several sleep studies. Alison was adopted and had never known her biological family, so genetic testing was pointless, and anyway not all cases were inherited. "Fatal insomnia, they called it." Danny laughed mirthlessly. "Jesus, I'd never even heard of the fucking thing before. First they thought it might be early-onset Alzheimer's, because a lot of the symptoms are alike. She started—"

"Danny," Tadhg interjected, "if this is too difficult—"

Danny shook his head wordlessly, and gathered himself. "She was having trouble falling asleep. At first we didn't think anything of it. She saw the doctor and got some sleeping tablets." Rather than helping to induce unconsciousness, the pills made Alison more alert than ever. "It took six months," Danny told him, "for her to die, completely sleep-deprived, demented by exhaustion. She was walking around dreaming while she was wide awake. When she died it was… such a relief. Is that a horrible thing to say?"

"No."

They were silent for a long time together, Tadhg holding him.

"So you can't ever die," Danny said after a while.

Tadhg laughed. "I'll make sure not to in that case."

"Dad?" There was a gentle tap on the door. "Are you guys decent or are you, like, doing it?"

"See what you signed up for?" Tadhg said, grinning. "Still time to back out, you know."

"Wouldn't dream of it," Danny replied. "We're decent, Lily," he called, his heart already warming to her presence. "You can come in."

Exclusive Excerpt

Dark Mire

A Kildevil Cove Mystery

By J.S. Cook

You never know what trouble will rise from the bog.

When the body of an unidentified woman is found in a Newfoundland bog, Inspector Danny Quirke must scramble his team of investigators to find her killer. But what initially seems like a straightforward case soon becomes mired in a tangled web of lies and deliberate obfuscation.

With the strange mutilation of the body—one eye gouged out completely—evidence seems to lead to a fringe religious group with bizarre beliefs. But while the pathologist indicates mushroom poisoning as the cause of death, Danny thinks circumstances point to something more sinister—especially when he begins to receive anonymous messages with links to horrific pictures of damaged human eyes.

Three more bodies join the first, with seemingly nothing to link them but a little girl in a yellow party dress who flits in and out of the mystery like a creature from the old legends. Then an old friend from his childhood reappears, and Danny is forced to confront uncomfortable truths about his own nearest and dearest.

On an island, everyone is a suspect….

Coming Soon to
www.dreamspinnerpress.com

PROLOGUE

MUCH TOO early to be out here picking berries, and she wouldn't be anyway. The old woman—Eileen, Azariah's mother—had made sure to fill her head with old wives' tales about the unwary being fairy-led, enticed away to some foreign country not of this world and made to live in slavery. "They'll play you the finest music you ever heard, my dear, and you mightn't want to dance, but you will. Oh, you'll dance all right. Dance till ye dies."

She shuddered reflexively, her usual response any time the old woman crossed her mind. Yes, she was Azariah's grandmother, and it was only right they take on the care and housing of her, especially now she was so feeble. "It's the right thing to do," he'd said. "She brought me up after Mam died. I owes her that much, and blood is blood."

Yes, blood is blood, she thought now. Blood drove her out here onto the barrens, away from Eileen's incessant complaining, her constant talk and dire warnings. It was blood that would bring her back, the hardening and stinging of her overfull breasts, ready to let down milk the moment young Barry cried for it. The baby, too, had driven her outdoors. Ever since she brought him home from the hospital, he'd seemed to do nothing but cry, wailing inconsolably, face red and fists clenched. The nurses told her she'd bond with him, but so far, the overwhelming love she'd expected to feel was noticeably absent. She hadn't even wanted children, but Azariah had insisted. Having children was what you did, and his Apostolic Pentecostal faith dictated you have as many as possible. Breeding and raising the Lord's army was the highest calling a woman could aspire to. If only she had known, she might have chosen differently, but she'd been mad in love with him, had willfully closed her eyes to his family's extreme beliefs. When he told her to stop cutting her hair, she'd obeyed; similarly, she'd agreed when he asked her to stop wearing cosmetics, to trade her skin-tight jeans for more modest, ankle-length skirts. He'd made it worth her while. She knew Azariah loved her, was utterly devoted to her, and she loved him. She'd spent too long living an ungodly life, ricocheting from man to man, selling herself cheap in the bars and nightclubs of St. John's.

But this latest was the final straw, the one that broke her back.

"We'll get started on the next one as soon as possible," he'd told her. "That's what God wants." Despite the fact that she was just out of hospital and still bleeding heavily, he'd forced her legs apart and drove himself inside of her.

"We're supposed to wait six weeks," she protested. "That's what the doctor said." The birth had been a difficult one, and the baby's head had ripped her open. "I'm too sore."

"This is what God wants," he said. When he finally rolled off her, the sheets were soaked in her blood. "Mam'll see to ye," he told her. The old woman had come with fresh cabbage leaves and made a compress for her. It didn't help. Eventually the bleeding stopped of its own accord, but the doctor's stitches had come apart where Azariah's zeal had torn her open again. Eileen gave her something to drink that made her nauseated and eventually sleepy, and she fell into a stupor. When finally she woke an entire day had passed, and the baby was crying. The baby was always crying. She rose and washed herself, dressed in jeans and rubber boots and a thick wool sweater, layered her raincoat over it. Still only April, and the weather was capricious this time of year. It might rain for days, or it might snow—you never knew. She pulled a knitted cap over her hair and put gloves on her hands. Eileen stopped her at the door.

"Where do ye think you're going?" she asked.

"I'm going for a walk."

"And that you're not!" The old woman was furious. "That baby has been in there crying. He wants feeding, and you're going to feed him." She grabbed Deborah's arm between her stick-thin fingers, pinching cruelly. "You get in that room and feed that youngster."

"Feed him yourself!" Deborah yanked her arm from the old woman's grasp.

Eileen was outraged. "Ye'll burn in hell for this."

Deborah spun away from her and reached for the latch on the outer storm door. It was rusted, in need of replacement or repair, like most things around this place. The house itself was little better than a tilt, a hastily built structure of salvaged wood and stone, a ramshackle dwelling that all but advertised the misery within. "I don't believe in hell!"

"It's shocking, that's what it is, pure shocking. Ye're his mother—"

Deborah rounded on her. "I never wanted the fucking youngster in the first place." She slapped her palm upwards against the latch, and it finally gave, but not before pinching her fingers painfully. She swore and then put her damaged fingers in her mouth to suck out the pain. With a push, she opened the door, and then she was out.

She was free.

A light but insistent drizzle was falling, the thin stream of water sifting down upon her, wetting her curly dark hair. She set out at a fast pace, moving uphill from the house and striking out across the strip of boggy ground that separated her from the road. She had no clear plan in mind. She'd get out to the high road and hitchhike into St. John's, get work in one of the clubs down on George Street. Sure, she'd just had a baby, but it would be no time before she got her figure back, and then they'd see something. She hadn't lost her confidence. She could twirl around the pole with the best of them. As for Azariah, she was finished with him. He could do as he liked, and his mother too. No doubt they'd decry her as a fallen woman, an unfit mother who abandoned her days-old infant to his fate. Well, that was just too bad. Needs must when the devil drove.

She had just crossed in front of the old United Church when she heard it, a thin sound like a cat's meow. At first, she thought the ever-present wind was playing tricks on her, the way there sometimes seemed to be voices in it, hissing and singing. The old woman said the dead were all around, and if you had ears to listen you could hear them whispering, but Deborah thought that was so much shite. Like most things Eileen said, one would be well advised to take it with a heavy dose of salt.

"Hello?" She felt like an idiot, standing by herself in the lane and calling out into the darkness, but what if someone was there? What if an animal or child had fallen into the ditch and injured themselves? She'd never forgive herself if she let an animal suffer. She loved animals. "Is someone there?" She heard it again, the same low cry. "Do you need help? Are you hurt or something?"

"Missus, I fell down." The voice came from behind her now, and she whirled around. A small girl stood there, grinning broadly. Her long, curly dark hair was pulled back in a pink ribbon and she was wearing a pink party dress. She was barefoot and wore no coat or hat. "Can ye help me go home?"

"Go home?"

"It's over there." The girl turned and pointed back in the direction Deborah had come, towards the barrens. "Mam'll be awful worried about me." As if on cue, she started to cry, such a sudden eruption of violent weeping that Deborah took a step back, startled and discomfited. "She'll smack me." The girl lunged forward and grabbed Deborah's hand, squeezed so hard it hurt. "I don't want to get smacked. Please, missus."

The drizzle thickened into rain: hard, spattering drops that felt like there was ice in them. Deborah pulled her hood over her head and squinted into the deluge. "Where are we going?"

"Just over here."

The girl tugged on her hand, propelling her forward with preternatural strength. They crossed the high road and continued, passing Driscoll's Road and the outskirts of the town, heading in a southerly direction. Deborah could smell the sea in the distance, but it was growing fainter, and the foliage around them began to thicken, the surrounding trees seeming taller now, almost blotting out the sky. They had long since left the road and were traveling down a narrow, muddy path that wound its way around boulders and tree roots. Several times Deborah stumbled and would have fallen but for the girl's insistent and nearly painful grip on her hand. It seemed she had been walking for hours, and her feet hurt.

"I can't keep going," she told the girl. "I don't think you're leading me anywhere at all."

"We're almost there," the girl assured her. She turned back, and in the darkness her face seemed lit with an unnatural glow. "You'll love it. Sure they'll be having a party."

"A party?" Deborah scoffed. "Yes, mind now."

And then she heard the music, accordions and fiddles, and a woman's voice singing something unutterably sweet and beautiful. They emerged into a grassy clearing, roughly circular in shape, with a neat white house at its centre, all the windows lit up with a warm golden glow. There would be people in that house, Deborah thought, and perhaps a cup of tea, and she could get in the warm and rest herself and think about what she wanted to do.

"See?" the girl said. "I told you." She called something Deborah couldn't make out, and the door was flung open, and a woman about Deborah's age was framed there.

"Noreen?" the woman called. "Is that you?" She peered into the darkness. "And you're after bringing us a visitor." As Deborah neared the house, the woman held out both hands to her, clasped her wrists, and drew her inside. "We're right glad to see ye," she said. She was beautiful. No, Deborah thought, not merely beautiful but... *luminous*. She seemed to glow from within, the same way the girl had. Her eyes were the palest green, her hair was the burnished red of a blasty bough, and her skin as pale as milk. "Come and warm yourself a while by the fire."

The house was larger inside than it had initially appeared, and a great round table, set with many places, was groaning with food: platters of roasted birds and wild game, whole salmon laid out glistening with salt, and bowls filled with boiled potatoes and carrots and fresh turnip greens. It wasn't even the season for greens. That was July or August, and this was April. It *was* April, wasn't it? It had been April when she left the house. It had definitely been April. The room was full of people, some sitting by the fireplace—enormous, vast, giving off a glorious heat— while others were lined along the walls. Several musicians were playing instruments and people rose to dance in the centre of the massive—yes, it was massive; the room was absolutely huge—ballroom, whirling each other merrily in a lively reel.

Someone rose from one of the chairs by the fire and pressed a glass into her hand. "Have a drop of stuff, my dear. It'll warm ye to the marrow of your bones."

The drink tasted of honey and lavender. The room was warm. A tall young man with dancing dark eyes whirled her into the reel, and Deborah was laughing as she hadn't laughed in years, not since marrying Azariah and coming to this awful place. She let the man swing her around, and the room went past at a dizzying rate; she could barely keep her feet. Her calves were aching from the strain, and she'd begun to bleed again between her legs. "I can't keep up," she gasped, her breath coming hard, a sharp pain beginning in her side. "I want to stop!"

Eileen's words were ringing in her ears. "...you mightn't want to dance, but you will. Oh, you'll dance all right."

The blade was at her throat before she could draw breath to protest, and then the house with its lights and music faded into nothing.

CHAPTER ONE

THE WET snow that had been falling all morning continued relentlessly, finding its way down the back of Deiniol "Danny" Quirke's collar. It was April, for Christ's sake, and it should be spring, or at least something like it. No bloody hope of that. Newfoundland didn't do spring. What it did was endless months of cold, wet misery. Unending rain and drizzle until the end of June, when the tiny fish known as capelin made it ashore to spawn and it could finally be summer. He sat back on his haunches, ignoring the creak in his fifty-year-old knees, and frowned at the body. A young woman lay face down in the icy bog, her long dark hair fanning out around her shoulders, a clump of soggy peat moss clutched in her fist. "Who found her?"

The assembled group of RCMP and Royal Newfoundland Constabulary constables, four of them in total, looked from one to the other. A tall sandy-haired young man who didn't look old enough to shave flipped through his notebook. "Hunter," he said.

Danny stood up, his knees cracking painfully. "Is that your name?" he asked.

The constable appeared confused for a moment but recovered quickly. "No, sir," he said. "My name's Carbage."

You poor bugger, Danny thought. He waited.

"A hunter found her," Carbage continued, "or should I say a poacher. He was out this way looking for rabbits."

Danny glanced around but could see only themselves. "I'm guessing he pissed off out of it."

Two of the constables exchanged glances again. "He was a poacher, sir. Reported the body on his cell phone." He was a short, burly young man with a rugby player's body type and something of an attitude. "Could be anywhere now."

"Help me turn her over," Danny ordered. Two of the constables moved towards the girl's corpse, one on either side. Danny crouched down, hands cupped around the nape of her neck. "Slowly, now."

She tumbled sluggishly through space and landed on her back. Danny examined her features, but he didn't recognise her. "Has anyone been reported missing recently?"

"No, sir," Carbage supplied.

"I want forensics out here," Danny said. "Now, if not sooner." He walked a short distance away from them and fished out his mobile phone. He didn't need to look up the medical examiner's number, since he knew it by heart. The line rang five times before Dr. Regan Lampe picked up.

"What?"

"Good morning to you too," he snipped. The wet snow began to fall harder, aided by a strong northwest wind. "Got a body for ye."

"Not yours is it?" she asked.

"No."

"Well, thank Christ for that."

"Don't fucking start with me, Regan." His cheeks flushed hot with anger, despite the cold day. "I've got a young woman lying dead in a bog in New Melbourne. How long until someone from the Carbonear hospital can get over here and collect the body?" The small cottage hospital in Old Perlican was closer, but the area's medical examiner was attached to Carbonear. Regan Lampe wouldn't have been his first choice in any case. She was young, overconfident, and hated men in general, not him in particular. Her snotty manner hadn't won her any friends.

"I'm sorry," she said, not sounding sorry in the least.

"How long?"

"I'll get someone over immediately."

"Fine." He didn't wait for her to say goodbye. When he'd ended the call, he made his way back to the body. The sandy-haired young man—Carbage, wasn't it?—was bent low, treading a careful path around the girl's corpse. He'd put on a pair of bright purple nitrile gloves and held a plastic evidence bag at the ready, along with a pair of tweezers. As Danny watched, he plucked a small piece of paper from the ground with the tweezers and dropped it into the bag without touching the sides.

"Nicely done," Danny observed. "Who taught you forensics?"

"Chief Inspector Fraser, sir," Carbage replied. "She's very thorough."

Danny bent low over the young woman. Something about her face wasn't quite right. It was—

Jesus. Her left eye was missing. He straightened and walked a few paces away, then stopped to stand in a grove of larch trees, steadying himself, breathing deeply through his nose.

Carbage was at his side in an instant. "Are you okay, sir?"

"I will be." The sight of that raw, ragged hole in her skull would stay with him for a while. Danny dismissed the other constables and waited with Carbage until the ambulance came and loaded the young woman's body inside.

"Sin," Carbage observed, as the ambulance doors were closed. "She was pretty-looking."

Danny turned to look at him. "Did you know her?"

"No, sir. It's just a general observation." He gazed after the ambulance, his open notebook in his hand and an unreadable expression on his face. "Too bad." He flipped his notebook closed and put it back into his pocket. "Do you want me to follow behind?" he asked.

"No, it's fine," Danny said. The snow had thickened, each fat flake hitting his skin with a wet slap. He shivered and huddled closer into his coat. "No point in getting in Dr. Lampe's way. She'll have a report for me soon enough. We might as well get back. You can ride with me."

"Strange thing to do," Carbage observed, once they were both in Danny's car. "Taking out her eyeball like that." Carbage's own eyes were a blue so brilliant they didn't look quite real. "Was it deliberate, or did the killer do it just for devilment?"

"I don't know," Danny said. He turned the key and started the car. Immediately a blast of cold air spewed from the heating vents. "I think T.S. Eliot was right," he observed wryly, with a look at Carbage.

"About what, sir?"

"April really is the cruellest month."

J.S. COOK was born and raised on the rugged, wind-swept island of Newfoundland in the North Atlantic Ocean. Her earliest published work was "The Magic Elf," printed in the local newspaper when she was eight years old. This incited an unquenchable thirst for literary notoriety that resulted in novels ranging from literary and historical to steampunk to moody atmospheric crime. The inspiration for her crime fiction often comes from real cases both modern and historical. To aid her research and ensure forensic accuracy, she designs and conducts her own experiments.

J.S. Cook holds a BA (Honours), an MA, and a B.Ed., all from Memorial University. She teaches English and Communications at the College of the North Atlantic. Along with her husband, Paul, and their 'dogter,' Lola, she divides her time between St. John's and Corner Brook, Newfoundland. Many of her books are set in Newfoundland and are written in a powerfully descriptive style that borrows heavily from the Newfoundland landscape, geography, and weather.

J.S. COOK

BECAUSE YOU
DESPISE ME

When Feldwebel Horst Stussel is murdered in Jake Plenty's Moroccan brothel, local police chief Nicolas Renard suspects Jake's involvement in the crime. Renard has loved Jake since their service in the Legion Etrangère during the Great War, but in this era of concentration camps, gas chambers, and the infamous pink triangle, his love for the American dare not speak its name.

When sadistic Nazi officer Major Danzig, a fanatic who excels at the arts of torture and interrogation, comes to Maarif, it isn't because of the Feldwebel. He is in search of Christophe Picard, Resistance leader and Jake's former lover. Danzig will stop at nothing to uncover Picard's whereabouts, to find him and destroy him, and in so doing, strike a fatal blow against everything Picard stands for.

With an Allied invasion of North Africa mere days away, Jake and Renard must combine their wits, cunning, and courage to help Picard escape to America and freedom. In the midst of war and struggle, the two men are drawn into the fight of the century—and each other's arms.

www.dsppublications.com

For more
great fiction
from

DSP PUBLICATIONS

visit us online.
WWW.DSPPUBLICATIONS.COM

www.ingramcontent.com/pod-product-compliance
Lightning Source LLC
Chambersburg PA
CBHW051542260626
47170CB00003B/1057